A HERO WILL RISE!

THE
MOUSE THAT ROARED

Revised Edition

NOVEL BY

DWAYNE MURRAY, SR.

Published By

Madbo Enterprises
1444 East Gunhill Road, Suite #32
Bronx, New York 10469
Website: WWW.MADBOENTERPRISES.COM
Email Address: Madbo726@AOL.COM

Warning!

This is a novel of fiction. All the characters, incidents and dialogue are products of the Author's imagination and are not real. Any references or similarities to actual events, people, living or dead, or to locales are intended to give the story a sense of reality. Similarities in names, characters, entities, places and incidents are purely coincidental.

Cover Design/Graphics/Photography: Marion Designs

Email Address: MARIONDESIGNS@BELLSOUTH.NET

Model: Heather Johns

Printing Company: United Graphics Inc

ISBN 978-0-9769855-4-9

Dedication

I dedicate this work to my loving wife Angie who stood by me, encouraged me, supported me and loved me from the first to the last letter. I love you and I am truly blessed to have you in my corner. Thank you for loving me.

Acknowledgments

First and foremost, I want to thank my ***Savior Jesus Christ*** for giving me the strength to complete this endeavor. It was His Grace that made this all possible.

To my wife ***Angie***, "Baby, You know the deal and nothing more needs to be said."

To my son ***Dwayne Jr.***, while I sat at that computer hour after hour, day after day, "Thanks!" for keeping me updated on all the games I was not able to watch on television. You were my personal "ESPN" newscaster.

To my son ***Daniel***, who had no mercy and played hard with me in basketball in the backyard. It was much needed leisure time to unwind after writing. Just one thing, "Danny, have mercy on your old man!"

To my mom ***Christine***, who always believed in me and encouraged me to pursue my writing. "Thanks Ma!"

To my belated grandmother ***Esther***, who would be so proud of me. I know if she was still with us, she would call me 3-4 times a day to see if I was finish with the book. "I miss you grandma."

To my niece ***Evelyn***, who spent her whole Saturday reading my book before I sent it to the printer. Thanks for your time, your willingness, your constructive criticism and honesty pertaining to the book. Your input was imperative and I really appreciate your help.

A special thanks to all my extended ***family*** and ***friends*** for your love and support. I recognize the importance of each and every one of you and I am blessed to have you all in my life.

To My editor **Susan Herriott** who helped me tremendously with this new and improved edition. Susan you are the best not only with your craft but with your warmth and professionalism. You're the best and it is a pleasure to have you as MY editor. We have big things to accomplish young lady.

To all the **book clubs** across the country that have supported me with their support. I love you and appreciate it.

I want to thank all the book vendors who helped me get my work to the people on the streets. Let's keep it going with the support that is needed. One love **Ace Boogie, Sister's Uptown Bookstore, My main man De'vine from Books in Da Hood, Bronx Bookman** and the rest of you.

Much thanks to **Moses Miller, Treasure E. Blue, Joy King, Kashamba Williams** and **Marie Antionette** for your friendship.

Finally I want to thank you **the readers** for your love, support and dedication. None of this is possible without you.

Chapter One

The Apple Doesn't Fall Far From Its Tree

In the Gunners' muggy Bronx apartment, a nine-year-old chubby-cheeked boy named Doug quietly looked through his parents' slightly opened bedroom door. His father was aggressively moving up and down on someone who was not his mother. As Doug continued to look at the moaning individuals under the blue sheets, Fred Gunner quickly turned around, catching Doug with his mouth wide open.

"Doug, I'm gonna bust your ass! Get the hell away from this door!" Fred yelled. "I was just looking for Mommy to tell her something," Doug explained.

Fred, who stood six feet three inches tall and weighed about one hundred and ninety pounds, jumped out of bed while dragging a naked Diana Cruz, the Gunners' next-door neighbor, with him. Quickly walking over and opening the blue-painted door, Fred revealed a shocked and frightened Doug, who had just urinated on himself.

"This look like your momma?" he yelled.

Not getting an answer, Fred reached down and yanked Doug by his gray T-shirt. He lifted him off the ground and held him directly in the face of a nervous Diana.

"Is this your momma?"

"No, sir." Doug swallowed hard. He was sweating and shaking as his feet dangled in the air.

Fred slowly let his son down as Diana watched in silence.

"Well that means she's not here, so get your ass in your room until I tell you to come out."

Fred smacked Diana on her naked backside and directed her back to the bed as Doug ran off to his room.

Doug's bedroom was painted with a flat red paint that was beginning to chip away in certain areas on the walls. Clothes were all over the dirty floor and white curtains hung from two dirty windows. A giant poster of a basketball player was on the wall, and a nineteen-inch television with a metal coat hanger substituting for an antenna was showing *Tom and Jerry.* Quickly removing his wet pants and underwear, Doug scrounged his room for dry ones.

* * *

Doug sat at an old wooden desk in a corner of his bedroom and played with his 1001 electronic set. As he lit up the small bulbs and made the bells ring, Fred Gunner violently pushed the bedroom door open. Doug jumped out of his seat in fear.

Relishing the sight, Fred spread a huge grin across his face. "You want some ice cream, boy?"

Doug stood at attention like an army soldier and nodded his head. "What the fuck does that mean?" Fred demanded. Doug's lips began to quiver. "Yes, sir," he answered fearfully.

Fred moved to the right side of the door and stared at Doug. "Bring your ass on then," he ordered. As Doug walked timidly towards the door, Fred quickly grabbed him by the collar, pulling his son's head towards his face. "What you saw today better stay away from your momma, 'cause if she ever found out it would kill her, and I would kill you."

* * *

On Friday evening, Margaret Gunner and Doug sat on their red velvet couch watching a drunken Fred. He was holding a brush in his hand, pretending as if it were a microphone, and trying to sing "Ain't Nobody." Reaching into his black dungaree jacket, Fred pulled out a pint of Bacardi rum. He took a long swig from the bottle and motioned to his wife to join him for a dance. Margaret gave her husband a half smile and jokingly shooed him away. With a puzzled look on his face, Fred reached down to the couch and pulled his wife by the wrist towards him, causing her to thrash her neck.

"Bitch, when your man tells you to dance, you dance." Squeezing her small wrist tightly, Fred grabbed Margaret by the hair and dipped her to the floor. "Fred, please, you're hurting me!" she cried. Using her right hand, Margaret tried to free herself from his grip.

"Give me some tongue, baby," a sweaty and smelly Fred urged.

With pain on her face and a bad bruise on her wrist, Margaret pleaded with her husband. "Fred, please…let's go to our bedroom." In one quick motion, Fred shoved his wife onto the couch and began to unzip his pants. With tears in her eyes, Margaret looked at her son, who was standing by the living room entrance in a daze. "Baby, go to your room right now," she said with urgency. After seeing his drunken father force himself between his mother's legs, Doug retreated to his bedroom and put his ear to his bedroom door. He could hear his father's wild moans over the music.

* * *

Saturday afternoon found Doug dribbling his Spalding basketball on the concrete pavement after leaving the park. He waved to some of the neighborhood kids. Most of them were wearing brand-name sneakers like Puma, adidas, and Converse. One kid in particular named Elvis pointed at Doug's old, worn-out Skips. "Hey, Doug," he yelled, "tell your drunken-ass father to get off his lazy ass and get a job. Maybe then he can buy your poor ass some new sneakers." Doug picked up his pace as the kids pointed at his sneakers and laughed.

* * *

Doug entered his apartment and found his father waiting by the door. "Dumb ass, where the hell you been?" Fred demanded. Doug looked past his father and into the kitchen at his mother. She was rubbing her cheek. Getting impatient, Fred snatched his son by the arm and pulled him closer.

Teary-eyed, Doug mumbled in a low voice, "I was at the park playing basketball." Still staring at his son, Fred released him and pushed him to the floor. "Leave him alone, goddammit!" Margaret yelled. Shocked, Fred stared at his wife. "Bitch, you lost your mind?" he snarled.

Despite her trembling body, Margaret moved herself in front of her son and shielded him from Fred. Now red-faced, Fred stared down Margaret and Doug, pointing his finger at both of them.

"Bitch, you ain't shit, that punk ass boy ain't shit, and you're never gonna be shit. You know why? 'Cause I ain't shit. If I'm going to hell, then you two are going with me," he fumed. He stormed out of the apartment, and Margaret turned and kneeled down to her son. "Doug, I will not mince words. I don't know how much I have left in me to take this. You are going to have to learn how to make choices in your life, and you'll have to pick and choose who you will follow. Do you understand?"

"Yes, I do," said Doug.

Margaret could tell by the confusion in her son's eyes that he did not.

* * *

On Sunday, the sun sent down hot summer rays into the crowded park on Valentine Avenue. Basketballs were making clanging sounds off the rim, and men and teenagers alike were yelling for the basketball so they might get a chance to take the next shot. Doug was wearing his Magic Johnson jersey and holding his basketball under his arm, hoping someone would choose him to play. He looked far off to the park entrance and saw his secret idol, Dollar Bill, conducting business with his many clients. Doug couldn't take his eyes off Dollar Bill's clean, crisp clothes and his always-fresh sneakers—he sported a new pair every day.

From his position at the top of the steps, Doug was about fifteen feet away from Dollar Bill. He could clearly see the exchange of money for aluminum foil between the clients and Dollar Bill. In a dreamlike state, Doug dropped his basketball and began to walk towards his icon. Suddenly, a huge, dark-skinned brother named Bucky grabbed Doug by the arm, scaring the living daylights out of him. "What do you want, shorty?" he demanded.

Wide-eyed, Doug barely whispered, "Just to say hello to Dollar Bill." Bucky—who was twenty years old, stood six feet three inches tall, and weighed about two hundred and forty pounds—looked at his boss for confirmation. Dollar Bill stared at the young boy, smiled, then nodded to Bucky, who in turn let Doug through. As Doug walked towards Dollar Bill, the little boy's hero grabbed him, violently pulled him closer, and felt around for a weapon or a police wire. Not finding anything, Dollar Bill rubbed Doug on his head in a playful but serious manner and turned him around to face him.

"Shorty, I have six eyes behind my head, and I've noticed you watching me for the past three weeks. What's up?" Mustering up valor, Doug tried to sound as cool as possible. "I just think you're dope," he said.

Dollar Bill looked at Doug, then at Bucky, and then at Doug again, who was now starting to perspire. Dollar Bill let out a colossal laugh that drew some attention from the people sitting on the benches. Doug still felt edgy, but he smiled. Dollar Bill hugged him around the neck and pulled him close to his chiseled chest.

"Shorty, do you know what I do in these streets?" he asked.

"You're a businessman," Doug answered, feeling a little more comfortable.

With a smile on his face, Dollar Bill reached into his pocket, pulled out a twenty, and placed it in the palm of the boy's hand. Doug stared at the crisp new bill. Then he looked up at Dollar Bill and said, "Thank you."

Dollar Bill pointed across the street to his new Pontiac Grand Prix and looked back at Doug. "Shorty, tomorrow at noon I expect that car to be shining and looking good. Cool?"

"Yes, sir," Doug answered, still holding the twenty. Dollar Bill shifted his attention to a skinny brother named Jackie, who was standing on the corner, lighting a cigarette. With his smile gone, Dollar Bill motioned to Bucky to look across the street. On the spot, the two young men took off after unsuspecting Jackie, leaving Doug where he stood. From a distance, Doug watched as Bucky ran up behind Jackie, punched him in the back of the head, and knocked him to the ground. Dollar Bill stood over Jackie and kicked him all over his entire body.

People began to look from the park and their apartment windows, and Doug started to exit the park—but not before catching Dollar Bill's eye. "Noon tomorrow, shorty. Don't forget me!" shouted Dollar Bill.

Doug started to jog home and then realized he'd left his basketball. He stopped and considered going back until he looked back across the street and saw the beaten and bloodied figure that no longer resembled Jackie. As he ran down Valentine Avenue, Doug repeated to himself, "Noon tomorrow, noon tomorrow."

* * *

Six cruel winters later, fifteen-year-old Doug stared at himself in the mirror as he put on his beige sheepskin coat and concealed his handgun in the waistband of his pants. He walked into the living room and stared at his father, who was sleeping on the couch with a quart of Jack Daniel's cradled in his arm. Doug looked down at his father for about thirty seconds and then walked to the door. Before unlocking it, he looked up at the picture of his mother that was hanging above. "I miss you," he told her. "I hope you're proud of me…and please forgive me."

* * *

The Tiger Lounge was packed and the stereo was blasting "Follow the Leader," the hit by Eric B. & Rakim. A well-groomed Doug walked inside and was greeted by men and women almost twice his age. He looked around the club until he saw his mentor, Dollar Bill, sitting at a private table flanked by three sexy women. Dollar Bill spotted Doug and waved him over to his table.

"My son, what's up?" asked a high Dollar Bill.

"Just chillin, what about you?"

Dollar Bill pulled one of his girls close to him and gave her a long, wet kiss. He looked up at Doug with a smile. "This is what I'm up to, baby."

Doug reached out his hand and gave Dollar Bill a pound. "Do you think we can talk outside for a minute?"

After taking a long taste of his Rémy Martin, Dollar Bill stared at Doug for a moment. "Shit, it's freezing outside. But hey, anything for my son."

* * *

Inside Dollar Bill's red Bronco, the two comrades shared a joint.

"Shorty, I can remember when you were just a snot-nosed bastard that washed my car. Now look at you, holding meetings and shit. So, what's up?" asked Dollar Bill.

Never taking his eyes off Dollar Bill, Doug let out a calm laugh. "Yeah, I always looked up to you, and I still do."

Dollar Bill passed the joint and looked straight into Doug's eyes. "I love you, shorty, like a son," he told his protégé.

Doug reached over, gave Dollar Bill an embrace, and then shoved him towards the driver's side window. Looking at Doug with shock and confusion, Dollar Bill watched Doug dive down onto the floor of the truck.

As a nice beat played from Dollar Bill's car stereo, Jackie popped up on the driver's side of the truck, pointing a twelve-gauge shotgun. Pumping the firearm once, Jackie yelled, "Payback, motherfucker!"

Dollar Bill turned his head towards the side window, and a big blast of light shattered the darkness of the night while the sound of breaking glass blasted through the air. Covering his face from the flying glass, Doug looked at his pants and saw Dollar Bill's brains and skull all over him. He wiped glass and blood away from his coat, and reached for his automatic weapon. Jackie's face turned to dreadfulness as he stared down the barrel of Doug's gun.

"Oh shit, shorty. What's up!"

Without hesitation, Doug let off four rounds, hitting Jackie three times in the head and killing him instantly. Hordes of people ran from the club, looking at the scene of the incident. Some women were screaming and crying while a few men got closer to the car and peeped inside. Before Doug crawled out of the Bronco, he grabbed three packages of cocaine that Dollar Bill had under his seat.

From out of the crowd, Bucky grabbed Doug by the shirt and pulled him up to his feet. "What the fuck happened!" he yelled. Blood- soaked, Doug pointed to the driver's side of the Bronco. Bucky ran over to the driver's side and came upon a dead Jackie and a half-headed Dollar Bill. Holding his head and falling to his knees, Bucky started to cry.

"I killed him, Bucky, but I couldn't save Dollar Bill," Doug explained.

The sound of police sirens was getting closer, and Bucky tried to gather himself. "Run, shorty, get the fuck out of here!" he told Doug.

With the speed of a gazelle, Doug took off down Webster Avenue. He felt for the bags of cocaine in his shirt and grinned.

Chapter Two

Meet Sandra Lyte

The city of Richmond, Virginia, was baking like hot peach cobbler as twenty-one-year-old Sandra Lyte stood in front of the full-length mirror in her bedroom, posing in a scarlet red two-piece bathing suit. Sandra smiled as she twisted, turned, and admired her thick hourglass figure. Her mother, Anna Lyte, sat on the edge of Sandra's bed, nervously looking at her wristwatch.

"Mama, there's no way I'm *not* going to win Miss Richmond. This is *my* pageant," Sandra declared. Anna shook her head with total doubt written on her face and looked at her watch again.

"Your father is going to hit the roof when he finds out you are defying his wishes," she warned.

Sandra gave her mother a frustrated look as she walked over to the closet and removed a very expensive gown adorned with rhinestones. "I am a twenty-one-year-old college graduate. I am not his little girl anymore, and he can't scare me with '*If Jesus was here*' speeches anymore." Jostled by their dog Sheba's bark, Anna jumped off the bed and looked at Sandra with a worried expression. "Okay, hurry up and put this stuff away. Since we agreed not to tell him until the day before the pageant, there's no use in him finding out now when he'll have so much time to fuss."

Sandra rolled her eyes. As she hid her things, she watched her mother ruffle her dress and hurry down the steps to greet her husband.

Annoyed, Sandra grabbed two decks of cards from off her table, shuffled them, and spread them all across her bedroom floor. One by one, she flipped over cards until gradually she started to match them not only by numbers but also by the exact same suits. Within two minutes, she had fifty-two pairs of matching cards. Looking at the neatly stacked piles of cards, Sandra blew on her knuckles and wiped her chest with bragger's bravado.

She headed down the steps and into the gigantic living room, which was decorated with beautiful artwork and sculptures. Sandra walked over to her father, Minister James Lyte, and kissed him on his cheek.

"Good evening, minister," she said.

James looked at his daughter from under his bifocals. "When do you plan to get those ghetto braids removed from your hair?"

"Minister, these are not ghetto braids," Sandra retorted. "They signify my African heritage."

The minister stood up slowly from his chair, rolled his eyes in disgust at his daughter, and left the living room. Showing the same frustration, Sandra returned to her room. Left alone, Anna looked up at the ceiling and just held her head in her hands.

* * *

Sandra and her best friend, twenty-year-old Karen Robinson, sat under a large tree on the sprawling and well-maintained Lyte estate, listening to a Luther Vandross CD. As they sipped on lemonade and sang along to "Superstar," Minister Lyte looked out at them from his window. His expression showed not only anger towards his daughter but also hatred.

Karen pulled a plastic bag from her handbag and showed Sandra the many pictures she had snapped while on her vacation to New York City.

"My goodness, Karen, New York looks so big," Sandra marveled. "What's it like there?"

"First of all, the men are *fine*, girl. I could not take my eyes off of them."

"What about the job opportunities? Is there room for another news anchor?" Sandra interrupted.

Karen rolled her eyes and looked at Sandra like she was stupid. "Sandra, I was not looking for any damn job. I was club hopping my ass off." The two women laughed as they sipped their lemonade.

"I have to get out of Virginia, Karen. If I can win this pageant, it just adds to my accomplishments, showing that I have the charisma and talent to sit in front of millions of people."

Karen reached out and grabbed Sandra to give her a hug. "That's why I've always admired you, girl. You go for what you want."

Sandra looked away from Karen and noticed that her father had come out and was sitting on the porch reading his Bible. She helped Karen to her feet and took her a few yards away to the lake.

"I know he hates me. He always has. My mother told me that when I was born he stood three feet away from the delivery-room window," she lamented as she looked down at her reflection in the water. "I get no support from my mother, and she is so damn submissive to him. But I have to take my chance."

Karen turned Sandra around and wiped a tear from her friend's face. "New York is nice, Sandra, but I have to be honest about something. I had a good time, but there are also some very shady people who will try to take advantage if you're not careful."

Sandra rubbed away a few more tears and gave Karen a smile. "I realize the risk I'm taking, but sometimes when you want something really badly, you have to be willing to stick your hands into the fire to grab it."

The two friends left the lake and headed back to Karen's car. Before Karen got in, Sandra gave her a hug and a kiss on the cheek.

"Have you mentioned the pageant to your father yet?"

Sandra looked back at the four-thousand-square-foot plantation-like home. "No, not yet," she sighed, "but in due time, I will."

After watching Karen drive away, Sandra walked up the steps leading to the front door of the egg-colored house. Her father was still sitting on the porch. "Good night, minister," she told him.

With his eyes focused on his Bible, Minister Lyte never looked up at his daughter, but he did direct a few words to her before she stepped into the house: "Peter denied his master three times before the rooster crowed."

* * *

On Sunday, the deacons stood at the top of the church steps greeting the many families who were filing in to attend the morning service. Meanwhile, inside the minister's quarters, Sandra stood off in a corner reading a journalism textbook while her father looked through his Bible. Her mother was busy steaming the minister's suit jacket. When she had removed all the wrinkles, Anna helped her husband put on his jacket and robe, and then kissed him on the cheek. With his Bible once again in his hands, and with his wife and daughter by his side, Minister Lyte marched to the pulpit.

* * *

The organist played "Rough Side of the Mountain," and the church choir and the worshipers sang and clapped along. From her seat in the first pew, Sandra was clapping way off tempo with an emotionless expression on her face. The singing and clapping died down, and everyone took their seats as Minister Lyte walked to the podium.

"Good morning, brothers and sisters," he greeted the congregation. As the worshipers responded, the minister opened his Bible and cleared his throat. "My God tells me that inwardly beauty is His joy, not outwardly adornments, such as jewelry and fancy braided hair," he started.

Most of the crowd nodded and voiced its agreement, but Sandra's eyes burned a hole through her father. Anna glanced at her daughter, who was tapping her manicured fingers against the leg of her black pants suit; then Anna quickly turned her attention back to her husband.

"My God tells me that our bodies are temples and should not be polluted by the evil products and messages of this world," he continued.

The crowd expressed its agreement with the minister a little louder. Some members stood to their feet, and the organist's fingers glided across the keys to symbolize his approval.

"Look at all the sex videos that our precious little children are being forced to watch by the so-called entertaining rappers and singers," shouted the minister.

Sandra bit her lip but did not take her eyes off her father.

"Brothers and sisters, I want to bring to your attention one of these so-called entertaining events being shoved down our throats in the next two weeks." In a dramatic pause, Minister Lyte walked away from the pulpit, wiped his brow, and gripped his microphone tightly before continuing. "Our beautiful city of Richmond has allowed a car magazine to sponsor an exploitative show to take advantage of our young women."

From a pew in the middle of the church, Karen watched her friend's stoic demeanor. The minister, who now had his congregation fired up on all cylinders, took a sip of bottled water and continued. "I will not hold my tongue, brothers and sisters. This so-called pageant exploits not only our city and our church but, most importantly, our misguided daughters who are involved."

The crowd yelled for the minister to continue and most of the worshipers were now standing. "I will not stand by and let them just walk into our blessed community and parade our young women around a bunch of immature men, whooping and hollering like these girls are prostitutes. No, not me!"

The noise in the sanctuary escalated, and Sandra turned around to witness the ruckus her father was raising. She was shocked to see people pumping their fists in the air.

"Brothers and sisters, I don't know about you, but when this magazine company arrives two Fridays from now, I will be standing at the gate waiting to protest in peace…but also in the presence of my God!"

People could barely hear themselves. The church was in a pandemonium of agreement about the protest.

"Within the next two weeks, the church and I will begin to organize our protest, and I know I can count on you, brothers and sisters!" As the crowd started to sing the church hymn, Anna leaned over to her daughter. "If you do this, you are on your own," she whispered. "This is my life and I will control my destiny," Sandra whispered back defiantly.

The two women turned away from each other and focused on Minister Lyte.

* * *

On Friday morning, the day of the Richmond pageant and Minister Lyte's firestorm protest, Sandra was jogging in place in front of her bedroom mirror in a gray panty-and-bra set. Dripping with sweat, she held two ten-pound rubber dumbbells in her hands. Every five seconds, she lifted the weights over her head and let out a deep breath. After running in place, she started on her crunches. She did one hundred and fifty in three minutes. After that, she did four hundred and fifty jumping jacks, breaking them up into three sets. When she completed her workout, Sandra stood in front of her mirror, admiring her thick but well-toned body. "The competition doesn't stand a chance," she smirked.

* * *

Minister Lyte stood before twenty members of his congregation inside the Richmond Baptist Church. Rolling up his sleeves, he gathered the group for prayer. "Dear Lord, we go to battle today not for recognition or for the spotlight, but we go to battle, Lord, because of what we believe to be right and true in Your name and glory." The people in the prayer circle all praised in unison as the minister continued. "We ask that You not only protect us in our journey, Lord, but we also ask that You free those behind this sinful act that they believe to be a pageant. We pray in Your name, amen."

Everyone lifted their heads, and the minister laid out his final instructions to the congregation. "Brothers and sisters, as I have said for the past two weeks, we will protest in peace and harmony, not anger. We will obey the laws of our police department and stay behind the barricades. Finally, we will not get into name-calling or any physical confrontations with the sponsors or attendees of this event. But rest assured, they will hear our voices, and our voices will echo our disapproval."

The members lined up to shake the minister's hand while two of the men loaded the church van with bull horns and large white cardboard signs denouncing the pageant. The minister watched his flock exit the church, one by one, until he stood alone. Looking up at the church ceiling, he assured himself, "If I pull this off, it will surely glorify me."

* * *

Four hours before the beauty pageant, Sandra gathered up her personal cosmetics and costumes, and put them inside her tan suitcase. As she looked at her new hairstyle in the mirror, she heard a knock at the door. She turned around as her mother entered the bedroom with her hands held out in a pleading manner.

"You have to reconsider, Sandra. Just for me, please?" Anna begged tearfully.

Sandra stared at her mother with disbelief. "Listen, everyone needs to get a grip on reality. It's just a pageant," Sandra said in disbelief.

Anna took a seat on Sandra's bed and grabbed her daughter by the hand. "I know we have not been the greatest parents, Sandra, but please look at it from our perspective. We have built a reputation in this town for being an upright family and a God-fearing one at that."

"As long as I can remember, I have played the sweet little minister's daughter. And I've played the part very well, I might add," Sandra said, picking up her bags. "So please don't stand before me and preach what is right according to God when you and the minister know fully well what's in our little secret closet and why I don't have the little brother or sister I should have had."

Anna's light-skinned face turned tomato red, and in a fit of rage, she leapt off Sandra's bed and got directly in her face so that their noses were touching. Thrown off balance from the invasion of her personal space, Sandra took a step back and bumped into her dresser.

"Be very careful what you dig up, Sandra, because you know and I know, this family can't handle repercussions very well. And since you're the weakest, you would surely crumble without us around. So be very fucking careful."

Sandra grabbed her pageant gear and then turned to look at her still red-faced mother. Anna was biting on her bottom lip so hard that blood slowly oozed from her mouth.

* * *

At seven o'clock in the evening, the Richmond College auditorium was slowly filling up with ticket buyers who were mostly men. The three men and one woman who were serving as the pageant judges sat in the first row of the middle section. The stage was beautifully decorated, and the electrician was rotating different-colored beams of light onto the stage. The sponsor's banner for the pageant was draped overhead and read, "HOT RIDES MAGAZINE." A man dressed in blue jeans walked on stage and tested the microphone by tapping it with his hand. Eagerly, the men in the audience began to make howling and barking noises.Backstage was total chaos as women ran all over, helping the contestants with their dresses and makeup. Inside the dressing room, Sandra calmly put the final touches to her hair and began to slip on her glittering black dress. Three other women walked in and started to crowd Sandra in an attempt to share the mirror. As the start time drew nearer, an older-looking woman entered the room. "Ladies, let's hurry," she said. "You have ten minutes before the curtain rises." All the contestants, including Sandra, began to move faster.

* * *

Across the street from the auditorium, Minister Lyte and members of his church gathered with signs in their hands. They formed a circle and began to march. Armed with a bullhorn, the minister declared, "Our women are God's gift, not the hot rods' thrift!" The members marched in a circle, repeating the minister's proclamation loudly and proudly.

As they marched, a News Channel 21 television van pulled up to the curb. Anchorwoman Sheila Brown exited the van, followed by her cameraman. Sheila positioned herself on the lawn with the college auditorium as her background shot. When her cameraman nodded to indicate that they were now on the air, Sheila showed her pearly whites to greet her audience.

"Good evening, Richmond. I am Sheila Brown and this is breaking news. Tonight, in the midst of what some say is a harmless beauty pageant, there is controversy brewing about ten feet away from me as protesters led by Minister James Lyte show disapproval. If possible, we are going to try to get a word with Minister Lyte." Sheila walked over to the protesters and put a microphone near the minister's face. "Minister Lyte, what is this protest about?"

The minister gave the newswoman a stern look for about three seconds. "It's about bringing to light what this event is all about. It's not just some pageant, as you might call it…No, this is nothing but an exploitation of the young women of this city."

"Minister, some would say this protest is somewhat overblown because this is nothing more than a showcase for some talented young women."

The minister held his sign high in the air. "You can call it what you like, Ms. Brown, but take a look at the sponsor magazine's promotion space in the back. They sponsor sex chat lines and escort services. So who knows what they have planned for some of these young women."

As she listened to the minister, Sheila pushed at her earphone to listen to a transmission. Looking at the minister with a concerned expression on her face, she turned to him with another question. "Minister Lyte, we at News Channel 21 have a second crew inside the auditorium covering the event, and we would like to show you live footage."

"Why would I want to see that filth unfolding, Ms. Brown?"

Sheila pointed to a live monitor inside the news van. "Minister Lyte, is that your daughter, Sandra Lyte, on stage wearing a swimsuit?"

Minister Lyte focused his attention on the monitor. In complete shock, his mouth fell open and he dropped the sign he was holding. The other protesters gathered around the news truck and witnessed a bikini-clad Sandra walking from one end of the stage to the other. Some of the members patted the minister on his back in a gesture of comfort.

"Minister Lyte, is that your daughter?" Sheila Brown asked again in a serious tone.

Without saying a word, the somber-looking man walked slowly towards his car. Two women from his church tried to escort him, but he gently yet firmly pushed them away. As he got into his Lincoln Town Car, the deacons of the church pushed away a camera operator who was trying to get a shot of him.

* * *

Two hours later, Sandra stood on stage waiting to hear who would be crowned Miss Richmond. The runners-up had already been announced, and she crossed her fingers that her name would be called next. The MC made the final announcement, and Sandra smiled victoriously. The other contestants rushed in to give her hugs and kisses. Then the chief editor of HOT RIDES Magazine crowned her as Miss Richmond, giving her a check for five thousand dollars and a two-foot trophy as her reward. As she walked off the stage, Sandra saw Deacon Frye of the Tuckahoe Baptist Church amongst the many men in the audience. The two stared at each other as if they were the only ones in the building. Deacon Frye finally stood and exited the building as two of the pageant contestants escorted a somewhat numb Sandra off the stage.

* * *

A little after midnight, a long white stretch limousine pulled up to the driveway leading to the forty-foot walkway to Sandra's home. As the door opened, loud music and screaming voices resounded from the car. Stacy and Patrice, two of the contestants, stood on the backseat with half of their bodies hanging out of the moonroof. Both girls held bottles of champagne and were clearly drunk. Sandra put a finger to her mouth, signaling for them to keep quiet. She waved her Miss Richmond crown in the air with jubilation, and then waved good-bye as the limousine drove off with the girls still exposed from the moonroof.

With her crown and trophy in her hand, Sandra began to walk towards the house. As she headed up the dark hill, she enjoyed the sounds of the crickets and frogs, and the feel of the cool moisture of the grass on the bottom of her soles. When the foyer lights went on and illuminated the glass entry door, Sandra flinched. She stopped for a moment and then slowly headed up the porch steps.

She was only two feet away from the door when it flung open. The usually immaculate minister stood before his daughter wearing nothing but blue jeans. His always perfectly combed hair was in shambles. Sandra looked up at her father and stared at him as if she were a deer looking into the headlights of an oncoming car. Coming out of her trance, she focused enough to notice her mother Anna standing behind the minister. Sandra started to back away, but her father reacted with cat-like reflexes. He snatched his daughter by her long braids and pulled her violently into their secluded home.

"You fucking bitch!" yelled Minister Lyte, tossing Sandra against the closet door in the foyer. Sandra smashed into the door. She winced as the doorknob jabbed her in the back. Fighting the pain, she quickly crawled towards the front door, but she was blocked and then pushed back down by the foot of her mother Anna. Now crazed, Minister Lyte reached down with both hands, grabbed Sandra by her left arm, and slung her into the dining room. Already hurting, Sandra smashed into one of the oak chairs, which escalated her pain.

"We are ruined, you dumb-ass bitch!" yelled a psychotic Anna.

Minister Lyte quickly walked over to his battered daughter and grabbed her by the throat. He dragged her to the back of the house and tossed her on top of four large garbage bags. Anna followed right behind her husband and unlocked the door. She proceeded to throw the garbage bags out onto the lawn.

In a tag team-like effort, the minister stepped forward to take his next turn in the assault. He grabbed Sandra by her legs and dragged her down the steps. As her back hit each step, Sandra continued to clutch her purse, which she had somehow managed to hold on to throughout the whole ordeal. "Why, oh please, why?" she screamed in pain.

As if on cue, Anna positioned herself over her daughter and began slapping her and scratching her across the face. Calling on strength from deep inside her, Sandra stunningly made it to her feet. She held her ribs as she stumbled and then ran towards the road. In a fit of rage, Minister Lyte grabbed the Miss Richmond crown and violently threw it at Sandra, barely missing her face. Sandra reached down, grabbed the crown, and hurried towards the road.

Holding her husband back by his blue jeans, Anna yelled at her daughter as she faded into the wooded path leading to the road: "Don't you ever come back here! Do you hear me, Sandra? Don't you ever come back here!"

* * *

An old red Dodge pick-up truck pulled into the Greyhound bus station, and an elderly white man wearing a black Pepsi-Cola hat ran to the passenger's side door and opened it. He reached inside and gently helped Sandra out of the vehicle. The old man stared at Sandra's beaten and scratched face.

"Young lady, are you sure I can't get you to a hospital?"

"No, sir. You have done so much for me tonight. Thank you," Sandra said softly, trying to smile through her pain. The old man stood back and watched as Sandra limped towards the terminal.

As she walked slowly towards the ticket booth, Sandra could feel the few people who were inside the terminal staring at her. Still wearing her torn and dirty pageant dress, Sandra walked up to the ticket window with purse and crown in tow. "Sir, when is the next one to New York City leaving?"

The ticket clerk was trying his best not to stare, so he looked down at the bus schedule. "The next bus is leaving in about thirty-five minutes," he told her.

Sandra dug into her purse and pulled out a credit card. She slid it under the glass towards the clerk. "I'll take a one-way ticket," she said.

While she waited, Sandra looked around for a bathroom. As soon as the printer spit out her ticket, she headed there to clean herself up.

* * *

The bus was practically empty. Sandra sat back and listened as the driver welcomed them all aboard and announced their destination. Leaning her head back on the headrest of her seat, she reached into her purse and took out a Hershey's candy bar with almonds and a photograph of New York that Karen had given her a few nights ago. As the bus pulled out of the depot, Sandra let out a sigh of relief and declared, "I am free."

Chapter Three

Welcome to the Big Apple

Sandra slowly opened her hazel eyes and looked out the window of the Greyhound bus. As they traveled across I-95, she could see the great New York skyline in the distance. She felt inside her purse and found the disposable camera she had purchased a few hours ago. Sandra smiled and wiped her wet, clammy hands on the jeans she bought and changed into during her layover in Washington D.C. "Welcome to New York City," the bus driver announced. He then informed his passengers that they would be pulling into the Port Authority bus depot shortly. Sandra reached under her seat and grabbed her duffel bag, which contained her cell phone and some toiletries. When the bus pulled into the terminal, she stood with the rest of the passengers and exited the bus.

"Excuse me, sir. I was told that an information booth is nearby," Sandra said to the bus driver.

The driver looked up from his bus schedule. "Up those escalators, and if you look straight ahead, you can't miss it," he directed. Sandra smiled and walked away.

At the information booth, Sandra grabbed all the information guides she could hold, including subway maps, bus maps, street maps for the five boroughs, and a miniature yellow page book. She sat on a bench inside the terminal and looked for the different locations Karen had mentioned when Sandra called her from the bus the previous night. She had jotted down the name of a cheap hotel where Karen and her parents had stayed. Gathering her things, Sandra held the paper with the hotel information in her hand and started her ascent up the escalator, which took her to a hot and muggy Manhattan street.

Totally shocked by the crowd of people and all the cars, Sandra stood by a pharmacy, almost too frightened to step into the middle of the busy sidewalk. She took a deep breath and gathered the courage to approach an

Indian man. "Excuse me, sir," she started, but the man looked right through her and quickly walked away. Trying not to get discouraged, Sandra waited a few moments before approaching a Caucasian woman who was dressed in an expensive suit and was talking on a cell phone. "Ma'am can you please tell me..."

Once again, Sandra was brushed off as the woman walked around her. Frustrated and tired, Sandra looked up at the tall buildings across the street. "Miss, are you lost?" she heard someone ask. She turned towards the voice and spotted a street-corner frankfurter-stand vendor who was waving at her. Sandra walked over to the old Italian man and gave him a smile. "You look lost. What are you looking for?" he asked. Sandra pointed to the hotel written on the paper and showed the man. "Oh okay, young lady, the Hotel International is three blocks down that way. If you walk straight three blocks, it will be on your left," he said.

Sandra smiled. "Thank you very much," she said as she proceeded to walk in the direction the nice old man showed her.

* * *

The hotel room looked a little dingy to be in the heart of Manhattan, but Sandra brushed it off and let the excitement of freedom take over her mind. She closed the door behind her and placed her belongings on a twin-sized bed that was covered with flowered linens like her grandmother had back in Virginia. She looked around the room. There were cracks running up the beige-painted walls and ceiling, and there was a nineteen-inch television sitting on an old wooden stand. She walked into the bathroom. White terrycloth towels sat on a rack above the toilet bowl, and miniature bars of soap were on the sink.

Sandra walked back to the sleeping area and sat at a small round table that had two dinette chairs. After removing her cell phone, her credit card, a notepad, and her five-thousand-dollar check from her bag, Sandra reached for the remote control and turned on the television. The audio came on before the picture, filling the room with the sound of moaning. As the picture came into focus, Sandra realized that a porno flick was on. She looked with slight curiosity, then quickly turned the channel and watched the news. With her mouth half open, she watched without blinking an eye as a black newswoman reported the stories for the day. Coming out of her trance, Sandra slapped her thighs and stood up. She walked to her window, which was draped with dingy white curtains and a slightly torn shade. "I will make it. I have to make it," she told herself as she looked out at the city. Grabbing her room keys, purse, and check, Sandra headed out the door and onto the streets of Manhattan.

* * *

Sandra walked down the street, passing the hustling people of the city until she came upon a pizzeria. When she entered, she took a deep breath and smiled at the smell of cheese and sausage. She had stepped up to the counter and ordered a slice of pizza and a soda when a tall, light-skinned, handsome brother walked up beside her. From the corner of his eye, the man looked Sandra up and down, admiring her nice plump backside. Trying not to pay attention, Sandra got her order and paid the Italian owner.

"How you doing, lovely?" the young man asked.

"I'm fine, and you?" Sandra replied with a half smile.

"What's your name, baby?" he asked, flashing a sly grin.

Sandra looked down and was shocked to see that the brother had no shoes or socks on, and his feet were filthy. She tried to act as if she hadn't noticed. "Sir, I just want to eat my meal, please."

The young man's smile turned to a smirk as he stepped back from Sandra. "Oh, so you gonna be like my bitch wife and brush me off, too?"

Obviously frightened, Sandra tried to walk away, but the young man stepped just inches away from her face and exposed a seven-inch piece of lumber. "Bitch, where the fuck do you think you're going?"

The owner of the shop turned around and grabbed a bat from under the counter. His son Mario, who was six feet tall and weighed about two hundred and fifty pounds, had just exited the bathroom. Like a gazelle, he leapt over the counter and hit Sandra's tormenter in the arm with a rolling pin, causing him to yell in pain while dropping the piece of lumber. "Get the fuck out of here, you sick bastard. I'm tired of you harassing our customers!" he yelled. The brother quickly ran out of the pizzeria, holding his injured arm. Meanwhile Sandra was backed up against the wall, holding her chest and trying to gain control of her heavy breathing.

"Miss, we are so sorry," the pizzeria owner said, walking over to her to offer some comfort. "I run a respectable business, and I meant you none of this. Please take your money back."

Still taking deep breaths, Sandra motioned no with her hands. "Thank you for your help and your offer," she said when she was finally able to speak "I just need to get some fresh air and find the nearest bank."

Mario took Sandra by the hand and escorted her out of the pizza shop. He pointed diagonally across the street to a bank. "We are so sorry, miss. Our deepest apologies, and if you ever come back, the slice is on us." Sandra smiled at Mario and he went back into the shop.

Before crossing the street to get to the bank, Sandra scanned the area for the no-shoes-having light-skinned brother.

* * *

Inside the bank, Sandra marveled at its size compared to the First National Bank in Richmond. A security guard tapped her on the shoulder and she flinched a little.

"Didn't mean to startle you, miss. I saw you looking around and figured you needed some help," he offered.

"That's okay. I've just had had a long day," she said as she wiped a braid from in front of her face and smiled at the guard. "Could you point out someone that can help me with opening an account with this bank?"

The guard looked towards customer service and gestured to Sandra to follow him. She walked over to the desk and stood waiting. When the customer representative called out for the next customer, Sandra walked over. She took out her check and her Virginia driver's license.

"Yes. I'm here to open an account and deposit this check," she said. The rep was a short Spanish woman whose nametag read 'Ida Martinez.' She looked at Sandra's check and then at her driver's license and then back at Sandra.

"Is there any reason you can't deposit this check in your home town?"

Sandra looked and felt distraught. "Ma'am, due to some unforeseen circumstances, I no longer reside in Virginia and I just arrived in New York today."

"Well, do you have a permanent place of residence?"

Sandra fidgeted with the chain pen on the counter. "No, I don't. Right now I am staying in a hotel a few blocks away until I find an apartment."

Ida looked at the check again and then looked up at Sandra.

"Well, Miss Lyte, this check has a sixty-day grace period until it expires. I suggest you find a place that you can call home and that you establish an account with Con Edison. Then bring the check back to us with your proof of address and we'll be glad to have you as a customer. However, right now, our bank policies will not allow us to cash your check. I am really sorry," Ida explained as she gently slid the check back to Sandra.

Sandra put her check and driver's license back in her purse. "Well, thank you very much for your help," she said. "Hopefully you'll see me again soon."

A huge lump filled Sandra's throat as she walked out of the bank.

* * *

Back in the hotel lobby, Sandra stopped at the front desk. "Is there somewhere nearby where I could get something not too expensive to eat?" she asked the hotel manager, Jeffrey. The middle-aged white man's hair was dyed black and he had a pencil tucked behind his ear. He looked at Sandra in silence for a few seconds before answering. "There's a Chinese restaurant two doors down…the food ain't bad," he suggested.

* * *

From her seat on the radiator, Sandra looked out the restaurant window. After a few minutes, she took her cell phone out of her purse and scanned her directory. She scrolled down until she came to her best friend Karen's number, then she abruptly flipped the phone shut. "Once I get settled, girlfriend, I will call you so you can come up and visit. I miss you already," she said quietly to herself.

"Miss, chicken wings and shrimp fried rice," yelled the Chinese man. Sandra got up from her makeshift chair and walked over to pay for her food. "Eight nineteen for you, pretty lady," said the old man. Sandra looked in her purse, pulled out a twenty-dollar bill, and handed it to the man. While she waited for her change, she took stock of the rest of her money. She had one hundred and twenty-four dollars.

"I have to cash this check. I can't keep charging my card," she said quietly to herself. She took her change and her food, and left the restaurant. From the corner of her eye, she saw a large cat jump up on the counter. She glanced at her bag of food. "That's just an old wives' tale," she told herself. "Get it out of your head."

* * *

Once again Sandra stopped at the front desk. But this time no one was there, so she rang the bell. Jeffrey emerged from a room in the back with an erection from playing with his penis. He walked up to the desk with a smile on his face. Trying to act like she hadn't noticed the bulge in his pants, Sandra sat her food on top of the counter.

"Hi, I just wanted to ask a quick question. I have a check that the bank could not cash for me. Do you know of any place that could help me?"

Jeffrey looked up from the mail he had started to flip through and peeped through his black bifocals. "How much is the check worth?" "Five thousand dollars," Sandra said as she grabbed her bag of food.

Jeffrey rubbed his fingers through his hair. "I need to see the check."

Sandra pulled the check out of her purse and handed it to Jeffrey, who examined it for a few seconds. "This is an out-of-state check. I can cash it, but it's going to cost you three hundred dollars. My bank frowns on out-of-state checks."

"Okay, no problem. Three hundred dollars is the charge," Sandra agreed.

Jeffrey handed her back the check. "Come back down and see me in an hour. I will cash it then. Oh, by the way, if you don't check out by noon tomorrow, the room is sixty dollars for another twenty-four hours."

Sandra nodded her head. "No problem, and thanks for helping me out," she said. As she walked to the elevator, Jeffrey rubbed his penis while looking at her large, firm backside.

* * *

A smiling and obviously happy Sandra sat at the tiny table in her hotel room and counted the forty-seven hundred dollars that she got from Jeffrey, the pervert. Still full from the large order of Chinese food, she pushed the remaining cuisine to the side. She pulled out the new notebook, pencils, and calculator that she had just bought, and began to add things up. On her pad she wrote down that two thousand dollars should find her an apartment in Manhattan near the broadcast companies, not realizing that two grand in Manhattan would get her two days in a cardboard box in a subway station. She also wrote that five hundred dollars should get her a week's worth of clothing until she received her first paycheck. The remaining money, she wrote, would be spent on used furniture and miscellaneous things. "It will be a little rough in the beginning, but I will accomplish what I set out to do," she assured herself.

Feeling giddy and energetic, Sandra decided to play her memory game. Since she didn't have her usual deck of cards, she turned the forty-seven one-hundred-dollar bills over so that the face of Benjamin Franklin stared back at her from each one. Concentrating on the first two letters and the first three numbers of each bill, Sandra scanned her eyes up and down the different rows for about one minute. Then she turned the bills over, face down. One by one, she began touching each bill and calling out its first five serials. After announcing each bill, Sandra turned it over. With very little doubt in her photographic memory, Sandra got all forty-seven bills correct. Blowing on her knuckles and then rubbing her chest, Sandra headed to the bathroom to take a nice warm shower.

* * *

Sandra lay in her bed wearing a pair of nylon jogging pants and a gray T-shirt. She could hear a few horns and the engines of a few passing cars. She looked at her watch. It was 2:37 a.m. "Sandra, take your ass to sleep. You have a big day tomorrow," she told herself. She rubbed her ears, lifted her head up, and listened to the couple next door having hot and heavy sex. As the bed rocked faster, it began to pound on Sandra's wall, which made her bed vibrate a little.

With a smile on her face, Sandra listened as the woman next door told her man to "pump it harder." Without thinking, Sandra instinctively moved her hands over her breasts for a moment. Within a few minutes, she could hear the man start to moan as the bed moved faster and faster, until the couple simultaneously let out yells of ecstasy and then got quiet. Sandra tried not to laugh. "I think I'll call him speedy," she joked.

* * *

An hour later, Sandra heard a sound coming from the table. Not able to tell if she was dreaming or awake, she tried to ignore the sound. When she heard the box of half-eaten Chinese rice hit the floor, she couldn't ignore it anymore. Now fully awake, she sat up quietly and listened to the scrambling that came from the table. Easing herself out of the bed, she reached over to the nightstand and slowly clicked on the bedroom light.

To her horror and disbelief, Sandra was face-to-face with two New York City rats that had to be at least seven inches long. She tried to scare them away by shooing, but one of the rats stood on his two back legs and sniffed at Sandra. "Oh, hell no!" she said as she grabbed her sneakers off the floor and quickly put them on while standing on the bed. Not taking her eyes off the unwanted visitors who were now climbing into the food container, Sandra heard about three sets of footsteps walking towards her door. As her food container magically made its way to the bathroom, there was a knock at the door.

"Yes, who is it?" asked Sandra.

"Open the door. Give me my money," the voice answered back. Sandra could hear whispering between at least three people and she saw the doorknob slowly turning. "Who is that?" she asked with a slight quiver in her voice. With a heavy jolt, the hotel door shook ferociously, making Sandra scream. "Open this fucking door now, bitch, and give me my money from your bogus fucking check!" demanded a heavy voice with a Spanish accent.

"What are you talking about?" Sandra's heart was racing.

In a low tone, the Spanish man demanded, "Jeff, open this goddamn door. I'm going to kill her, then you, for fucking with my money."

Sandra heard the jingling of keys and knew she had to move quickly. She grabbed her purse and jumped off the bed. She ran over to the table, grabbed a chair, and stuck it under the doorknob, jamming the door. Frantically glancing around the room, Sandra looked at the window and ran over to it. She pulled it up quickly and climbed out onto the fire escape.

Cautiously, Sandra climbed down the steps of the fire escape as quickly as possible. When she got to the next floor, she heard three popping noises. She looked up while holding on to the rail and saw Jeffrey fall backwards out the window. He landed on the fire escape. Gripped with fear, Sandra continued climbing down, almost slipping on the now rain-soaked metal steps.

"You're next, bitch. I'm coming for you!" the Spanish accent yelled.

Breathing fast and crying, Sandra made it down to the first floor, but she was still ten feet above the ground, and she could hear feet running down the hallway staircase. She climbed over the rail and let herself hang over a metal Dumpster filled with what looked like pig slop and cow manure mixed together. Sandra closed her eyes and let go. She landed dead center in the garbage slop.

Ignoring the stench and the pain shooting from her ankle, Sandra grabbed her purse, climbed out of the Dumpster, and ran out of the alley. With no clue of where she was, she ran in the direction of a light that was straight in front of her. As she got closer, she recognized the red, white, and blue neon sign for the drug store. She exited the alley, looked both ways, and noticed two figures, both tall and dark, looking up the other direction of the block.

Quickly Sandra darted between two cars and crawled to the other side on her hands and knees. She looked cautiously from behind a parked car and spotted a yellow cab that had its off-duty sign on. Sandra held her hands up towards the driver in a begging gesture and he motioned for her to come. Sandra ran to the cab, got in, slammed the door, and slumped down to the floor.

"Take me to the place where I can catch the different buses, please!" she begged.

"Okay, lady. I'll take you to the bus terminal," the driver said, turning on his meter. As the cab took off, Sandra faced her bitter reality. She wanted to go home.

* * *

Curled up under a staircase in the Port Authority Bus Terminal, Sandra held her head in her hands and sobbed uncontrollably. Her clothes were filthy and her ankle throbbed with pain. Clutching her purse like a running back clutches a football, Sandra opened it and stared at her forty-seven hundred dollars, a pack of Juicy Fruit gum, and her cell phone, which had one bar left on the battery indicator. Sandra lifted herself up and limped over to a closed Taco Bell. As she walked, she passed many derelicts and homeless teenagers sleeping on floors and benches, but no police officers were present.

Sandra walked to the ticket booth area, stopped, and pulled her phone out of her purse because it had started beeping. She looked around the large bus terminal in desperation. She wiped away her tears and cleared her throat, and then she dialed home. Her heart was pounding as she swallowed a large lump down her throat.

Awakened from her sleep, Anna Lyte answered on the fourth ring. "Hello, who is this?"

"Momma, it's me, Sandra," she answered nervously. There was complete silence for a few seconds, and then Sandra's phone indicated that the battery was low. "Momma, I'm lost in New York City. Can I please come home?" The phone beeped again, and Sandra heard a click and a violent voice.

"Don't you dare call here again. You have no home here anymore!" Minister Lyte bellowed.

"Daddy, I am so sorry. Please, can I come home?" Sandra begged her father through her tears.

"No you cannot, and don't call me Daddy again, you little tramp. Do you know how you ruined my name and my church?" Sandra looked up at the sky for help. "Daddy, I've been assaulted and chased by angry men claiming that my check from the contest was not real. Daddy, please can I come home?"

"Hell no!" the minister declared without sympathy. "You made your bed, now you lie in it. As far as I'm concerned, I never had a daughter!"

Before Sandra could respond, her phone sounded one final beep and went dead. "Hello! Hello daddy!" a crying Sandra yelled. She dropped her phone to the floor and fell to her knees. She was crying hysterically when she felt a tap on her shoulder. She turned around and was face-to-face with a tall, slim, black woman who reached out to Sandra with a sandwich and a small container of orange juice.

"Here, sweetheart…take this. You look like you've had a long night." Sandra studied the woman, then slowly reached out and took the food and the drink. "My name is Brenda Taylor and I work with Project Outreach for the homeless. If you like, I have a van outside with a few young people like you. We can offer you a bed for the night, and in the morning we can sort some things out for you. How do you feel about that?" Sandra looked at Brenda for a while and then nodded in agreement. Brenda put her arm around Sandra and walked her outside to a waiting blue van. Four young girls were seated inside.

Chapter Four

Decisions Are Made

This particular winter was a brutal one in the Bronx. There were about thirteen inches of snow still on the ground from the previous snowstorm. Inside Doug's large three-bedroom apartment, Fred Gunner was lying on an Italian leather couch wearing silk pajamas and smoking a Cuban cigar as he watched a porno film on the fifty-inch big-screen television. Doug entered the living room decked out in a two-piece alligator suit with alligator shoes to match.

"Damn, boy. Where're you going looking like you just got back from Africa?" Fred mocked.

At twenty-three, Doug now stood six feet two inches tall and weighed two hundred and thirty pounds. He stared at his father for a moment. "I told you last night that I have an important meeting to attend."

Fred sucked his teeth and stared at his son from the corner of his eye. "Just remember to bring home those steaks I like," he ordered.

Doug put on his leather coat and grabbed his car keys. "If I make it home," he told his father.

"Confidence, son. Confidence," Fred said, half-laughing.

Doug walked past his father and exited the apartment.

* * *

Forty-five minutes later, Doug held his arms in the air as two large brothers, each weighing over three hundred pounds, seized Doug's coat, cell phone, and 9mm handgun. Doug opened his shirt and revealed to the two men that he was not wearing a wire. The men escorted him up a white flight of stairs and stopped in front of a door that had no doorknob or peephole. Within ten seconds, a buzzer went off, and the door slowly opened to an all-white room. Inside there were two white chairs, four very large bullmastiffs, and a man wearing a two-piece black silk suit and gold jewelry on his neck and wrists.

"Doug, my new friend or enemy…that will depend on you. Please come in!" Mario Chavez yelled with laughter.

A wary Doug stepped into the room, leaving the large brothers on the other side of the closing door. With a smile on his face, Mario pointed to the chair. "Sit, my man. Let's get acquainted."

Doug took a seat and another door opened. Two Cuban women who were in their twenties walked out wearing nothing but black thongs. They were in perfect shape with not one ounce of body fat and not one wrinkle or blemish on their faces. The women carried champagne and caviar to Doug, pouring him a glass while offering him the caviar on a cracker. Another Cuban woman entered the room from the same door, toting an all-white poodle on a leash. She gestured for the dog to heel, and the poodle lay at Doug's feet. Mystified by the whole scenario, Doug sipped on his champagne while Mario nodded his head and watched all three women leave the room.

"Babies, make Doug comfortable for daddy," commanded Mario, and all four bullmastiffs formed a square around Doug. "Doug, long meetings aggravate me because most meetings are ninety percent bullshit," Mario said as he took a seat. "We don't need to bullshit. All we need to do is become good communicators."

Doug looked at the dogs and nodded his head slowly in agreement.

"I have many associates in your part of town who tell me you are an up-and-comer who enjoys hard work," Mario said.

"I have been fighting for this opportunity for eight years now, Mr. Chavez. I have no problem putting in long hours and spending the majority of my days away from home."

"I like that…a man not afraid to get dirty. Good for you, Doug."

Mario reached into his jacket pocket and pulled out a two-pound bag of cocaine that was wrapped in plastic and tape. He tossed it to Doug, who caught the package and read the label, which said "Baby Powder" in red letters. "Uncut and uncensored, straight from Columbia. I have no competition and no equal," Mario bragged.

Doug stuck his pinky fingernail in the bag and put the product on his tongue. After ten seconds, he rubbed his mouth and stared at the cocaine and then at Mario with an astounded look on his face. Mario burst out in laughter as he rose from his chair. "This is worth fifty thousand dollars to me, Doug. But I promise you—out there it is worth two hundred thousand. They will pay for my pleasure. That I guarantee."

In an instant Mario's expression turned stone cold as he stared at Doug with dark, menacing eyes. "I welcomed you into my home and treated you with love and respect, right Doug?"

"Yes, you have," Doug answered, returning Mario's intent gaze.

"I hope I can trust you, Doug. Because you understand that between love and rage is a razor-thin line, yes?"

Mario averted his eyes and stared down at the floor, rubbing his hand through his dark, curly hair.

"You can trust me, Mr. Chavez. And yes, it is thin," Doug agreed, nodding his head up and down.

With ice-cold eyes, Mario looked up at Doug without blinking.

"RAGE!" he yelled.

At that moment, the four bullmastiffs jumped up on their feet and proceeded to rip the defenseless white poodle apart. Doug leapt to his feet, leaving his chair and hurrying to the side where Mario stood. The floor that was once white was now covered with the poodle's blood and the few body parts that could still be identified. The dogs were covered in blood and sat side by side, staring at their master. Smiling again, Mario put his arms around Doug.

"One week from today, we make two hundred, yes?"

Doug looked at the large package in his hand, and then looked up at Mario and answered, "No doubt."

* * *

Inside a cold and damp basement, Doug, Troy, Buster, and Fish stood at a table. Troy, a light-skinned brother with a college degree, possessed the brain of an accountant. Buster, a muscular, dark-skinned brother with a long, ugly scar on his face, was not much for words and would carve a man like a turkey at the drop of a hat. Finally, there was Fish. He was the eldest of the crew, and he knew anyone and everyone when it came to the game of hustle.

The four childhood friends stared down at the old wooden table, transfixed by the package of "Baby Powder" that was lying there. Doug cleared his throat, breaking the silence.

"My brothers, today is the day when we will no longer be looked upon as small-timers. In one week, we will separate ourselves from the others."

Troy looked at Doug. "We only have one week to move this?"

Fish reached down and rubbed his hand across the product. "One week is a lifetime if this shit is as potent as your contact makes it out to be," he assessed.

Doug smiled and looked across at Buster. "We have to carve out a niche, my brothers—take what is ours."

"I have been waiting all my life to get paid like this," Buster proclaimed. "I'll carve our names into the other brothers' faces so that they know a new product and merchant is on the street."

Doug grabbed a large duffel bag, reached in, and pulled out four portable cell phones. He handed one to each man. "It took me a little while, but I have rigged these to last only two days after the initial time we use them," he explained. "So when the time runs out, just throw them in the trash and meet up at the spot for another." He reached in the bag again and took out four electronic hotel room keys. "There are Baker Motels in the five boroughs. I got the hook-up through someone who owed me a huge favor. Each one of these keys will open room twenty-one at each motel. When I give you the word, we will meet to settle up for that night's work."

"Do you have any idea where we can go to start moving this?" Troy asked, smiling from ear to ear with anticipation.

"We put a little out there and watch them come looking for us," Fish predicted.

Doug nodded his head in agreement. "Tomorrow morning, Buster, you gather your forces together and see who's hungry and wants to put in work for us. Fish, tonight you start putting the word out to your partygoers about the new brew in town. Troy, you and I will meet up at my place in the afternoon to prepare the powder for distribution." Doug motioned for his men to get close to one another. As they huddled close, Doug declared, "This is our time, right now."

* * *

On Friday at 6:00 a.m., Doug and Troy sat inside a spare bedroom in Doug's apartment, packaging their new product. There was a large brown table in front of them with scales, sifters, a large plate of glass, ten playing cards, a box of at least one thousand miniature Ziploc bags, a box of baking powder, and a large amount of cocaine. Both men were sweating while they put together their supply. Doug stopped suddenly, paying attention to a knock at the door.

"Doug, are you in there? What are you doing up so early?" asked Fred Gunner.

Doug motioned to Troy to keep going. "Yeah, it's me...now go back to sleep." Doug walked over to the door, cracked it open a few inches, and passed a bottle of Johnnie Walker Black and two hundred dollars to his father. "Please, Pop, go back to bed," Doug urged as he closed the door quickly. He walked back over to the table, and he and Troy continued bundling the product.

* * *

Later that afternoon, Fish sat at a bar surrounded by numerous associates he dealt with on a regular basis. The men were all drinking Rémy Martin and Courvoisier. All eyes were on Fish as he stood and took center stage. "My brothers, we have been dealing with each other for some time now. I have always been forthright with every one of you, and I have handed out numerous favors to you."

Nine men formed a circle around Fish, bobbing their heads in agreement. One of the men was Jay Black, the owner of Class Barbershop. "What you say is true, Fish. Any way I can help while making a little dough, I'm with that."

Fish patted Jay on the back and smiled. "That's good to hear and know, because what I am about to propose is an excellent opportunity for all involved." Fish pulled out his laptop computer and revealed a graph showing how much product the men were to sell from their establishments and how much they would profit. As the men sat and listened to Fish, everyone had a smile on his face except a heavyset brother named Willie, who owned a meat market.

With his face twisted in anger, Willie stood up and pushed his chair to the ground, causing a loud bang and bringing complete silence to the room. "Fish, how is this shit fair? I've worked hard to create my business. Now you want me to sell this product and risk my shit? I want double!"

Never taking his eyes off Willie, Fish continued to smile. "Brother Willie, I love you, baby. I would never cheat you out of anything. When you couldn't afford to pay for your meat, who got it for you at almost half price? C'mon, I know the money doesn't look long now, but you have my word: Within the next few months, everyone will be satisfied."

Willie was breathing hard. "Fuck that, Fish. I'm out," he shot back.

"No problem, Willie. I'm sorry we couldn't do this. I truly understand how you feel," Fish said, still smiling. The room was so silent that everyone could hear the breath moving through Willie's nostrils. He put on his coat, grabbed his briefcase, and exited the bar. After watching the bar door close, Fish continued with the meeting.

* * *

Willie had stopped his red Chevy Blazer at a red light on the Grand Concourse when a black Suburban with all tinted windows rolled up next to him. The front passenger window rolled down and the driver honked the horn, gaining Willie's attention.

"What do you want?"

"You got a light?" the passenger asked.

"No, the hell I don't," Willie snapped, looking very pissed off.

"Then what the fuck are you good for?" Buster asked, pulling up a sawed off shotgun that he fired at Willie, blowing his head off his shoulders. Willie's body spasmed and the Blazer crashed into a tree. In an instant, the Suburban sped off. Buster put the shotgun under his seat and announced to his driver, "We will not be denied."

* * *

Doug sat in his brand-new Acura watching his corners bring in the cash. It was summertime, and the east side of the Bronx now belonged to him and his small but efficient family. It couldn't get any better or easier. While Doug's workers handled the corners, Buster made sure they stayed protected by the forces. Troy had a girl he was dealing with who owned a string of check-cashing spots in the Bronx. Through these businesses, Doug laundered his money. Meanwhile, Fish kept his promise to his associates that if they allowed the product to be sold in their establishments, they in turn would receive under-the-counter cash and protection.

Mario Chavez was ecstatic for a few reasons. For one, Doug was always on time and never missed a payment deadline. Secondly, Mario liked the fact that Doug never revealed to anyone who his contact was. The less people knew about him, the better. Finally, Mario's product was being sold all over fresh territory that he hadn't tapped himself. As for the cops, Doug had that under control to an extent. He had become quite physical with a female rookie cop over the winter. Through romance and dining, Doug was able to purchase "get-out-of-jail-free" cards and "free-to-sell" permits while obtaining information about the "Dirty 24" of the neighborhood precinct. The Dirty 24 was a drug-and-gun unit whose main task was to freeze up drug trafficking. Through this female cop, Doug had found out that the salary being paid to these men was peanuts, so he set up a meeting and made the commanding officer of the unit a little offer in exchange for his corners and freedom for his sellers. Doug was now rolling in milk and honey, and everyone involved seemed to be happy. As he watched his masterpiece unfold, Doug pulled out his phone, dialed a number, and waited for an answer on the other line.

"Hello, Dad. Please be ready. I'm on my way to pick you up. Okay, I'll see you soon." Doug started his car up and began to drive off when a Ford pulled up next to him. "What's up, Doug, my man?"

Doug looked at the driver of the vehicle and smiled. "Detective Tommy Davis, how are you today?" Doug reached for his car visor and pulled a yellow envelope from under it. He passed it to Davis.

"My man, good looking out," the detective responded.

"Looking forward to seeing you fellows at my party palace this Friday," Doug smiled. Both men nodded their heads in agreement and then drove off.

"Sorry, Pop," Doug said to himself as he turned on his music.

* * *

The sun was beginning to set and Fred Gunner looked at the tall trees that lined both sides of the roadway. With complete silence engulfing the car, Fred clutched his traveling bag when he saw the very large Westchester residence: The Shadybrook Retirement Home. The brown building had to be at least a city-block wide and seven stories high. Doug drove through an iron gate and parked in the visitors' parking lot. He exited the car and looked at Fred as he walked to the passenger side, where he opened the door, helped his father out of the vehicle, and began to walk him to the main entrance.

"You motherfucker, you think I don't know what this place is?" Fred spat.

Doug stopped at the front entrance and looked his father in the eyes. "I can't be home with you all the time and this place has everything you need to keep you busy and healthy."

"Fuck you, Doug. I knew you planned to get rid of me from the get-go!" Fred said, still clutching his travel bag.

"That's not true, Pops. I'm just too busy to care for you anymore. My life is going in a different direction and you're getting in the way."

Suddenly Fred hauled off and slapped the shit out of Doug. "Boy, who the hell do you think you're talking to? Did you forget who spit your ass inside your dead mother? I know what you're doing and I know you're making money, so if I don't like this fucking place, you will find me another. You understand, you little bastard?"

Still standing at the entrance of the residence, Doug felt belittled and embarrassed by the way his father was speaking to him. Not knowing how to respond, he handed a bottle of Jack Daniel's to his father.Fred looked at his son and threw the bottle on the ground right at Doug's feet, destroying his eight-hundred-dollar alligator shoes. "Fuck you, boy. I don't need you to walk me in."

Chapter Five

A Friend Named Pamela Brown

Inside a small bathroom colored with baby blue paint, Pamela Brown, an athletically built, dark-skinned sister with beautiful, long silky hair, was giving her four-year-old son Derrick a bath before bed. She sat on the toilet bowl watching as the curly-haired tot splashed his plastic wrestling men along with his pet dinosaur in the sudsy warm water.

"Wash behind those big ears for Mommy," she encouraged.

Revealing his white baby teeth, little Derrick grabbed his washcloth and did a masterful job. "Look, Mommy, like this?" he asked.

Getting on her knees, Pamela leaned towards the tub to give him a big kiss, but she couldn't because of the vodka bottle that encased her. Derrick stood up in the tub, smiled at his mother, and waved good-bye. Now crying hysterically inside the large vodka bottle, Pamela motioned to her son to sit down in the tub. Derrick slipped on the bar of soap that was lying at the bottom of the tub and fell backwards, landing on his delicate head and submerging in the tub of water. Using all of her strength, Pamela hammered her bloodied fists on her unbreakable glass prison, but she couldn't save her son.

"Mommy, help me!" Derrick cried from under the water.

Still on her knees, Pamela sobbed, "Oh God, no! I am so sorry, baby! Please God, no!"

Sitting up quickly in her bed, Pamela held her chest, which was drenched in sweat. She looked out her window and saw the full moon in all its glory.

"I miss you so much, baby, I miss you so much," she sobbed, getting out of bed. She walked to her dresser where there was a picture of little Derrick, smiling ear to ear. Pamela stared at the picture for a moment then lit a candle. "Mommy has been doing so well," she told her son. "I hope you can forgive me."

* * *

The afternoon, Pamela sat amongst twenty people. When it was her turn, she stood and announced, "Hi, my name is Pamela, and I'm an alcoholic."

"Hello, Pamela," the group responded.

"It's been two years and one month since my last drink," Pamela said as she took her seat. The people in the room broke out in applause. "It has been three years to the day that my son has been gone, and he helps me so much, as does my higher power."

The director, a white woman named Ms. Clarke nodded in acknowledgement. "How has Derrick helped you, Pamela?" she asked.

"I talk and listen to him every night before I go to bed, and there is no barrier between us," Pamela explained, wiping a tear from her eye. "He tells me as long as there is no barrier, he will always be there to help me through this."

The Spanish man seated on Pamela's right side rubbed her shoulder for support.

* * *

Pamela put on her sunglasses to fight the glare of the beaming sun as she walked to the train station. A little boy, who was about six years old and was carrying a baseball bat, walked up to her. "Excuse me, Ms. Lady, can you tie my sneaker please?"

"Sure, sweetheart," Pamela said with a smile. She grabbed on to the boy's laces, tied his sneaker, and rose back up.

"Thank you," said the little boy.

As Pamela began to walk away, a heavyset woman quickly ran to the boy. "What the hell did I tell you about talking to strangers?" she yelled.

Pamela watched the boy's smiling face turn to a frown. "It's all right. He just asked me to help him with his shoes," she explained.

The woman looked at Pamela suspiciously. "Derrick, you bring your ass on, and you better not do that again!"

As the mother walked down the street pulling the boy by his arm, Pamela said softly to herself, "Bye, Derrick." She pulled out money from her pocket and walked down the steps of the subway.

* * *

In the Hunts Point section of the Bronx, the warehouse where Pamela worked was smelly and damp. The conveyer belt rolled out no- frills boxed and canned foods as Pamela worked her post wearing earplugs and goggles. Feeling a tap on her shoulder, she turned around and was face-to-face with a huge Spanish woman named Gladys, who looked about fifty years old and had huge bumps on her face. Gladys looked up at the supervisor's office and pointed Pamela in that direction. Although the office was poorly lit, Pamela could see her boss, Tyrone Jones, motioning to her with his index finger to come upstairs. Pamela removed her protective gear and began her ascent.

"Close the door behind you, Pamela," said Tyrone as he lit up a cigar. He was sitting at his desk with his huge potbelly sticking out. "Sit down, baby," he invited.

"I'll stand, and I'm not your baby," Pamela said coldly.

Letting out a loud, ugly laugh, Tyrone blew smoke in Pamela's direction. "Baby, you owe me a whole lot of money because of your many cash advances, and I'm growing impatient with your twenty-five-dollar-a-week repayments. So let's stop playing games and clear this debt up the right way."

Pamela looked down to the factory floor and saw a few of the female workers sneaking a peek up at the office. "You better take that twenty-five dollars I pay every week and go meet one of your women on 'the Point,' because that's all you're getting from me."

Tyrone's smile vanished and he spat tobacco residue at Pamela's feet. "I control many aspects of your life Pamela, like bills, getting paid, and food going into your stomach, so you should show me some respect."

"Fire me," she smirked. "I'll have you brought up on charges with the union. Keep talking and I'll file sexual harassment charges too. But know this, Tyrone, I will never in a fucking lifetime give you anything but your twenty-five dollars. And like I said, that should get you a lot from some girls on 'the Point.'"

The two stared at each other until Pamela made the first move and exited the office.

* * *

With her three-dollar umbrella destroyed, Pamela hurried to the train station, four blocks away. Wiping her face with her free hand, she began to jog towards the train station. When she was a block and a half away, she could see the green light above the subway entrance. Deciding that the horrendous rainstorm had given her umbrella enough of a beating, she threw it in a nearby trash bin. Her newly done hair was getting drenched as she reached into her pocket for some money to get on the train.

Suddenly, Pamela was grabbed by the arm, violently thrown to the ground, and dragged to an abandoned building's alleyway. Even as she kicked and thrashed her legs, she could hear her assailant's deep breathing. She tried to get her hands on the assailant's face, so he threw her into some garbage cans, causing some major bruising to her ribs.

"Help me! Help me!" screamed a battered Pamela. As she struggled to make it to her feet, she felt a cold, hard smack across her face that released blood in her mouth. She grabbed a garbage can lid and swung wildly, connecting with the predator's head and causing him to stumble backwards. She made it to her feet but stumbled as she tried to keep her balance.

"Somebody, please! Help me!" she continued to scream as she tried to hurry out of the alleyway without taking her eyes off her assailant, who was now making it to his feet. She looked around frantically and found a piece of broken brick that she quickly picked up. With her arm cocked halfway up in the air, Pamela ran down the alley towards the tall figure. Using all the strength in her body, she smashed the rock across his face and pushed him into the garbage cans. They both fell to the ground, and Pamela heard her attacker screaming in pain as he held his face. Using his writhing body as support, Pamela pushed herself up to her feet. She felt her swollen lip and unmercifully kicked the man in his balls, spitting her blood on him as she stumbled out of the alley.

Gathering herself, Pamela held her bruised ribs and ran to the Town Car cab that she saw sitting at a red light. She knocked frantically on the back passenger window and quickly jumped in when she heard the door locks pop up.

"Where you going?" the Spanish cabdriver asked.

"Get me to Lincoln Hospital," she instructed. Exhausted and drenched from the rain, Pamela laid her head back and let her tears flow as the cab took off. "Thank you, God," she cried softly.

* * *

After removing the building keys from the door, Pamela gingerly walked to the staircase leading to her fourth-floor apartment. Gritting her teeth, she slowly began to climb. Each step was a struggle, and she could barely find the strength to continue to the next one. She held the cold compress she received from the hospital against her swollen lower lip and ignored the commotion coming from the various apartments on each floor she passed. Painfully, she made it to her floor. Pamela was unlocking her door when her next-door neighbor approached in a stealth-like manner and tapped her on the shoulder.

"Oh shit," she yelled as she quickly turned around, ignoring the pain coming from her sore rib cage. "Damn, Doug! Don't sneak up on me like that. Say something."

Doug, who was wearing a black silk shirt with slacks to match, smiled at Pamela as if she were the last piece of apple pie in the world. "Baby, what happened to my luscious lips," he asked.

Trying to ignore him, Pamela continued to unlock her door. Doug put his hand in front of her in an attempt to stop her from entering.

"Come on, Doug. Please, I need to go inside."

Pamela could smell the alcohol on Doug's breath. She turned her head away from him, sucking her teeth in frustration.

"When you first moved into this motherfucking apartment, I was the only person to show you some respect. And now all you do when I try to talk to you is act all bitchy, like your shit don't stink!" Doug yelled.

Still holding her ribs, Pamela jingled the keys in her other hand and looked at the white ceramic tiles that decorated the hallway floor.

Frustrated by her failure to respond, Doug became irate. "You better start to realize, Ms. Bitch, that it would be to your advantage to accept me as a friend rather than to have me as an enemy." After a few seconds of silence, Doug slowly removed his hand. "Sooner or later, I will have you, baby. So you should make it sooner," he said as he stepped away.

Once inside, Pamela violently slammed her door so hard that it sounded as if an M-80 firecracker had exploded in the hallway. With her back to the door, she could hear Doug laughing loudly in the hallway. She removed her shoes from her swollen and sore feet, and slowly walked to her dark bedroom. She felt for the light switch and turned on the light. A beautiful smile came across her face as she looked straight ahead at her personal shrine for Derrick. Mesmerized by his radiant smile, Pamela held her ribs and walked over to her dresser where her son awaited. She caught a glance of her own battered face in the mirror, but she never let her smile leave as she lit the vanilla-scented candle that she dedicated to her son, a lover of all things vanilla. As the flame from the candle flickered, Pamela told her boy, "I am here, baby. We made it through another one." Bowing her head, Pamela closed her eyes and meditated to her higher power.

Chapter Six

A Rose is Still a Rose

The stands were jam-packed at Dade High School in Miami, Florida. Some of the fastest track and field boys and girls were competing in the three-day event. Nine girls were lining up at the starting line for the one hundred-meter dash. A fourteen-year-old freshman named Rose Garden was representing Dade High.

With long cornrows that extended down her back, the very dark-skinned Rose wore an orange mesh suit over her slim, tight body that rippled with muscles. Rose loosened her legs as she removed her warm-up suit. Hearing the judge over the loud speaker, all nine girls walked up to the starting line, wedged onto their starting blocks, and arched their backs while remaining on their knees. The judge announced, "Runners set," and the women rose and waited until they heard...*Bang*!

Like greyhounds chasing a rabbit, the girls were off and running. Rose was in fourth place and pumping her legs hard. The crowd roared as a light-skinned junior from Pensacola High named Tammy Johnson took the lead with about fifty meters to go. Finding another gear within her, Rose made a move and passed two girls on each side of her until she was neck and neck with Tammy. The crowd was in a frenzied state and other competitors looked on as Rose and Tammy separated from the pack with about twenty meters to go. Tammy gained a fraction of an advantage on Rose, who bit her lower lip and asked her slender, powerful legs for more. They responded by gaining back the deficit and taking the lead with ten meters to go. Seeing the yellow tape in front of her, Rose sucked in a quick gulp of air and exploded towards the tape while Tammy gave it everything she had but was unable to respond to Rose's challenge. Sticking her chest out, fourteen-year-old Rose broke the yellow tape and caused the six thousand spectators that filled the stands to cheer in unison. As the other runners crossed the finish line, Tammy grabbed Rose gently by the arm. "Your ass better stay ready because you may be Miami's pride and joy, but we *will* be meeting again at the Olympic trials," she whispered. "Thanks. I'm looking forward to it," Rose said through heavy breaths.

* * *

On the center podium, Rose bent her head down and received her gold medal. As she waved to the crowd, she looked around for her track coach, Eddie Wright. Spotting him on the side of the field with her other teammates, Rose ran off the podium and into his waiting, open arms.

Rose's teammates picked her up and she spotted her father, Butch Garden, slowly clapping his hands together in the stands. As Coach Wright helped her down, Rose's smile faded from her face. Her teammates noticed and wondered why. Grabbing her coach by the neck, Rose forced him down to her level.

"Coach Wright, do you think I could catch a ride home with you?" she asked.

"Sure, sweetheart, no problem," he said with a smile.

Rose looked at her father and gestured with her hands in a steering motion. Then she pointed to her coach.

Butch smiled and gave Rose the okay sign. "Daddy will see you when you get home," he whispered as he put on his straw fedora and exited the stands.

* * *

When Coach Wright pulled up to Rose's small, modest-looking Miami home, all five of the female members from the team hugged and kissed her.

"Young lady, we are all so proud of you, and you deserve all of the credit for getting us into first place. You be sure to tell your dad I said hello, and make sure you study tonight," Coach Wright said as he reached over to the middle row of the van and patted Rose on her head.

"Good night, everyone. See you in class tomorrow," Rose said as she got out of the van. She stood and watched as the van carried her teammates down the dirt road. When the van was no longer visible, she turned and looked at her home. Then she went inside.

* * *

Rose turned on the light in her small but neat pink bedroom. Her eyes glanced over its furnishings—a canopy bed, a nineteen-inch television, a computer, a printer, and a couple of wooden dressers—until her eyes finally settled on her favorite part of the room. In the center of the wall, a picture of a stunning, dark-skinned woman with the smoothest skin you had ever seen was hanging in a beautiful oak frame.

The woman's eyes were hazel, her lips were plump, and her skin was without blemish. At least one hundred medals from track and field competitions throughout the country surrounded the picture. Newspaper clippings were pasted all over the wall as well. A pair of ruby red track shoes dangled from the corner of the picture frame. Setting her bag down, Rose removed her gold medal from her neck and smiled. She walked over to the picture, lifted the shoes off the frame, and turned them over to read what was on the bottom of the sole: "Baby girl, I give you these wings so that you may fly wherever you want. Love, Mommy."

Rose held the shoes close to her chest and hung her gold medal on a new nail she put in the wall. "This is for you, Mommy," she said as she kissed the picture and admired her mother's beauty.

"Get your ass downstairs and cook our supper!" Butch roared.

Terrified, Rose dropped the track shoes to the ground and quickly spun around to face her bare-chested father.

"Yes, Daddy. I'm going down now," a quivering Rose answered.

"Now, goddammit! I'm hungry!"

Rose headed to the bedroom door with her head bent towards the floor, too afraid to look at her father. Smirking, Butch slowly moved to one side so Rose could go to the kitchen.

* * *

Later that evening, Butch got out of the shower, dried off, and splashed cheap cologne on his body. He took out his comb and ran it through his nappy beard, causing popping sounds as the comb fought its way through the tangled hairs. He then walked into his bedroom and put on a two-piece pajama suit that looked like a uniform an orderly would wear in a hospital. Turning on his radio, Butch grunted as he lay across the bed, smiling and looking up at his chipped ceiling.

Also preparing herself for bed, Rose put on her mother's favorite blue pajamas and a pair of pink cotton socks. She gathered her books for school and put them inside her schoolbag. She looked at the outfit she had draped across the chair for the next day. Finally, Rose looked over to her mother's picture.

"I miss you and I will always love you," she said as she reached for the small brown Bible that was on her dresser. Rose opened it to Psalm 23 and laid it at the foot of her bed. She got down on her knees and prayed: "Heavenly Father, thank You for all of the blessings You've given me and for taking care of my momma. I don't know if You will be angry with me for asking this, but could You please bring me to my mother tonight? I just want to feel safe again. Please, maybe tonight, bring me to my momma. Amen."

Rose got up from her knees, put her Bible back on her dresser, and got into bed. She turned off her lamp and waited.

* * *

About an hour had passed and Rose was starting to feel a calm come over her. Her eyes were just starting to close when she heard heavy footsteps getting closer and closer until they stopped in front of her door. She looked towards the bottom of her door and saw a black shadow, then she heard the turning of the doorknob. The door slowly opened and the smell of cheap cologne penetrated Rose's nostrils. With tears running down both sides of her cheeks, Rose looked at the dark and hairy six-foot-two-inch monster standing over her.

"Move over for Daddy," Butch ordered in a firm voice.

Rose was crying and shaking. "You said no more after the last time," she pleaded. "This is not right, Daddy, please." The bed made a loud creaking sound as Butch's hulking two hundred and seventy pounds engulfed his defenseless daughter.

The moans of Butch Garden and the creaking of the white canopy bed traveled throughout the house.

* * *

Rose clicked on the light in her bathroom, barely able to look at herself.

"You won't take me, God, because I'm dirty, right? Well I didn't make myself this way. He did." Removing her pajamas, Rose examined her body in the full-length mirror and gently rubbed the bruises between her sleek, athletic thighs. Bowing her head down in self-pity, she turned on the water in an attempt to cleanse herself in the shower. She stepped in and let the hot, pulsating streams of water hit and penetrate her skin. Ignoring the scalding damage to her beautiful skin, Rose built up her threshold for the pain.

"You refuse to take me, so I guess I will send him to You. You refuse to protect me, so I will protect myself," she proclaimed. She turned off the shower, dropped her face cloth to the tub floor, and stepped out into the steamy, sauna-like bathroom. Barely able to see what was in front of her, she wiped the fogged mirror and stared at her welted body. "I will hurt no more," she declared.

* * *

The clock that hung crookedly on the hallway wall read 3:45 in the morning. Setting her duffel bag and her red track shoes on the hallway floor, Rose put her ear to her father's bedroom door and heard his loud, disgusting snores. Gently turning the doorknob, she slowly and quietly pushed the door open. She stuck her head into the slightly opened door and smelled the repulsive mixture of Old Spice cologne and Jack Daniel's whisky. Sure that he would sleep forever, she stepped into the unclean bedroom that was lit by a small nightlight. Butch was sprawled face up and naked in his bed.

Rose walked directly to Butch's closet, which was missing a door, and reached for the brown shoebox at the bottom of the closet. She removed the cover and stared at its contents for a few seconds before reaching in and removing the black .38 special. Feeling the weight of the gun, Rose could barely level it with two hands. She walked slowly over to the comatose Butch, trembling as tears began to fall from her eyes. Using all of her strength, she raised the gun and took two more steps forward, accidentally kicking a green metal case the size of a sneaker box. The sound of the box caused Butch to shift his naked body in the bed and change his snoring pattern. As she watched the scene, Rose held her breath and was as still as a boulder. Seeing her father fall back into a deep sleep, she gently bent down and sat on the dirty wooden floor. She laid the pistol in her lap and gently lifted the box off the floor, setting it in front of her. The box wasn't locked, so Rose lifted the cover and looked inside. Not sure of what she had found, Rose removed a handful of white plastic cards that resembled postcards. Evening them out in her hand, she turned them over to see if the other sides would make sense. She brought the cards up to her eyes and then grabbed her mouth in horror. Rose held her breath and tried not to scream as she looked at the Polaroid pictures.

Little boys and girls who looked no more than seven years old were engaged in horrific and graphic sexual acts with grown men. Unable to hold her dinner, Rose crawled over to a corner as quietly as possible and vomited. She looked at the pictures again, empathizing with the innocent little ones with frowns on their faces and black bags under their eyes. The children were black, white, and Asian. They looked as if they suffered from malnutrition. The men, who looked like businessmen from corporations, had smiles on their faces.

Rose stepped over the loaded gun and stood directly over her father. Wiping away her tears, she gently spread the pictures around his body and on his bed, and promised, "I'll be back, you fucking sick pervert."

* * *

When she reentered her father's room, Rose had a red metal can in one hand and a book of matches in the other. Not paying attention to her still-snoring father, whose leg and arm were now hanging off the bed, Rose screwed the cap off the can and began to spread the kerosene throughout the bedroom. She made sure not to get any fluid on Butch's face as she soaked his bed and the pictures.

As she looked down at the snoring monster, Rose removed a set of pantyhose from her jacket pocket and proceeded to tie Butch's dangling foot to the bottom post of the bed. She made sure her knots were tight, then she soaked the rest of the bedroom leading to the door. Standing in the doorway of her father's bedroom, Rose removed the keys to his truck from her pocket, then she grabbed her bag and track shoes. She calmly lit the entire book of matches, tossed it on the bedroom floor, closed the door, and exited the house with her belongings.

* * *

From the rearview mirror of the black truck, Rose watched the flickering red light in her father's bedroom get brighter and brighter. She started the truck and clutched the gold medal that hung from her neck. "I'm sorry, Coach Wright," she said through her tears as she drove off down the highway towards the Trailways bus depot. Behind her, the Gardens' house was going up in flames.

* * *

The sun was beginning to rise as Rose listened to the engine start up and watched the door of the bus close. The bus was three-quarters full when it finally pulled out of the depot. "This is the six fifteen to New York City. Our travel time is twenty-two hours," the bus driver announced over the loud speaker. Looking at the bottom of her red track shoes, Rose read her mother's message: "…you may fly wherever you want." Then she closed her eyes and went to sleep.

Chapter Seven

Let's Be Friends

It was Friday evening and Doug was wearing a two-piece Hugo Boss suit as he prepared for the party at his Bronx co-op that none of his partners knew he owned. Inside the large living room, there was a large Italian leather sectional and a marble coffee table. In one corner of the living room sat a fifty-inch rear-projection television, which was hooked up to a state-of-the-art Bose home theater system. On the other side of the room, there was a large table with heated pans of lobster tails, imported Alaskan crab legs, filet mignon, baked salmon, pasta with Alfredo sauce, and five different types of vegetables. Forty-eight bottles of Dom Pérignon and forty bottles of imported beer were on ice. Admiring his set-up, Doug slowly rubbed his hands together in anticipation.

He walked down the long hallway and stopped to open a door that was to his left. Stepping inside, he inhaled the smell of jasmine that filled the large room, which was lit by scented candles that sat atop oak armoires and nightstands. Three full-sized beds with Egyptian bedspreads and sheets were equally spaced apart. A beautiful woman wearing Victoria's Secret lingerie sat on each bed. There was a thick Asian woman named Kim, an hourglass-shaped Spanish woman named Maria, and a dark-skinned sister named Moesha.

Doug looked at each of them and smiled. "Ladies, you do understand how important this is to me, right?"

The three women smiled at Doug. "Yes, Daddy," they giggled in unison.

Taking one last look at the women, Doug smiled and closed the door behind him. Two steps to his right, he opened another door that had the same set-up as the first, except for two differences. This room had the smell of cinnamon, and on each bed sat three Russian women named Abir, Helena, and Tabitha. All three women were wearing identical one-piece leopard-print teddies and were listening to classical music. Doug walked into the room and kissed each one on the cheek and asked, "Will you ladies screw their brains out tonight?"

"All night long," they responded in their native accent, smiling at Doug. He exited the room and made his final stop at the last bedroom, which was at the end of the hallway, directly in front of him. Before entering the room, Doug stopped and stared at the door, shaking his head slowly. He grabbed on to the doorknob and entered the room, his eyes widening as he looked at the three-hundred-pound German woman named Mabel. Wearing an all-black leather get-up with a motorcycle cap and boots to match, Mabel slowly stood to her feet. The fat from her pale body overhung from the various openings of her outfit.

Wearing fire-truck-red lipstick and black mascara, the woman smacked a black leather whip that she held in her right hand. "Where is my fucking man?" she demanded.

"Easy, big girl. Your man is on his way," Doug answered, snapping out of his temporary trance.

He closed the door and muttered to himself, "Whatever turns you on, partner."

* * *

The doorbell rang and Doug got up from his seat on the couch to answer it. He looked through the peephole and then opened the door to greet his guests.

"Detective Davis, what's going on?" he smiled.

Tall, blonde-haired, well-built Tommy Davis entered the apartment with eight other police officers. They greeted Doug with handshakes and pats on the back.

"Doug, my brother from another mother…where the party at?" Davis asked.

Doug laughed aloud with the rest of the officers as he closed and locked the door behind him. "Right here, my brother, right here." Inside the living room, Doug observed the nine high-ranking officers from three different precincts as they chowed down on his spread and drank beer and champagne. Detective Tommy Davis, Detective Sam Daniels, a sixteen-year African American veteran, Detective Joseph McCarthy, a thirty-year-old Irish American who headed the Bronx drug task force, and Detective Tony Harris of the homicide division were sitting on the couch admiring Doug's apartment.

"Hey, Doug, you have to give me the number of your accountant so I can be like you," Davis joked. The three other detectives burst out in laughter and then continued to enjoy their meals.

* * *

An hour later, Doug walked down his hallway again. This time he could clearly hear moaning and groaning coming from the rooms where six officers were having their own little orgies. Walking straight ahead, he covered his mouth to smother his laugh as he heard the sound of the whip being smacked on Detective Tony Harris by three-hundred-pound Mabel. Before returning to the living room, Doug removed a remote control the size of a credit card and pointed it towards a light fixture that hung from the ceiling. Looking carefully at the light, Doug saw a small, glowing red light come on. With a devilish smile on his face, Doug went into the bathroom.Closing and locking the bathroom door behind him, Doug bent down to the vanity under his sink and opened the locked door. He moved toilet paper and cleaning products to one side, then slid open a small door and smiled at six VCRs that were recording everything going on in every room of his apartment. Each VCR had a label that described the room it covered: "Living room," "Bedroom #1," "Bedroom #2," "Bedroom #3," "Kitchen," and "Outside front door." Doug slid the door closed and locked it. Then he put the cleaning products and toilet paper back where they were. "Just in case, motherfuckers, just in case," he said softly to himself as he stood back up and brushed himself off. Doug returned to the living room with three thick brown envelopes in his hand. The detectives stopped the conversation amongst themselves and focused on what was in Doug's hand.

"You really want to make an impression on us now, don't you?" asked Sam Daniels.

"Business is business," responded Doug, who handed each officer an envelope. As each man removed five thousand dollars, Doug looked over at his grandfather clock and winked at the pinhead camera that was in the screw that held the hour and minute hands together. All three officers stood by Doug, who then turned his attention to Detective Tommy Davis.

"Doug, as long as you stick to the agreement, you will have our loyalty and protection. We will see to it that you have your corners with no hassle," said Davis.

Nodding his head up and down, Doug focused on Detective McCarthy, who added, "I will always give you a heads up when my department is ready to conduct a sweep of your district. That way you can give your men a rest while the competition gets caught up in the web."

The six officers who had been having sex returned to the living room and began to fix plates of food. One of the officers, Sergeant Carlos Ortiz, sat on Doug's couch and put his feet on the marble coffee table.

"Brother, that's a three-thousand-dollar table. Can you please remove your feet?"

Ortiz looked at Doug from the corner of his eye and ignored him, but Detective McCarthy took control of the situation.

"Hey, Ortiz, respect our friend's home and take your fucking feet off his table," he ordered.

Somewhat embarrassed, Ortiz grumbled, "I apologize," and took his feet down.

"Yeah, no problem," Doug said, playing it cool even though he was steaming.

The three detectives removed their coats. "Okay, partner, we're ready to get deep into some poontang right about now," Detective Sam Daniels told Doug. Putting his arm around the detective's shoulder, Doug instructed, "Right this way, my friends."

* * *

At 4:00 a.m. on Saturday, all nine police officers gathered in the living room, making plates of food to go. Doug put bottles of champagne in plastic bags and handed them out to all of the officers. Conscious that his camera was still recording the festivities of the long evening, Doug sneaked a peek at his grandfather clock. As the men began putting on their jackets, Doug announced, "I want to thank you for this opportunity to establish what will hopefully be a long and prosperous relationship with you all."

The men held up their champagne bottles as a sign of toasting and said, "Hear, hear!"

Doug walked them to the apartment door, opened it, and watched them leave one by one, until he was face-to-face with Detective Tommy Davis. "Just remember, partner, this can go two ways. We can have a good working thing where everybody wins…or you can fuck us, and then in turn—I promise you—we will bury your ass. But I believe you will do the right thing, Doug." Smacking Doug on his shoulder, Tommy exited with the rest of his comrades.

Doug closed the door behind him. "You motherfuckers are already buried. You just don't know it," he said to no one but the camera.

* * *

All cleaned and dressed up, the women received two thousand dollars apiece from Doug as he shook their hands. "Ladies, you hooked me up. Every one of those men left with a smile on his face this morning, and I want to thank you all for helping me. I have everybody's numbers, so when another event comes up, you'll be the first I'll call. There are three limos waiting for you downstairs, so please get your asses out of my place," he said. One by one, the women left the apartment until they were gone.

Inside his living room, Doug pulled his laptop from underneath the couch. He turned it on, put in a disc, and pulled up some private files on all nine officers. Smiling ear to ear, Doug said, "I guess that Coke-bottle-glasses-wearing Timothy is good for something. That bookworm bastard was able to hack into the precincts' computer systems with no problem. That was the best fifteen hundred I've spent in a while." Looking at the officers' files, Doug accessed their salaries, their family histories, all the reports they had filed, and most importantly, all of the people they had busted. To top it off, Doug even had access to their major purchases for the past two years. "This motherfucker has a Porsche and a Yukon? Yeah, okay. Duly noted," Doug said in a surprised tone as he looked at Detective Davis's file.

After a few minutes, Doug decided to get a little sleep, but before lying down, he made a phone call. When he heard Troy answer with sleep in his voice, Doug responded, "Yeah, boy, get your ass up and make some more dough for the baker man. Nah, I'm just fucking with you. Listen, tell Buster and Fish that we will all meet up at the club tonight for dinner, dancing, and sticking hood rats with big pieces of meat. I just might find my future ex-wife for the summer. Okay, partner, I'll see you there." Doug hung up the phone, pulled a remote control from his pocket, and shut down the cameras throughout his apartment. He stared out of the window, watching the sun rise. "See, Mama," he said, "Pop was wrong. I am doing well for myself. I know you're looking down on my black ass and I hope you are somewhat proud of me. I wish you could see me now."

He walked slowly to his couch and plopped down on it. Within twenty seconds, he was sound asleep.

Chapter Eight

What Have You Been Up To, Girl?

It had been a little while since that rainy night at the bus terminal, and Sandra had come a long way since then. She was sitting at a small round table that could only seat two, looking over her cell phone and light bills. She got up and walked over to the dresser to get her paycheck from American Temps. For the past three months, she had been doing clerical work at small businesses in the Bronx and Brooklyn.

Her kitchenette on 119th Street and Fifth Avenue was tiny but very comfortable. Unable to afford anything from Macy's department store, Sandra had decorated her place very nicely with secondhand goods. Her walls were covered with beautiful African art she bought for three dollars each from the local street vendors, and her bed was covered with colorful Afrocentric throw pillows from the Saturday flea market on Lenox Avenue. She had made a multicolored bookshelf out of plastic milk crates she received from Alvin, the manager at the local grocery store who had a thing for her. The crates held at least sixty books, with topics ranging from African history to how to make anything out of chicken broth. She also had a nineteen-inch television, which wasn't bad for something out of a pawnshop. Her cooking area consisted of a tiny stove and a very small refrigerator, but you could eat off her floor, and there wasn't a single dirty dish in her sink. She had managed to put away about twelve hundred dollars from the pageant prize money she won in Virginia, even though she had found out the hard way that the check was bogus.

The only thing she hated about her place was sharing the bathroom with the other tenants. The three women, Missy, Pearl, and Anita, all seemed to be nice, but Missy and Pearl were nasty when it came to cleaning up after themselves. Anita, who was a party girl, was the first to welcome Sandra to the two-story brownstone and from time to time, they hung out.

Sandra kept a Bible at her bedside. She had received it from Brenda Taylor, the woman who had befriended her at the Port Authority. Almost like a guardian angel, Brenda helped Sandra get her place, recommended her to the temporary agency, and wrote her encouraging letters from time to time. The other book Sandra kept at her bedside was the New York University master's degree program directory; she had picked it up at work a few weeks ago. She still held on to her dream of becoming a news anchor, but seeing how tough the job market was in the city, she realized it would take some more education and a lot of hard work.

Glancing at herself in the mirror, Sandra played with her braids and put a stick of gum in her mouth. She was just about ready to go to the bank when there was a knock at the door. She looked through the peephole, saw Anita, and let her in. The two women embraced and then sat at the dinette table. Anita was wearing tight stonewashed jeans and a blue wifebeater. She was light skinned with an hourglass figure and an attitude to match. A white gold necklace adorned her neck and a titanium Movado watch decorated her wrist. She looked at Sandra's check that was sitting on the table.

"Girl, how the hell do you make it on two hundred and thirty-six dollars a week?"

"It's not that hard. I just have to budget and avoid spending what I don't have."

Anita held the check up to the sunlight shining through the window. "Baby, when will you learn that you can have anything you want? You just have to go and take it. We have plenty of assets at our disposal—you just have to know who to use them on."

Sandra looked down at the floor. "I was brought up to believe that hard work always pays off in the end. God says, 'If one does not work then one does not eat,' so although my check may not be much, it helps me maintain until things get better."

Anita let out a high-pitched laugh and looked into Sandra eyes. "Listen, baby, all that sounds good, but that shit does not pay for the things on my neck and wrist. There are a lot of motherfuckers out here with big dollars to spend, looking for a trophy to show off to their homies. I know I am fine as hell and can cook my ass off. My momma says there is one way to get what you want from a brother—walk into the room butt-ass naked with a plate of food, and he will get you anything you desire. Why spend my shit when I can spend his?"

Sandra shook her head and put her check in her pocket. "I'm going to the bank. You want to come?"

"Yeah, sure, but only if you come with me to Macy's afterwards."

"Okay, no problem," Sandra said as she grabbed her apartment keys. The two young women left the apartment and headed into the sun-splashed streets of Harlem.

* * *

Sandra was in total awe of Macy's as she walked around the department store, looking at the clothes, smelling the fragrances, and admiring the many appliances she wished she could have. After allowing a Spanish woman to spray her with a nice-smelling perfume, Sandra turned her attention to Anita, who was now making her way to the cash register. Sandra met her before she got to the cashier.

"Oh Anita, can I see what you have, please?" Sandra asked.

Anita was holding a Coach bag, a Donna Karan suit, and two pairs of Tommy Hilfiger jeans. Sandra looked at the items and checked the price tags on the merchandise. She added everything up quickly in her head and was stunned.

"How can you afford this, Anita? I would have to work for three months to have this."

With a wide grin, Anita pulled out a credit card and a fifty-dollar bill. She walked up to the cash register and handed her things to the white cashier, who started ringing everything up.

"Will you be paying cash or charge?" the cashier asked.

Anita handed the woman the credit card and watched her swipe it on the card reader. "Mr. Clarke, I will need some identification, please," requested the cashier.

"Is that sufficient proof?" Anita asked as she reached across to the cashier and handed her the fifty-dollar bill.

"Yes, and I will need you to sign here, please." The cashier smiled as she passed a receipt to Anita.

Anita grabbed a pen and signed the paper as the cashier packed her bags. "Thank you very much," she said as she took her merchandise.

Dumbfounded, Sandra stared at the cashier, who just smiled and took care of the next customer. Anita put on her sunglasses and left the store with Sandra not too far behind.

* * *

As Sandra sat on the third step of the brownstone, she watched Anita lean over into a red Cadillac driven by a dark-skinned brother who could pass as an offensive tackle in the NFL. Anita reached into her jeans pocket, pulled out the credit card she had used in Macy's, and gave it to him. Meanwhile, Sandra could clearly see that his hand was down Anita's shirt, rubbing on her breast. A few moments had passed when Sandra saw the guy attempting to stick his tongue in Anita's mouth. Before he could, Anita waved her finger from side to side and walked away from the car. The brother smiled, flipped on a pair of shades, and slowly drove off. Anita returned to the stoop wearing a huge grin.

"Assets, baby. You've got them too," she told Sandra, "and if you stop acting so damn shy, I'll show you how to use them."

* * *

At 7:00 p.m. Sandra was relaxing on her bed, eating Breyers strawberry ice cream, and watching a rerun of the old game show *Concentration.* With little effort, she picked the numbered blocks one by one, revealing the matching cubes that contained prizes or money.

"Oh my goodness! What kind of memory malfunction are you people going through?" she yelled at the two contestants in frustration. "Choose four, not nine…Oh, forget it! You have no hope."

She got off the bed and removed her nylon jogging pants and T-shirt, then she lay back down with nothing on but her panties and bra. Tuning out the television, Sandra closed her eyes and thought about the tall, dark-skinned brother who delivered packages to her temporary job site.

Imagining his hands caressing her face and her thighs, Sandra slowly slid her hand into the front of her panties and lifted her bra, revealing her plump but firm breasts. As she rubbed her nipple, Sandra let out a moan. She could almost feel the strong, dark brother grabbing and lifting her large but shapely thigh in the air while he slowly gave her soft, wet kisses. Creating a rhythm while she caressed herself, Sandra slowly arched her back in the air as a cool summer breeze came through her open window and moved gently over her body.

Visualizing her strong, confident lover above her, Sandra extended and bent her legs as if she were wrapping them around his wide back as they moved to the Isley Brothers' "Between the Sheets." Letting out a louder and more intense moan, Sandra felt the eruption getting near. She decided she could no longer wait for her lover and she let herself go. "Oh shit, yes!" she yelled, drowning out the contestants on *Wheel of Fortune.*

Sweaty and somewhat drained, Sandra lifted herself off the bed and looked at the television. "Choose a vowel," she instructed the blonde-haired man who was trying to figure out which letter to pick.

As Sandra put on her pants and T-shirt, there was a knock at the door.

"Who is it?" she asked.

"Girl, you are going to go blind doing that shit," Anita answered from the other side of the door. "Get your ass up so we can party tonight."

Letting out a long sigh, Sandra walked to the door to let Anita enter.

* * *

After spending an hour or so getting ready, Sandra was looking good in her short but not too skanky skirt, a sleeveless baby blue silk-like shirt, and a pair of Anita's black pumps. Sandra fixed her cornrows in a ball that sat on top of her head with a few braids coming across her face, making her look very sexy and exotic.

Although she was very pretty herself and was wearing the most expensive clothes and jewelry, Anita couldn't hold a candle to Sandra's pure, natural beauty.

"How do I look?" Sandra asked her friend, who was sitting on the bed watching her.

"You look nice with my bad-ass shoes on," Anita said with a grin.

"Thanks, Anita," Sandra said, glancing down at the borrowed footwear.

"Okay, baby doll. We have ten minutes to get outside," Anita announced after calling a cab from her cell phone.

"Where exactly are we going tonight? I really don't want to be out too late." Sandra sounded hesitant.

Anita rolled her eyes up to the ceiling. "Oh, girl, please…shit. I found out about this hot new spot where the players hang out. It's called the Baby Powder Club, and it's run by this guy named Doug or something." Hearing the horn blow outside the window, Anita grabbed Sandra by the hand and pulled her towards the door. The two women headed into the neon lights of Harlem.

Inside the cab, Anita told the driver to take them to 144th Street and Malcolm X Boulevard. The cab took off and Sandra felt like she was part of the scene.

Chapter Nine

Blinded By the Light

The club was jam-packed and a song by the Fugees was being blasted through the sound system. Sandra was in total awe of how well the Baby Powder Club was coordinated. The bar resembled an oval-shaped racetrack with over one hundred plush leather chairs, and several bartenders were mixing drinks. The large dance floor was made of polished white-stained oak. At the back of the club, there were beautiful tables with white linens and flowers for those who wanted to eat. Looking around, Sandra noticed that all of the men were wearing designer two-piece suits with expensive shoes to match. The women were also dressed eloquently, which made her feel a little out of place.

"This is nothing like Richmond's night clubs," said Sandra.

Anita grabbed Sandra by the hand and led her to the bar, where handsome and distinguished brothers were present.

Trying to keep her composure, Sandra fiddled with her hair nervously.

"Girl, relax and have some fun. This is a party and we're going to have a good time…shit," said Anita.

As Sandra continued to look around the club, a tall, light-skinned, handsome brother approached with a slight smile on his face. "Good evening, ladies. My name is Greg. Can I buy you ladies a drink?"

Smiling at Greg, Anita took stock of him from head to toe. "No thank you, Greg, but that was very nice of you," she gently declined.

Greg smiled and quietly walked away, looking somewhat dejected but trying his best not to show it.

A puzzled Sandra stared at Anita. "He seemed to be very nice and sincere. Why did you turn him away?"

Anita smirked. "Baby, if you want to survive in my world, you've got to pay better attention to the real players and the pretenders. First, the brother was wearing shoes from Payless. Second of all, he was wearing a

Timex watch. Finally—and this shit tops the cake—he had three teeth missing from the back row of his damn mouth, which means more than likely no benefits, which probably means no job, which makes me wonder how the hell his ass got in here."

Sandra couldn't help but burst out laughing as Anita rolled her eyes in Greg's direction.

Destiny's Child's "No, No, No" came on and Anita yelled and announced to the club, "Damn, that's my song!" She grabbed Sandra by the hand and pulled her off the barstool. They quickly made their way to the dance floor. Sandra tried to keep up with Anita as she broke out in all the new dance moves, but she couldn't, so she created her own moves. Slowly and seductively moving her body side to side, Sandra finally let her hair down—literally; her braids were flinging from side to side. Men who were once enjoying their drinks and private conversations were now focusing on the brown-skinned sister with the thick, tight body, who was letting it all hang out on the dance floor. As Anita and Sandra danced with each other, neither girl noticed the small circle that was forming around them.

Sitting in his owner's box that overlooked the club's patrons and employees, Doug relaxed in a leather executive chair with a glass of champagne in his hand. The room was off-white with cherry wood molding around the ceiling and floor. The lights were soft and somewhat dimmed, giving off a mellow ambiance. Inside the room with Doug were his associates Fish and Troy. Everyone except Doug had two women, one sitting on each side of him, nibbling on his ear, and feeding him lobster with butter sauce.

Doug couldn't take his eyes off the brown-skinned sister on the dance floor with the shapely thighs, firm breasts, small hips, and plump backside. However, it was not her body drawing Doug's attention; it was the innocence in her face. She had a look that said *I would never hurt a soul. If a puppy were in the street on a rainy night, I would take him in.* Doug's experience in the game of making money and making enemies had taught him one thing: Nobody could be trusted and loyalty was as definite as winning the lottery. One of the lessons Doug had learned from Dollar Bill was never to trust a woman totally because she would do and tell you anything to stay close to your stash. Sex them and treat them with the respect they earned, but never let them wake up in your kingdom. Doug knew Dollar Bill was right, but looking at Sandra brought a sense of calmness to the storm in which he lived. Continuing with his fixation on Sandra, something felt right and pure about her.

"Damn, Doug, wake the hell up! What are staring at, boss?" asked Troy.

"Troy, see that woman with the baby blue blouse on dancing with the light-skinned female? I need you to go down and give her a bottle of Moët and dinner on the club."

Troy was kissing on a Spanish woman while feeling on a light-skinned sister. "Come on, partner. I'm a little busy, as you can see."

Doug cut his eyes at Troy so hard it could have cut a rock. "Goddammit, man! Fuck these women. I asked you to do me a solid!" he demanded. As Fish stared at an enraged Doug, Troy got up to do as he was told.

Downstairs, Sandra was sweating and smiling from ear to ear as she watched Anita return to their table with two bottles of water. "Shit, this is nothing but faucet water and they're charging me six dollars. The next time we'll just drink from the johnny pump."

Sandra laughed so loud that a few women sitting in the vicinity stared at her. As the two friends sipped their water, a short Cuban man approached their table with a large serving tray on his shoulder. Right behind the man was a handsomely dressed brother, who had a forced smile on his face. As the two puzzled women watched the waiter place lobster, leg of lamb, two bottles of Moët, and two dozen pink roses at their table, Troy excused the waiter and stepped up to the table.

"Good evening, ladies. I hope you are enjoying yourselves tonight. My name is Troy and this dinner, along with the bouquet of flowers, is a gift to you from the owner, Mr. Doug Gunner." Troy pointed up to the owner's box, showing the women where Doug was sitting. Anita picked up a bottle of champagne and waved it wildly in Doug's direction while Sandra shyly and slowly waved her hand up to Doug.

"Thank you, Troy, and please let Doug know we appreciate the hospitality," Anita said. Troy nodded his head in acknowledgment and headed back up to the owner's booth. Anita immediately went berserk on her dinner and champagne, but Sandra said her grace before tasting hers. Chewing and savoring every bite, Sandra inconspicuously looked up at Doug, who was staring back down at her.

* * *

After refreshing themselves in the women's room, Sandra and Anita moved slowly with the crowd towards the exit. Still holding her flowers in her hand, Sandra was sticking close to Anita, who was making her own path out into the summer night. The sidewalk was jam-packed with people who were waiting for cabs or for their cars to be retrieved by the club's valet attendants. As Anita looked to hail a cab, she felt a tap on her shoulder.

"Hi, pretty lady. I'm Troy. Do you remember me?"

"Hi, Troy. Yes, I remember you," Anita smiled. Troy pointed towards the corner a few feet down the block, bringing to Anita's attention a white Cadillac limousine.

"Who is that for and where is it going?" Anita asked with suspicion and disbelief.

Troy rubbed Anita across her face gently. "It's for you. The driver has been ordered to take you wherever you like."

Anita saw Sandra's puzzled expression. "What about my girl? Can she ride also?"

"Actually, *that one* is for your friend," Troy explained, pointing in the opposite direction, where a driver was standing by the passenger side of a blue Mercedes-Benz limousine.

Anita grabbed Sandra by the arm. Cautiously and curiously, she walked her over to the shiny blue limousine. When the two women got near the car, the tinted back window slowly rolled down, revealing a well-groomed and handsome brother wearing an all-white Giorgio Armani suit. Removing his black shades, Doug smiled at the women while tapping on his door with his finger. The tuxedo-wearing driver opened the door for Doug, who slowly stepped out of his car, revealing his blue gators.

"Good evening, ladies. I really hope you enjoyed yourselves tonight," Doug said.

Anita took a step forward. "Yes, we did, and you have a classy club."

Never taking his eyes off Sandra, Doug continued, "Thanks a lot. I have put much time into my place."

"Thank you for the flowers. They smell very nice," Sandra said, wearing a girlish smile.

Doug nodded his head and grinned like a kid at Christmas. "May I ask your name?"

"My name is Sandra Lyte and this is my friend Anita Crane."

Doug reached out, shook Anita's hand, and smiled. Two cars that were driving by stopped and honked at Doug, who in turn acknowledged them. Quickly turning back to Sandra with a sly grin on his face, Doug asked, "Do you have any idea why I gave you those roses, Sandra?"

Sandra thought about it for a second. "No, I don't. Why don't you tell me?"

"Because I wanted the roses to know what real beauty looks like," he said, rubbing his hands together slowly.

Anita had a *you-are-full-of-shit* look on her face, but she was somewhat caught up in the moment. Then it happened: Sandra's and Doug's eyes met and locked, remaining that way for a few seconds. Doug, who stood six feet two inches tall, weighed two hundred and fifty-five pounds, and had the physique of Adonis, was melting inside. Anita watched the whole scene unfold and then finally broke the silence.

"Well, it's getting late and it's been a long day," she said.

Doug nodded his head in agreement. "Do you think you would like to spend your Sunday afternoon with me tomorrow, Ms. Lyte?" he asked Sandra, who looked at him for a few seconds before answering.

"What did you have in mind?"

"Whatever pleases you is fine. You know, New York is a big place," he replied, twisting his shades between his fingers.

Sandra looked at Anita and saw that she was smiling. "Okay, you have a date. Noon will be fine."

Doug reached into his pocket and pulled out a card with his name and number. "Sandra, you call me when you're ready, okay?"

Sandra studied the card and then looked into Doug's eyes. "Okay, I will," she agreed.

Doug looked at his limo. "Well, I was hoping we could have gone for a ride tonight, but that's cool. So, why don't you and Anita take the Cadillac home?" He shook Anita's hand. As he shook Sandra's, on the down low he slipped her a miniature box of Godiva chocolates. Smiling at Doug, Sandra slowly walked away and headed down the street with Anita to their waiting limo. Still standing outside his vehicle, Doug watched in a daze as he admired the perfect shape and proportion of Sandra's knock-out figure.

Inside the Cadillac, there was complete silence as Anita opened Sandra's box of chocolate and began to eat them. Savoring the sweet taste of the creamy chocolate, Anita glanced at Sandra and rolled her eyes, mumbling to herself in a very low tone, "Bitch."

Sandra looked up from the radio dial that she had been adjusting. "Anita, did you say something?"

A smiling Anita responded sweetly, "No, boo. I didn't say anything."

* * *

Across the street from the club, a horn honked to get Doug's attention. Doug looked over and saw Buster's black Suburban. He put his shades in his jacket pocket, walked over to the truck, and was let in by one of Buster's soldiers. Inside the vehicle's backseat, Buster was holding a meat cleaver on the wrist of a man named Dexter. His mouth was taped shut and his hands were bound with plastic and duct tape.

"Yo, boss. I hate to disturb you on your get-out night, but this is the motherfucker that has been stealing from the Laundromat's cookie jar, and we have him on film," Buster explained. Dexter was crying and shaking, trying to get a word out, but he couldn't.

"Damn, Dexter. When you were dirt-ass poor, who gave you a job and paid your sister's rent? Who loved you like a son, baby?" Doug asked.

Sweat and tears were pouring down Dexter's face as he began to shake uncontrollably. "You can't pay me back, Dexter. You don't have shit that I need. But you know what, my man? I'm going to show you what it feels like to come up short." Doug stepped out of the truck. Then he stuck his head in the window and nodded at Buster, who raised the meat cleaver and chopped down on the wrist of Dexter, who was going berserk while a soldier named Dave held him. The plastic was filling up with blood, and Buster raised the cleaver again, landing with another swift blow that caused Dexter's hands to dangle by their skin.

Doug watched without flinching. "Drop him off at Harlem Hospital and call me tomorrow. I need some rest," he told Buster.

Buster smiled at Doug and punched a wailing Dexter in the jaw, knocking him out completely. "I hear you boss. We'll talk tomorrow."

Doug tapped on the hood of the truck and walked back to his limousine. "Home, my good man," he told the driver.

* * *

Sandra stood in front of the mirror nailed to her door, nervously making some final changes to her long braids. She was wearing a white blouse and a pair of new black slacks from New York & Company. Sandra looked at her black shoes and wondered if she should wear them. After a moment, she decided that she would keep them on. Looking at her full lips, she reached in her purse and put some strawberry lip gloss on for good measure, believing that most men liked sisters with big, glossy lips.

A horn blew out front, and Sandra quickly turned and went to her window. Peeping through the mini-blinds, she saw Doug looking fantastic in a gray two-piece Calvin Klein leisure suit. Sandra admired the elegance and style that Doug gave off. She watched him blow his horn again before she exposed herself to him from the window with a smile and a wave. Smitten by her beauty, Doug waved back and walked to the other side of his brand-new shiny red Lexus that wouldn't be available to the public for another seven months. He opened the door and motioned with his finger for Sandra to get in. Trying not to rush, Sandra mouthed "okay" and left her apartment.

As she walked down the staircase, she ran into Anita, who was walking up the stairs to her apartment. Sandra had a huge smile on her face. "Girl, I'm so nervous! He looks so handsome. Doesn't he?"

Anita was holding a bag of food she'd bought from the Chinese restaurant. She gave Sandra a half smile. "Yeah, I saw him and the motherfucker didn't even speak to me when I said hello. Just be careful with him."

Sandra looked puzzled, but she started smiling again as she walked towards the door. "I'll let you know everything that happens when I get back," she promised.

As Sandra walked out into the sun-splashed street, Anita said to herself, "Your dumb ass won't last two days with him."Outside, Doug admired how Sandra's face and hair looked in the sunlight. "It's good to see you, my lovely sister. You look very nice, Sandra."

"Thank you very much. You look very nice yourself," she replied, trying not to blush.

Doug gently grabbed her hand and Sandra allowed him to lead her into his car, where the scent of Grey Flannel cologne was lingering in the air. As she put on her seat belt, she discreetly looked in the rearview mirror, watching and admiring her tall, muscle-bound date walk around to the driver's side of the car.

Looking deeply into Sandra's eyes, Doug smiled. "Are you ready to have a good time, Sandra?"

"Yes, I am," she said, returning his gaze. As the sound of smooth jazz played through the car speakers, Doug and Sandra headed down Fifth Avenue.

* * *

As the couple sat in Tavern on the Green, Doug was enjoying his swordfish as he watched Sandra eat her lobster and steak. Reaching across the table, he poured her some more red wine and then did the same for himself.

"May I propose a toast?" he asked, holding his glass slightly in the air.

"Yes, you may."

Sandra held her glass next to his and Doug looked into her eyes from across the table. "To a new and hopefully long, exquisite relationship between two people."

Sandra didn't say anything at first. "I agree, same here," she finally concluded. They gently tapped glasses, took sips of wine, and continued to eat and talk.

"Sandra, what part of New York were you born in?" Doug asked.

"I wasn't, Doug. I was born and raised in Richmond, Virginia."

Doug looked surprised. "Oh. How long have you been here? And what made you come?"

A little sadness reflected from Sandra's eyes. "Maybe once we get to know each other a little better, I can tell you my story."

Doug nodded his head slowly up and down. "I understand, Sandra, and I respect that." Smiling at each other, they finished their meal.

* * *

Later that afternoon, Doug led Sandra out of the theater on Broadway where they had just seen *Bring In'Da Noise, Bring In'Da Funk*. Sandra held a T-shirt and a program from the show, and was smiling from ear to ear in awe of the bright lights and the excitement coming from the entertainment capital of the world.

"How did you like the show?" Doug asked.

"I have never seen anyone dance like that before," she answered, shaking her head back and forth in amazement. "The show was great. Thank you."

Putting his arm around her shoulders, Doug turned Sandra around to face him and pulled two more tickets out of his pocket. "The night ain't over yet, baby." In Doug's hand were two tickets to Radio City Music Hall to see Luther Vandross in concert.

Looking at the tickets, Sandra grabbed her mouth and then threw her arms around Doug's neck, yelling, "Oh my goodness. Luther is my man! Thank you."

Doug held her by her thin waist and savored her sweet-smelling perfume. "Come on. Let's go see your man." Heading in the direction of Radio City, Sandra put her head on Doug's massive arm and walked side by side with him.

* * *

As Doug drove Sandra back to her place, the moon and stars illuminated from the sky directly into the open moonroof of Doug's car. "Cherish" by Kool & The Gang was playing on the radio, and Sandra rested her head sideways on the passenger seat, gazing at Doug. When they got on the FDR Drive, Sandra admired the lighted skyline of the city.

"Doug, I just want you to know that this has been the best time I've ever had out with anyone, and I want to thank you again."

"I had a nice time too, and like I said, hopefully we will remain friends."

"If you don't mind me asking, what is it that you do?"

Doug cleared his throat. "I own my club and I also work in exporting for a good friend of mine, which earns me some extra cash."

Sandra sat up straight in her seat. "That's really interesting work. Do you travel much?"

They were coming towards their exit when Doug answered, "Every now and then I have to leave town." As they got closer to Sandra's place, he asked, "Do you need anything from the store before I let you off?"

"No, thank you, Doug. I'm fine," she said after contemplating for a minute.

They pulled up in front of Sandra's place and Doug put the car in park. As the two of them stared into each other's eyes, Doug moved in for a goodnight kiss and Sandra moved in also. They slowly kissed and held each other until they both began to moan.

Taking control of the situation, Doug slowly pulled away. "You better go before something gets started," he warned.

Sandra let out a childish giggle. She slowly opened the car door and gave Doug one more kiss before exiting.

"Sandra, I'll call you tomorrow when you get home from work," Doug told her. Nodding her head in agreement, Sandra entered the brownstone as Doug watched from his car. After a few moments, Doug saw her light go on. He started his car and drove off.

While driving, Doug dialed a number on his cell phone. "Mr. Chavez, this is Doug. How are you? Just wanted to confirm my pick-up tomorrow morning. Okay, very well. I'll see you then."

Smiling and happy, Doug threw his phone on the passenger seat and said to himself, "Time to go stick it deep into my Spanish mommy, Jasmine." Pressing the CD button on his dashboard, Doug nodded his head to the jam "Gangsta's Paradise" by Coolio as he drove to the Bronx for some wild sex.

* * *

It was Wednesday and Sandra hadn't been to work since Friday, but work was the last thing on her mind right now. She was holding Doug's hand as they walked into Tiffany & Co. jewelry store on Fifth Avenue. Doug looked across the store and spotted Cindy, a white salesperson who recognized him and waved as she walked over. Doug whispered something in Cindy's ear, then he moved to the side and watched as Cindy and another girl made a fuss over an overwhelmed Sandra.

When they left the store, Sandra was in a trance-like state as she admired the diamond bracelet and the gold Movado watch that she now sported on her wrists. The couple walked briskly down Fifth Avenue until they came to Saks Fifth Avenue, where they stopped to purchase some clothes for Sandra. Before entering the store, Doug turned Sandra towards him.

"I know this is fast and to the point, but I have to say this, so please just listen. You are my woman right now. As my woman, I have to be able to trust you. Loyalty and trust are more important than clothes, money, or jewelry. Because if at any point in time things go bad, I have to know that you will be there for me and that you would never betray me. Do you understand?"

Sandra had a serious look on her face. "I have never met anyone like you, and yes, I believe in the same things as you. So please believe me when I tell you I would never betray or hurt you in any way. I will always stick by you as long as you want me to. I would never do you dirty, and for some reason, right now I feel like I really love you, Doug."

Taking Sandra in his arms, Doug kissed her in front of the store as people walked around them. They were interrupted by Sandra's cell phone ringing.

"Hello, Ms. Jones. Yes, I'm sorry. I have just been under the weather for the last couple of days, but I promise I will be in tomorrow."

Doug reached for Sandra's phone and gently took it from her hand. "Hello, Ms. Jones. I'm Sandra's man and I'm letting you know that at this moment, she quits."

He hung up the phone and handed it back to Sandra. "You will no longer work for anyone," he told her. "I'm your man, so anything you need or desire, you come to me. Also, I want you to start looking for a real apartment tomorrow. I will take care of all the expenses. Now come, let's go shopping." Walking in front of her, Doug extended his hand backward for Sandra, who reached out and grabbed hold of him.

* * *

Only candles lit Doug's bedroom, and the scent of cinnamon filled the air. He looked up as the bedroom door slowly opened, revealing a luscious Sandra, who was wearing a purple two-piece teddy. She walked over slowly to her man, who was sitting at the foot of the bed. Sandra stood between his large, strong legs and gently rubbed his bald head. With his large hands, Doug slowly felt Sandra's thighs and her smooth behind as he pulled her close to him.

Sandra slowly pushed Doug back on the bed and sat atop him. Seductively, she removed her top and showed her perfectly shaped breasts. Rubbing her back, Doug reached up and began kissing her nipples softly. Sandra moaned uncontrollably, then she slowly removed Doug's silk boxers and took his large manhood into her hands. Squatting up slightly, she helped Doug make his way inside her.

As they both moaned and kissed with passion, Sandra swiveled and began grinding on top of her man with fierce desire. The candles flickered throughout the room as Doug and Sandra made slow, beautiful love throughout the night.

Chapter Ten

Diamonds Are Not Forever

The Manor Ballroom in the Bronx was decorated with care and elegance for Troy's thirtieth birthday party. Red and white balloons were spread throughout the room and a large number-thirty ice sculpture was sitting in the middle of the floor. The waiters were all dressed in black tuxedos, ready to serve lobster, crab, fish, and steak to the fifty friends and family members who were scheduled to attend. Bottles of champagne and wine sat atop a long table, along with a five-layer birthday cake for Troy. To set the tone throughout the evening, a professional disc jockey was in a booth playing music on state-of-the-art equipment.

As guests began to take their seats, Troy arrived with his beautiful wife Beverly. Wearing a white silk suit and white alligators to match, Troy was smiling and waving at the guests, who clapped and yelled his name.

"Where's Doug? I see everyone but him. Damn, I thought this was *my* night," Troy griped to his wife.

Beverly smiled at the guests, then leaned in to whisper in Troy's ear. "Don't worry about where he is. You just enjoy your night with your friends and me," she comforted.

Troy smiled at his wife and admired how beautiful she looked. He kissed her and then they walked around the hall to greet everyone in attendance. The first ones to hug him were Fish and Buster, who were sitting at the large round table that had been reserved for the crew. As Troy and Beverly made their rounds, people started looking towards the entrance of the hall where Doug and Sandra had just arrived.

Decked out as usual, Doug was wearing a tailored midnight blue two-piece suit with a velour white hat and blue alligators to match. He was also sporting a diamond-studded cane. His finger displayed a two-carat blue diamond ring and his wrist boasted a diamond Rolex watch. Walking next to Doug and holding his arm, Sandra looked stunning. She wore a white silk gown with high splits on both sides that revealed her thick, firm thighs. Her hair was in cornrows, and her fingernails and toenails were painted red. A three-carat diamond necklace hung from her neck, and a diamond Rolex watch that matched Doug's adorned her wrist.

As they walked to the center of the floor, Doug stopped and twirled Sandra around slowly so that everyone could admire her. Although she looked a little embarrassed by the gesture, Sandra kept a smile that showed her pearly white teeth. Doug looked towards the large round table and saw Troy, who was wearing a fake smile.

"What's up, baby!" Doug yelled at Troy as he walked towards the table with Sandra behind him. Doug grabbed Troy, giving him a hug and swinging him from side to side.

Doug smiled at Fish and Buster. "My partners in crime…who loves you more than me?" He hugged both men, and then he walked over and gave Beverly a quick kiss on the cheek.

Grabbing Sandra by the arm, Doug paraded her to the side of the table. "Everyone, I want all of you to meet my polished and unflawed diamond…my baby, Sandra. Hey, ain't she the most beautiful rose in this room?" Everyone looking at Sandra smiled and waved, including Beverly, who was doing her best not to let her true feelings show.

"Good evening, everyone. Nice to meet you all," said Sandra, who took her seat next to Doug.

"Hi, Sandra, this is my husband, Troy, the guest of honor at this occasion," Beverly said.

Sandra looked at Troy with a smile on her face. "Happy birthday, Troy, and may you have many more."

"Thank you, Sandra. It's nice to see you again," he said, reaching for his wife's hand.

Doug, who was listening to every word at the table, sat in silence with his face twisted in a knot and his lips almost pouting.

On the sound speaker, the disc jockey announced, "Ladies and gentlemen, we at the Manor Ballroom want to thank you for taking the time to come out and share in the thirtieth birthday celebration for our good friend Troy Collins. To start it off, I would like to spin this first record for the birthday boy."

The crowd awaited the song and everyone yelled "Happy birthday!" as the song of the same title began to play. Smiling, Troy stood and waved at the crowd as Beverly got out of her seat, grabbed Troy's hand, and led him to the dance floor. Sandra smiled and applauded them while Doug just looked on. The dance floor was flooded with people having fun and dancing. Some looked good doing what they did while others just looked plain out of rhythm. But the one thing they all had in common was fun. They all had smiles on their faces, and they were having a ball. Out of about fifty people, the only two still sitting were Sandra and Doug.

Sandra was smiling, clapping to the music, and patting her feet. "Sweetheart, come on and dance with me. I bet I could show you a step or two on the dance floor."

"Listen, I'm not one for dancing," he said without looking at her. "I'm just here for my man, Troy. Besides, this disc jockey ain't playing anything I like."

Sandra played with her earrings. "Well, would it bother you if I took the floor by myself? I love to dance and I like the music."

Letting air exit from his mouth, Doug looked at Sandra calmly. "Sweetheart, if your man ain't on the dance floor, what makes you think I'm going to allow you out there?"

"Allow me, Doug?" Sandra asked, letting out a small chuckle.

Doug turned to Sandra and looked at her with dark, shark-like eyes. "I'm not going to speak on this matter anymore. I am done," he said firmly.

As the record ended, Sandra's smile also faded away. She turned her head and watched Troy and his wife walk back to the table.

"So, Sandra, what do you do?" Troy asked, still holding his wife's hand.

Sandra's radiant smile emerged on her face again. "Well, Troy, I'm actually…"

"She does nothing," Doug interrupted. "My woman doesn't need to work for anything or anybody. It's my job to take care of her. The only person she needs to depend on is me."

Beverly looked in the other direction and dabbed her sweaty forehead. "Baby, I will be right back. I want to freshen up," she said to Troy. "Sandra, you want to join me?"

After looking at herself in her pocket mirror, Sandra agreed. "You know what, Beverly, I need to use the bathroom also. Sure, I'll join you."

The ladies got up and excused themselves. "Make sure you hurry back," Doug told Sandra.

Not saying a word, Sandra acted as if she hadn't heard Doug and laughed as she walked with Beverly.

"Sandra, did you hear me?" he asked a little louder, drawing eyes and attention from other nearby guests.

Sandra stopped and turned around. "Yes, Doug. I heard you… damn," she answered.

As the women walked to the bathroom, Fish and Buster joined Doug and Troy at the table.

"What's up, partner? You okay tonight? You seem kind of edgy," Fish noted.

"Yeah, man, I'm cool," Doug answered after taking a long sip from his glass of champagne. "That meeting with my contact has me a little worn out, but I'm cool."

Buster smacked Doug on his shoulder. "Come on, Doug. This night belongs to our partner Troy. Let's show some love tonight, man. No business tonight, just pleasure, okay?"

Doug reached across the table, hugged Troy, and kissed him on the cheek. He spotted Sandra and Beverly making their way back across the dance floor. With a smile, he jumped out of his seat and rushed over, surprising Sandra. Grabbing her by the hand, he led her to the dance floor where the disc jockey was spinning a song entitled "Still Not a Player" by Big Pun.

Doug danced like he was having an epileptic fit while Sandra moved her hips smoothly from side to side. As Doug's boys laughed and yelled at him from their table, Sandra took his hands and tried to get him to dance to the beat. She put her arms around his enormous shoulders and pulled him towards her to give him a huge kiss. At that moment, all seemed well between them.

* * *

Doug and Sandra, along with everyone else at the table, were taking their last bites of dinner. Sandra took a long swallow of club soda, which caused her to release a belch that had the sound of a passing tugboat in the night. She quickly covered her mouth, and with embarrassment in her eyes, she looked at everyone at the table. They all stared back at her in shocked silence. Within a couple of seconds, Beverly let out a huge laugh, followed by Fish then Buster. Troy pointed at Sandra, who was smiling and giggling.

"Excuse me, everybody. I'm sorry," she apologized.

Everyone was laughing and patting Sandra on the arm to show her that it was no big deal—everyone except Doug. He was staring at Sandra as if she were the last person he wanted to be around. Under the table, he quickly kicked Sandra's foot in disgust.

"Ouch! Doug, what the hell is wrong with you?" Sandra asked.

Doug wiped steak sauce away from his mouth.

"What the fuck do you mean what's wrong with me?" he asked angrily. Getting up from his chair, he looked down on Sandra with anger in his eyes.

Totally embarrassed, Sandra reached into her bag to retrieve her cell phone. "Can you give me a number for a cab company?" she asked Beverly. "I'm going home."

"Doug, come on, partner. She just burped. It's no big deal, man," said Troy, trying to soothe the situation.

Tears started to roll down Sandra's face and Beverly walked to her side of the table to console her.

"Come on, baby, let's go to the ladies' room to freshen up," she suggested.

The women began to leave the table but stopped suddenly because of the yelling and commotion coming from outside the hall. Beverly looked towards the door and held her chest. At the ballroom entry, seven to eight masked men ran into the room with guns drawn.

As people got up from their tables with fear on their faces, one gunman started firing in the direction of the dance floor. It was sheer pandemonium as three women and a man hit the floor from bullet wounds. At Doug's table, Buster reached into his jacket and removed two automatic handguns. He fired at the masked men, hitting one in the leg.

Troy looked at his screaming wife, who was holding Sandra.

"Get down, Beverly! Get the fuck down!" he yelled.

People were crashing into each other and one man ran into the table holding Troy's birthday cake, knocking it to the floor. Fish threw Sandra to the floor and covered her with his body while he looked for a target.

Bullets were flying as the masked gunmen planted themselves behind tables and the disc jockey's booth. Looking for his wife while he crawled on the floor, Troy finally spotted her. She was screaming as one of the gunmen stood over her, reloading his weapon and pointing it at her face. As the gunman cocked the trigger, Doug came from the gunman's blind side holding a nickel-plated Magnum. He pumped one round into the man's head, removing half of his skull. Crouched behind a table, Buster reached out and grabbed Beverly by her arm, dragging her to safety behind a table. Fish spotted a shooter in the DJ booth, squatting behind the turntables. Rolling over Sandra, he fired at least twenty rounds from his two handguns, destroying the DJ equipment and the masked gunman, who screamed before falling out of the booth onto the floor.

Doug saw Sandra sprawled out on the open floor and started rushing to her side. Twenty feet in front of him, two gunmen appeared with guns aimed right at him. Raising his weapon, Doug fired, hitting one of them right between the eyes. Pointing at the other, Doug fired but was out of ammunition. The masked man's finger was on his trigger, ready to fire, when an injured man named Harry plunged a huge chunk of ice from Troy's sculpted number thirty into the shooter's head, causing blood to splatter. Harry looked at Doug and fell back to the ground fatally. Doug quickly regained his faculties and hurried over to Sandra. He dragged her behind a wooden column for safety.

"Are you hurt!" screamed Doug. Not getting an answer, he looked into her eyes and could tell that she was in shock. "Fish, how many of them are left?" Doug yelled.

"How the fuck do I know!" Fish fired back.

Calm came across the hall for a moment. Then Buster, who was still guarding Beverly, saw two masked men rushing for the door. They began to shoot aimlessly in the air. Buster shot back, hitting one in the back of the head. The other made it out the door. Taking in the scene, Buster observed the many injured and dead bodies lying all over the dance floor.

"Doug, I think it's all clear," Buster said. "We have got to get out of here, man. The police will be here soon."

Soaked in sweat, Doug carried Sandra in his arms as Troy consoled Beverly, who was crying.

Fish still had his weapon in his hand. "Everybody, come on. There's an exit through the kitchen," he instructed.

Following Fish, everyone made their way to the kitchen, stepping over bodies and blood. As they walked through the kitchen, Troy noticed cooks, waiters, and servers hiding behind two freezers.

"It's over…there are people out there hurt. One of you call an ambulance!" Troy ordered.

A waiter, trying to put on a brave face, reached into his pocket and took out his cell phone.

* * *

As the crew got to their vehicles, Doug said, "I have to get her to a hospital. I will call everyone tonight. Troy, is Beverly okay, man?"

Troy rubbed his wife's face. "No, Doug. She was almost killed tonight, man!"

Doug looked in silence as an angry Troy put his wife inside their car and drove off. Hurrying while at the same time being gentle, Doug got Sandra into the car and ran to the driver's side. He paused for a second to look at the scene of Troy's party. Hearing the sirens getting closer, Doug entered his car and sped off to Albert Einstein Hospital.

Chapter Eleven

An Unwanted Blessing

As Doug sat in the waiting room, he observed the elderly and the children who were in need of medical care. He looked up at the television that was positioned up near the ceiling and watched the news report from the Manor Ballroom, wondering who might have been behind the attack and how they could have known about the event since it was an exclusive party for Troy. The scene on the television showed pure havoc. Doug was not worried about the cops figuring out that he was there because all they had to do was look back on the reservation list. His only two concerns were making sure the murders would not link back to him and making those responsible pay. Getting up from his chair, Doug walked to a secluded part of the floor and dialed Fish on his cell phone.

"Fish, it's me. Is everybody all right? Good, what about Beverly and Troy? Listen…everybody's heat was untraceable, right? Okay, listen. Everybody stay out of the club except Buster and me. I'm going to have to smooth this shit over with the blue crew first. So whatever we put on the street will have to go through the back door for a minute…The doctors are looking at her now so let me get back. Remember what I said. Tell Troy and Buster…Okay, talk to you later."

Doug hung up the phone and saw a doctor who looked like he was searching for someone. Doug ran up behind him. "Excuse me, doctor. My name is Doug. I brought Sandra Lyte in about an hour and a half ago. Are you looking for me?"

Dr. Meng, a short and stout Chinese man, held his hand out for a handshake, which Doug obliged.

"Hello, Doug. I'm Dr. Meng, and yes, I was looking for you." The doctor, who was wearing a shirt and tie with his black pants, put his hand on Doug's back and led him to a small office."Please have a seat, Doug. There are some important things we need to discuss."

As he sat down, Doug looked around the room and observed the many charts of the body and all of the different equipment used to examine the body, which in a strange kind of way made him a little squeamish.

"First off, your friend Sandra is going to be fine. She has just suffered a little rise in her heart rate. By the way, what caused her heart rate to increase?"

Doug looked around the room and took a deep breath. "Two men attempted to rob us at gunpoint. Sandra panicked and started losing her mind a little, which caused her to pass out. After giving them my money, they took off, and that's when I brought her here."

The doctor nodded his head up and down. "Doug, do you know any reason why they didn't take the expensive jewelry she's wearing?"

"When she started screaming and panicking, a few people started looking out of their windows and stopped to look out their cars. This must have made the robbers nervous, so they took what they could from me and ran off, leaving her things alone."

The doctor stood up and patted his feet on the floor while listening to Doug's story. He seemed a little skeptical about the whole thing.

"Well, I am here to tell you that Sandra is responding much better than when she first arrived, and her blood pressure is back to normal. Secondly, and most importantly, she asked me to inform you that she is in the very early stages of a pregnancy."

Doug's head was spinning a thousand miles an hour as he stood up. He remembered what Dollar Bill said, which felt like a hundred years ago: "Females are just mules you hump—nothing more, nothing less. Never let them set up base in your camp."

Dr. Meng looked at Doug with some concern.

"Doug, are you going to be okay? By any chance, are you the father of this baby?"

With his head buried in his hands, Doug let out a long, exasperating sigh. "I'm not sure, but I could be, doc."

The doctor patted him on the shoulder and helped him to the door. "Come, Doug. Let's go see if Sandra is up and able to talk," he suggested.

Walking down the corridor made Doug feel as if he were being led to a room where he would be given a lethal injection for all the shit he had done in his short but busy life.As soon as they got to the room, the doctor patted Doug again and left him alone with Sandra. After all she had been through, she still looked gorgeous. Doug removed his jacket and pulled a chair next to the bed. The silence was deafening as he looked at the blue and almost-too-clean floor while Sandra focused on the smooth white ceiling that was above her head. Doug stared at Sandra, who looked as if he was the last thing she wanted to see.

"Sandra, how are you doing?"

"I'm fine, Doug," she whispered in a low tone.

Doug got up and pulled his chair closer to Sandra. "So, the doctor told me the news," he started.

"Yes. I'm pregnant."

"How do you feel about that, Sandra?"

"Right now I don't know what I feel. I was just in a violent shootout at your friend's birthday party. Listen, Doug, I know I'm from someplace that you consider country, but my brain is not country. You told me you were an exporter. What exporters carry big guns to a party and get involved in a gunfight? I'm not stupid, Doug. Maybe a little behind in the times, but I'm not stupid."

Doug felt as if his pants were down in front of an audience. He got up from his chair and took a seat on the edge of Sandra's bed. He slowly and gently grabbed her hand. He held it a little tighter when he felt her pulling away. "Sandra, from the minute I laid my eyes on you, I knew you were someone I wanted to be with. I'm a hustler, Sandra, and I'm sorry I had to lie to you about that. Please try and dig where I'm coming from. I just thought the less you knew about what I was doing, the better it would be for both of us. Besides, I know you're not stupid. I knew that sooner or later the shit would hit the fan."

For the first time, Sandra looked at Doug and something inside her felt sorry for him. He had surrounded himself with people, but in all reality, he was a lonely person.

"Doug, listen to me, okay? This is really going to sound crazy, but you know what shocked me the most about you tonight? Not the violence, not your lack of respect for your friends, but more than anything, the way your mood swung from right to left in a matter of moments. I mean, all I did was belch and you almost crushed my foot. What did I do that was so bad? It didn't change the kind of person I am. Can you answer that?"

Doug rose to his feet and faced Sandra. "Up until this day, life has always been tough for me. Nobody has ever given me anything—not a piece of bread or a cup of water. My father never loved me and my mother died on me, so I never learned to trust anyone. So now, I finally meet someone who is pure as snow. I admit I can act a little crazy, Sandra, but please try to understand. You are the best thing that has come into my life. Now the doctor is telling me you're pregnant. Please, Sandra, forgive me and I promise you'll see a new man."

Unable to hold the tears back any longer, Sandra let them escape her eyes. She sat up in the bed and reached out for Doug's hand.

"Doug, you said to me that all you wanted was loyalty and trust from your woman. I know it has not been that long between us, but have I given you any reason to doubt me?"

Realizing that this young woman from Richmond, Virginia, was no dummy, Doug decided that he must be honest for once. "No, Sandra, you have not given me any reason to doubt you. That's why I'm asking you to start over with me so I can show you that I'm down for you as much as you are for me. I know what I'm doing isn't right, but it's all I know how to do. Please don't leave me like everyone else has in my life. Please, Sandra, I want to be a part of you and what is growing inside you."

Pulling Doug slowly towards her, Sandra put his hand on her face and he began to caress her softly.

"Doug, I don't have anyone in this city but you. You promised that you would look after me and I believed you. So please don't let me down. I have no place to go and no one to turn to except you."

He slowly kissed Sandra on the mouth and looked into her eyes. "I promise things well get better between you and me," he told her.

Sandra pointed towards the chair and motioned for him to sit.

"I'm ready to go home tonight. Can you get me out of here?"

"The doctor said he wanted to take a few more tests in the morning," Doug said, looking at the clock on the wall and then back at Sandra. "Besides, we have been through a lot tonight. I really think you should stay here and rest. I promise I will be here first thing tomorrow to get you out of here, okay?"

With a smile, Sandra nodded her head in agreement. Doug bent down and gave her one more kiss.

"If you need anything tonight, you tell them to charge it to me," he insisted. Then he gave her one final hug.

Before shutting Sandra's light off, Doug smiled and winked at her. With the moonlight shining through the window, Sandra said softly to herself, "I know I can change him."

* * *

As he stood outside on the street, Doug's phone began to ring. He looked at the caller ID.

"Oh shit. I do not need this right now," he complained as he looked up at the stars that illuminated the sky.

On the other end of the phone, Detective Tommy Davis started screaming at the top of his lungs as soon as Doug picked up.

"Listen to me, okay? Look at the book. It was a legitimate party for my best friend. I have no idea where they came from or who they were. All I know is that my guys did not fire back, and no guns or ammo that will be found there can be traced back to us."

Staring up at the sky and shaking his head, Doug continued to respond to the irate detective. "I understand that I have to lay low. What's it going to cost to keep me out of this? Okay, let's meet at Echo Park on the Tremont Avenue side tomorrow night, just you and me. We can make this work. Talk to you later."

After hanging up with Davis, Doug called Fish. "Listen, tomorrow night I need some birds in the trees at Echo Park. I'm setting up a payment that should clean this shit up. So get some birds ready just in case some shit jumps off. Okay, I'll be in touch."

As he walked back to his car, Doug looked up in the direction of the hospital. He picked a window, assumed that Sandra was in there, and wondered aloud, "Just for humping and bumping, what the hell did I do?"

* * *

The next morning Doug held Sandra's belongings as he unlocked his apartment door. He moved to the side so that she could enter. At that moment, Pamela Brown was leaving her apartment. She sadly stared at Sandra then at Doug without uttering a word. Sandra walked in and stood in the long hallway decorated with nice-looking artwork. Doug closed the door behind him. "Please make yourself at home, because it's your home also."

Doug showed Sandra around the large three-bedroom apartment that he had beautifully decorated himself. Then he sat Sandra down in the living room.

"Sandra, in another nine months, we will become a family, and our lives will change forever. Therefore, I think it's very important that from this point on, you should spend most of your time here at home. Also, you should find a private doctor that can see you on a one-to-one basis."

"Doug, I want to thank you for letting me stay here, and I promise that for as long as I can, I will help out around the house by making sure things stay clean."

"There's no need for you to do anything because I have a cleaning service come by once a week to clean the place up."

Touching her belly, Doug smiled at Sandra and told her, "From this point on, things will be nice and peaceful."

Chapter Twelve

Seven-Year Sentence and Counting

What started as a promising beginning had become nothing but a relationship of lies, deceit, and worst of all, abuse on both the mental and physical levels. Things had changed drastically in the lives of Sandra and Doug. The mood swings that Doug had were no longer there; instead his mood was now nasty all the time. With the rise in the usage of crack and crystal meth, which were cheaper to produce and purchase than cocaine, Doug had seen his clientele drop dramatically. This meant a drop in sales and cash flow. On top of that, his large three-bedroom apartment, which he had once considered his own private Idaho, was now very crowded with Sandra and the two most beautiful twins in the world, Chaka and Kareem.

That's right—nine months after moving in with Doug, Sandra dropped a load on his ass weighing a grand total of fourteen pounds and nine ounces. As Sandra held and smiled at her two babies, a mystified Doug stood about four feet away from the visitors' viewing window. While fathers rushed from work to see and hold their bundles of joy, Doug was too busy trying to find that new contact, which was another reason for his bitterness.

Mario Chavez, who had been the king of cocaine in most of the five boroughs, was like a champion prizefighter. Because he was on top, there was always someone waiting to knock him down and claim his throne. As Mario got older, he didn't have the sense to share the wealth and keep the young pups happy; instead he was greedy, which was not smart. Those young pups got larger and hungrier every day. They formed a wolf pack and attacked Mario until he could not fight anymore. After a few bloody battles in the Bronx, Doug's connection was no more, and that left Doug scrambling for fresher product. Not being perceptive enough to change with the times, Doug fell off in the city. To his credit through, he learned to enhance what he was receiving from a new Italian cat named Johnny from Bensonhurst, Brooklyn. Johnny's supply was not as good as Mario's was, but it kept Doug's loyal customers returning to the club, which he still owned and maintained.

Doug's other problem was that his buddies at the police department still had their hands out every month and their zippers unfastened with penises hanging out, ready to attend another orgy at Doug's expense. Eventually, something had to give. Either Doug would have to cut them loose and risk losing everything he had left, or he would have to cash in his chips, putting them up against the wall.

The one thing Doug didn't lose was his sense of security when it came down to covering his own ass. As time went by, he kept himself educated in the advancement of video electronics. Over the years, he bought new equipment that allowed him to transfer all of the video of the cops' sexual escapades on to DVD discs. What started out as four detectives and five regular police officers involved in sex parties had expanded to include their indulgence in drug and alcohol use as well. Doug recorded everything that went down in that co-op apartment. He had about ten discs that could blow the police department out of the water, creating the biggest scandal the city would ever see. So keeping this information a secret was no game; it was about life and death. This was Doug's life insurance policy against anything that came against him from the NYPD. He cherished those discs more than he loved his own children.

Finally—as if he needed any more pressure—Doug was losing his grip on his crew. Fish, Troy, and Buster had become very fond of the life that Doug had introduced them to, and they got a little cranky when they had to leave the club to hit the corners again to sell for Doug. This left them in a very dangerous situation; those young cats that had started prowling the streets to sell their product did not take kindly to some old-timers still trying to play the game. Doug knew this. He wasn't stupid, and he knew it would only be a matter of time before the boys wanted to come inside again—even if it meant setting up three against one.

Doug knew nothing was fair in the streets, which was why he decided to go a little old-school and look up an old friend of his from when he was new to the game: his man Bucky. Even though he was forty-eight years old, Bucky was sharp, in shape, and loyal. Bucky loved Dollar Bill, and Dollar Bill had loved Doug. Doug knew this gave him a strong connection with Bucky. So why not use it to his advantage? As long as Bucky never figured out that it was Doug who set up Dollar Bill, everything would be okay. Bucky would be in the club and on the streets for one reason—to watch Doug's back while keeping an eye on the boys in the crew—period. If anyone got out of line, Bucky would do them for Doug in a heartbeat. Then there was Fred Gunner, who resided at the Shadybrook Retirement Home in Westchester. On the first day of every month, Doug took a ride up there to visit Fred. He had to pay eight hundred dollars a month and give his father three hundred for his pocket. Doug wouldn't admit it, but deep down inside, he had always feared and loved his father at the same time.

With all of this drama hanging over Doug's head, he still had to send what he called "two crumb-snatching kids" to private school, pay off cops, pay off members of a crew who might not even like him, and pay rent for an apartment that he couldn't even enjoy. Someone had to suffer for Doug's woes, and that person had been beautiful Sandra. Giving up hope that she would ever hear from her parents again, Sandra had come to the realization that all she had to build on were Kareem and Chaka, who were now seven years old and always put a smile on her face whenever they entered the room. Sandra understood that she was not totally blameless when it came to the situation she was in. Most women would have left the very first time their men laid hands on them, but this situation was a little different because Sandra had no outlets or support. She trusted and loved Doug, and he controlled her decisions and clouded her judgment. It was a huge mistake to make when she had been striving for independence. She became accustomed to the lifestyle she and the kids enjoyed under Doug's care. Realistically, how was she ever going to pay rent in New York City? Kareem and Chaka were very intelligent and excelled in every school subject. How was Sandra going to pay for the excellent private school they attended? Deep inside she knew she could not provide for her children like Doug could. So Sandra endured the smacks and sometimes the punches, as well as the bitches, hoes, and other names Doug decided to call her on any given day.

One thing stayed constant with Doug though—the way he made up with Sandra. He always asked for forgiveness, which Sandra always gave. After that came the expensive gift to smooth things over, which she always took. She loved Doug in a way that allowed her to take a lot of shit that another person would not. Sandra loved him, but she loved her kids even more. When she realized that Doug didn't love their kids as a father was supposed to, it made her question how much shit she was supposed to take. Sure, he was paying for the best private school in the city and Christmas was always spectacular. But he showed them very little love and something had to give.

Sandra went to all the school functions alone and took it upon herself to do the things a father should do with his son and daughter. She even taught them not to hate their father, but above all, to love and protect each other exclusively. Doug put fear in Sandra through mental and physical intimidation, and he had her believing he watched her every move. If she ever thought of trying to leave him, bad things would happen. Knowing Doug for as long as she had and seeing what kind of lifestyle he lived, Sandra knew that if he wanted to touch her, he could. Doug had Sandra and the kids on a time clock. Everything was set up for Sandra to do at specific times—cleaning, cooking, picking up the kids, and even having sex. She had better be on time or she would pay.

After two months of begging, Doug became tired of hearing Sandra's mouth and allowed her to do something that gave her pleasure. He allowed her to volunteer four hours a day at a soup kitchen that was on Jerome and Burnside avenues. This was her outlet and a way of giving back in hopes that she would receive some blessing or forgiveness for what she had allowed herself to get into. From 10:00 a.m. until 2:00 p.m., Sandra was in heaven because she helped those less fortunate than herself. From time to time though, she asked herself was it not the other way around—weren't they really helping her?

So now, a new phase in Doug and Sandra's life together had begun. Neither one of them knew where it would lead, but they both realized that something had to give. It was just like the old saying: A master can only kick his dog so many times before the dog begins to growl back.

Chapter Thirteen

You Are Late

There were about two hundred people inside the community center on this cold December day. Some were in line getting served lunch, and others were at the tables eating. Sandra, who was wearing a black sweater with black jeans to match, had her braids covered with a scarf and her hands covered by plastic gloves while she served the food. By her side was Carla Smith, a fifty-nine-year-old black woman, who had started the program six years ago by feeding people in train stations. Her service had grown and she now fed people from all over the Bronx. The food consisted of sandwiches, soup, salad, vegetables, and fruit. There were about twenty volunteer workers carrying out various tasks, from serving the food to maintaining crowd order. Serving the food brought great joy and comfort to Sandra, and she never lost her smile while serving.

"Good afternoon, James, and how are you?" Sandra asked the twenty-something-year-old homeless man from Tremont Avenue.

James tried not to make eye contact with Sandra.

"Good afternoon. Is it possible for me to have an extra piece of fruit?"

Sandra looked at James with a smile and compassion. She reached inside the fruit basket and gave him an extra banana. James looked up at Sandra for about a second and smiled. "Thank you for the fruit and for remembering my name," he said. Sandra nodded her head as he walked to a table to eat.

The line was moving at a rapid pace when Carla returned from the pantry looking confused. "Sandra, I know for a fact that I bought a large container of garlic on Monday, but for the life of me, I can't remember what I did with it."

"Ms. Carla, look in the pantry, inside the third cabinet on the second shelf and to your far right. It should be sitting next to the half-full jar of oregano," Sandra said, looking up from the mother and daughter she had just served. Carla twisted up her eyebrows as she looked back at Sandra, and then she left the room.

A slim, dark-skinned girl with twists in her hair walked up to Sandra with a tray in her hand. She looked straight ahead at the clock behind Sandra. The young woman looked no older then twenty and seemed to be in pretty good physical shape.

Sandra carefully placed the food on the girl's tray. "Good afternoon, Rose, and how are you doing on this cold, blustery day?"

"I am fine, thank you."

"You are in great shape, Rose. Do you work out?" Sandra asked, admiring Rose's posture.

"No, not much anymore. How do you know my name? I don't remember telling you."

"Yes, you did—three weeks ago when you first came in here. You were soaking wet from the rain," Sandra said as she placed a small container of apple juice on Rose's tray.

The slim girl with the track-star body looked at Sandra for a second and then walked to the back of the center and sat in a corner.

Carla returned with the garlic in her hand. She shook her head as she stared at Sandra. "Girl, you better gets you a hotline like that Ms. Cleo had," she joked. The two women shared a chuckle while feeding the hungry.

* * *

The center was closed until dinner, and Sandra was in the kitchen with Carla and a Spanish woman named Jasmine. They were washing and drying dishes by hand, laughing at something Ms. Carla had said. With the big, tin-like salad bowl in her hand, Sandra glanced up at the clock on the wall and noticed the time. Her hands started to tremble and she dropped the bowl on the floor, startling Carla and Jasmine.

"Oh, my goodness, Sandra. Baby, you all right?"

"Ms. Carla, I am really sorry but I have to go. I have to get home, okay?"

Looking very concerned, Jasmine rubbed Sandra on her back, trying to comfort her shaking and trembling friend. Sandra glanced around nervously, quickly removed her apron, and tossed it to the floor.

"Please, Sandra, tell me what's wrong. Maybe we can help," Jasmine offered.

"It's okay. I promise I'll be back tomorrow. I just have to get home in a hurry," Sandra said. As she rushed out of the kitchen, the other two women watched with concern.

* * *

Sandra stood in the middle of the street and vigorously waved down a cab. She got inside, told the cab driver her destination, and asked him to hurry. As they drove down the Grand Concourse, the driver got caught in a slew of red lights and came to a halt. Sandra looked at her watch and at her surroundings. Tears fell from her eyes as she looked at her watch again. It was now 2:20 p.m.

The traffic lights started turning all green down the long stretch of the Grand Concourse. As she looked at the many buildings that she passed, Sandra was also counting the blocks. She was now two minutes away from her building. As the driver made a right on Bedford Park, Sandra finally saw the big beige building that she called home. When the cab stopped, she pulled a ten-dollar bill out of her pocket and exited without taking her two dollars in change.

Once inside the building, Sandra ran up the stairs. She took two steps at a time until she reached her floor. Out of breath, she walked quickly to her door and fumbled with her keys. Finally getting the keys in order, Sandra unlocked the three deadbolt locks and opened the door to the apartment.

"Hello, everybody. I'm…" Suddenly it felt as if a shotgun blast had hit her chest. Sandra fought for air while grabbing her left breast. The room was spinning at about a hundred miles an hour as Sandra fell back towards the living room wall. She could vaguely see Kareem and Chaka sitting on the couch, still wearing their green school uniforms. After about two seconds, everything just went black.

* * *

Feeling an ice-cold gush hit her face, Sandra gasped for air as if she were drowning in Niagara Falls. She sat up quickly, spit up water from her mouth, and grabbed her chest in pain. She was barely getting oxygen into her lungs, but she gained some focus and saw that she was still in the living room. As she struggled to get on her hands and knees, she spotted her children, who remained seated on the couch with terrified looks on their faces.

Sandra slowly turned her head to the right and pushed her braids out of her face. Two large muscle-sculpted legs were in front of her. As she slowly lifted her head upwards, Sandra saw Doug, who was wearing nothing but a pair of black silk boxers and a pair of blue slippers. Still weak, Sandra started to fall back on her backside. As she tried to regain her balance, Doug grabbed her and forced her to her feet. Smelling his gin-and-tonic breath in her nostrils, Sandra braced for the worst. Doug dragged her to the kitchen like a rag doll. Then, with a show of brute force, he threw her in the direction of the stove, causing her to skin her hand on the floor.

"What fucking time did I tell you to come home, Sandra?"

Trying to regain her composure, Sandra avoided looking at Doug. "You said two o'clock. I'm sorry, Doug."

Sandra's muscle-bound tormentor looked down on her. He quickly walked over to her and arched his foot to her face. Sandra raised her hand in an attempt to block the oncoming kick, but it never arrived. Instead, Doug slowly lowered his leg.

"I'm going to the back and by four o'clock, my meal better be ready on that table. The next damn time I have to go pick up these kids from school, I'm going to bust your ass again. Do you understand?"

"Yes, Doug, I understand."

Doug grabbed Sandra's keys off the table and took them to the door. He found a key and turned the top bolt on the door, locking Sandra and the kids inside.

* * *

Next door in her apartment, Pamela Brown had her ear close to the wall that was adjacent to Doug's living room. "I hope she kills your ass," she said softly to herself as she grabbed her keys and headed to her A.A. meeting.

* * *

When their father closed the bedroom door, Kareem and Chaka rushed to their mother's side to help her make it to her feet. Chaka began to gather pots and pans while Kareem wiped Sandra's face with a towel that had been hanging from the refrigerator.

"Hurry, momma, hurry! We don't have much time!" Chaka urged. Barely able to look at her children, Sandra hugged them and opened the freezer to get the food she would prepare for dinner.

* * *

As Sandra stood next to her children, who were both overly dressed for an at-home meal, she examined their groomed heads and made sure their hands were clean. Then she looked at the dinner that she had placed on the white Italian lacquer table. The roasted duck was piping hot. There were vegetables, rice, baked rolls, and salad sitting alongside the duck. Sandra positioned the children behind their chairs, kissed them both on their heads, and went to get Doug.

"Doug, dinner is ready," Sandra said after making three light knocks on the door.

"Go wait for me by the table. I will be there in a second," he responded coldly.

When he heard the slow taps of Sandra's shoes moving away from the bedroom, Doug went back to what he was doing. He carefully weighed each scoop of cocaine that he placed atop the scale. Then he gently sifted the product into a small plastic bag. He flicked the bag with his index finger and a smile spread across his face. "Those young boys don't know who they're dealing with," he said with satisfaction as he wrapped the last bag of cocaine for his men to sell that night.

He got up from the fold-up table in the bedroom and walked into the dining room. There was complete silence as Doug looked at his family, who stood by the table waiting for him to sit. Taking his time, he walked over to a brown maple console table that displayed a beautiful old-fashioned radio. He turned a knob, a light illuminated, and the soft sounds of jazz music started to play.

Doug walked over to the dinner table, took his seat, and watched Sandra hurry over to him. She grabbed a white napkin, unfolded it, and gently laid it in his lap. Then she stepped back to rejoin Kareem and Chaka.

Sandra watched Doug prepare to eat his dinner. He cut up the duck and stuck a piece on his fork along with some vegetables and rice. He looked at his daughter, then at Sandra with suspicion. He pointed the food that was on his fork at Chaka. The girl looked up at her mother and then slowly walked over to her father, who put the food to her mouth and stuck it inside. As he watched Chaka chew, Doug studied the girl's throat to make sure she swallowed, and he observed her face for any reaction. Fully satisfied, he motioned with his finger for the rest of them to sit down and eat. As the smooth voice of a woman came through the radio, Doug savored his food.

Chaka and Sandra looked at each other simultaneously, then at little Kareem, who was clutching a butter knife with his tiny hands. Looking straight ahead, Doug chewed his food and swallowed.

"Anytime you're ready, my man," he challenged. "Anytime you're ready."

* * *

Laughter filled the apartment as Sandra and the kids decorated their Christmas tree. Sandra, who was wearing a Santa Claus hat, began stringing the lights around the tree as Kareem jumped around, tossing icicles. Sandra stood to her feet and pulled her son close to her waist.

Chaka, though, was staring straight ahead with fear in her eyes. Unbeknownst to her mother and brother, Doug was right behind them. He took one of the candy canes Chaka was holding, put it near Sandra's ear, and snapped it in two, making Sandra flinch. He walked away laughing and then returned to his bedroom.

* * *

Later that evening, Sandra was lying with the kids on their bed as they watched the last of *Animal Planet* on a fifty-inch plasma television. Grabbing the remote control, Sandra clicked the television off.

"Okay, my precious little ones, it's time for prayers and bed."

As Chaka got on her knees, Kareem ran out of their room, laughing up the long hallway. Trying not to get frustrated, Sandra motioned to Chaka to wait where she was. Then Sandra got up and stuck her head out of the bedroom door.

"Boo, Mommy!" Kareem yelled playfully.

Sandra grabbed her chest and acted like the little boy had frightened her. She playfully grabbed him and carried him to where his sister was.

"Y'all better take your asses to sleep back there," Doug yelled from another room.

Sandra put her finger to her mouth, warning the children to be very quiet. Then she motioned for them to say their prayers.

"God bless Mommy and my sister, Chaka. God please let it snow on Christmas so that me, Mommy, and Chaka can build a snowman. Amen," Kareem prayed.

As Sandra tucked her children away, she gave each of them a long hug and a kiss to go along with it. Chaka held her mother tightly and refused to let go. Only when Sandra used a little strength was she able to break herself free. She walked over to the doorway, blew them a kiss, and turned the light out.

* * *

Now in her bed, Sandra was wearing a two-piece pajama set with thermal underwear underneath. She was burning up, but she hoped the extra layers would serve as a deterrent for Doug, who was in the bathroom three feet away from her.

"Please give me strength," she quietly whispered. She could smell the aroma of musk oil and hear heavy footsteps coming towards her. The door slowly opened. Doug was wearing pajama bottoms along with a huge white gold necklace around his neck. He walked over to the bed and took a seat, causing Sandra to sink. He reached into his pocket and pulled out a long, thick, platinum necklace that he placed on Sandra's chest.

"I know you don't believe in me anymore. But I know deep down inside, I can change to a better person. I'm sorry for how I've been lately, but I've been under a lot of pressure. So please take this as an early Christmas gift."

Leaning over Sandra, Doug kissed her on the mouth and gently began rubbing her breast. Sandra looked Doug in the eyes and saw sadness and anger, but most of all she saw anger.

As Doug tugged at her clothes, tears welled up in Sandra's eyes. *I am nothing but a weak woman and mother*, she thought to herself. With Doug's weight pressing down on her, Sandra turned her head towards the window where she gazed out, imagining the children and herself far away from Doug.

* * *

As Doug slept like a log, Sandra quietly got out of bed and put her pajamas back on. Using the light of the moon as her guide, she walked over to the armoire that sat across the large bedroom. Getting on her hands and knees, she felt around for something under the armoire. As she glanced back at the bed where Doug was shifting his body to another position, Sandra found her well-kept secret. Under the armoire, she had taped a brown packaging envelope.

Without taking her eyes off Doug, Sandra sat on the floor and slowly opened the flap of the envelope with her fingernail. She gently shook the contents onto a throw rug that sat under the armoire, revealing an abundance of expensive jewelry that consisted of diamonds, gold necklaces, watches by Movado and Cartier, and bracelets. Sandra removed the platinum necklace from her neck and placed it in the envelope with the rest of the jewelry Doug had given her for accepting her bruises like a good little girl. After returning the package to its hiding place, Sandra crept back into bed. She laid her head on her pillow and forced herself to sleep.

* * *

Inside the waiting lounge of Dr. Joanne White's office, Doug looked over some old issues of *Psychology Today*. The office was posh and upscale, which it should be for two hundred dollars a session. Doug was patting his feet to the jazz music playing softly in the waiting area when the door to the back office opened. Doug smiled at the middle-aged Asian psychiatrist he had been seeing sporadically for the past nine years to help him cope with his mother's suicide. She walked over to Doug, greeted him with a handshake, and showed him to her office.

The walls were covered with cherry wood and the floor was covered with plush beige carpeting. Fresh flowers were beautifully arranged on two tables in the room. The wall behind the doctor's desk displayed laminated plaques of her numerous degrees, while another wall held a thirty-five-inch plasma television and DVD player to match. Dr. White had spared no expense.

Doug took a seat on a beautiful leather couch. He studied the doctor as she opened her pad and took out an expensive gold pen.

"First off, Doug, how have you been since the last time we met?"

Doug smiled at the doctor. "I have been fine and the exercises you gave me have helped a lot."

Dr. White scribbled on her pad. "What about visiting your mother's gravesite? Have you thought about that?"

"Well, that's the good news, doctor. I have gone to see her twice, and both times seemed to relieve the stress that we discussed last time."

Happy with his compliance in treatment, Dr. White smiled. "Doug, that is fantastic. You don't know how proud I am of you. That's a really big step you've taken in releasing the anger and fear that has been inside you for a very long time."

Doug felt all along that he was nothing but a guinea pig for his doctor's psychological bullshit: If she could prove that he was making progress, it would validate her skills as a psychiatrist. At the same time, Doug also knew that as long as he kept his visits, it could pay off for him in the end. Like serial killers who get off because their psychiatrists prove them sick, so could Doug if he ever got in a jam. As long as he fed her ego, he could lie until his nose fell off and she wouldn't know the difference.

"Dr. White, I don't know if this helps any, but I also went to see my father last week and we discussed some things concerning my mother. I also told him that with a little more time and healing, I could forgive him also."

"You are truly amazing, Doug, and you should be proud of yourself," Dr. White said, shaking her head in amazement. "I remember a while back at one of our sessions when you said you thought your father ruined your chances of ever being a good husband and father. Well, in my opinion, Doug, I truly believe with the progress you have made, one day you are going to make a great husband and dad."

With a smile on his face, Doug looked at the grandfather clock and saw that he had twenty more minutes to bullshit the Harvard graduate, so he did.

* * *

Aware that she had some time to spare with her shopping, Sandra pushed her cart down the aisle, passing all the food that contained sugar and was high in fat—the kind of food she loved—and made her way into a section that shelved organic food. She jumped with fear when her cart was hit from the side.

"Hey, Sandra, you have got to keep your eyes on the road, girl," Pamela laughed.

Feeling relieved, Sandra looked inside Pamela's basket and was very envious. Banana crunch ice cream, Entenmann's chocolate donuts, and chicken fingers were just a few of the delights it held. Wondering how the hell Pamela kept her body so tight, Sandra finally stopped staring at the food.

"Hi, Pamela, how are you doing?"

Sandra's eyes darted back to the junk food in Pamela's cart.

"You know you're welcome anytime you want to come over, watch the stories, and pig out with me, right?"

"I know I have not been very neighborly, Pamela, and I am sorry for that. But your invitation sounds nice. Maybe one day we can."

"Your kids eat brussels spouts and drink soybean milk? What is that? Squash? Now, Sandra, I *know* you eat some Popeye's fried chicken?"

Sandra tried unsuccessfully to hold in her laugh. "My goodness, I have not had fried chicken in a while. That sounds good right about now."

Pamela looked at Sandra with a smile but with a touch of sadness. "Well, Sandra, like I said, when you're ready to free yourself, you and the kids knock on my door and I will show you what a good time is all about."

Sandra smiled and tried to hold back the tears welling in her eyes. She touched Pamela on the hand and walked to the organic section to select her goods. Looking behind her secretly, Pamela stared at Sandra and put on her sunglasses to hide the tears in her own eyes.

* * *

Typical of kids their age, Kareem and Chaka surrounded their mother, anxious to see what would come out of the grocery bags. Chaka helped her mom put things where they belonged, and Kareem's eyes widened every time Sandra removed the bags' contents. His face showed his disappointment at the sight of vegetables and liver. After making sure that Doug was not around, Sandra pulled out a half gallon of banana crunch ice cream, which brought silent jubilation from the two children. Sandra rearranged frozen vegetables and meat inside the freezer, making room to hide the ice cream behind the bags of frozen food. She gave her children a smile and put her finger to her mouth, letting her kids know that this was their secret. Their faces showed their determination to keep the ice cream a secret.

"Let's meet under the bed at eight o'clock, and don't be late, okay?" she said as she handed each child a plastic spoon.

Both of her children, who were her spitting images, smiled. "We won't be late, Mommy," they promised before returning to the living room floor to continue painting their mother and themselves in the park on a sunny day.

* * *

The atmosphere at dinner was quiet and calm. Sandra had prepared lamb chops smothered in apricot sauce, served with linguine and broccoli. For once the kids did not complain about only being able to drink water and not soda, and they both cleaned their plates. Sandra made sure Doug got the best lamb chops and that his water glass had four ice cubes like he always demanded. When his glass was half empty, she instantly refilled it. Doug seemed a little more at ease at the dinner table. He even asked the kids how school was going, which was something he never did. Sandra and the kids made sure they cleaned the dishes so Doug could not complain. Yes, all was well in the Gunner apartment, and it hadn't been that way in a while.

* * *

Kareem and Chaka were lying on the floor with half of their bodies under the bed. They silently hugged and smiled as they waited for their secret treat, their spoons ready in their hands. Kareem got to his feet and started doing a little dance until Chaka banged him on the foot. "Get your ass back under this bed," she whispered angrily. Not wanting to feel the wrath of his seven-year-old sibling, Kareem obeyed his sister.

Down the hall, Sandra was on the toilet reading an issue of *Jet* magazine. Her attention was broken when she heard Doug's heavy footsteps heading towards the bathroom. When she heard him pass, Sandra got back to admiring the R&B hunk that was featured in the magazine. A few moments later, her attention was abruptly drawn away again by a loud slamming sound in the kitchen. Sitting on the toilet and getting tense, Sandra lowered the magazine. She could hear Doug returning, but this time at a much quicker pace as his footsteps pounded on the wooden floor much harder. He stopped at the bathroom door and Sandra placed the magazine in front of her on the white tiled floor. Her heart was ready to jump out of her chest and she began to perspire.

Doug's footsteps sounded as if he were returning to the bedroom, and Sandra felt like a load had lifted off her shoulders. She leaned her head on the cold bathroom wall. Then *BANG*! The door busted open and sweaty, muscle-bound Doug stood in front of Sandra, breathing hard and glaring at her with eyes red from smoking reefer. He held the box of banana crunch ice cream in his hand.

"Doug, please. I'm sorry, it was for the..."

Missing her head by a fraction of an inch, the box of ice cream crashed into the window, knocking down cologne and shampoo. Doug pressed his foot against Sandra's thigh and knocked her off the toilet and onto the floor.

"What the fuck did I tell you about bringing this shit in my house, bitch?"

Sandra tried to push Doug's foot off her aching leg, but she couldn't budge it. "Doug, you're hurting me. Stop!"

Doug reached down and grabbed Sandra by her braids. He lifted her up and threw her into the bathtub. Having some presence of mind, Sandra grabbed on to the shower curtain in an attempt to break her fall. Still falling back, she hit her head on the metal spout, opening a slight gash on the back of her head.

"I'm the boss, bitch! I have the power. Do you understand me!"

Doug reached in the tub, grabbed Sandra by the arm, and flung her into the wall, causing her to break the towel rack with her back.

"Doug, just let us go, please. Just let us go!"

Breathing hard and fast, Doug looked down on her. "Go ahead. You go, bitch. But those are my kids and they are not going anywhere! I pay for everything in this motherfucker and everybody owes me! What you gonna do without me? You are too stupid to make it without me! Go ahead and try to leave me. See what happens!"

Sandra was still lying on the floor, holding the back of her head as blood from her wound trickled down her hand. She looked over at the toilet and spotted the ice cream. Gathering her strength, she slowly began to crawl in that direction. Doug watched and was somewhat amazed and shocked to see Sandra grab the partially melted ice cream. He wore a curious expression as he watched her crawl on her hands and knees towards the bathroom door.

"Kareem and Chaka, Mommy's coming with your ice cream!" she called out to the children. With half of her body out in the hallway, Sandra grimaced in pain as she slowly rose to her feet. With her face directly in front of Doug's sweaty chest, she tried to move around him without touching his body.

"You ain't giving them shit. Give me that damn ice cream!"

Defiantly, Sandra reached for the box and snatched the ice cream away from Doug. Enraged, he knocked it out of her hand and pushed her into the wall so hard that she heard the plaster crumbling from within. Sandra moaned and fell to the floor, where she lay motionless.

"Like I said, you are weak and dumb. You can do nothing to me or without me. Keep your ass on the floor where you belong." Doug reached down, grabbed the ice cream, and walked away. As he passed his kids' room, he threw the box in the wastebasket that sat near their bedroom door.

Doug walked back to his bedroom, slammed the door, and locked it. Chaka and Kareem ran from their bedroom to come to the aid of their mother. As they rubbed Sandra's face, Chaka began to cry. Sandra reached up with her hand and caressed her daughter's hair. Kareem, who was standing over his mother, squeezed his plastic spoon until it broke, leaving a jagged piece of plastic in his hand. He began to walk in the direction of his father's room.

"No, baby. You're better than him," Sandra said, sounding hoarse and weak. "Our time will come soon."

Listening to his mother, Kareem returned and stood near Sandra and Chaka in a protective stance.

Chapter Fourteen

The Great Escape

"Do not be late picking up those kids, Sandra. I am dead serious," Doug warned.

Not saying a word, Sandra got out of Doug's truck and went into the community center. While taking her coat off in the basement supply room, she felt the back of her head and gently rubbed the cut that she had sustained from Doug. She took a seat and looked at her watch. She had about forty-five minutes before people would start to arrive. At the sound of the footsteps coming from the hallway, Sandra stood with a serious look on her face. Ms. Carla and a skinny white man in his sixties entered the room.

"Hi, Sandra. This is the gentleman I was telling you about, Mr. Smith. Peter, this is my friend Sandra."

Sandra and Peter shook hands, and Carla left the room so they could be alone.

"I will cut right to the chase, Sandra. Whatever I estimate your merchandise to be worth will be at market value. The price that I give you will be fair and honest. I collect ten percent of the fair price in cash and there is no room for negotiations. Do we understand each other?"

Remembering the drama she'd gotten into with the slimeball Jeffrey and the phony check from the pageant, Sandra was fully aware that she had to be extra cautious when dealing with people's money.

"Listen, Mr. Smith. I really appreciate you taking time from your busy schedule to come all the way uptown to see me. I really hope you understand that I can only let you estimate what I have right here and not at your store. I trust that you will be fair with me, and I have no problem with your ten percent fee. After you give me a price, I will bring the merchandise back here so we can exchange my possessions for the cash."

Nodding his head in agreement, the wrinkled man reached into his pocket and removed a small eye scope. "Okay, let's see what you have," he said.

Sandra reached behind her back and removed the brown envelope from the back of her pants' waistline. She slowly emptied the contents onto a small green table. Taking a seat, Sandra anxiously watched the man look carefully at her things. From time to time he wrote on a small yellow pad. Sandra leaned forward and looked at each piece of jewelry that Doug had given her, remembering the pain she endured physically and emotionally to receive it. Leaping out of her seat in sheer terror, Sandra stood in front of the old man, blocking the view of Jasmine, who had entered the room without knocking.

"Oh, Sandra, I'm so sorry. I didn't realize you were using the room. I just wanted to sit these plates in the closet," Jasmine apologized. She looked like she too had been startled.

"That's all right, Jasmine. You can sit them right on the floor and when I'm through, I will put them away myself," Sandra instructed. She glanced back quickly to check on Peter. He looked nervous and his hands were shaking. When she turned back around, Jasmine gave her a smile and tried to sneak a glimpse at the person Sandra was trying to conceal from her.

When Jasmine finally left the room, Sandra walked to the door, locked the latch, and tested the door for good measure. Then she walked over to a refrigerator and retrieved a bottle of water for Peter, who was wiping seat off his forehead.

"Here you go, Mr. Smith. Please continue," Sandra requested. Peter took a sip of water, which seemed to calm him down. Then the old man continued to estimate Sandra's goods.

* * *

After about half an hour of figuring with his calculator and notepad, Peter finally rose to his feet and stretched, letting out a moan.

"Sandra, you have some very nice pieces here. Based on what I have determined to be true and fair, I would be willing to offer you thirty-two thousand dollars minus thirty-two hundred, which covers my fee," he advised.

With the best possible poker face that she could muster, Sandra studied the pieces that were on the table. "That seems to be fair, Mr. Smith," she answered. "We have a deal."

The two met in the center of the floor and shook hands.

"Sandra, today is Tuesday. Why don't we meet at this same time and location on Friday to complete the transaction?"

"Friday will be fine, Mr. Smith. I will see you then."

Sandra opened the door for the man and watched him leave. She closed the door behind him, locked it again, and walked back over to the table. She put her jewelry back inside the envelope, which she tucked back down inside her pants, covering the bulk of the envelope with her sweater. She fixed her braids and wiped her pants, then lifted her fist to the sky and said, "Thank you." Then she put away the dishes Jasmine had left and made her way upstairs.

The sweet aroma of Ms. Carla's cooking put a smile on Sandra's face. The dining area was busy as usual, as the men who volunteered set up the tables and chairs while others began bringing out the lunch for the day. In her usual friendly manner, Sandra waved to everyone as she headed over to the kitchen area where Ms. Carla was handing out pans of food to be placed on the tables.

"Everything okay, Sandra baby?" Ms. Carla asked.

"Everything went fine, and thank you so much for your help," Sandra said, rubbing the gray-haired woman's shoulder. Ms. Carla passed a long pan of vegetables to a volunteer and gave Sandra a quick squeeze.

Jasmine walked into the kitchen and got a pan of tossed salad. She looked at Sandra and smiled. "Sandra, I'm sorry about barging in on you earlier. I should have known better to knock."

"Don't worry, Jasmine. It's okay. No harm was done," Sandra assured her.

The two women exchanged smiles and continued helping Ms. Carla.

* * *

At 3:00 a.m. on Wednesday, Sandra was in the living room on the computer. Doug had arrived home at midnight smelling like Alizé and he was now dead asleep. To make sure of it, Sandra had even held back her vomit long enough to allow him a fifteen-minute sex session.

On the computer, Sandra entered her credit card information to pay for a reservation on December 11th at 10:35 p.m. from Kennedy Airport. Doug had planned some type of get-together at the club for his friends at eleven o'clock, and Sandra figured that he would be there when it was time for her and the kids to catch a cab to the airport. He always liked to be at least three hours early when he was planning an event.

Sandra read an e-mail that had been sent to her earlier in the evening from a real estate company in Virginia Beach. It confirmed that they had vacancies in a nice apartment complex that had been built sometime last year. Sandra looked at the clock on the computer and decided that she shouldn't stay online much longer. Hurriedly, she deleted the e-mail and logged off. Then she went into the "C" drive, erased the history for all activity for that day, and deleted the Web sites she had visited. She shut down the computer, then quickly and quietly returned to bed.

* * *

As Doug drove Sandra and the kids to school, Sandra flipped the visor down and glanced at her kids through its mirror. They had somber looks on their faces. Understanding the despair and anger they must be feeling, she tried to lighten the mood. "Hey, Kareem…knock knock…"

Smiling at his mother, he answered, "Who's there?"

Doug turned down the radio. "I am here and I'm trying to listen to the goddamn music. So can you please shut the hell up!"

Kareem cut his eyes at his father from the backseat and was silent again while Sandra looked straight ahead. When they pulled up to the school, there were about sixty kids all bundled up and dressed in green uniforms. Sandra got the kids out of the car.

"Sandra, I can't take you home. A bus will be on that corner in fourteen minutes, so make sure your ass is on it. At nine thirty I will blow the horn to take you to feed your animals, so you make sure your ass is home waiting for me. Do you understand?"

"Yes, Doug. I understand," Sandra answered. As she got out of the Cadillac Escalade, she and Chaka overheard one of the children proclaim, "Man, that is a nice truck. They must have it made." Sandra looked at the child, then at Chaka, thinking, *If they only knew.*Sandra kissed her children on their cheeks and watched them enter the classroom. Then she hurried to the main office. Phones were ringing and women in their forties were helping students with different issues. Sandra looked at her watch. Doug had left her with nothing but a MetroCard, so she had to hurry.

"Excuse me, ma'am. Who do I need to speak to in regard to getting school records sent to another state?" Sandra asked the black woman who was writing on a pad.

The woman didn't even look up at Sandra. "You must give us two weeks' notice and provide us with an official letter from the school the child will be attending so that the necessary paperwork can be sent."

"Well, two weeks is too late because we're planning to move in a few days. I was hoping someone could help me."

The woman looked up at Sandra with an expression that said, *You must be kidding.*

"Like I said, we need two weeks' notice. The assistant principal, Ms. Duncan, should be here in about an hour. Maybe she can do something for you."

With her watch telling her that she had seven minutes until her bus arrived, Sandra backed down. "Okay, thank you. I will try back then," she told the woman.

Her escape came down to timing, so Sandra understood that she would just have to pull the kids out and deal with the school records when they arrived in Virginia. She fixed her coat and hurried out of the school to get to the bus stop.

* * *

In her bedroom, Sandra was carefully packing away a three-day supply of clothing for the kids and herself. She figured that with the money she would get from Mr. Smith, buying the kids new clothes would not be a problem, especially with the prices being much cheaper in Virginia. She removed a bag from the top of the closet and took out brand-new toothbrushes, toothpaste, a couple of coloring books, crayons, and a deck of cards. She put them in the small carry-on suitcase, closed it, and put it in the back of the closet, where she concealed it with her winter coats and sweaters. She closed the closet door and walked over to her dresser mirror. Sandra fixed her hair and clothes, and took a deep breath. *Everything is going to work out. Just don't panic. Just be cool. Tomorrow I will have my money and we will be away from here*, she told herself.

Outside the window, a horn blew. Sandra grabbed her coat and keys, and hurried to get her ride from Doug to serve lunch to her friends.

* * *

It was Friday and Sandra was back home after dropping the kids off at school. She looked at her watch. It was 9:35. In about an hour she would have a little over thirty thousand dollars for a new beginning with her children, but most importantly, she'd be away from the man she both loved and feared—Doug. The only problem was that the bastard was sitting in a chair right across from her, and the jewelry was under the armoire that he seemed to be guarding.

The room was silent except for Doug, who was biting on a pretzel stick and making loud chewing noises. He always prided himself on leaving on time and sometimes a little early. So if he told her to get ready, how could she get to the stash right in front of him? Sandra felt beads of sweat begin to form on her forehead and she knew if Doug saw that, a thousand questions would soon follow. She had to do something—even if it meant taking a small beat down—because this was possibly her only chance. She slowly got up from the bed and walked to the door.

"Where the fuck are you going, Sandra? It's almost time to go."

"I'm a little thirsty. I need to get some water."

Doug stared at her for a minute. Then he took another bite of his pretzel and looked away from her. Sandra left for the kitchen, trying not to look suspicious.

As she got water from a pitcher inside the refrigerator, Sandra looked at the cat clock with the eyes moving from side to side. She always hated that clock because the cat was a reminder of how much time she had wasted with Doug. Not knowing what to do, Sandra bit her bottom lip as tears welled up in her eyes. She put the water back inside the fridge and saw something that gave her an idea. There was a whole glass bottle of protein drink that cost Doug $150 per bottle once a month. Even if it meant a beat down, what more could he do to her that he hadn't already done? Sandra checked behind her to make sure she was still alone, then she slowly nudged the glass pitcher inch by inch along the shelf until *SMASH*!

"What the hell was that!" Doug yelled from the bedroom in the back.

Wondering if she had done the right thing, Sandra looked at the thick purple liquid that had splashed all over the white kitchen floor. "I spilled your drink by accident," she answered meekly. She moved to the side and stood next to the refrigerator, listening to the loud, heavy footsteps of the beast arriving. Doug stood at the doorway of the kitchen wearing a designer sweat suit. He looked at the mess and then at Sandra with a pissed off stare. He walked slowly over to her and stood with his hands on his hips, not saying a word. Sandra cowered and flinched in anticipation of his reaction.

"Sandra, get a fucking mop and clean this shit up. You have six minutes before I have to leave and drop you off. If it's not cleaned up, I promise I will use your head as a mop," Doug threatened.

Sandra walked towards the bathroom, where the mop and bucket were kept. She looked in the dining room mirror in front of her and saw that Doug was opening a roll of paper towels and laying the sheets on the floor. She knew that this was her chance. She quickly grabbed the bucket from behind the bathroom door and sat it in the tub to fill it with water. While the bucket was filling up, Sandra ran to the bedroom.Breathing hard but silently, she quickly knelt down and reached under the armoire, scraping her knuckles on the wood, but still managing to retrieve the envelope. She quickly stuffed it down the back of her pants and covered it with her sweater. Hearing an agitated Doug walking towards the bedroom, Sandra quickly stepped into the bathroom, just missing his eyesight. She turned off the water, picked up the bucket, and grabbed the mop. She began to walk past Doug towards the kitchen, focusing on the floor and not Doug's stone-angry face.

"Hurry the hell up, Sandra," he yelled, causing Sandra to flinch and almost spill some of the water.

* * *

Inside Doug's truck, Sandra was trying to sit straight up in her seat, but she was beginning to squirm a little because the envelope was irritating her back. Knowing that they were only a minute away, she sucked it up and handled the pointy edge sticking in her back. They pulled up to the community center and Doug stopped the truck so Sandra could exit. Rose Garden, who was standing by the door wearing a thin coat, caught Doug's attention. Sandra walked up to Rose, gave her a hug, and started to walk inside.

"Sandra, come here!" Doug yelled before she could get in the door.

Sandra motioned to Rose to get out of the cold and walked back over to the truck.

"Yes, Doug?"

"Who is that girl that you just spoke to?"

"She's just a girl that comes in to eat lunch. That's all."

Doug looked furious. "What is her goddamn name and how old is she, Sandra? I didn't ask you that. Obviously she eats here. I'm not stupid. I said what's her name?"

"Her name is Rose."

Doug rubbed his chin and grinned as he thought about Rose. "Yeah, okay. You go inside now and feed the animals. You just make sure you're not late picking up those kids."

Sandra shook her head as she walked away from the truck and inside the center. She was hanging her coat in the coatroom when Rose entered. The girl looked very cold and hungry, but she managed a smile when she looked at Sandra.

"Ms. Sandra, I know how busy things can get for you here, but I saw two of the workers bringing a Christmas tree and decorations in here right before you came. I was wondering if I could help decorate the tree?"

With so much pressure and anxiety on her shoulders, Sandra wanted to feel human again. Maybe decorating the tree with this broken young woman could help them both.

"I tell you what, Rose, after lunch I think I can sneak away for a couple of minutes. You and I can work on the tree then, okay?"

"Okay, Ms. Sandra, thanks," Rose answered happily.

Sandra looked at her watch and saw that in about forty-five minutes, Mr. Smith would be there with the money for the exchange of the jewelry.

* * *

Like always, Sandra stood behind the many long tables with the other volunteers and served lunch to the many people entering the center. Jasmine was working right beside her.

"Are you okay, Jasmine?" Sandra asked. "You've been rubbing at that wrist since you got here this morning."

"Oh, no, Sandra. It's fine. I just banged it on the dresser by accident last night. It's a little sore, but it will be okay."

Sandra looked at Jasmine with concern and suspicion but she didn't want to pry, so she smiled and continued to serve food. She neatly placed mashed potatoes on a little girl's tray and then saw Ms. Carla waving to her to come over. As she sat her large spoon down, Sandra looked around to make sure no one else was watching.

"Jasmine, do you think you could cover for me for a few minutes?" Jasmine grabbed Sandra's spoon, smiled, and nodded yes.

When she met Ms. Carla at the staircase, Sandra had a look of anxiety and of jubilation.

"Sandra, baby, Mr. Jones is downstairs waiting for you. Will you be okay?"

Sandra smiled at the gray-haired woman and kissed her on the cheek. "I am going to be fine," she said, squeezing Ms. Carla's hand. "Thank you for all the support and kindness you have shown me since I started here. You will never know what it has meant to me."

The two women shared another embrace and then Sandra walked down the steps leading to the basement. Like always, the basement was warm and a little dim, but it was still illuminated enough to function. As she approached the storage door, Sandra reached behind her and removed the envelope that she had been hiding since that morning. She felt a little pride that she never rubbed or attempted to remove the nuisance, even though the corner of the envelope had been sticking her in the back. She wondered if her tenacity was a sign of something good happening. She wiped away the little sweat beads that popped up on her forehead and gently turned the doorknob.

As she entered the room, she was greeted by a gentle smile. Mr. Smith was sitting at the small table wearing an old pair of bifocals and clutching a very old but well-maintained brown bag that looked like the kind doctors used to carry to people's homes on visits.

"Good day, Ms. Lyte. How are you?"

Sandra held her envelope tightly with both hands. "I'm doing fine, and how about you?" she answered, feeling less fretful.

"I am fine, just preparing for the holidays. Please take a seat so we can get down to business."

Sandra grabbed an old wooden chair and sat across from the old man as he began to reveal crisp, clean stacks of brand-new one-hundred-dollar bills from the U.S. Treasury.

"Ms. Lyte, this is your total share of twenty-eight thousand eight hundred dollars, and this is my share of three thousand two hundred dollars."

Sandra stared at the stack of money sitting on the table, almost hypnotized, until the sound of Mr. Smith clearing his throat brought back her attention. Feeling a little embarrassed, she reached down and grabbed the envelope that contained her freedom from the years of hell she had suffered. She opened the envelope and gently poured the contents on the table.

The room was spinning and Sandra's head was pounding as if someone had smacked her with a baseball bat. Shocked and red-faced, Mr. Smith stared at the copper and aluminum scrap metal that Sandra had emptied onto the table. Sandra held her mouth and rocked back and forth in her chair. Then she began to sob uncontrollably.

The old man quickly grabbed his stacks of money and put them back into his bag. He looked around the room suspiciously, as if someone would bust into the room and rob him at any moment. Sandra reached towards the dirty scrap metal. "Why, God, why!" she cried.

Mr. Smith hurried toward the door and unlocked it. Before stepping out of the room, he stopped and looked back at Sandra, who had crumbled to the floor in disbelief.

All kinds of thoughts ran through Sandra's mind as she tried to figure out who she could have wronged in her life to deserve what she was going through now. As she fiddled with the metal, the door slowly opened and Ms. Carla walked in. The smile on Carla's face disappeared when she saw Sandra sitting on the floor and shaking her head. The older woman strained to bend down in front of Sandra.

"Baby, what happened?"

"I am being punished," Sandra said, lifting her head slowly. Swollen red eyes looked back at Ms. Carla. "I am being punished and maybe I deserve to be."

Ms. Carla grabbed Sandra and began to stroke her head.

* * *

With the dishes washed and the garbage disposed, a few volunteers remained to help with small miscellaneous items. Sandra, who had somehow found the strength to finish her day and had even kept her promise to Rose to decorate the Christmas tree, put on her coat. She looked at the smile on Rose's face as the girl admired the seven-foot imitation pine tree. Sandra realized that she would have to return home and face Doug, but she was not concerned about the possibility of another beating because that was a foregone conclusion. What really was on her mind was how he had found out. Who or what gave her in? What was not easy for her to swallow was how he always stayed on point. Sandra knew it was time to pick up the kids and face the beast, so she left the pantry.

* * *

At 10:00 p.m., Sandra was sitting in the living room looking at the walls that surrounded her and waiting for Doug to come out of his lab, where he had been making his product for the last eight hours. The kids were fast asleep, which was a relief. She didn't want them subjected to what would happen even though she knew they didn't have to see the actual beatings to know what Mommy was going through.

Finally, there it was—the squeaking of the door followed by the footsteps of the beast. Sandra sat on the couch looking straight ahead. She tried not to notice the large obstacle that was now in front of her, but how could she not? Would this be the last of the many beatings? Would she awaken as she had from the others? Or would she finally meet her maker? Sandra was about to find out.

"Baby, I want you to know that I cannot let you go. You are a part of me, and you know too much about me. As I told you a while ago, Sandra, I know every move you make before you do. I really don't care how people perceive me or my lifestyle because I understand my intelligence and my limitations. But, Sandra, you don't understand yours," Doug started, sounding relatively calm.

"You see, Sandra, dealing with me is not a mystery. I am what I am…no more, no less…and you knew that, so don't act stupid. Any strong, independent woman would have walked away years ago, but you elected to stay for the lifestyle. Sandra, you are weak and unappreciative. Many hood rats would relish being where you are. You're too stupid to see and appreciate a man like me. If you did as I told you, do you think I would have touched a hair on your head for the past seven years? Sit back and think. Whenever I disciplined you, it was because of some dumb shit you did," Doug said, pausing to take a sip of white wine. "Like this last shit you tried to pull—saving the jewelry and trying to pawn it, which I have to admit was pretty smart. Nevertheless, baby, you have to realize that even when I sleep, I am awake. Every time I gave you something, I saw how you stashed it. I bet you're asking yourself how I knew about your little plan to get some cash and head to Virginia Beach to your nice new apartment. Well guess what? When a woman doesn't enjoy my sex anymore, I don't get upset—I just find another. That's what I did, Sandra, with a nice Spanish mommy named Jasmine. You probably know her. She serves the animals right alongside you."

For the first time since he started talking, Sandra flinched with emotion. She looked up at Doug's grinning face and could not believe her ears, but her hearing was perfect.

"I told you, Sandra. I may not have your little journalism bullshit degree, but I am street savvy and I have a think-ahead attitude. Now, you may want to go after her on Monday, but you will not get the chance because as of today, I had her removed. But ask yourself, did I plant someone else in her place? Maybe or maybe not."

Doug reached under his chair and pulled out a folder. "Baby, I had the feeling that you would start to use my computer, so look what I did," Doug said as he removed a sheet of paper and held it in front of Sandra's face. With a menacing smile, Doug watched her eyes move from side to side as she read her Internet activity on the night she bought her airline tickets. "Isn't technology a motherfucker, baby? I never knew you could watch and take pictures of other people's Internet activity until I watched *Jerry* on television one morning. I went out and bought myself a program for your sneaky ass. I know about the airline tickets, the e-mails to the property owner in Virginia…shit, baby, I even saw those dark, fine-ass brothers you've been looking at on those online muscle calendars. Damn, boo, I stay in shape. You don't love me no more?" he asked sarcastically. Sandra could only sit still and absorb the humiliation and torment as Doug showed her pictures of everything she had done on the Internet. Doug reached out and took Sandra's wallet, which contained her New York State ID, her bank card, her credit card, and even her Virginia driver's license. Doug also took away her cell phone.

"At this point in time, you will be on lockdown a little harder now, baby. Your cell phone belongs to me, and I will be sure to have someone always watching when you pick up those kids. Now this is the last thing I'm going to say to you. Sandra, you are stupid and weak. We agree?"

Sandra answered in a low, meek voice, "Yes, I am."

"Very good, baby. Now we're getting somewhere. Now I want you to listen to me very carefully. Christmas is only two weeks away, and I love Christmas. Therefore, one of two things will happen for the holidays: You will be on your best behavior and the kids will have the biggest Christmas they could ever imagine. On the other hand, baby—and I want you to listen carefully, because you know I do not bullshit—you can try to fuck with me again. And I promise you, when those crumb snatchers wake up and rush to the Christmas tree to open their little neatly wrapped gifts, they will find Mommy instead with a bullet in her fucking head. Do you understand, boo?"

Sandra looked into Doug's eyes and tried to find a glimmer of doubt that she could turn into hope, but she could not. All she saw was a pair of cold brown eyes.

Doug picked up his glass of wine and the folder and started to walk away. As he passed Sandra, he took his right hand and backslapped her, causing her to fall off the couch onto the floor. As he headed back to the bedroom, Sandra held her bleeding bottom lip and said quietly, "He is right. I am weak and stupid."

Chapter Fifteen

Kids, Let's Go For a Ride

It was Saturday morning and Sandra watched from the fourth-floor window as Doug got the kids inside the truck to visit his dad at the Shadybrook Retirement Home in Westchester, New York. Since Doug put a block on the house phone and took away her cell phone, Sandra could only hope that he would have the decency to call her when they arrived. Putting the palm of her hand on the cold, frosted windowpane, she waved good-bye to her babies as the truck left from in front of the building. She looked around the large but empty apartment and tried to keep herself upbeat. She turned on the radio and looked over at the door, but she knew that she would spend the rest of her day inside the apartment, too afraid to encounter Doug's street surveillance.

* * *

There was little traffic on the north side of the Hutchinson River Parkway and Doug was making great time. He looked in his rearview mirror and saw Kareem opening up a granola bar while Chaka, whose mouth was hanging wide open, looked at Kareem as if he were crazy.

"Boy, what the hell do you think you're doing? You know damn well I do not allow food in this truck."

Giving his father a sarcastic look, the seven-year-old tyke chomped down on the granola bar, creating a loud crunch and causing crumbs to scatter on the Escalade's cream-colored leather interior.

"You little bastard, I know you heard me! Put that damn bar down!"

Kareem stared at his father with hatred that no child should have inside him. "Why should I listen to you? You hit my mommy!" he shot back.

Chaka attempted to cover her brother's mouth with her hand but to no avail. He continued, "I know what you do to my mother and when I get big I am…"

The children's heads and bodies jerked forward as Doug stomped hard on the brakes, bringing his vehicle to a screeching halt in the center lane of the highway. Doug snapped his huge torso violently in Kareem's direction.

"When you get big, you gonna do what, you little bastard? What you gonna do? You are from the same flimsy cloth as your dumb-ass mother! Like I told you before, my man, anytime your little ass is ready, come on!"

Tears were in Chaka's eyes as she listened to the blasting horns from the passing cars. She held her brother by his arm as he tried to lean towards Doug. Father and son stared at each other until Doug blinked first. He turned around and started to drive. As the trio made their way to the residence, Doug took a quick glance up at his rearview mirror. Still stone-faced, Kareem was burning two lasers through the back of Doug's head with menacing brown eyes while Chaka rubbed his hand in an attempt to keep him calm.

* * *

The tall iron-gated entrance led to the visitors' parking area. Doug drove through and parked his vehicle. Before they exited the truck, Doug turned to Kareem and Chaka. "I don't want any running or playing inside this place. When we get inside, I want you both to sit down and keep quiet. Do you understand?"

Chaka sat up straight and looked into her father's eyes. "Yes," she answered softly.

Kareem was looking out the truck window, admiring the trees and the well-manicured grass. "Why are we here? Who do we know here?" he asked.

Doug looked at the little boy as if he were an enemy instead of a son. "You don't worry why we're here. I asked you a damn question. Do you understand?"

Kareem continued to look out the window. "Yeah," he answered in a nonchalant fashion. Doug got out of the Escalade and walked to the other side to open the door for the two youngsters. Chaka took her time climbing out of the truck, but Kareem quickly hopped out, jumped over the low chain-link fence, and started running in a circle in the grass. Doug looked around the grounds to see if anyone was watching.

Chaka looked at her father's face and saw that he was furious. "Kareem, come on. Let's go. I'm going to tell Mommy you're misbehaving," she yelled to her brother.

Kareem stopped in his tracks, then he slowly walked over to where his father and sister stood.

"Get your dumb ass inside this place," snapped Doug.

"Don't call him dumb. He received three A's and two B's on his report card last week. You can even ask Mommy," Chaka defended her twin. As the three of them walked towards the entrance, Doug realized that he had never seen his children's report cards from that expensive school he was paying to send them to.

Doug signed the children and himself into the big green book on the mahogany desk, and the kids admired the many paintings that covered the tall walls and the statues that sat on the mantles. The children looked in the many rooms that they passed. Most of the people they saw were old. They also noticed that the hallways and the floors were spotless, smelling like the dentist's office where their mom took them for check-ups.

They walked up a flight of stairs and Doug led them to a large community room that had a pool table, a Ping-Pong table, three card tables, and tables set up for games of chess. Doug looked around the room where about twenty senior citizens were busy doing things from arts and crafts to listening to the baseball game on the radio. Finally, Doug spotted a man watching an animal program on television. He was wearing a silk robe and designer pajamas.

"Go sit down until it's time to go," demanded Doug. The children walked over to a loveseat against the wall and did as they were told. Removing the black Kangol hat from his head, Doug walked over to where the man with the big gray Afro sat. He reached out and tapped the man on his shoulder.

"Where is my fucking pastrami sandwich, boy?" Fred Gunner asked without turning around.

Doug glanced down at his empty hands. "Sir, I am really sorry, but I was in such a rush to get here that it slipped my mind."

Fred sucked his teeth and slowly turned around in his swivel chair. "Nothing changes, right, son? You're still the same sorry motherfucker that I spit out from my balls, huh?"

"So, how have you been? Are they treating you okay?" Doug asked, ignoring his father's insult as he took a seat next to him."You got my money, man?" Fred questioned back. Doug reached into his pocket, removed some money, and handed it to his father. "Also, my room is feeling a little small, so make some arrangements to get me moved to a larger room. Understand?"

"Yes, sir. I will get on it right away," Doug answered, looking down at the black-and-white tiled floor.

Fred looked over in the direction of the love seat, where Kareem and Chaka were talking to each other. He slowly turned his head back in the direction of his son. "Stupid ass, tell me you did not? Those are yours?"

"Their names are…"

"What did I tell you many years ago?" Fred interrupted. "The less baggage you carry, the easier it is for you to move. Now look what you've done. You got some profit-eating crumb snatchers on your hands now."

Doug still had not found the courage to look his father in the eyes. "I send them to private school and house them in a nice apartment. They eat the best foods, and I don't allow them any candy or sweets."

The two men looked at the two children. Forgetting what her father told them, Chaka got out of her seat and walked over to two elderly women who were playing bridge. She sat down with them and the old women both smiled at Chaka, and one patted her on the cheek. Chaka reached into the little purse that Sandra bought for her and pulled out two sticks of sugarless gum. She handed a stick to each woman. The women looked as if they had won the lottery. They smiled and blushed as they enjoyed their treat from Chaka.

Meanwhile, Kareem had followed his sister's lead. He walked over to a table where a man who looked to be in his late sixties sat at a chess table, waiting for a formidable opponent to take a seat across from him. The old man stared at Kareem with curiosity on his face, then he nodded to the board as if to say to Kareem, "Your move." Kareem reached out his hand to offer a handshake and received one from the wrinkled old man. As Kareem made his first move, the old man smiled with approval. Then he made his move.

Fred and Doug watched this all unfold.

"I see you got them trained to listen, huh, boy?" the older Gunner criticized. "You married the momma, too?"

Doug exhaled slowly. "No. I did not marry her, sir. But we've lived together for the past eight years," he admitted, clutching his hat in his hand.

"What you gonna do when things get tight?" Fred asked, looking up from counting the money Doug had given him. "I told you what would happen if you didn't listen to me. I'm about one hundred miles away from your ass, and I know for a fact things are getting tight."

"Sir, you don't have to worry. I have enough to survive for a while."

"Just survive? Is that what you've become, just a survivor?" Fred shook his head and looked at his son as if he were a complete idiot. You better start living, my man, because that bullshit you call a life will not last forever. You better start thinking ahead for yourself and fuck everybody else."

Doug reached into his pocket, pulled out a Movado watch, and handed it to his father. "I almost forgot—Merry Christmas. I know it's still two weeks off, but I wanted to get it for you."

Fred studied the watch. Then he looked back at his son and tossed the watch back at him. It hit Doug's knee before it fell to the ground.

"I told you I don't wear leather bands. I only wear metal bands. Get me what I like."

Doug picked the watch up off the floor and responded, "No problem, sir."

* * *

After an hour of humiliation from his father, Doug began to gather his things. He looked over at the table where Kareem was playing chess. A number of old men had formed a circle to get a chance to beat the seven-year-old chess master. He looked to his left and saw Chaka knitting with three elderly women who marveled at how fast she had caught on. Doug looked at his father, who was counting the money he had received.

"Sir, I have to get going," he said softly.

"Well, get going," Fred answered. "By the way, when you come up here next month, you will bring *two* pastrami sandwiches instead of one. Maybe this will teach you about what is important, like accountability."

"No problem," Doug said, putting on his coat. "I will see you next month. Kareem and Chaka, let's go," he called to the children.

Kareem twisted his face with frustration. "Can I finish this game please? It's almost over."

Doug looked back at his father and saw Fred grinning and shaking his head. Doug clearly knew what that gesture meant: *You have no control and on top of that, you are weak.* Doug walked away from his father and headed over to Chaka first. He took the knitting utensils away and put her coat on. Looking sadly at the elderly women, Chaka just waved good-bye and so did the women. Next, Doug went over to the chessboard where Kareem was in deep thought.

"Kareem, it's time to go. Put on your coat," he ordered.

"Oh, come on, sonny. Let us get a chance to beat the young wizard. You should be proud of him. This kid is going places when he gets older," a wrinkled-face man said. Not paying any attention to the wise old man, Doug gave Kareem his coat and the boy reluctantly put it on. Kareem shook hands with the elderly men and received numerous pats on his head. As Doug and the children began to exit the recreational room, Chaka quickly ran over to Fred and touched him gently on his shoulder.

"Good-bye, granddaddy," she said.

Fred looked at the beautiful girl from the corner of his eye. "Good-bye and that is Mr. Gunner," he said. Chaka looked at him for a second or two, kissed him on the cheek, and returned to Doug and Kareem.

Kareem looked at his sister strangely. "That was nasty. Why did you kiss him?"

"Because he is sad," Chaka said, rolling her eyes at her brother.

* * *

As the sun sent its rays through the windows of the Escalade, Doug looked in his rearview mirror and noticed that his children were sound asleep. He dialed a number on his cell phone and got through to Fish, who was at Doug's club.

"Hey, what's up? How much did we move last night?"

Doug's mouth dropped open as he listened to Fish on the other end. "What the fuck do you mean Buster got jacked last night? By who? They got all of it? Damn. Listen, get everybody together tonight. We need a sit-down," Doug said. He hung up his phone and threw it in the seat next to him.

"Can we stop at McDonalds? I'm getting hungry," Kareem asked as he awakened from sleep.

"Hell no! I told your little ass to eat something before we left this morning! Now just wait until you get your ass home to eat!" Doug answered angrily. Not saying a word, Kareem sat back in his seat and looked out of his window.

* * *

Doug watched his kids run and jump into the open arms of their loving mother, who was preparing lunch.

"How are my babies doing?" she asked with excitement.

Chaka kissed her mother all over her face. "I learned how to knit a sweater today!" she exclaimed proudly.

"You did! That's wonderful. I knew you were a smart girl."

Kareem started doing some sort of crazy dance for his mother, which made his sister crack up laughing. "I beat five men in chess today," he bragged. "One of them even called me a wizard."

Sandra smiled at her son proudly. "Well, you practice enough on me. I can see why you are so good."

Meanwhile, Doug stood at a distance in the living room, looking on with anger in his face. Sandra could sense that he was standing behind her, but she didn't dare look.

"Sandra, come to the bathroom for a second," Doug demanded.

"Okay, Doug. Can you give me one second? I want to get their coats off and give them some hot chocolate."

"Excuse me?" Doug questioned her audacity.

Sandra kissed the children on their cheeks and walked over to Doug, who led her to the bathroom.

He closed the door behind him and then looked Sandra up and down. She was wearing a corduroy skirt with no stockings. Doug slowly pinned her to the front of the vanity. His face was dark and menacing, and he was so close to Sandra that she could smell his breath. He rubbed his large sweaty hands on her smooth, toned thighs.

"Do you miss your man, baby? You miss me, right?" he asked as he pushed himself against her harder, making Sandra grimace with pain because of her aching back.

"Yes, Doug. I miss you," she answered nervously.

Quickly and forcefully, he spun her around so that she now faced the mirror over the sink. With very little regard for passion or gentleness, Doug quickly jerked up her skirt, revealing blue silk panties. Sandra grimaced at the reflection of the beast in the mirror as he pulled her panties to one side, ripping them in the process. Biting her lip and gripping both sides of the porcelain sink, Sandra winced every time he thrust his penis inside her.

She was trying to be strong, but she kept thinking about how Doug never made true love to her and how she found him repulsive. She only hoped this rape would be over soon. As he pushed himself harder and farther inside her, Sandra spotted a disposable razor Doug used to keep his large skull clean. For a split second she thought, *It is right there, Sandra. Grab it, and at the precise moment that he releases his nasty, slimy sewage inside you, decapitate the nasty serpent attached to his balls. Then you can grab the kids and just go.*

Then reality set in. *Wake up, stupid!* It chastised her. *You know you will only have one chance, and if you blow this chance, he will definitely break your neck while your skirt is still up. Do you want that for your kids? Just deal with this. It's almost over—just look at the ugly-ass faces he's making. Just use your head and think of a better plan.*

Moaning louder, Doug pulled out of Sandra and released himself on her skirt. He pulled up his pants and smacked Sandra on the backside, making a loud noise.

"Hurry up and get my lunch ready. I'm hungry," he said as he walked out the door.

Sandra looked at herself in the mirror. "Yep, Sandra, you are pathetic," she told her reflection. "Now go do what Massa told you to do."

Chapter Sixteen

Can't Beat 'Em, Join 'Em

The Harlem streets were paved with fresh white snow thanks to the nor'easter that had swooped down on the city. Driving slowly and carefully, Doug turned up his wipers to help his vision and wondered what had happened to his friends on Friday night as they peddled his product on his corners. He didn't want to speculate or assume, but Doug was sure about one thing: He had to get his men back out there because his lifestyle cost money.

He pulled up to his nightclub and got out of his vehicle. Covering his face from the wind-blown snow, Doug quickly stuck his key in the door and walked inside his quiet and dark club, which, to the disappointment of many, was closed for the night. Doug brushed off his coat and stomped the snow off his feet, then he walked to the back of the club toward his office. As he walked, he admired and appreciated how the staff kept the place clean and well managed. Doug stopped, removed his coat, and laid it across a barstool.

"Yo, Fish, Troy…yo, Buster," he called out, but he got no response. Feeling a little suspicious, Doug felt for his gun in the back of his pants waistline as he walked into his office.

"Doug, my brother, please don't," said the man dressed in all black who was sitting at Doug's desk. From Doug's left and right, two men standing six feet six inches tall and wearing white full-length cashmere coats pointed silver pump shotguns to his head. Letting his senses take over, Doug lowered his hands to his sides.

"That's right, brother. Just relax and all will be fine. It's almost Christmas and we want you to spend many more with the ones near and dear to your heart."

Doug looked around rapidly with only his eyes and took a deep breath. "Who are you and what do you want? Better yet, how the fuck did you get in here and where are my men?"

The man in black removed his sunglasses. He had light hazel eyes and no eyebrows.

"Okay, Doug, here we go. My name is X, and I represent the Lords of the Underground. We control ninety percent of all the drugs on the street. Whether it's cocaine, smack, marijuana, ecstasy, or crack—if someone is getting high in this city, chances are it came through us. As for what we want, Doug—we want you. We have watched you since you visited one of our distributors, Mario Chavez. You remember him, right?"

Doug looked at the man with curiosity and fear, but mostly fear, because after sitting under the hot lights in the room, Mr. X had not one drop of perspiration on his forehead.

"Your organization killed him? I lost sixty percent of my profit because of that shit!"

Mr. X motioned with his fingers for his men to lower their weapons. "Business is business, Doug, and Mario went beyond the organization's rules when it came to promoting on the side. He never asked for permission, and he was very dishonest in sharing his new mule, which happened to be you."

Doug took a seat in front of his desk and looked around the room.

"Come on, Doug. I admire your intelligence," the man in black continued, "but for a kid who started with nothing and now enjoys the many things that you have, you are not getting the big picture right now. We just cut out your middleman—the guy who was getting seventy percent of your profits. If you make some long, hard decisions, there is a chance you could be making a lot more without him."

Doug tried to picture what he could do with better profits.

"Tonight I was supposed to have a meeting with my men about who robbed them and how. Well, I already know now who did that, but my other concern is for my men."

Mr. X stood up out of his chair and removed his coat. Then he took his seat again. "Doug, I have some good news and some bad news. I will give you the bad news first because I believe in silver linings. When we entered the club, your men had not arrived yet, so we waited. When they came, your friend Troy began to act very immature and disrespectful by pulling his gun and spitting on my shoes—a very nasty act that we dealt with swiftly."

Reaching under the desk, Mr. X revealed a mid-sized cardboard box. He slowly opened the flaps on the box and slid it forward to Doug, who was now very apprehensive about looking inside. Doug looked at the men that were in the room with him and then slowly pulled the box close to him, swallowed hard, and looked inside. He quickly jumped out of his seat and pushed the box to the floor, staring at the contents of the box with disgust.

"Calm down, Doug, and let me explain the scene to you. Troy pulled his gun out with that hand. That pinkish slime is his lips and tongue. That is what he used to create the saliva he so rudely spit on my fifteen-hundred-dollar shoes."

"You did not have to do this. He has a wife. He was a good man," Doug sobbed, unable to hold back his emotions.

Looking at Doug as if he were a child, Mr. X shook his head. "Hey, Doug, pull yourself together. He had a choice. Troy could have been a gentleman and lived, or he could have been rude and died. He chose the latter. Besides, his wife is not that stupid. We ran a background check on Troy. That wife of his had a substantial insurance policy on him, so she understood his lifestyle. So please wipe your eyes. You look weak.

"Now, as for your friends Buster and Fish, listen up. Some time ago, Buster killed a man on Fish's command by the name of Willie Parker, who owned a meat market in the Bronx—all because Fish thought he was out of line at some meeting he held. Now you look a little shocked because I know so much, so I will tell you why I am so informed. Fish has worked for us long before you met Chavez. That's why he had those contacts for you. His mistake was made when he gave the hit on Willie. Fish had no authority to give such orders. Why he would be that stupid is unknown to me. So because of the rudeness of your men, they had to pay for past sins. As we speak, your man Buster is being ground up in Willie's meat market for pulling the trigger."

Feeling as if the room were spinning, Doug looked at the ground. "So that leaves Fish. Where is he?"

Doug was visibly shaken and Mr. X looked amused. He motioned to one of his cronies, who then left the room.

"Ah, here is our friend now," said Mr. X when he heard the sound of rolling wheels approaching the office. A moment later, Fish was pushed into the room in a leather chair wearing nothing but his underwear. Fish's face was beaten unrecognizable, and his right leg was broken in at least three areas. His hands looked like pulverized stumps because they had been smashed with a sledgehammer. His eyes were swollen shut and his lips were mangled, causing him to spit up blood.

"Doug, let me be the first to say that this is cruel, without a doubt," Mr. X began, "but this is a business and like any business, rules and regulations have to be abided by. Fish was treated well by this organization—and so was his family—because we believe in loyalty not only for our workers but also for their loved ones. So when a person has been treated as well as Fish has been over the years, there is no excuse for his stupidity. The consequences of that stupidity are on display for you tonight, Doug."

With his mouth gone dry and his eyes fixed on the childhood friend who had been living a hell of a secret life, Doug couldn't think straight. "Please, get him to a hospital and I will listen to your proposal. I just ask you kindly that you please get him some help. He doesn't deserve to die like this. Please," Doug pleaded.

Mr. X nodded his head and the same man that wheeled Fish in the room pulled him out backwards. Doug watched until the man that had fought and worked side by side with him for so many years was taken out of his view and he could only hear the squeak of the chair's wheels on the floor.

* * *

It had been about twenty minutes now and silence permeated Doug's office. The only thing that had changed was that Doug had been given a drink and a grilled chicken salad that he had not touched. Mr. X finally spoke.

"Doug, tonight we have witnessed much and learned a lot. So now before I let you go home, let me lay it on the table for you. We all agree that my employers are in charge of this city and very soon, most of the entire east coast. The canals that feed and furnish you are closing up real fast. What you have on your side are your brains and your will to eat, which we admire. The proposal I am offering to you is an interesting one at that. We offer you an entry-level position in our organization as a worker that we will pay handsomely for hard work. You will also have a great opportunity for advancement."

Doug did his best to regain his composure. "Like anything in life, I am well aware that nothing is free. If I was interested in becoming a part of your organization, what would I have to do?"

"Doug, we realize you are not stupid. We know that you have some very high-ranking cops on your payroll. They have no idea how quickly we have risen in the ranks, but sooner or later, they will. We want this to be a nice transition for all, and the last thing we want is a firefight with the cops. Therefore, if you would become a part of our organization, we would help you continue to fund them. In exchange for our funds, you would give us information on the higher-ranking officers, such as their family histories, who they shake down, and the judges they get their search warrants from."

Doug looked and felt a little bit more confident that not only could he leave his club tonight with his life but, very possibly, with a new start as well.

"I am pretty sure there is another stipulation involved, right?"

Mr. X gave Doug a knowing smile. "Yes, Doug, and it comes with a deadline attached to it also. The start-up money for joining the organization is one million dollars, and you have until New Year's Day to have the money. If you do not make the deadline, the deal is off and you will be lucky to sell a nickel bag on an abandoned corner in Staten Island. Which in turn means you will lose everything you have, and that father of yours that you're paying so dearly to keep in that upscale retirement home—well, I wonder how it would make you feel to see him living in a cardboard box. Therefore, Doug, you have what looks like a mixture of a dilemma and an opportunity on your hands. Either way, the clock is ticking."

Mr. X got up from his chair and put on his coat. He reached into his coat pocket and slid a white card in front of Doug while one of the guards opened the door for him.

"Doug, listen very carefully. The phone number on that card is a private and exclusive number. You will only have one chance to dial that number and that will be to inform us of your answer. If you do not call, the organization will assume that you will not be joining us."

Before Mr. X left the room, he patted Doug on the shoulder and took away the grilled chicken salad that he never touched. "Waste not, want not," Mr. X said as he exited.

Doug sat in his office wondering what had just happened to his friends and, most importantly, to him. He looked at the card with the phone number on it and remembered what his father asked him at the retirement home: *Do you want to live or just survive?* He looked at the card again and said to himself in a low tone, "Let's see what you are made of,

Doug." He got up from his chair, turned off his office light, and left the empty club.

* * *

The weather was bad, but Doug was home in his apartment, which was dark and quiet. He walked quietly from the living room to his children's bedroom and slowly opened their door. Their nightlight gave a dim illumination to the room. Chaka was lying on Sandra's chest while Kareem was lying on both of them, as if he were shielding them from danger. Doug looked at his family for another minute then he slowly closed the door and went to his bedroom.Doug sat on his bed, deep in thought, wondering what had to be done on both fronts. How would he get the money together, and what would he do if he couldn't get the money? When he finally put his head on the pillow, Doug passed out quickly from exhaustion.

Chapter Seventeen

Bad Decisions, Horrible Circumstances

There was only a week until Christmas, and Doug had used every source available to raise cash for the proposition. With total liquidation of all he had, including the jewelry and coats he had purchased for Sandra, he had put together roughly $250,000. It was not nearly enough to join what could possibly be the most powerful moneymaking machine in New York history from a street perspective. Doug knew he was smart and he did not need a flunky like Mr. X to tell him this. With his father's question still ringing in his mind—*Do you want to live or just survive?*—Doug thought about a wolf he saw on an animal program that had waited five days in one spot before it went in for a kill. The wolf knew this would be his last opportunity to eat well, so he practically starved himself to death just to make the perfect kill. As he sat in his office on this cold, blustery morning, Doug decided he would be that wolf. Wolves needed weak prey, and Doug had already decided what to hunt. Picking up his phone, Doug dialed an old wolf to form a pack: his old friend Bucky.

* * *

Inside a black van that was parked in a snow-covered parking lot at the Bay Plaza Shopping Mall in the Bronx, Doug, Bucky, Al, and Clyde sat waiting. Doug, being the youngest of the four, considered them old-school but in a good way. They were smart, hungry, and fearless. The last credential was very important because even when a transaction like this seemed like it was so simple and clean, it usually was not.

Doug looked at his watch, which read 1:59 a.m. He pulled out his weapon and checked it. Satisfied, he sat with a briefcase on his lap that contained $250,000. Doug figured that he would have little problem selling back the kilos he would acquire tonight. When he combined the profit with the money on his lap, he would easily reach his goal.

As he looked at the entrance next to the Checkers restaurant, Doug spotted the white Lexus he was expecting. It pulled in and stopped about one hundred feet away. Not to dare insult his crew, Doug didn't ask if they were ready. He just nodded his head and flashed his lights three times. The Lexus, in turn, did the same and slowly drove up to where Doug and his crew were parked.

Simultaneously, the doors of both vehicles opened, and both crews exited. The leader from each side was holding a suitcase. Michael Marino, an Italian cat from Bensonhurst, Brooklyn, was Doug's counterpart. He couldn't be any more than twenty-three years old. Standing alongside him were three more Italian guys who were about the same age. Scouting his prey, Doug noted that they were wearing nice coats with suits and shoes. In the dead of winter with so many ice spots in the parking lot, Doug knew these people were not dressed for warfare. With his men wearing sweat suits and Gore-Tex hiking boots, Doug's crew was prepared. After each posse checked the other out, the two leaders came face-to-face.

"Thank you, Doug, for being on time. I was a little worried with how your people are always late for everything and all," Michael smirked.

Drawing a few chuckles from his crew, the young Italian looked behind him and smiled.

"I know what you mean, partner. We're always late for everything," Doug responded.

"Let's get something straight. We ain't partners or friends," Michael said, obviously feeling his oats. "The only thing happening is a nice, simple transaction that I would like to get done right now so I can get the hell out of the Bronx."

"Fair enough. Let's get it done."

Not taking his eyes off Doug, the now serious-looking Michael snapped the latch and slowly opened his briefcase, revealing neatly packaged bundles of pure cocaine. Looking as cool as ever, Doug slowly opened his case and showed Michael the cash, which was neatly stacked in five-hundred-dollar bundles. The men slowly exchanged briefcases and each man inspected his package, one by tasting and the other by speed counting. They looked up at each other, reluctantly nodded their heads in agreement, and then closed their briefcases. Michael looked over at his car, which was about forty feet away, and spotted a young teenager circling around his vehicle.

"Hey, what the fuck are you looking at!" yelled Michael.

The young kid held up his arms and shook his head from side to side. "Sorry, mister. I was just admiring it. I didn't know it was yours. Sorry!" the kid yelled back.

Michael nodded to one of his men, who pulled out his weapon and started to walk toward the teenager. The young man turned and ran out of the parking lot.

"What the fuck is this, Doug?" Michael demanded.

"Take it easy, man. He was just some kid looking at your ride. That's all. Relax."

Suspicious and angry, Michael quickly grabbed his money and motioned to his men to back up. As they did, Doug picked up his suitcase. His men pulled their weapons to cover him as they led him back to the van. As each team of men entered their respective vehicles, they watched each other closely. Michael looked at the money in the briefcase, smiled and began to chuckle with his men. "Stupid-ass eggplant. He never saw it coming. Let's pull out first, boys. I have a feeling they are going to be very angry." Michael started his car. As soon as he began to back up, there was a loud bang.

"Holy shit! What the fuck!" The men all looked up, but the lights of the oncoming van blinded them. Letting out a blood-curdling scream, Michael and his partner in the front passenger seat held up their hands as the van crashed head-on with the Lexus, causing the air bags to deploy and hit them hard in the face."Let's do it!" yelled Doug as he and his band of men jumped out of the van and rushed the totaled Lexus. Without hesitation, Bucky and his friends fired upon the passengers in the backseat before they could even pull their weapons. Doug fired and killed Michael's friend that was sitting next to him, leaving a dazed and bloodied Michael still clutching the briefcase with his hand. Doug motioned to his men to get back in the van and hurried to the driver's side of the Lexus to meet Michael. He punched the injured man in the face and grabbed the briefcase that contained his money. He looked down at the blown-out tires of the Lexus. The spikes he had paid the teenager to put under them had worked perfectly.

"I guess I am on time, huh, Mike?" asked Doug.

"Fuck you," Michael responded, gasping for air.

Doug smiled and stared at Michael one last time before pumping bullets into his body. Then he hurried back to the van and drove off towards the exit leading to I-95 South.

With blood coming from his mouth, Michael was in the last few seconds of his life. He reached into his coat pocket and removed a small red detonator. As he watched the black van speeding away, the bloodied young mobster gave one last smile, pressed the button, and died quietly.

Meanwhile, Doug was headed up the ramp that led to the nearly empty highway when the briefcase filled with cocaine exploded. The van came to a complete stop and the four men coughed and gasped for air as the van filled with a powdery white dust. Doug rolled down his window, allowing fresh air to enter and helping him gain some vision. He looked at his hands and his clothes, and couldn't believe his eyes. The van and the men were covered with cocaine, and the briefcase was practically destroyed.

Bucky wiped his mouth and eyes. "Doug, get the hell out of here before someone catches us!" he yelled. Doug grabbed the steering wheel and took the highway back to his club. As the cold winter air blew in from the window and hit Doug's dejected face, he knew only two things: He had to lose the van, and he had to arrange for his only and last resort to raise the money.

* * *

Doug let the warm water hit his baldhead and run down his back. "*Do you want to live or just survive?*" He quietly questioned himself as he turned the water off and got out the shower. He wiped the steam off the mirror and looked at himself. "It's time for a new beginning and I want to live," he told his reflection. He picked up the cordless phone that was resting on the sink and dialed the number of his long-time associate, Detective Tommy Davis.

"Good morning, it's me, Doug. Listen, I have a proposal for you that involves a nice piece of change. I was wondering if we could meet at our usual spot this afternoon? Okay, very well. I will see you then. Later," he said into the phone and then hung up. Through the bathroom door, he could hear Chaka and Kareem laughing in the kitchen with Sandra.

* * *

In a beautiful five-thousand-square-foot house in Bensonhurst, Brooklyn, Tony Marino, head of the Russo crime family, was asleep in bed with his wife, Connie, when the phone rang. Aroused by the sound, he moved around under his goose-down comforter, finally reaching over his wife and grabbing the phone on the third ring.

"Hello?" he answered, clearing his throat. "Yes, this is he. Oh no…Oh please no!"

Frightened, Connie quickly sat up in bed, holding her mouth with one hand and grabbing her husband with the other. Tony began to sob uncontrollably.

"Honey, what is it? Please answer me. What is it?" Connie pleaded.

Tony put the phone back on its base and turned to his wife, who was now shaking. "Honey that was the city morgue. They want us to come down right away. Baby, they say Michael is there."

Connie screamed and Tony grabbed his wife, trying to comfort her. As the two of them cried together, their sixteen-year-old daughter Kathy burst into the room with a look of fear on her face. "What happened? Mom and Dad, what happened?" she cried as she sat on the bed with her parents, forming a tiny huddle of support.

* * *

Inside the Boston Road Diner, Doug and Tommy were sipping on cappuccino and eating English muffins. Doug reached under the table and gave the detective an envelope that was four inches thick.

"Do we have all bases covered, Tommy?"

Tommy let a grin come across his face. "All bases are covered. Just understand that after this, we will sever our alliances for a while. Doug, I have to ask, are you sure about this?"

Doug sipped from his cup and nodded his head yes. "I have never been more sure about anything. I appreciate your services." The two men shook hands and finished off their food and drinks. Doug threw a twenty-dollar bill down to cover the food and left the detective at the table.

"Yeah, it's me," Tommy said to someone on the other end of his phone. "Everything is a go. We have the green light. Just let the other two men know and we'll meet up at my place to discuss the situation. Oh, by the way, did you hear about Michael Marino? Yeah, I know. It could not have happened to a better grease ball." Tommy hung up his phone, slithered out of the booth, and left the restaurant.

Chapter Eighteen

Merry Christmas

It was Christmas morning and Doug was in the bedroom closet kneeling over a safe that he had installed into the floor. He slowly turned the dial from right to left and then opened the safe door. He pulled out a leather binder and studied its contents, DVDs marked with dates and events. After carefully zipping the binder shut, Doug put it inside the safe, closed the door, and spun the combination dial to ensure its security. Then he stood up, brushed off his knees, and turned off the light inside the closet. When he turned around, he was surprised to find Sandra standing right behind him.

"Oh shit!" he said, startled.

"Merry Christmas, Doug. I'm sorry. Did I scare you?"

Doug looked at Sandra as if he had been doing something wrong. "How long have you been standing behind me, Sandra?" he asked as he quickly closed the closet door.

"Not long at all. I just heard some rumbling and I thought it was the kids, so I got up to see. Merry Christmas once again."

Doug began to gain his composure. "Why don't you go wake them up so they can open their gifts?" he suggested, giving Sandra a smile before he walked off to the living room. Sandra smiled back and as she walked to the kids' bedroom, she felt like a kid herself.

Smiling ear to ear at her bundles of joy who still had cold in their eyes, Sandra led Kareem and Chaka to the living room. Doug stood by the couch, looking at the children's expressions as they spotted the many gifts that awaited them under the tree.

"Merry Christmas, boo-boos. Look what Santa brought you," Sandra said. After focusing on the colorful packages, the two children looked at each other with excitement. Grabbing and hugging each other, they both ran into the arms of their mother. Doug took in the whole scene and then sat on the couch. "Merry Christmas, kids," he told them.

Sandra turned the children to face Doug. "What do you say to your father?" she asked them.

The twins looked up at Doug and they responded together, "Merry Christmas."

Kissing them both on their cheeks, Sandra released them and watched as they began to happily rip open their many presents. "Doug, would it bother you if I put on some Christmas music?" she asked.

Doug watched the kids laugh and hug each other with the surprise of each newly discovered toy and said, "Sure, Sandra. No problem. Turn on your Christmas music."

Sandra found a red Christmas hat and put it on her head, which brought laughter from Chaka. Then she put on a CD of R&B singers performing different Christmas carols. Sandra walked over to the tree, kissed her children once again, and took a seat next to them to share in their happiness. As she sat down, Doug looked at his watch. He got up from the couch, grabbed his coat, and put it on.

"Sandra, listen, the kids have toys that need batteries and I forgot to get them. I'll run out to get them and be right back."

"Okay, we'll be right here," Sandra said, trying not to say or relay with facial expressions anything that could spoil the moment.

Doug removed his keys from his pocket and began to exit the apartment, but before he left, he took one more look at Sandra and the kids sitting by the Christmas tree.

* * *

It had been about an hour now and Doug still had not returned with the batteries. Sipping on a cup of eggnog, Sandra started to gather up shreds of wrapping paper and put them inside a black garbage bag.

"Come on, kids. You still have a whole lot more to unwrap, so let's go." She gave each child a cup of orange juice and a breakfast bar. Then she heard the locks on the door turn and the door close. Sandra bent her head towards the hallway. "Doug, we're still in the living room opening gifts. Do you have the batteries? Doug?"

Sandra slowly walked past the kids, who were oblivious to her concerns. She was cautiously walking towards the door when four large men dressed in black and wearing ski masks knocked her backwards to the floor in a mad rush.

"Kareem and Chaka, run to your room! Run!" a terrified Sandra screamed. The children, however, didn't run because they never had a chance. Two of the men had each grabbed a child and covered its mouth. Sandra made it to her feet and attempted to run in the direction of the kids, but one of the assailants tripped her, causing her to fall into the Christmas tree. Another one of the men turned up the volume of the Christmas CD to drown out the noise in the apartment.

Sandra looked to her left and saw that her children were terrified. They were kicking and squirming while being held by the two men. She looked to the right, under the tree, and grabbed a radio that belonged to Kareem. One of the men grabbed Sandra by her hair and she swung with all her might, striking him across his face. The radio cut through his mask and left a long, jagged gash. Falling backwards and holding his face, the attacker screamed in agony. Raging with determination, Sandra rushed at the man holding Chaka.

With a sudden jolt of force, Sandra crumbled to the floor from a sharp kick to her ribs. She felt as if her ribs were broken, because at that moment she could hardly breathe. The man she cut rushed towards her, kicking her in the face with the bottom of his black cowboy boot and causing her to violently sprawl out in the middle of the floor.

Meanwhile Kareem was going berserk. He managed to bite down on his captor's arm, which caused the giant figure to jerk his arm back and smack Kareem hard across the face.

"Listen, enough of this shit. Someone is going to hear us. Let's get this over with," said the man who kicked Sandra in the ribs. One of the other men grabbed Sandra by her arm and dragged her over to the couch. Making a very feeble but brave attempt to get up again, Sandra felt the hard and painful pressure of a boot pushing her back down to the floor. An assailant grabbed her by her braids and yanked her head up violently, putting a large amount of strain on her neck.

"Look at this, baby!" he demanded. In disbelief and horror, Sandra watched as the living room window was opened, sending a cold and blustery wind chill through the room and across her face. Her beautiful daughter Chaka was being carried towards the window. Sandra moaned and managed to stretch one of her arms out towards her daughter.

"No, please. Not my baby!" she cried. With tears streaming down both their faces, Sandra's and Chaka's eyes met and locked. The only thing Sandra could think of was holding her baby girl in the operating room on the day she was born. The animal holding her daughter twisted around as if he were throwing a discus in the Olympics and tossed Chaka out the fourth-floor window. Feeling the warm sensation of urine coming from her body, Sandra lowered her head. She felt herself losing consciousness but just as she tried to close her eyes from what was coming next, she was slapped across the face and made to watch.

Kareem, who always tried to protect her, was fighting to get loose and make it to her. Her little man was kicking and punching as hard as he could. Miraculously, he almost squirmed loose but couldn't because of the power of his assailant. With very little strength left in her body, Sandra lowered her head to the floor and watched as her little warrior was sent to meet his sister.

"We have got to get out of here," one assailant yelled over the song "Jingle Bell Rock," coming from the speakers. As three of the men hurried to the hallway that led to the door, the man who had been holding Sandra down yanked her head up by her braids. He reached down with a solid steel military knife and pressed it against Sandra's throat. She was catatonic from her state of shock, but Sandra managed to see two things: a white wrist and a green dragon. The dragon moved slowly across her face, and she felt the suffering and torment start to leave her body as her throat was slit open. With her eyes slowly closing for what she believed to be the last time, Sandra's head fell with a thud on the oak wood floor.

* * *

Pamela Brown was returning from the neighborhood bodega with a few things for her private Christmas dinner. While climbing the stairs between the second and third floors, she looked up in sheer fright as four masked men rumbled down the stairs in her direction. Not being quick enough to get out of the way, Pamela was shoved into the staircase wall, causing her to hit her back and drop her bags. As she sat on a step trying to get herself together, she heard the men reach the first floor and exit the building. She bent her head upward in the direction of her floor and started making her way.Holding her bags, Pamela stood in the middle of the fourth-floor hallway and stared at two apartment doors. Slowly and silently, she took out her keys and tried to take that first step towards her door, but something would not allow her to do it. She looked over again at the slightly opened door of apartment 4B, where "Silent Night" was playing from the inside. Pamela gathered courage from somewhere deep inside her to move towards Sandra's door. With much apprehension, Pamela knocked on the door three times, which caused the door to open a little more.

"Sandra, are you there?" Pamela asked. Feeling the hair on the back of her neck stand, she stuck her head halfway in the door. "Sandra, Merry Christmas…are you there?" Now shaking a little, Pamela slid her body between the door and found herself inside the long, dark hallway. As the stereo completed the playlist of songs, there was a deafening silence.

Setting her bags on the floor slowly and as quietly as possible, Pamela made her way down the hallway. She saw light coming from the living room a few steps ahead. As she walked through the entrance, her attention was immediately drawn to the brown curtains that blew back and forth because of the cold wind coming from outside. Looking to her right, Pamela saw the many toys that sat under the Christmas tree and many more that remained unopened.

When she turned to her left, Pamela screamed so loud that people throughout the building opened their windows to see what was causing the commotion. Holding her mouth and falling to her knees, Pamela looked in horror at Sandra, who was lying in a pool of blood.

"Sandra, please no, Sandra. Somebody help us! Somebody help us!" Pamela yelled as she crawled over to her friend and neighbor. Kneeling in the blood, Pamela rubbed Sandra's head as she tried to find a pulse. She felt a light, pulsating throb coming from Sandra's neck. Pamela quickly removed her coat and sweater. She rested Sandra's head on the coat and wrapped the sweater with pressure on Sandra's ugly open wound.

"Please, somebody, help us, please!" she yelled while holding Sandra's unconscious body in her arms. Pamela's heart rate jumped higher as she heard footsteps running into the apartment. She looked up with fear in her eyes.

"Oh God, Luis. Call an ambulance, please. She's dying!" Pamela begged.

"Oh shit, where are the kids? Where are the kids?" The superintendent walked over to Pamela and tried to comfort her. "Pamela, I already called 911, but I will call again!" As Luis dialed 911 on his phone, Pamela softly kissed Sandra on her head. In the distance, they could hear sirens approaching. Luis walked over to the window to close it but he heard screams coming from the back alley of the building, so he looked out. The short Spanish man quickly pulled his head back in. He couldn't stop his breakfast from coming up from his stomach and projecting from his mouth onto the floor.

"Luis, what did you see?"

Letting his body slump to the floor, the now sobbing man responded, "It's her kids."

Pamela was now crying harder as she rocked Sandra back and forth. EMS workers busted into the apartment holding all kinds of medical equipment. A worker quickly grabbed on to Pamela. "Okay, miss, you have got to let us take over from here, please!"

Still crying, Luis gently grabbed Pamela and pulled her to the side.

"Let's move. Her pressure is going! Close her up, and let's move! Heart rate is dropping!" yelled the EMS worker. Pamela and Luis watched as the medical unit hooked tubes and machines to Sandra. They put her on a stretcher and quickly rushed out of the apartment.

An EMS worker quickly turned to Pamela and Luis. "We are going to need you two to come down to the hospital because your friend has lost a lot of blood. We need to see if either of you can donate."

Quivering, Pamela nodded her head up and down quickly in agreement.

* * *

Outside the front of the building, there was pandemonium and outrage as police cars lined up throughout the street. Uniformed officers were asking numerous tenants questions. From a distance, cries of anguish could be heard as the paramedics wheeled Sandra out of her building with Pamela by her side. A black sedan with a flashing light in its window quickly pulled up to the building. Two detectives got of the car. Observing the scene carefully, they walked over and looked at Sandra, who was about to be lifted into the ambulance.

"Is she gonna make it?" Detective Tommy Davis asked the EMS worker, who was frantically trying to get in the vehicle.

"I really don't think so. She has lost a lot of blood. All we can do is get to the hospital quickly. Her life depends on it."

As Pamela entered the ambulance from the back, Doug's truck pulled up in front of the building. The crowd looked at him and several people pointed at him. Doug got out of the truck and examined the scene.

"Oh God, no! Not the babies!" yelled an old woman who was wearing an old red coat over her pajamas. Everyone then focused on another set of emergency workers carrying out the small bodies of Kareem and Chaka, who were inside what looked like black plastic duffel bags.

Doug looked over at the alleyway, dropped the bag of batteries, and began to run towards his children. "No! Please no, please! My children!" he yelled. As he got closer to their bodies, Doug was grabbed by three uniformed officers and was gently subdued.

"I am so sorry, sir, but we cannot let you see them like this right now. We are so sorry," said one of the officers. Doug fell to his knees and began to sob loudly as onlookers also cried in sympathy.

"Where is my lady, Sandra?" he cried. People pointed at the EMS truck that was now turning the corner.

"Sir, your wife is being taken to Bronx North Central Hospital," said another officer. As Doug turned and walked towards his truck, he was confronted by Detectives Davis and McCarthy, who had somber looks on their faces.

"Doug, hello, I'm Detective Tommy Davis and this is Detective Joseph McCarthy. We want to express our deepest sympathy to you and your family. Here are our cards; we'd like to speak to you as soon as possible while this is fresh. But right now we suggest that you go to the hospital to be with your wife. As soon as anything comes up, you will be the first to know. We'll be the lead detectives on this case, so please believe and trust that whoever did this horrible crime will be caught and prosecuted to the highest extent of the law."

The officers shook Doug's hand and led him to his vehicle so that he could hurry to the hospital. As the detectives watched Doug speed off, Detective McCarthy rubbed the fresh bandage on the left side of his cheek.

"Damn, this hurts," he complained.

"Look at it this way, partner, consider it a very expensive battle scar," Davis suggested.

* * *

The waiting room was jam-packed with people who were there to support Sandra. Ms. Carla and people who volunteered at the food pantry were standing together in prayer. Pamela and Luis were sitting with a nurse with their sleeves rolled up, ready to give blood. The nurses were checking to see if anyone else had the right type of blood to donate to Sandra. Rose had quietly entered the waiting area and had taken a seat in a corner where no one would notice her. In all there had to be about twenty-five people in the room talking, crying, and praying. Everyone came to a hush at the sight of Doug, who was very surprised by the number of people there to support Sandra. One by one, neighbors approached Doug and gave him hugs as a show of support.

"Hi, my name is Carla. Sandra has helped me so much at the pantry. We all just want to give our deepest sympathy for your loss."

Doug had a somber look on his face. "Thank you all for your support but I have to see Sandra right now." As Doug received the last of the handshakes and hugs, his eyes locked with those of the only person who had not expressed sympathy towards him—and that was Pamela. She stood on the wall holding a cotton ball on her arm where blood had been drawn. Their eyes remained locked until they both looked away in the direction of the doctor, who had just entered the waiting area holding a clipboard.

"Who is the next of kin to Sandra?"

Doug stepped up to the forefront. "That would be me. Is she going to be all right?"

After introducing himself, Dr. Mackey looked somberly at Doug. "Right now, sir, Ms. Lyte has lost a lot of blood and her heart rate is unstable. The nurses have informed me that this woman, Pamela Brown, has O type blood, which is somewhat unique because of its ability to donate universally. Sandra is also O type, which means she can only receive from a person with type O. So, Doug, as you can see; we do not have time to waste. We need to get Ms. Brown inside for a transfusion and even after that, you have to understand that the next twelve hours will be critical."

Doug turned to Pamela. "Please, Pamela, help her," he pleaded.

Without even looking at Doug or responding to him, Pamela walked right to the doctor. "I am ready, Dr. Mackey," she said.

Pamela let the tears fall down her face as the nurses laid her on the bed next to Sandra, who was unconscious and had several tubes coming out of her mouth, arms, and nose. The nurse wiped Pamela's arm and inserted a needle attached to tubing. As Pamela watched her blood enter a filtering device, she listened to the beeping of Sandra's heart monitor. All she could do was hope and pray that Sandra would live to see another day.

Chapter Nineteen

Now On to More Important Matters

On New Year's Day, Doug stood in front of the mirror in his empty and quiet apartment. He had not been staying there much since the horrible incident one week ago, but he'd arranged for a cleaning service to come in and thoroughly clean the apartment. Without remorse or regard, he even had Chaka and Kareem's toys and clothes thrown away, trying to erase anything with sentimental value.

With one million dollars from life insurance in his possession, Doug spared all expense when it came down to his children's funeral. He had no sense of shame or embarrassment as throngs of people came to witness the children being buried on top of each other in the same plot of land, their tiny bodies squeezed inside two unfinished pine boxes that a dog owner would not use for his pet. The flowers that adorned their caskets came from the local bodega. Doug also spent the minimum amount of money on their shared tombstone. Just their names, date of birth, and the date of death engraved it.

Doug was now preparing for his new life with the Lords of the Underground. Dressed in a very conservative suit with shoes to match, he looked inside the suitcase at the clean and neatly stacked blood money that he would turn over for his entry into the organization. He picked up the card that Mr. X had given him a few weeks ago and dialed the number from his cell phone. "This is Doug. I am calling for the sit-down. Yes, I have it. I have it all. Yes, I know where it is. Very good. I will be there at three o'clock. Okay, good-bye."

A smile spread across Doug's face as he looked himself up and down from head to toe, making sure he looked perfectly debonair for the meeting.

* * *

The Plaza Hotel worker took the keys to his vehicle and a stunning black sister greeted Doug.

"Good afternoon, Mr. Gunner. My name is Gloria Henderson and I would like to welcome you to the Plaza Hotel. If you follow me, I will take you to meet with my associates."

Doug couldn't help but look at the elegance of the woman as he followed her to the elevator. As they traveled to the fifteenth floor, Doug thought about the possibility of his new life. The elevator doors opened and Doug was taken to a luxury suite.

As Gloria and Doug stood in the living room, a man dressed in a white suit entered with a huge smile on his face.

"Good day, Doug. How are you today?" The man walked over to Doug and greeted him with a handshake and nodded his head at Gloria, who smiled and left the suite.

"Doug, please sit down. My associates will see you in a few minutes. Meanwhile, please enjoy your choice of entrée, which has been prepared especially for you." A waiter removed the covers from the trays that sat on a table in the dining area, offering Doug lobster, Alaskan crab legs, roast beef, and poached salmon. Doug indicated that he wanted the lobster. He sipped on Johnnie Walker Blue while the waiter prepared his plate.

* * *

After his meal, Doug walked to another suite on the same floor and took a seat on the couch. Two black men who looked to be in their early forties entered the room. Both men were well dressed and well groomed, looking as if they had stepped off a GQ magazine cover. Taking a seat on a couch opposite Doug, one of the men pulled out a long Cuban cigar and ran his tongue across it while the other man pulled out a lighter and lit the cigar.

"Doug, can we have our money please?" asked the man wearing the tan-colored suit. Doug grabbed the suitcase and slowly handed it to the man. He and his partner examined the money inside and closed it back up, setting it between them.

"Doug, my name is Mr. Brown and this is Mr. Green. We would like you to think of us as your sponsors. This basically means that we are putting our reputations on the line with the organization, trusting that you will prove to be a worthwhile acquisition."

Doug paid close attention to every word. "I want to thank you for the chance to become a member and I promise, I will not let you down."

Mr. Brown nodded his head at Doug. "First of all, Doug, never make promises, because when you do, you automatically put yourself in debt to someone…and that is not intelligent. Secondly, if you are not beneficial to us, please understand that you will not be letting us down—you will be letting yourself down. Always remember, Doug, your actions and decisions might reflect on our judgment of character, but it will definitely impact your life even more."

Feeling isolated and alone, Doug realized that for the first time since he had been involved in the game, he was not calling any shots. He recognized that these cats were serious and in a polite kind of way, they were letting him know that the organization didn't believe in using erasers to correct mistakes. You had better be on your toes when it came down to business because if you were not, chances were you would be out of business for good.

"Doug, I want to make something very clear to you. Lords of the Underground doesn't tolerate loose ends, and I will make myself clear about what I mean by 'loose ends.' If by any chance you have bodies, cases, unpaid debt, broken promises, vendettas, or even an unhappy woman, do not bring it to us because we don't want any part of it. It's your problem from your past life and it's your duty to handle these affairs before you enter into matrimony with our organization. As of this moment your new life has begun, but it is up to you how you want this transition to go—either smooth or bumpy," Mr. Brown explained.

Doug nodded in agreement. "Without a doubt, I fully understand and accept the terms of the agreement. As a new employee, I am ready and eager to do all I can to make myself a profitable asset."

Mr. Green grabbed a duffel bag off the Italian marble table and handed it to Doug. "Doug, inside that bag you will find an untraceable disposable phone, twenty-five thousand dollars in cash, and keys to a brand-new vehicle that awaits you in the parking garage of this hotel. At this moment, Doug, I want you to think of yourself as one of a thousand ants that spends the day working to please the queen. As a worker, your task is to carry out our instructions to the finest detail and always bring us back a profit.

"You will never use your phone to make calls, only to receive them from us. Your car is strictly for transportation, not for women or any other childish use. Your money is your livelihood, so spend it wisely. We will contact you at noon for your first assignment, so please stay on point because we will only call once. If you miss the call, you lose the assignment and the wages that go with it. You will not get another call for three weeks, and by that time you will be hungry again. Continue to show sloppiness and you are done. Do I make myself clear?"

"I understand clearly what you have said and I will be ready when the call comes in," Doug assured, feeling rejuvenated by the opportunity.

"It has been a long, productive meeting, Doug," Mr. Brown said with a smile, "and I really hope this relationship will be productive for everyone involved. It's about time that Mr. Green and I headed back to let the organization know that we have a new employee. Doug, I want you to get a taste of how we treat our employees. I want you to enjoy this suite here in The Plaza for the rest of the day. Whatever you need, just charge it to the room and the organization will cover it. In addition, here are two tickets to the Broadway show *The Phantom of the Opera.* I have seen it twice and I enjoyed it even more the second time. One more thing, Doug..." Mr. Brown dialed a number from his phone and Gloria entered the suite with two black sisters that looked like runway models, except they had bodies like Amazons. The two women were both dressed in designer pinstriped suits and they smiled as they looked at Doug.

"Doug, this is Jayne and Samantha," Mr. Brown continued. "They will be your guests tonight and would love to spend some time getting to know you a little better. I hope you do not mind the company?"

Doug couldn't help but smile. "Not at all. It would be my pleasure to have them join me tonight."

The three men stood and exchanged handshakes, then Mr. Green, Mr. Brown, and Gloria exited the room, leaving Doug with his guests for the night. Without saying a word, the two women walked up to Doug, kissed him on the mouth at the same time, and slowly began to remove their clothes. Gently and slowly forcing Doug to sit on the coach, the women put on a sex show for Doug that even he had to admire. While sitting there on the couch with a huge erection, something continued to pop up in his head. Doug thought about the "loose ends" he had to take care of. He knew if he really wanted a new beginning, the "loose ends" had to be disposed of at all costs. This was Doug's last and final chance to scratch his way back to the top. As dismal as that sounded though, Doug did not let it get him down because the one thing he had that no one could take from him was his will to achieve at any cost. True, the men in this organization were elaborate, but they got that way by being hungry and ambitious. As he saw it, no one was more hungry and ambitious than he was.

With his mind focused back on his dates for the night, Doug smiled as the women climbed on top of him and removed his clothing.

Chapter Twenty

Loose Ends Starting to Form a Noose

A table lamp next to Sandra's bed lit the hospital room, which was filled with balloons and flowers sent by caring individuals from her building and the pantry where she volunteered. It had been nine days since that horrible Christmas morning when Sandra experienced what no human being should ever have to go through. The news coverage had lasted for about three days, but as usual when dealing with certain neighborhoods and individuals, the unsolved crime became just another cold-case file.

There was now only one tube in Sandra's arm and the doctors said her recovery had been nothing short of a miracle. During this time, as she continued to fall in and out of consciousness, her main support system had been Pamela. Reading to Sandra and fixing her hair had become a regular routine. A couple of the nurses had explained to Pamela that Sandra's scar would always remain and that she would soon remember what happened to her children. She would need psychological therapy that would last months, maybe years.

Doug had not visited Sandra once since he left her in the hospital, which made Pamela try to come up with about a thousand reasons why. Pamela had noticed the quiet young woman named Rose who came by to look at Sandra through the door at different times of the night. Pamela always wondered how she got by security but did not think too much about it. She just thought it was nice to see that Rose cared.

Pamela looked at her watch and saw that it was four in the morning. She took out a picture of her son, Derrick, kissed it softly, and laid her head on Sandra's stomach. She closed her eyes and drifted off into a light sleep.

* * *

At the Checkers hamburger spot in the Bay Plaza Shopping Center, the drive-through window was closed and people were waiting and wondering why they couldn't order food at two o'clock in the afternoon. Getting inpatient, the majority of them drove over to a nearby Burger King, which was about three hundred yards away.

Inside the restaurant, in the back of the supply room, there were twelve workers—two managers and ten regular shift workers—who ranged between the ages of seventeen and thirty-five. They were all sitting against a wall, face-to-face with Tony Marino, the reputed crime boss. They all knew who Tony was, which was evident by the tears streaming from everyone's eyes. The room was silent but filled with tension and fear because Tony had a few of his soldiers with him, and they looked as if they hadn't beaten anyone in a while and were eager to make up for the idle time.

Tony stepped forward. "You all know who I am," he started, "however, what you may not know is that I am a loving husband and father who cares about my family very deeply. Now I know you all have families that you care about, so I think you can relate to what I am going to say. I know this restaurant operates twenty-four hours a day, and I am here with you today because a few days before Christmas—in this same parking lot—there was a tragic shooting that took the life of my son."

All the workers were trying not to disrespect Tony by looking away from him, but some couldn't help themselves. Their eyes strayed to the yellow rain gear that sat on the floor next to two chainsaws.

"Now, what I want you to know is that I am not a monster, just a businessman. So as bad as this scene may look right now, I want you to understand that I want you all to go home and continue to live your lives as usual. But before I can let you do that, I need some answers that could possibly help me and my family," Tony explained.

A shaking and now sobbing Spanish girl raised her hand. Tony took notice and nodded his head to her with a slight smile.

"Sir, I'm really sorry about your son, but I didn't see anything because I was not here. Sir, I'm just sixteen years old. Can I please go home? Please?"

Tony looked at the girl with some compassion. "Please don't cry, sweetheart. I have a daughter your age at home, so please understand that having you in this situation really pains me. I promise you that once I get my answers, everyone will be free to go."

* * *

Thirty minutes had gone by and Tony had shown patience and understanding as he questioned everyone about what happened on the night of his son's murder. Feeling like he wasn't getting anywhere, he nodded to one of his soldiers who then began to put on the rain gear. Chaos ensued as the workers, who were all sitting with their feet bound together, started sobbing louder and begging for their lives. No longer smiling, Tony looked at them all from one end of the room to the other.

"All I wanted was your help today. Everyone in this room knows the police will not help me because of who I am. They are probably gloating because of my loss. So, please…I beg of you…somebody, please do not allow me to change your lives the way mine has been changed."

Tony looked around the room and now just saw frightened faces. He nodded to his soldier in the rain gear, who in turn walked over and grabbed a manager named Alfred, a skinny man who was about thirty years old. Terrified, Alfred trembled as the other soldier's foot held him facedown to the floor. He urinated on himself when he heard the chainsaw's motor crank up and start running, its fumes penetrating his nostrils with the smell of death. As the blade headed towards Alfred's neck, he closed his eyes and began to pray silently.

"Wait, oh God, please wait!" yelled eighteen-year-old Tasha.

Tony looked at the distraught black girl's face and motioned with his finger to his man. The man in the rain gear turned off the chainsaw, and two men picked Alfred up off the floor and helped him to sit up. Tony walked over to Tasha and pulled out a handkerchief. He gently wiped her face clean of tears and sweat. Looking deeply into Tasha's eyes, he asked, "Sweetheart, do you have something you would like to say? Take your time."

The young girl bravely gathered herself together and swallowed. "I was emptying the trash that night when I heard some yelling coming from the parking lot. I was a little nervous and it was very cold, so I stayed close to the door where it was warm. I put the garbage in the bin and that's when I heard a loud crash, which sounded like two cars hitting each other. After that a few seconds went by, and then I heard the gunfire."

Tony studied the young girl. Because he believed he was an expert at knowing if a person was lying or telling the truth, he never took his eyes off of her as he handed her a bottle of water.

"Please, Tasha," he said, reading the name on her employee nametag, "tell me what happened after that."

Tasha took a small sip of water and looked at her fellow workers. They all stared back at her. Knowing that all their lives might depend on her, she continued, "After the gunfire, I wanted to go downstairs and get Alfred, but I knew he was counting inventory. With us being the only two there, I didn't want to leave the counter unattended. I was so scared, but something kept pushing me to go look. I stuck my head around the wall of the restaurant. I saw a big, bald black man standing by the driver's side of the car with a gun pointed at the driver. He fired about two or three times into the car. After that, he reached inside the car and removed a black briefcase."

"Tasha, did you get a clear look at his face? Or did you hear anything anyone said?" Tony asked.

"No. I'm really sorry. I couldn't get a clear look. It was dark and the lighting in the parking lot is not great. As for any words being said—no, sir. I did not."

The description Tasha had given him fit almost anyone in the five boroughs. Frustrated, Tony took a long, deep breath and exhaled.

"No, wait!" Tasha suddenly cried out. Everyone in the room quickly focused back on her. "I did hear something. When the big man with the suitcase was staring at the person he just shot, I heard one of the guys yell from the van they were in, 'Come on, Doug, let's go!' That's when the man named Doug got in the van and sped off."

"Tasha, I am pretty sure the police asked you the same questions that I did, so tell me, sweetheart, why did you keep this away from the police?"

Tasha took another sip of water. "I had a brother that would be in college if he was alive today. He was very smart. Four years ago, my brother was shot for holding a bottle of orange juice in a black plastic bag. Two cops investigating a robbery in my building thought he had a gun they never found. My brother died in my mother's arms. The trial found them not guilty because the jury said it was an accident committed by two decorated cops. I will never help or rely on the police department for as long as I live. I'm really sorry about what happened to your son, but I was scared and not willing to help the cops."

Looking at the workers in the room, Tony motioned to his men to untie the staff's feet and help them to stand. "Tasha, you are a brave young girl and I am sorry about your brother. I hope you and the rest of your coworkers understand that this was personal to my family and me. I had no other choice but to go to this extreme. When we leave, you can go on with your lives as usual."

The men picked up their tools of destruction and exited the restaurant with their boss. Feeling like a ton of bricks had been moved from their chests, the workers at the hamburger restaurant hugged and sobbed together. A few walked over to offer comfort to Alfred, who was still visibly shaken.

"We need to all go home and never tell anyone about what almost happened here today," Tasha said, looking at everyone. All the workers gathered their belongings and went home for the rest of the day.

* * *

Back inside the hospital room, Pamela was now awake but was still resting on Sandra's stomach. "Why couldn't you just leave, girl? You could have brought those little angels of yours to my place and we could have figured something out. I had everything all worked out for us to enjoy our time together. I had banana crunch ice cream in the freezer along with tacos and chili for the kids. We could have watched the stories together and figured out who was dishing out the dirt. I could have told you about my little baby, Derrick, and showed you all of his pictures. I could have been your ear to listen and to try to understand all that you went through living in that hellhole. I am no angel either, Sandra, because I heard your suffering and I did nothing about it. I was scared and somewhat of a coward not to speak up, and now it is too late. I just hope one day, when you are able and well, you can find it in your heart to forgive me."

As tears left her eyes, Pamela felt her face moving up and down on Sandra's stomach. She shivered as Sandra's smooth hand rubbed her face and head, stroking it gently. Lifting her head and turning it slowly in Sandra's direction, Pamela could see the determination of a woman who had lost it all except her will to live. She watched with complete awe as Sandra tried to speak. Not saying a word, Pamela gathered herself on the bed and brought her ear close to Sandra's mouth to make out what she was trying to say.

Sandra slowly pulled oxygen into her body and gathered the strength to speak. "Get me away from here…the dragon is coming for me. The dragon will find me here…get me away from here." Exhausted, Sandra lay back on her pillow. Pamela stood to her feet and looked into Sandra's eyes. "Don't worry, my sister, I will get you out of here," she promised.

Chapter Twenty-one

Checking Out

Inside a roach-infested Queens flat, Detective Tony Harris sat on his couch checking his unregistered silver-plated semi-automatic weapon. He fed it a clip of fourteen bullets and took a sip of the warm beer that was on his dusty coffee table from earlier. The twelve-year veteran could hear the reassurance of his fellow detective replaying in his mind. "It doesn't matter if she survives because she could never identify us," Tommy Davis had said. "And secondly, her mental state would be so screwed up that she could never face the challenge of revisiting that day again, so just relax."

Relaxing was easier said than done, and besides, Tony hadn't become a detective by playing it safe. He got there because he believed in his instincts, and those instincts told him Sandra was better as a dead corpse than as a live one with the will to seek justice. It was easy for Tommy Davis to tell him to relax; he was the only one in the apartment that day with no blood on his hands. All he did was give orders and turn the volume up on the radio. No, Tony was going by his instincts tonight and those instincts said he needed to let Sandra smell the Downy on the pillowcase she laid her head on. He looked at his watch and felt it was the perfect time to pay her a visit. Because it was the graveyard shift, no one would even notice he was there or, for that matter, notice that she was gone. Tossing the pornographic magazine off his lap, Detective Harris inserted his weapon in his holster, kissed the magic dragon on his wrist, and left to pay Sandra a visit.

* * *

The hospital had a quiet, comatose aura and there weren't many doctors and nurses on duty—maybe because of the snow, or perhaps it was because only the unlucky had been stuck working this shift. Inside the emergency waiting room, only a handful of people sat with fevers, cuts, and bruises. At the nurses' station, there was only one nurse, and she was too busy flirting with the porter to see anything right away. The majority of the patients were asleep in their beds. The few who were awake were waiting for daybreak, hoping loved ones would visit, or desiring to go home.In room 613, Pamela was gathering up Sandra's personal belongings while Sandra sat on her bed holding her neck and letting the tears fall from her eyes as she thought about her babies. Still wearing her hospital gown, Sandra made a feeble attempt to put her jeans on as she watched Pamela stuff her duffel bag to its full capacity. Moving as if she were seventy-five years old, Sandra could barely bend down to put her legs into her pants. Taking deep breaths, she tried again but to no avail. Pamela looked at her and could only feel hurt and despair as she watched this once vibrant woman with so much of her life ahead of her reduced to this.

"Sandra, try not to do so much, okay? I will be right there in a minute. I just want to make sure I have everything," Pamela whispered. Accepting that she was helpless, Sandra listened and gave up until Pamela came to help. She sat on the bed while Pamela slipped her gown off. Then she lowered her head so Pamela could pull on her sweater; next she got help with her jeans. Pamela looked around and found a clean pair of white socks that she gently put on her friend's feet.

"Sandra, baby, in a few minutes, we will be getting out of here," she said.

* * *

After parking his car in the hospital parking lot, stone-faced Tony Harris looked up at the Bronx North Central Hospital. He glanced at his watch; it was about three hours before daybreak. Tony adjusted his coat collar and put on the same pair of black leather gloves that he had used to open Sandra's throat. Then he entered the hospital to finish the job.

* * *

With Sandra all bundled up and ready to go, Pamela quietly used her cell phone to call a cab.

"Sandra, sweetheart, I will be right back. I just want to make sure the coast is clear," Pamela whispered. She left Sandra sitting in a wheelchair wondering to herself why Doug had not been by to visit her. She knew he never loved her or the kids, but she figured sympathy would justify at least one visit. Putting the thought out of her mind, Sandra refocused on getting out of the hospital. She didn't care what anyone thought or believed; she could feel the dragon looking for her to finish what he failed to do previously: You do not slaughter a family and leave loose ends.

Turning her head and snapping back to reality, Sandra saw Pamela return with a look of purpose on her face. "Okay, Sandra, you have everything? We have to move right now because the cab will be here in ten minutes." In her chair, Sandra took a deep breath and let Pamela push her out the hospital room.

Making a sharp left and walking away from the nurses' station, Pamela pushed Sandra towards the intensive care ward, which had another set of elevators on the north side. Looking cautiously from side to side, she gently opened the swinging doors with the wheels of the wheelchair. Now in the other ward, she made a sharp right and saw two security guards having a coffee break. She made her way to the elevators and breathed a sigh of relief as she pushed the button and waited with Sandra.

* * *

Riding on the elevator, Detective Harris adjusted his gloves on his hands and waited for the elevator doors to open on the sixth floor. He knew that the hospital would be on a skeleton crew, and he believed that his mission should be quick and without difficulty. When the doors opened, he stepped out and walked towards the nurses' station. As he walked along the ward, Harris quickly glanced into rooms where the doors were open, hoping that maybe he would locate Sandra without having to ask a nurse. The less he was noticed, the better.

* * *

Pamela was getting frustrated at this point. The elevator had stopped at their floor twice, but both times the custodians had it filled to capacity with mops, buckets, and other cleaning supplies. She decided to try to sneak on the elevators back in the west wing where Sandra's room was. It was a huge risk, but knowing she only had a few minutes until the cab arrived, she had no choice. Sandra was in no condition to walk down six flights of steps. "Hang in there, girl. I'll get us out of here," Pamela promised.

* * *

Detective Harris walked down the quiet corridor and found himself at the nurses' station where Nurse Collins, an attractive young white woman in her early twenties, sat reading a magazine. Putting a smile on his face, Harris slowly and calmly approached the unsuspecting nurse with his badge in his hand. "Good morning, nurse. I'm Detective Harris of the homicide squad and I am looking for a Sandra Lyte, whom I believe is on this floor. I know it's very early in the morning, but I will only be a few moments and my questions are crucial to our investigation."

The nurse typed in Sandra's name and looked at Harris with a pupil's crush. "Detective, Sandra Lyte is located in room six thirteen, but I really do not want to get in any trouble. I'm kind of like new on the job. So please, if you could make this as short as possible, I would appreciate it."

Putting on the charm, Harris smiled at the nurse and briefly rubbed her hand. "I promise I will make it quick and it will be our secret," he assured, and she pointed him in the direction of the room.

The smile on Harris's face faded as he prepared to kill Sandra, and now he was convinced he would have to do the same to the nurse. Slowly opening the door, Harris stuck his head in and saw the curtain pulled around the bed. He stepped inside the room, gently closed the door, and walked towards Sandra's bed.

"I never miss twice, bitch," he whispered, smiling as he slowly pulled the curtain back. The smile quickly disappeared and sweat beads started to form on Harris's forehead. Sandra was gone.

The detective looked around the room in a slight state of panic. He stared at the empty bed for a few seconds before quickly exiting the room. He walked back to the nurses' station and stood by the desk in a dazed-like state. He scanned the ward, hoping to see something or someone.

"Detective, that was quick. Did you get the information you were looking for?" asked Nurse Collins.

Cautious not to give himself away by wearing his frustration on his face, Harris played cool. "Nurse, Sandra Lyte is not in her room. Did you see anyone leave with her? Did anyone come visit her today? Can you check your visitors' log, please?" As Nurse Collins looked over the log, Harris held his badge in his hand. He glanced over at the elevator bank that was about sixty feet away and saw a woman in a wheelchair and another woman standing with her. Ignoring the nurse as she tried to tell him about Sandra's last visitor, he walked away from the nurses' station.

"Excuse me, ladies!" Harris yelled towards the elevator.Pamela looked up and saw Harris walking towards them with his hand raised, revealing a badge. Sandra, who was trying to keep herself up and awake, was somewhat drowsy because of all the medication that she had taken during her stay in the hospital. She looked up, saw the dragon on Harris's wrist, and began to tremble. Using all of the strength she could muster from her throat, Sandra's dry, raspy voice warned Pamela, "The dragon is here! The dragon is here!"

As Pamela's eyes locked with Harris's, the red light over the elevator door illuminated and the bell dinged, signaling down. "Stay right there. I need to talk to you!" demanded Harris. The doors opened, and Pamela quickly spun Sandra around in the chair and wheeled her into the elevator. "I am an officer. Do not move!" yelled Harris as he sprinted towards them.

Pamela frantically pushed the lobby button and the close button at once, and the elevator doors finally began to close. Hearing the footsteps of the dragon getting closer, Sandra shook even more. Before the doors closed completely, Pamela got a quick glance of the well-built man who was pursuing them.Harris stood in front of the closed doors and looked up to see which direction the elevator was going. He looked around the ward and located a stairwell. Moving quickly, he pushed the door violently and ran downstairs, hoping to catch his prey.

Still pushing hard on the button for the lobby level and hoping the elevator would not stop, Pamela used her other hand to hold on to Sandra's face, trying to keep her calm. She looked up at the digital screen and watched the numbers slowly descend. Pamela reached into her purse and removed her house keys. She held them inside her hand in such a way that two of the keys protruded between her fingers, creating a jabbing weapon. The elevator screen read "lobby" and as the doors slowly opened, Pamela put her body weight on the back of the wheelchair, making sure to get a good push out the door.

* * *

Picking himself up off the first-floor steps, Harris looked at the orange soda that someone had spilled. He rubbed his sore ankle and hurried down the last flight of stairs leading to the lobby level. Not paying any attention to the sign on the door that read "EMERGENCY EXIT ONLY- ALARM WILL SOUND," Harris pushed the red arm on the door and in an instant bells were ringing. Ignoring the alarm, Harris limped out of the hallway and into the back of the lobby where he saw Pamela and Sandra exiting the elevator. "Stop! I said stop!" Harris yelled at the top of his lungs.

Frantically pushing Sandra towards the three revolving doors leading to the street, Pamela turned and looked for the yelling voice that she somehow heard over the ringing alarm. She looked behind her and saw the madman limping towards them with his gun showing at his side. With all her strength, Pamela pushed forward without bothering to look behind her. She pushed Sandra as fast as she could until she reached the security desk where three guards were trying to figure out why the alarm had gone off. Pamela could hear Detective Harris's screams getting louder, which meant he was getting closer. "Please help us! That man's got a weapon. He's trying to kill us!" she yelled at the security guards. The three guards looked at Pamela and then at the limping man coming towards them. He looked like a sweating maniac.

"Get out of here now!" a husky guard named Bernard yelled at Pamela and Sandra. He pulled out his mace and his nightstick. "Oh yeah, fellas, we got some action. Let's take his ass down," Bernard rallied. As the three guards ran towards the detective, Pamela pushed Sandra outside the door into the cold winter morning where the wind was howling.Pamela looked for the cab and saw that it was beginning to drive away from the hospital entrance. "Taxi, right here!" Pamela yelled, causing the red brake lights to illuminate. "Come on, Sandra. Let's go!" She pushed Sandra as fast as she could and they made it to the cab's back door. Pamela quickly opened it and used all her strength to push Sandra inside. Sandra felt helpless, but she used all of the muscles in her body to crawl inside the backseat of the cab.

Once Sandra was safely inside the cab, Pamela opened the front door on the passenger side. Before getting inside though, she took a quick peek at the revolving doors of the hospital and saw the guards wrestling her pursuer on the floor. She got inside the cab and looked at the Spanish driver. "Jerome Avenue on the corner of Burnside Avenue. Please hurry!" she pleaded.

When the guards had finally subdued Harris, Bernard noticed his badge and weapon. "Oh shit! Everybody calm down! This guy's a cop!" he said, sounding shocked. The other two guards looked at Bernard and then at the furious, red-faced detective. They all slowly released him, moving away and leaving him on the cold tiled lobby floor.

"You are fucking idiots! I was yelling at you three assholes that I was a cop! I am telling you, not only will you lose your jobs, you will also be arrested for obstructing an officer." As the three guards stood in silence, Harris made it to his feet and looked towards the revolving doors where he had been inches away from capturing not only Sandra but Pamela also.

"This ain't over. This ain't over by a long shot," the sweaty detective mumbled.

* * *

The cab pulled up to the curb and Pamela quickly exited the cab. She ran to open the other door where Sandra sat. Carefully grabbing on to her, Pamela assisted her out of the cab.

"Sandra, are you okay, baby?" Pamela asked. Still trying to catch her breath, Sandra slowly nodded her head up and down.

Pamela walked over to the driver's side of the cab, took a twenty-dollar bill from her pocket, and gave it to the driver. "You did a great job in this bad weather. Keep the change, and thank you."

"No problem, mommy. Thank you." The cab driver smiled and took the money.

As the car pulled away, Pamela grabbed Sandra's bag and walked towards the delivery entrance of the pantry. Pamela knocked three times on the door and hugged Sandra in an attempt to keep her warm. She heard the turning and clicking of locks, and then there was a heavy pull of the door that forced it to open. Standing on the other side with welcoming smiles were Ms. Carla and Rose Garden. All four women hugged and embraced each other as they assisted Sandra into the pantry.

After helping Sandra get her coat off, the women sat at a table covered with breakfast food. Shaking from their ordeal, Sandra looked up at Pamela. "I will never be able to repay you, Pamela. You saved my life," she said hoarsely.

Pamela reached across the table and rubbed Sandra's sweaty forehead. "You don't owe me anything. You are my sister."

Ms. Carla made everyone grasp hands around the table and led them in grace before they ate.

Chapter Twenty-two

A Discovery at the House of Horrors

A week had passed and Sandra was sitting on an old cot that Carla had stored away in the basement. Pamela was next to her. "I don't want to bombard you with too many questions, Sandra, because I don't want you straining your throat," she began. "Do you plan to see a counselor to help you through this ordeal? Sandra, you haven't had the chance to sort through the horrific death of your babies."

Sandra looked straight ahead at the cinder block wall and gently cleared her throat. "Pamela, my life is over. My dreams of raising my children are over. My dreams of starting a career, being a devoted partner and wife to someone are over. My trust in the people of this world is over. I fully accept that my parents hate me and want nothing to do with me. Pamela, I even accept that I have never done anything malicious to anyone in my life but someone wants to kill me, and chances are he will probably succeed. You know what I will never accept though? To die knowing I never tried to bring my children's killers to justice. That would be a shameful and cowardly way to leave this earth."

Pamela listened intently to every word that came out of Sandra's mouth while getting the courage to share her secret. "Listen to me, please. I lost my son Derrick many years ago because of my stupidity and selfishness. For many years, I needed someone to talk to and a shoulder for support. Sometimes it helped and other times it did not, but at least I had the assurance of knowing I could go somewhere. Sandra, you have suffered and gone through more than what the average person would ever face in a lifetime. Trust me. You have to seek counseling now and I will help you."

Sandra didn't want to make it seem as if all Pamela had just said had gone in one ear and out the other, but she needed to express herself. She grabbed her faithful friend's hand. "Pamela, I want to let you know something and please never forget this, okay? I love you for being a friend to me from the day we met until this very moment. Please understand that I mean no harm, but at this moment, fuck a counselor. The reality is that more than likely I could die before even finding out the truth about Kareem and Chaka. But you see, Pamela, I do not care anymore. What can they take from me now? I was always told by my father and Doug that I was useless and that I was not worth a pile of shit. You know what Pamela. Looking back at my life, maybe I am not. I couldn't even get the courage to get my children out of a violent environment. What kind of mother was I? Therefore, all I have left is vengeance. Chances are I will probably screw this up, but be forewarned…I will die trying. I will not visit my children's resting place without trying to make amends first. I miss my babies. What did they do to deserve this?"

As Sandra began to cry uncontrollably, Pamela hugged her and rocked her slowly. "Whatever you need me to do, let me know. Whatever you need me to do, I am here," Pamela whispered into her friend's ear.

Standing at the door and looking on in silence, Carla and Rose looked like they wanted to help Sandra as well, but they had no idea what to do. Calming herself down, Sandra gently pulled away from Pamela and wiped her face with a napkin.

"Has anyone heard from or seen Doug?" Sandra asked. All three women shook their heads no. "Who arranged for Kareem and Chaka's burials?"

"Doug did that, Sandra," Carla answered, stepping forward. "To be honest with you though, I wish he would not have. Your children deserved a better service than what he gave them. At least they knew you loved them."

Rose stepped forward with her head tilted to the ground and began to cry. "I hate him. He is a wasted sperm. Doug cares about no one but himself."

As Carla tried to comfort Rose, a now subdued Sandra stood on her own. "Pamela, when you're at home, have you heard him come or go since the funeral?" Sandra asked.

Pamela took a few moments to ponder the question. "Come to think of it, Sandra, no. I haven't heard him come or leave since the funeral."

"Pamela, did you really mean what you said about helping me?"

"Of course I did. Anything you need, I am here for you."

Sandra looked straight into Pamela's eyes. "Help me get back into the apartment. I need to gather a few things." All three women looked at Sandra as if she had completely lost her mind.

"Sandra, you can't be serious, girl. Please take my advice and seek out counseling before you dare enter that place again. I don't have much but I will pick up some things for you, and I am pretty sure Ms. Carla wouldn't mind you staying here. But Sandra, you cannot go back there," Pamela pleaded.

There was rage in Sandra's eyes. "You just said not even a minute ago that you would help me in any way that you could. So, I'll ask you one more fucking time. Pamela, will you help me get into the apartment or not?" Pamela looked at Carla and Rose for help but saw that none was available. She feared she would lose Sandra's trust if she answered wrong. "Yes, Sandra, I will help you," she finally agreed. "Do you have a plan to get inside without being found out?"

"Yes, I have a plan. But for this plan to work, I need you to do exactly what I say, okay?"

"Yes, I understand and I will do exactly as you tell me," Pamela promised, feeling queasy.

"If you all do not mind, I need a few moments to myself, just to think. So if you would excuse me, I would appreciate it."

Everyone left the small, chilly room and Sandra sat back down on the cot and stared at the ceiling. "This is for you, babies," she said, rubbing the wound on her neck and thinking hard about how she would go about finding some answers.

* * *

By the second week after Sandra left the hospital, she had started digging for information, just as she had promised her children she would. Spending hours down at the precinct, she tried to get information about the ongoing investigation but had turned up nothing new. Detective Sam Daniels, who Sandra found to be quite polite, spilled his coffee when she walked into the large office. His reaction had seemed strange, but it evaporated quickly from her mind because her main concern was getting any information on her case as quickly as possible.

Giving the detective all of the details of that Christmas Day was crucial to Sandra, who even explained to the detective about the man with the dragon tattoo who had cut her throat and had paid her a visit at the hospital two weeks ago. Showing compassion and understanding, Detective Daniels reassured Sandra that they were doing everything possible to bring her children's killers to justice.

Somewhat satisfied with the detective's position, Sandra took his card and left the precinct feeling like the ball was rolling in the right direction. The minute she left the stationhouse, though, Detective Daniels wasted no time calling Detective Davis and explaining the two major problems that had arisen: Sandra's memory to detail and Tony Harris's dumb-ass decision to visit Sandra in the hospital.

* * *

Sandra's watch read 1:00 a.m. on Tuesday morning, and based on the sounds coming from the walls of the basement, the wind was howling. Since Pamela had confirmed that Doug had not been home since she had returned to her apartment, Sandra had decided that this was the right time for her to return to the scene of her bloody Christmas. The plan was for Pamela to sit by her phone in the kitchen and look out of her window, which was directly over the one-way street leading to the building. What was great about Pamela's view was that it gave her a clear view for about three blocks. Since no one else in the neighborhood had a black Escalade, chances were that if Pamela spotted one, it would belong to Doug. But there was always the possibility of human error. What if somehow Pamela missed the car? This almost seemed impossible, but they had a backup set of eyes that belonged to Rose, who begged Sandra to let her help.

Rose would stand inside a building on the corner where Doug would have to make a right turn to get to his street. Using Pamela's cell phone, Rose would dial Pamela's home number if she saw anything that resembled Doug's vehicle. Once Pamela received that phone call, she would make sure it was Doug. If Pamela made a positive identification, she would call Sandra on the cell phone that she had borrowed from Ms. Carla, and Sandra would have adequate time to exit the apartment, lock the door behind her, and enter Pamela's apartment, which was right next door. If all of this went according to plan, then they would call Rose and tell her to go back to the pantry where Ms. Carla had a bed set up for her to sleep.

Knowing that Doug was not a stay-at-home type of man, Pamela and Sandra would sit by the door all night, drinking coffee and listening for Doug to leave. When that happened, Sandra would return to the pantry with her possessions, particularly her wallet and the cell phone that Doug had taken from her. She hoped they were in the same place where he had hidden them from her. If she found her things, she could withdraw the three thousand dollars she had accumulated from the many ass beatings she had endured. She figured maybe she could get a fresh start in a little kitchenette apartment somewhere away from the house of horrors, but that goal was far away right now because what she was attempting to do was almost suicidal. What if the dragon and his friends were waiting for her like a pack of wolves waiting for a deer to return to its drinking pond? Deep down Sandra knew Pamela was right about seeking counseling and letting the detectives do their jobs. She wondered to herself who she thought she was since she hadn't even mustered the wisdom to recognize the warning signs to protect and shield her children from the violence and abuse of Doug Gunner.

Sandra looked at Ms. Carla's cell phone, which was fully charged, and did her best to push the negativity from her mind so she could focus on the task—getting in and out of the apartment as quickly as possible with her most important possessions. Just maybe, she thought to herself, after all she had been through, a blessing could be sent down to her and she would find a clue or sign that the detectives had missed—something that would lead to the capture of Kareem and Chaka's killers.

Quickly jumping to her feet as if someone had stuck a pin in her butt, Sandra glanced at the cell phone, which was now ringing. She read the caller ID in the blue illuminated glass, which indicated that it was Pamela calling. Taking a deep breath, Sandra slowly flipped open the receiver. "Hello...Thank you, Pamela. I am on my way…Don't worry. I will be careful." Sandra hung up the phone and put on her coat, hat, and scarf. She made sure that she had her keys in the pocket of her jeans, and then she walked out the door of her little room. She looked back at the cot that Ms. Carla had been nice enough to give her, and at that very intense moment, she realized that she might not return to this room. Pushing that thought out of her mind, Sandra turned the light off and closed the door. At the side door of the pantry, Ms. Carla was waiting for her with a smile of concern, but nevertheless it was still a smile. Outside the open door, a cab was waiting for Sandra, ready to take her to the apartment. Without saying a word to each other, Sandra and Carla hugged each other for a moment, both fighting back tears.

"I love you, Ms. Carla, and I always will."

"I love you too, baby, and you call me Mom, okay? You are the daughter I always wanted." Slowly releasing each other, they gave one more look before Sandra headed out into the dead of night, stepped inside the car, and drove off. Ms. Carla stood at the door watching the taillights of the car until she could see them no more.

* * *

Five blocks away from her destination, Sandra now thought to herself, *What if he changed the locks? What if someone in the building sees me and tells him?* Pushing those thoughts not totally out of her mind but way to the back of it, Sandra focused on achieving her objective as fast as possible. As the cab got closer to the building, she made the driver stop at the alleyway that led to a back entrance of the building. After paying the cabby, Sandra got out and stared up at the brown building.

As Sandra entered the alleyway, a cold chill sent shivers throughout her body. She realized that somewhere in this area, her children's bodies had landed, ending their hopes and dreams forever. Doing everything within her power to control her emotions, Sandra walked straight to the steel steps that would take her to the back entrance of the building. With each move she made, coldness ran through the soles of her shoes to the top of her now throbbing head. After each step, something in the back of her mind tried to convince her that she was in over her head. With determination, Sandra continued to climb until she stood at the top of the steps in front of the large steel door. Reaching into her pocket, she removed the keys that would possibly lead her to justice.

"Turn the key and get this over with, Sandra," she said quietly to herself. Taking a deep breath, she slowly pushed the door open and saw the mailbox that Kareem always opened to get the mail for her. She turned her eyes away from it and headed to the stairs. Grabbing on to the banister, Sandra quietly began her journey up to where it had all ended.

With the first step came a slap in the face. At another step, the name-calling, "bitch" and "stupid," came. A few steps later it was hair pulling and crashing into walls. Another step brought the looks of confusion on her children's faces as they wondered why Mommy had to go through this. The next step conjured up the nasty, drunken sex she had endured for years. After a few more steps came the belief that she was useless and weak, adding nothing positive to the life of her kids or herself. The last step, which put Sandra six feet away from the apartment door, invoked the images of Chaka reaching out to her for help and Kareem fighting with all of his strength to free himself to help his mother.

Then it hit Sandra like a ton of bricks all at once. As much as she blamed herself, and she really did—she now realized that she hated Doug. She not only hated him, but she wished things on him now that her minister father had told her many lives ago that God would not approve of. She couldn't help it, though. The hatred filled her body as she got closer to the door. Now a sick thought entered her head: She hoped sl would find Doug asleep right now so she could stab or burn him to dea so that he could feel a small portion of her pain.

Sandra looked at the peephole of Pamela's door, and although s couldn't swear by it, she could almost feel the eye of her friend looki out for her as usual. Sliding the key into the top lock, Sandra turned u she heard the clicking sound. Now for the middle lock, this had to jiggled a little until it made a clicking sound. Finally, there was the lock the doorknob that she only had to turn halfway to the left, and with t Sandra gave the door a slight push and gained access to her perso hellhole.

Looking down the long, dark hallway that got its only light from opening of the door, Sandra ignored the heavy footsteps of the dra and his accomplices running inside, rushing the kids and herself Christmas. She closed the door as quietly as possible, locked it, reached for the light switch in the hallway. Able to see what was in of her now, Sandra slowly and cautiously walked up the hallway that l the living room. Remembering as if it were yesterday, she walked ov the big lamp that sat on the end table and turned it on. The Christma and all the gifts that were under it were gone. The blood that poure of her throat onto the wooden floor was gone. In fact, the apartmer cleaned spotless and gave off an eerie lemon smell.

Get in and get out. You are wasting time, Sandra reminded herself. Tu her back to the living room, Sandra was frozen by the voices coming the window: "Help us, Mommy! Help us! Come with us, Mommy. leave!" Almost frozen in her steps, Sandra's legs felt as if they w two tons each, and she couldn't move them. Anxiety built up insi and she felt sweat breaking through her skin.

Get away from the window and out of this room, Sandra told herself. *them. They know your purpose and they understand. They know you love the get out of this room because time is wasting.* Feeling like she was pushing car, Sandra managed to get away from the room and the voices th pleading to her.Now inside the bedroom, Sandra was determ accomplish her task quickly and effectively. She looked throu dresser drawers for her wallet. Not finding it there or in the nigh she swiftly looked inside the armoire drawers. Instead of her owr she found Doug's underwear and shirts. Pushing back the though throwing her things out, Sandra walked to the closet and gently the many expensive suits and coats to the side in order to look o the shelves. She moved the shoeboxes from one side to the othe

Sandra found were automatic weapons and some pornographic DVDs. Feeling as if her time were running out, Sandra became somewhat dejected and lowered herself on her knees in the closet, hoping Doug had mistakenly thrown something on the floor. She moved more shoeboxes to the side and was now leaning in the closet when she felt a bump on the closet floor. She felt with both of her hands and pulled on a ring that lifted a wooden plank, revealing the safe Sandra had seen Doug open on Christmas morning. Looking at the safe with deep thought, Sandra pushed everything else out of her mind and focused on the three numbers that Doug had dialed that morning.

"You can do this, but you must hurry", Sandra's inner voice told her. With the only light coming from the brightness of the full moon, Sandra turned on the closet light and knelt down. Putting her face inches away from the safe's knob, she could see Doug dialing those three sets of numbers from right to left and right again. With her right hand, Sandra turned the knob slowly and stopped at thirty-three. Turning back one full rotation, she now stopped at fourteen. Finally, she turned the knob slowly to the right again, stopped at twenty-six, and exhaled. She grabbed the silver handle and closed her eyes. Hoping and praying with her eyes still tightly shut, Sandra gently pulled the handle in the down position and heard a clicking sound. She slowly opened the safe door and gazed inside to inspect the contents.

Sandra removed and unzipped a small black case, finding what looked like ten gold DVDs. She quickly zipped the case back up and set it between her thighs. She moved bundles of money out of the way and found her wallet and her cell phone. Quickly grabbing them, she frantically looked through the wallet's contents and found everything was still there. Most importantly, Sandra's bankcard was still there, which was the key to getting a new place. Paying no attention to the money, the two guns, and a bag of reefer that she found, Sandra closed the safe, spun the knob, and made sure it was locked. Remembering exactly how the shoes were placed, Sandra closed the wooden plank that hid the safe and put the shoes back.

* * *

As Rose stood in the hallway of the cold building looking out of the front door, she was unaware of the red Lincoln Navigator that had just sped past her. Holding Pamela's phone in her hand, she continued to wait.

* * *

Sitting at her window wide awake and alert, Pamela looked at her watch and saw that it had been twenty minutes since Sandra had entered the apartment. She stood up and looked out of her window. Then she looked at her telephone and wondered if it was working; it was a stupid thought, though, because she had never been late with a bill payment. As she walked closer to her window, Pamela noticed a red truck coming to a rolling stop and then parking in front of the building. With a concerned look on her face, Pamela watched two women exit the truck first. They seemed to be laughing and giggling with one another. Pamela's face of concern turned to horror as Doug got out of the driver's side of the truck holding a suitcase. Quickly running over to her phone, Pamela called Sandra and hoped she had remembered to put Ms. Carla's phone on vibrate.

Speaking as softly as possible as she watched the threesome walk up the courtyard steps leading to the front door, Pamela said, "Sandra, get the hell out now! Doug's on his way upstairs. Please hurry up. I am going to open my door right now. Hurry!" Pamela ran quickly to turn the locks and open her door. From a distance, she could hear the party of three talking. It sounded like they were on the first floor.With the black DVD case under her arm, Sandra swiftly and quietly locked all three locks, having to jiggle the middle lock just a touch. Hearing footsteps and talking getting closer and clearer, Sandra began to tremble. She was almost frozen in her steps when Pamela grabbed her by the arm and snatched her into the apartment. Neither woman noticed the piece of paper that fell to the ground from the top of Doug's apartment door.Pushing Sandra towards the kitchen, Pamela locked her door and held her breath as she could clearly hear Doug and his two playmates making their way to his apartment. Sandra sat on the kitchen floor with her head buried inside her hands while Pamela stood by her door, listening to Doug and the two women.

As Doug fiddled with his keys, he took notice of the white-tiled hallway floor. He bent down, picked up a small yellow piece of folded paper, and turned to the two women. With his hand, he gestured to them to go stand one floor below. Pulling out his gun, Doug opened his apartment door and cautiously entered.

A couple of minutes later, Doug came out of the apartment. "Ladies, everything is cool. Come on up," he called out.

They came up but one of the girls still looked concerned. "Doug, baby, you sure everything is okay?"

Doug looked at the woman with a bit of anger. "What did I just say? Just bring your asses in here now."Hearing Doug's apartment door close, Pamela let out a long sigh and turned to Sandra, who was still sitting on the kitchen floor. Pamela got on the floor next to her and gave her a long hug. "Please call Rose and tell her we are okay and that she did really well," Sandra suggested. Without hesitation, Pamela did just that.

Chapter Twenty-three

Dirty Deeds

Covering his eyes from the bright sunlight coming from his bedroom window, Doug gathered his thoughts. He looked at both sides of his bed and realized that he must have put Bernice and Sharon out when it was still dark, even though he couldn't recall doing so. Slowly he got out of bed and headed to the bathroom when he suddenly stopped and took notice of his nightstand, where he had laid the yellow paper that he had picked up off the hallway floor. He looked at the paper for another few seconds and then went to the bathroom.

With a slight look of amusement on his face, Doug stood at the doorway of his bedroom and scoped the entire room from left to right. As he tried to decide if he should make some breakfast, an overwhelming feeling of paranoia came over him. Doug turned and started to walk to the kitchen and then stopped. He walked over to his nightstand and checked inside. Everything was in place. Next, he checked the other nightstand and the armoire. Satisfied, he walked to the kitchen to make himself some breakfast.

* * *

Disgusted with the slop that he had prepared, Doug panned around the dining room and looked at the three empty chairs where Sandra, Kareem, and Chaka sat just a month ago. Then, in an instant, visions came to his head of the doctor asking him if he was sure he wanted to wait outside the operating room and lose the chance to see his kids being brought into the world. He only visited Sandra and the kids once, and that was to bring them home. As the kids grew in those dining room chairs, Doug had not taken the time to play basketball or baseball with Kareem, or even to teach him how to ride a bike. Sandra was the one who did all of those things. Doug looked at the other chair where, every morning, Chaka would fight and struggle to get herself seated to eat. She would gaze at him, hoping he would help her, but the only help came from Sandra, as usual. Focusing back on the garbage on his plate, Doug remembered how well Sandra could cook and deep down inside, he loved her meals. He pushed the slop away from himself. "What did anyone ever do for me?" he questioned. "I gave and everybody took! Nobody ever gave me anything!" He got up from the table, still seeing the three people that never did him any harm. Not wanting to give in to regrets, sorrows, and disappointment, Doug left to take a shower without looking back.Wearing nothing but his bathrobe, Doug stood in front of his closet looking over his wardrobe and trying to decide what he would wear. He pulled out his beige two-piece suit and found the shoes and shirt to match. He closed the closet door, turned on some soft music, and began to get dressed.

* * *

It was a little before ten in the morning and Doug was prepared to head out to make his afternoon meeting when, once again, he stopped and looked at the piece of paper that sat atop his nightstand. Deep inside Doug knew he had not checked every hiding space. As he removed his jacket, he felt anxiety pumping through his body. He walked over to the closet, opened the door, and turned on the light inside.

Doug slowly removed the many boxes of shoes on the floor. When he could see the plank of wood with the metal ring on it, he gently grabbed it and slowly pulled it up, revealing his safe. He arched his body so that he could get closer, then slowly turned the dial from right to left and back to right, just as Sandra had done eight hours ago. Doug slowly turned the handle and lifted the safe door. He fell backwards and hit his back on the closet door, looking as if he had just seen not one ghost but three. Doug could feel the saliva fall from his mouth. Tears, for the first time in many years, filled the eyes of the man built like steel. He tried to gather himself, but it was difficult because the closet felt as if it were spinning three hundred miles an hour.

He held his throbbing baldhead in his hands until he was finally able to sit up on his knees. Kneeling back over the safe, Doug removed the weapons, the reefer, and the four thick stacks of one-hundred-dollar bills. As he stared at the empty safe, Doug felt as if he were having a nervous breakdown. He sobbed like a six-year-old boy who had lost his favorite toy. "What the fuck! Not my DVDs! Who the fuck took my DVDs!"

Doug struggled to make it to his feet. He came out the closet and plopped himself on the bed with a thud. The only word that came to his head was "leverage." It had taken him years to build it up, and just like that, his advantage was gone. Without it, Doug knew if things hit the fan, it would be over for him. He looked at his watch and realized that he should have been out the door already to head to his meeting. As he slowly put on his jacket and grabbed his car keys, it was now obvious to Doug that someone had been in his apartment and the yellow paper had not been lying to him. He put everything back in the safe and did his best to pull himself together. Before he left, he looked back at his bedroom, trying to process his thoughts. His brain was working five times harder than usual.

* * *

As he drove down Webster Avenue towards the Cross Bronx Expressway, Doug grabbed his phone and scanned for the telephone number for North Bronx Central Hospital.

"Yes, this is Doug Gunner. I'm calling to find out about the condition of a patient by the name of Sandra Lyte. She was admitted in your hospital on Christmas Day. No problem, I can hold. She left unauthorized two weeks ago? Listen, how could she just leave the hospital without anyone seeing her? So, did anyone in the hospital notice anything strange around her room? Yeah, okay. Thanks for nothing." He hung up the phone and drove onto the expressway saying, "No fucking way. There has to be another answer. There has to be."

* * *

Sitting by herself in the basement, Sandra looked at the two items she had taken from Doug's safe. She picked up the wallet and slowly examined the contents—her Virginia driver's license, her social security card and, most importantly, her bank ATM card. Sandra looked up to the chipped white ceiling with relief. Feeling wary of the DVD case, she looked it over, wondering about its contents. She set the case down on top of the table, slowly unzipped it, and revealed ten gold discs secured in plastic sleeves. She flipped the plastic pages and read what was on each disc: "April 23, Sexcapade," "May 16, Orgy Time," "January 1, Pretty

Young Bondage Girls," and other dates and names of sexual parties were written on the discs.

After turning the last page, Sandra started to close the book until she noticed a small bulk inside the last sleeve. Feeling with her fingers, she found the opening and carefully removed some pink-colored paper. She slowly unfolded the two sheets and began to read the top of the first document. The letterhead read "National Insurance Agency Inc., Syracuse, New York 13215." She looked further down the page and realized she was reading a receipt for payment of an insurance policy for $500,000 in the name of Chaka Lyte. With her hands starting to tremble, she quickly flipped to the other pink document and saw that it read the same, except on this page the insured was Kareem Lyte. Both documents named Doug as the only beneficiary and both documents had Doug's signature. Sandra looked at both pieces of paper and then bent her head towards the floor beneath her feet. With her body beginning to tremble, she once again stared at the insurance policy receipts. She glanced up at the cinder block wall and quickly ran at the cot and the wooden table, turning them over and causing a loud crash. Grabbing hold of the wooden chair, Sandra hurled it at the wall, smashing it to pieces. She grabbed at her shirt and began to dig into the fabric and pull at her skin. Staring at the receipts that now lay on the floor, Sandra yelled, "You no good son of a bitch! You motherfucker!" She ran over to a cabinet and proceeded to throw dishes onto the floor.

Ms. Carla and Pamela quickly ran into the room, both wearing shocked looks on their faces when they saw the damage Sandra had done inside the room. Pamela gently grabbed her from behind and was able to get her down to the floor. "Okay, baby, I am here. I'm here," she comforted. As she rubbed Sandra on her head in an effort to calm her down, Pamela looked up at a mystified Ms. Carla.

* * *

It had been an hour since Sandra's outburst. While Pamela and Ms. Carla cleaned the basement, they managed to keep Sandra cool. She never explained what triggered her outburst and she had managed to hide the receipts from them both. She felt remorseful for breaking Ms. Carla things and offered to repay her, but Ms. Carla would have none of it.

"Please talk to me anytime you feel like it. I am here for you girl," Pamela encouraged. Feeling grateful, Sandra gave her a hug. When she released her, Pamela continued. "I just wanted to let you know that my cousin Kenny is ready to drive us to the apartment I mentioned to you a few days ago. It's pretty far from Doug, almost on the border of Yonkers. Most importantly, it's very secluded with rent you should be able to afford until you're ready to really get out of here."

Sandra walked over to her friend and gave her a hug and a rub on the shoulders. "Okay, I'm ready. I just want to say good-bye to Ms. Carla before I leave." Sandra grabbed her two duffel bags, opened one, and put the case holding the DVDs inside.Pamela and her cousin stood next to his blue sedan, watching Sandra and Ms. Carla embrace each other, almost looking as if neither one of them would ever let go. When they finally ended their good-bye, Sandra bent to pick up her bags. While she was gathering her things, Rose came running towards her from across the street. As Pamela observed the exchange, she could see Sandra mouthing the words "Good-bye, baby" to Rose, who began crying and pulling Sandra's arms in a gesture for her to stay. Sandra grabbed Rose and held her close, stroking the young woman's hair softly.

Still crying uncontrollably, Rose had to be subdued by Ms. Carla, who gently but forcibly took her into the pantry. Knowing that she wouldn't be able to stand seeing the pain on Rose's face, Sandra walked to the sedan without looking back. Kenny shook her hand and put her bags in the trunk. As they drove off down Jerome Avenue, a white Cadillac STS waited a few seconds, pulled off, and began to tail them.

* * *

Sandra, Pamela, and Kenny stood on the porch of a three-family brick house in the Riverdale section of the Bronx. A small Russian woman, who looked to be in her mid-sixties, opened the door and said, "Yes, how can I help you?"

Kenny put a smile on his face and calmly stepped forward. "Hello ma'am. My name is Kenny Brown. A few days ago I called you about the studio vacancy you advertised in the newspaper." The old woman looked at all three of them, closed the door, and yelled for someone in her Russian tongue.

After a few seconds, a tall, slender man in his thirties came to the door. "Yes, who come for studio?"

Sandra raised her hand. "Good afternoon, sir. That would be me. My name is Sandra Lyte." Looking at all three of them with some suspicion, the man slowly opened the door and waved them in.

It had been just a few moments, and Sandra felt that all the place needed was a paint job and some nicer curtains. The apartment was already furnished, and even though the furniture was a little outdated, Sandra seemed satisfied. She walked over to the man who had introduced himself as Boris. "Sir, I like the place very much and would like to move in right now, if possible."

Boris turned from staring out of the small kitchen window and looked at Sandra. "One month rent, one month security, and no pets, okay? You pay rent always on first of month, yes?"

Sticking out her hand to Boris, Sandra shook the man's hand. He did not crack a smile.

"You have a deal, and I promise never to be late with the rent."

* * *

That evening, Sandra was exhausted from all of the tidying up she had done around her new place. Before Pamela and Kenny left her to be alone, she got Kenny to do her one more favor, and that was to drive her to a local pawnshop to purchase a television and a DVD player. She ended up getting a nineteen-inch television/DVD combo set for half its original price. The set was not brand new but it was in excellent condition. Most importantly, it spared Sandra the time of trying to figure out how to hook two separate units together.

Sitting on her old but comfortable wooden bed that creaked a little when she moved, Sandra looked around at her surroundings and couldn't help but think about how bad her life had turned out. How the many choices she had made had turned out to be horrible ones, not only for herself but also for the ones that meant the most to her—her children. What was she doing here? Why not just make a run for the border and start again? She had not heard from the police since she'd made her visit a few weeks ago, so as far as Sandra could tell, her kids' case was turning cold very fast.

As she sat on her bed, a voice inside Sandra's head began to speak. "You have been spared, Sandra, not because you are special or because the world needs you. It's simply because of the dirty hand you've been dealt. You deserve a shot at redemption and with that chance; you owe it to your children to fight back. Your children never got the chance to live and grow like they deserved to." Sandra tried to drown out the voice by looking at the pictures on the kitchen wall. The voice just got louder. "You see, Sandra, in spite of what you've been told for the past seven years about how dumb and weak you are, I will no longer let you use that as an excuse to keep running and hiding from finding the truth. No, that shit stops today! Today the mission begins and the tears end. You will find those responsible for killing your children, no matter what it takes. However, Sandra, I do promise you this—if you try to run away, give up, or give in to excuses, make no mistake—I will haunt and torment your mind until you die. I will never go away and will always remind you of how you crumbled in the face of adversity. When you had one last chance to do what was right for your children, you faltered. I will also make you realize that you did not love your children because even in their deaths, you would not stand up to protect them. Then those seven beautiful years of love that your children abundantly poured out to you will turn to infinite hatred, because they will soon begin to talk to you also. They will not speak of how they miss and love you; instead, they will tell you how they despise you because of your weakness. So now it's time to think about your next move."

The room once lit by the setting winter sun was now dark, and the only thing that Sandra could clearly make out was the DVD case that sat atop her bedside dresser. She got up from the bed, walked over to the dresser, and grabbed the black case. She sat down in front of the television and turned it on. From reading the manual that the pawnshop owner had given her, Sandra remembered that she needed to press the AV button on the television, which brought her to a black screen that flashed, "No Disc." She looked at the buttons on the DVD part of the set and located the open/close button. She pushed it, causing the door to slide forward. After unzipping the case, Sandra looked through the various discs, finally choosing the one that said "Sexcapade." She loaded it into the player and pressed play. Then she adjusted the sound and watched the screen. As clear as day, there was Doug in some apartment that Sandra didn't recognize. There was food and champagne in the living room. Not taking her eyes off the screen, Sandra watched as black and white men entered the apartment. It was hard for Sandra to make out who the men were because of the angle and blurriness of the overhead camera shots. Using the fast-forward button, Sandra sped the disc ahead hoping to see something better, but she only found various scenes of the men having sex with different women. She got frustrated and was about to remove the disc and try another when she observed a black man putting his clothes on in one of the rooms. It was not the clothes that caught her attention but the badge he put around his neck. She looked more closely and intently at the screen and was positive that it was a police badge. The officer, who Sandra still couldn't make out, was balding on the top of his head. She watched the man walk over to the Chinese girl he had sex with and give her one last kiss. He put on his gun holster and walked out of the room. Temporarily stopping the player, Sandra grabbed a notepad and a pen to write down what she had observed. Then she pressed the pause button again and continued to watch.

* * *

After spending almost three hours stopping and rewinding the DVD player, Sandra had done her best to observe and memorize everything she felt was important. As she looked over her notes, she was positive that the men on the discs were part of law enforcement, but at what level, she was not clear. What she hoped, though, was that the next set of discs she watched would be a lot clearer and would have more concrete details. Feeling hungry but not at all tired anymore, Sandra walked to the kitchen and prepared a sandwich.

* * *

Six hours had vanished in the blink of an eye and Sandra could hear the sound of garbage trucks rolling down the street. The sun had not begun to rise yet, but with the chirping of the sparrows, it would rise soon. Taking a sip of warm soda, Sandra wiped her dry and drooping eyes with a wet rag. She finished off her drink and put the can on the floor where there were about nine candy bar wrappers and several other empty soda cans. The pad on Sandra's lap, to her total disappointment, contained only one page of notes with a few thoughts that could help solve the crime of *her* century.

She had scanned through several discs and had only gained insight about a few things: Doug was pretty clever in many ways, making sure he had law enforcement on his side for protection while at the same time obtaining dirt on them just in case they came after him. As for the law enforcement officers, they were nearsighted in doing all of this illegal activity, knowing it was wrong and could jeopardize their careers. Finally, Sandra was now fully aware that if she was going all the way with this, she had some legitimate proof. A southern girl from Virginia was about to bring a lot of important people down and, at the same time, maybe find the truth about Kareem and Chaka's murders. Unfortunately, however, all nine discs had terrible camera shots and grainy pictures. The only reason

Sandra was able to make out Doug was that his dumb ass at times looked directly into the camera. Now looking down at the final disc that read "Pretty Young Bondage Girls," Sandra loaded it in the player. After forty minutes of viewing had passed, the sun began to rise and Sandra's pencil was moving quickly across the paper. To her surprise, this last disc was as clear as the blue sky. The views were no longer overhead but at face and shoulder level where she could make out without a doubt everyone's identity and burn those images in her mind. So far, Sandra had not seen anything special, just the men and Doug sitting around eating, drinking, and snorting blow. She got up without turning the player off and quickly ran to the bathroom with a glass in her hand.With the sound of the flushing toilet preceding her, Sandra walked back to her chair with a fresh glass of water and focused back on the television. Her eyes suddenly widened and she mistakenly dropped her glass of water. Getting closer to the television screen, Sandra fell to her knees as she witnessed Doug smiling as he paraded a shaking and crying Rose around on a leash in front of the law enforcement officers.

"Oh my goodness, no. Rose, how did he get to you?" Sandra asked herself aloud. Unable to move or turn away from the image on the screen, Sandra looked on as Doug forced the terrified Rose to remove her clothes as the men formed a small circle around her and waved their arms in the air as they poked and spanked her petite body. Forced to the floor by a yank to the collar around her neck, the naked young woman sobbed, obviously pleading to be let go. With his free hand, Doug smacked Rose across the head, knocking her to the floor and causing Sandra to shiver. "You son of a bitch!" Sandra blurted out, her face turning red. Sitting in an upright position, Sandra rocked back and forth, continuing to watch as a much older woman, maybe in her late thirties, entered the room wearing a black dominatrix suit. The woman was dark-skinned and had blonde hair. As Doug smacked the woman on her backside, he gave her the leash that held Rose.

* * *

After about forty-five minutes of watching Rose being sexually assaulted and conquered by the dominatrix bitch, Sandra didn't know what pained her most—knowing now why Rose hated Doug so much, or realizing that she had sat through the ordeal, never turning her head away from the television. It made Sandra ask herself if she was becoming numb to all of the pain and suffering she witnessed. Then, just as quickly as she asked herself that question, the voice that had told her how things were going to be from now on answered, "No, Sandra, not numb—but stronger and wiser. The pain and sorrow you feel for Rose is right. Turn that pain and sorrow into ambition and determination." Just like that, the voice was gone.

Sandra had noticed from the previous discs that they only ran for about one-and-a-half hours. As she looked at the DVD counter on the television, she calculated that there would be about three or four minutes left to view. The dominant woman, who Sandra despised, was dragging a sweaty and naked, almost zombie-like Rose out of the room. As hard as it was, Sandra continued to take notes until she noticed something in the living room that caused her to shiver. One of the men, a white man who was very drunk, jumped up from the coach, removed his hat, and began to jump up and down, causing the others around him, including Doug, to laugh. The man removed his sweater and undershirt, revealing a well-chiseled body. What put Sandra in a shock-like state was what she saw plastered on the man's right wrist: a tattoo of a large fire-breathing dragon. The dragon that held her down and made her watch the murder of her children, the dragon who opened her throat and left her to die, the dragon that chased Pamela and her in the hospital was the same fucking dragon that was eating with that bastard Doug.

The DVD ended with the man with the pet dragon dancing on the couch. Sandra snapped the number-two pencil in her hands and stared at the frozen image on the screen.

Chapter Twenty-four

Doug Mixes the Past with the Present

As he sat in front of his new superior, Doug listened to the orders and objectives instructed. He looked around and admired the large apartment on Seventy-second Street and Park Avenue, but he tried to keep focused on the job at hand.

Mr. X sat at a large ivory desk in the living room, which was painted all white. "In a four-hour span, you will meet with three men at three different locations within the five boroughs. Each man will give you one-third of two million dollars in exchange for a special key. After the last pick-up, you will bring the two million dollars to me at another location that I will disclose to you later."

Doug did not respond right away. Instead, he let his thoughts wander. *Four hours, three meetings. I have to fit my selling time into finding my discs. I have to locate that bitch Sandra. I can't prove it yet, but I know my hunches are leading me in the right direction. Just have to flush her ass out, that's all.*

Mr. X snapped his fingers to get Doug's attention. "Excuse me, Doug. Are you okay? Are you with me? You have a very important task, so I suggest you listen carefully. When each man gives you the money, you are to turn over a key to him. The first man from the Bronx will get a red key while the man in Brooklyn will get a blue key, and finally, the man in Queens will get a black key. After each drop, you will do as I instructed, you understand?"

"Yes, I understand clearly," Doug said.

Mr. X took a sip of cappuccino. "Doug, when we first met, I told you in order to be successful in this organization, your mind had to be clear and all debts from your past life had to be taken care of before you worked for us. Do you remember?"

Doug nodded his head yes. "I assure you, my mind is clear and I am ready for this assignment," he asserted.

"Doug, don't try to reassure me or the organization of anything. You just keep telling yourself that. I would like to discuss your performance so far. To date, we have been satisfied with the way you have followed our instructions. We also understand that we have been keeping you relegated to your club for the past month, selling our product and entertaining our clients. We just want you to know that we thank you for your cooperation in handling the situation. We also want to let you know that as long as you continue to perform at your very best, we will continue to reward you as we did with your new vehicle."

Doug looked intently into his boss's eyes as he spoke. Knowing that the meeting was ending, he reached down by the chair he was sitting in and grabbed a gray briefcase. He gently set it atop the desk in front of Mr. X, who motioned over to his lieutenant named Blue. Spinning the briefcase towards him, Blue slowly opened it and turned it back to his boss for inspection.

"One hundred and fifty thousand. Right, Doug?"

"Yes, that's correct. One hundred and fifty thousand."

Mr. X reached inside the briefcase, removed $22,500 and slid it across the table to Doug. "Here is your fifteen percent. Now this meeting is over. Remember what we discussed, and I will see you at our next meeting." Doug stood up from his chair, shook his boss's hand, and left the plush apartment, making his way down to the garage where his Navigator awaited.

* * *

Doug drove down the cold but sunny streets of Manhattan, headed for home. He needed to get some rest before he started his night of work at the club. He drove up Broadway and made his way to the 145th Street Bridge. The only word on Doug's mind was "leverage" because he knew the man with the most advantages stayed out of jail. He also knew that he had lost a huge part of his, and what pounded at his head the most was the fact that he had possibly lost that advantage to some dumb bitch with a nice body who he should have dumped seven years ago.

As he crossed the bridge leading him back to the Bronx, all he could hear was his father's voice saying, "They are only to hump and pump—no more, no less."

Shaking his head back and forth, Doug pounded his steering wheel and pressed a button, which dialed a number. "Yeah, what's up?" a voice answered on the second ring.

"Bucky, what's up? This is Doug. Listen, I need to ask you something. Have you seen or run into anyone who has seen Sandra?" Doug asked.

"Nah, dog. I thought she was still in the hospital."

Doug stopped at a red light on the Grand Concourse. "No, Bucky. It has come to my understanding that she checked herself out, and I am very worried about my boo, man. I need to find her and make sure she is okay. Listen, Bucky, please do me a favor, man. Put the word out on the street and when you're out there, please call me right away if you hear or see anything, brother. This shit is killing me now. Where the hell could she be?"

"Yo, dog. You just stay calm, okay? I will put the word out and trust me…we will find her. You just stay calm."

With a conniving smile, Doug said, "Thanks, brother. I will talk to you later, one."

"One, Doug."

Doug pressed the receiver button on the steering wheel. He was about three minutes away from his apartment when he said to himself, "Sandra, baby, we'll soon see if my hunch is right or wrong. For your sake, you better hope I'm wrong. Because if I'm not, baby, your ass is through this time, and I will personally make sure the job gets done correctly." As he pulled up to his building, Doug rolled his eyes and sucked his teeth because Detective Tommy Davis was sitting on his stoop reading a newspaper and drinking a cup of coffee.

Shit, I am dead fucking tired. What the hell does he want? Doug exited his vehicle, put on a fake smile, and turned on the charm as he walked towards Tommy.

"Detective, to what do I owe this honor?"

Tommy looked up and smiled right back at Doug, giving him a look of phoniness. "It's been a little while since I've spoken to my brother from another mother, and last I noticed, that check them folks pay me at the department ain't supporting my lifestyle."

Doug leaned on a concrete pillar, about to fall on his face from exhaustion. "Listen, Tommy," he started, "I know shit has not been rolling in like the old days, but things have been a little tight for a brother."

The detective took a sip of his coffee and gazed at Doug's brand-spanking-new red Navigator. "Man, who you telling about tough? The old woman asked me for her three-hundred-dollar day-spa money and I had to tell her for the time being she would have to go around the corner to the Korean woman. She almost took my damn head off. Doug, brother please, the last thing I want to hear about is how tough things are for you.

Not once have I harassed you with phone calls or visits, but now I'm getting a little hungry and I want to eat, baby."

Doug knew this day would come. He stared at the detective, seeing him as a crack addict that begins to know your every move. When you make a move, there his ass is standing at the train station or the bus stop, waiting for you with his hand sticking out.

That word entered Doug's mind again: "leverage." He was starting to come to grips with the reality that he was losing it. "Listen, Tommy, I got a little something, but you are going to have to give me a little space, partner, until things heat up again." Reaching into his pocket, Doug pulled out a roll of hundred-dollar bills and gave Tommy some. "Tommy, this is twenty-five hundred and like I said, when things heat up, you know I will look out for you."

Tommy looked at the money like a child who hadn't received the Christmas gift under the tree that he expected. He smiled, put his newspaper under his arm, and got up from the steps. He held his arms up to the sky and stretched. "Okay, partner, being that we cool and shit, I'm going to give you some room. You won't have to worry about my soldiers coming around messing with you. Just continue to have a little something for me every week, cool?"

Doug looked at his watch. He could feel his eyes getting heavier as each second went by. "Okay, Tommy. No problem, but we can't meet in front of my place like this. When I have your stash, I will call you to set up an exchange." Tommy smacked Doug on the back, got in his car, and started the engine. He gave Doug a wave and a smile before he drove off down the street. Doug could only think of two things now. One of them was, how long had Tommy waited for him on those steps? It was only about thirty-three degrees outside; he had to be freezing. Then Doug realized that Tommy really was like a crack addict, except his drug was money. But just like any addict, he would do whatever it took to get his fix. That bothered Doug. What would Tommy do next? Wait by his door the following week? The second thing that concerned Doug was what Tommy said about his soldiers staying away and not making any visits. If the money got slow, would they start shaking him down? Of course they would. Removing his keys from his pocket, Doug began to walk up the steps, making his way into his building.

* * *

Doug looked at the mail he had just taken out from his mailbox, but he could no longer fight it. He threw the mail on his living room coffee table, plopped himself on the sofa, removed his shoes, and began to shut his eyes. Suddenly something flashed inside his head—the mail. Sitting up on the couch, Doug reached for the pile of envelopes with a new-found energy. Scanning through it quickly, his eyes focused on a blue envelope. He looked at the piece of mail like it was a winning lottery ticket, then he opened it and saw that Sandra's cell phone bill was for fifty-two dollars. Doug flipped through the pages until he came upon the list of numbers that she had dialed during this billing period. As he examined the list of numbers, Doug could clearly see she had made many late-night calls and the dates indicated this was right before he took her phone away. Two numbers stuck out, though, and they were both 718 numbers. Finding a boost of energy, Doug got up to retrieve the cordless phone that sat on the television set. He looked at one of the frequently dialed numbers, dialed it, and placed his hands over the receiver. He got an answer on the third ring.

"Good afternoon, Burnside Pantry, this is Carla. Hello? Hello? Hey, it's your dime." Doug heard a click on the other end of the line. He held on to the phone and now put on a big thinking cap, trying to understand why Sandra made all these calls at strange times of the night. Now looking at the other number, Doug dialed that one also and waited as he listened to the phone ring four, five, and finally six times with no answer, not even an answering machine.

Hanging up the phone, Doug took a walk to his living room wall to admire one of the paintings he had purchased a few years ago. He pushed the redial button and stared at the picture while listening to the rings again when something dawned on him. He listened more intently and swore he could hear a phone ringing on the other side of his wall. With the phone still in his hand, Doug slowly leaned toward his living room wall, pressing his ear against it. Sure enough, though it was low, he could hear a ringing phone. He pressed the off button on his phone and sported a look of curiosity because he could no longer hear the ringing through the wall. Doug pressed redial again and now could hear the ringing more clearly, as if it had gotten louder. Doug hung up and redialed three more times to reassure himself that he was not crazy. Sure enough, his discovery was true.

Doug tossed the phone on the couch, stared at the wall with anger and a bit of admiration mixed in, and said, "Okay, bitch. I think you just fucked up. I'm not totally sure, but soon enough I will find out. And if you did fuck with me, all of you fucked with me."

Chapter Twenty-five

Sandra Moves Forward

It was Saturday afternoon, 3:00 p.m. to be exact, and Sandra had just awakened from a nine-hour nap. She still had all of her notes etched in her mind and on paper from what she witnessed on Doug's DVD collection. She also figured a few things out while she prepared her clothes and got ready to shower.

Doug was not stupid, and sooner or later he was going to narrow down all those around him who could have entered the apartment and taken his DVDs. Figuring out how that person got into his safe would not be important to him though, because all he would want to do is catch the individual and make that person suffer. The other thing Sandra figured to be true was that those discs were very important to Doug simply because he enjoyed having the upper hand. As long as he held those discs with the cops engaged in illegal activity, Doug held an advantage just in case he got in trouble. Without the discs, his word carried little weight in a court of law if he was busted.

Sandra looked at her watch and rushed to get herself together. Soon after waking up, she had called Pamela on her cell and asked her to come over for lunch and a meeting. Being a stickler for time, Pamela would be there in about thirty minutes. Sandra grabbed her personals and hurried to the bathroom.

* * *

Sandra and Pamela sat at the small dinette table eating hero sandwiches in silence and drinking diet sodas. The sun was already beginning to set over the quiet Bronx street, and Pamela could tell her friend had a lot on her mind.

"So, girl, how do you like your new surroundings?" she asked, attempting to get Sandra to open up.

Sandra took a swig of her soda. "I think I finally know why things happened on Christmas Day, Pamela."

Having just finished her sandwich, Pamela adjusted her chair so that she was facing Sandra and looking directly into her eyes. "Okay, baby. You tell me why, and take your time."

"Pamela, I've spent about ten hours straight, maybe more—I can't be sure—studying what I took from Doug's apartment that night. You see this leather case? It contains discs of Doug and people who work for the police department doing some terrible shit that could get a lot of important people locked up."

She slid the case towards Pamela and watched her open it slowly, reading the titles and dates of each disc. "Sandra, please tell me what you saw, and what does it have to do with Christmas Day? Because if it can help you get those bastards responsible for Kareem and Chaka, you have to do something right away."

Sandra stood up from her chair and slowly paced back and forth in the small cooking area. "First of all, Pamela, what I am about to discuss with you can go no further than this room, because you are the only person I can trust, okay?"

Pamela nodded her head and hung on to every word coming from Sandra's mouth.

"This disc holder also had a set of insurance policy receipts totaling one million dollars made out in Kareem's and Chaka's names with Doug as the sole beneficiary. He never discussed these policies with me and I don't remember any insurance agent coming to the apartment when I was there."

"Wait a minute," Pamela said in disbelief. "Sandra, are you telling me that Doug is responsible for the deaths of his own children?""Yes, Pamela. That motherfucker had my babies slaughtered for the fucking money! You hear me, Pamela?" Sandra's voice rose with anger. "He killed my babies for fucking money!"Pamela leapt out of her chair with anger burning from her eyes. "What the fuck are we waiting for? Let's deal with that cold-hearted bastard right now! I know where I can get a burner. Let's blow his motherfucking brains out!"Sandra almost gave in to the temptation but quickly changed her mind. "Pamela that would be too merciful for that son of a bitch. I've got other plans for his monkey ass that will include pain and suffering as he has never felt. When it all goes down I will be there, and that son of a bitch will have no choice but to look into my eyes before he goes to hell. That I promise. I know you think I should react now, but this will take time and patience. Are you with me Pamela?""All the way, sister," she said, looking straight into Sandra's eyes. She calmed herself down and continued to listen to Sandra, who had determination written all over her face.

"On one of the last discs I watched, Doug had Rose on a dog leash, on her hands and knees, performing sex acts. Those motherfuckers stood there watching as she cried and begged them to stop. That's why she said she hates Doug and that he's a bad man. How could she be so brave and help us when she holds so much pain inside her?"

Pamela grabbed a napkin from the table and wiped her eyes. "Sandra, maybe that's just it, baby…maybe Rose's way of dealing with all that she has been through is by helping you and bonding with you. Obviously she knew more about Doug then we were aware of."

"On the last disc I watched, there was a man that I recognize from Christmas Day."

"Oh shit! Who Sandra?" Pamela said as she quickly jumped out of her chair and grabbed Sandra by the shoulders. She looked mad as hell.

"When those men ambushed us on Christmas, they all had on black clothes and black masks to match, so I could never match a face to them. What I vividly remember is the hand that went across my face as he slit my throat. Pamela, on his wrist was a tattoo of a green dragon. Just like the one on the man who was chasing us in the hospital. Do you remember him?"

Pamela twisted her face in thought and then answered, "Yes, Sandra, I remember him." Slowly and gently, she rubbed her fingers across Sandra's freshly scarred throat. "Sandra, let's sit down and take a break from all this shit. We're gonna make ourselves sick."

"No, I want to continue," Sandra protested, shaking her head. "On the last disc that I watched when they humiliated Rose, a man stood up and applauded, taking off his shirt. While the majority of the discs were a bit fuzzy and were shot at poor angles, this disc was perfect in every way. On this man's wrist was the tattoo, and clipped to his waistband was a gun and a police shield. Pamela, I can't totally prove it yet, but I am pretty positive Doug and these men are responsible for what happened to my children."

Pamela studied Sandra's face. "No, Sandra," she said defiantly. "Don't you dare doubt yourself or your feelings. They did this shit. And I'm going to help you figure out how to get their fucking asses back."

* * *

It was 10:00 p.m. and Sandra had been sitting by her window looking at pictures of Kareem and Chaka while Pamela had been looking angrily at DVDs of Doug and the detectives. Turning off the television after witnessing what was done to Rose, Pamela felt numb throughout her body. She walked back over to the dinette table and stared at the stove.

"Sandra, you are right in waiting. We can't go to the police because they have that secret blue-wall bullshit. We have to figure out how to get this information into the right set of hands. We also have to watch our backs because I'm pretty sure, sooner or later, Doug will put all of this together and will begin searching for his discs."

As she set the pictures of her dead children back inside a shoebox, Sandra tried her best to push the fear that she still had of Doug from her mind. "I have a few ideas on what we can do, Pamela. But the first thing I must do is get these discs into the right hands, and I think I know someone. Her name is Maria Copper, the special investigative reporter on channel four. She is always getting shady companies and people in trouble by exposing their wrongdoings. I remember last year when she got those meat markets in Hunt's Point closed down because of the bad meat they were selling to the supermarkets in the poorer neighborhoods. My plan is to give her a call as soon as possible next week."

"Sandra, I want you to know and realize something, okay? This is some deep shit we are about to get involved in. Once we set one foot into motion, there is no turning back. Now I want to tell you this also, Sandra—I love you. And as I said before, no one in this world is going to convince me that you deserved what happened to you. Understand that once this ball starts to roll, it is going to pick up some nasty shit along the way and you can't let it scare or intimidate you. You have to promise me that you will not give up, okay? As long as you stay strong, I am with you all the way."

"I love you too, Pamela. Thank you for all the help and support you have given me. And no, I will not give up, because this is not about me anymore. It's about my two babies."

As the women embraced each other at the dinette table, the unpredictability of the future entered their minds and bodies, but at the same time, the power of love and determination bonded them together, pushing all fear away. Slowly they let go of each other.

"Pamela, I promised myself that I wouldn't do this until I brought my children's killers to justice, but I miss them so much and my heart aches so much. I need to visit them. I need to speak to them, Pamela."

"Are you sure you're ready for this? You don't have any idea what visiting the gravesite could do to your mind. It could crush you and cause you to abandon the whole plan. Can you handle that?"

Sandra grabbed Pamela by the hand. "I thought that at one time. That's why I said to myself that I would not visit them until this was done. Now I realize that decision was the wrong one because of the danger and seriousness of this matter. Pamela, I want to see them for strength and comfort. So please...I don't even know where they rest, so can you tell me, please?"

Pamela walked over to the dinette table, grabbed the pad and a pen, and wrote the address down. "Sandra, this is the name of the cemetery, the address, and the location of their plot. Do you need me to go there with you?"

"No, this is something I have to do by myself. I'll tell you when I'm leaving and where I've hidden the discs. In addition, I'm going to make a copy of the apartment key so that you will have one. When I get back from visiting Kareem and Chaka, I will call you and that's when you can come over so we can contact Maria Copper, okay?"

Nodding her head up and down, Pamela looked at Sandra as if she were a baby chicken about to walk into a slaughterhouse, but she managed to put a smile on her face.

"Baby, let's call you a cab because it's getting late and it's freezing outside," Sandra suggested. The dispatcher told them a driver would be there in three minutes. Sandra helped Pamela put on her coat and gave her one last hug before walking her to the street.

* * *

It was Sunday morning, and the air was brisk but amazingly fresh and clean. Sandra sat in the back of a red Lincoln Town Car about three minutes away from the Pelham Cemetery on Earley Avenue in the Bronx. Holding two brown teddy bears in one hand and a small bouquet of flowers in the other, Sandra was doing her best to hold it together as they approached the entrance gates of the cemetery. The driver pulled inside the graveyard and Sandra handed him a piece of paper with the plot number and directions to where her children rested. As the car slowly moved on the asphalt driveway, Sandra gazed at the fancy and large monuments and headstones that families had adorned on the gravesites of their loved ones. The car came to a slow halt and the driver turned to face Sandra.

"Miss, I think this is the location. Would you like me to wait here for you?"

"No, sir. That won't be necessary. I have your company card, so I'll call. Thank you very much. You're a good driver." Sandra got out of the car and watched it drive away. She looked at the instructions Pamela wrote down for her while walking towards Kareem and Chaka's resting place. Buttoning her coat collar to protect her neck from the sudden burst of wind, she removed her sunglasses and looked at the concrete tombstone that had her children's names with their dates of birth and death on it. Letting a smile come on her face, Sandra slowly kneeled at the tombstone and wiped some old snow from the top of it. She laid the teddy bears on the ground and placed the flowers near them, making a decorative display. The sky was becoming very cloudy and the wind had begun to pick up, making the thirty-two degrees feel like fifteen. Looking at the dates of her children's short existence on the tombstone, Sandra felt it wasn't fair that she was above ground while her precious little ones were below it. Deep inside, Sandra wished she were with them.

"The first thing Mommy wants you to know is that I miss both of you very much. Kareem, I hope you are taking good care of your sister. Chaka, you make sure your brother stays out of trouble, because we know how mischievous he is."

Trying unsuccessfully to hold back the tears, Sandra looked to her far right where an elderly man was standing alone at a gravesite with flowers in his hand.

"Mommy said she would hold it together, but I can't because I miss and love you both so much. I know I should have tried harder to get us out of that place, but I had no other place to go. And there was no way I could afford to give you the education that you were receiving, so I took the beatings, hoping they would stop. Instead, the beatings turned your mother into this lonely woman before you."

Feeling as if two thousand pounds were weighing on her heart, Sandra tried to swallow but couldn't because of the peach-sized lump in her throat.

"I don't know if you two will ever forgive me for what I allowed to happen, but I hope and pray that you will give me the chance to make up for it. I want to make a promise to both of you that I will never sleep or rest until I have used up all the energy in my mind and body to find who did this to us. I swear before both of you that I will find them and they will pay."

Still on her knees, Sandra held on to the tombstone with both hands as she cried uncontrollably. Her warm tears fell into the snow and dirt beneath her. She didn't even feel the hand that came from behind her and touched her shoulder.

"It's okay, sweetheart. God has them in His bosom and they are in a better place now." Sniffing and trying to gain some control, Sandra shivered a little at the sound of the low but positive voice. She slowly turned her head and brushed her braids away from her red, swollen eyes.

"Please let me help you up from the snow, young lady," said the frail Jewish man standing behind her. He grunted but was successful in getting Sandra to her feet. "I miss my Edna like you miss your loved ones. I see they were very young and vibrant. They are probably doing much work for God right now and they know that you love and miss them, but they want you to live—just like my Edna told me last year before she passed." The old man removed a handkerchief from the pocket of his old black coat and gently wiped Sandra's face.

"Where did you come from?" asked Sandra, still upset.

Allowing a smile to come to his face, the old man replied, "From a far off place hoping for a better life. That was sixty-eight years ago, and it was then that I met my Edna. My life had never been happier until it was time for her to go. Did you have a good time with your loved ones?"

Sandra looked down at the ground and then back at the old man. "I enjoyed every minute with them, and I made sure they knew that I loved them all the time."

"Well, you have done a great thing that many mothers in this world cannot say they have done, which is a shame. They love you and will always love you, like my Edna loves me. You must never stop talking to them because they like that, but a time will come when you must continue on, holding them near your heart but still moving on."

Feeling a little comfort from this total stranger, Sandra reached out and rubbed his slouching shoulders. "Thank you very much for the encouragement. You are a very nice man. My name is Sandra and these are my babies, Kareem and Chaka."

"My name is Albert. It's nice to meet you, Sandra, and you must stay strong for them because whether you know it or not, they will always depend on you to continue to carry their legacy."

Sandra looked at the two teddy bears that sat on the gravesite. "I will Albert," she said, turning back to him. "I made them a promise that I would."

The old man moved closer to Sandra and gave her a gentle hug. "He knows your pain and will help you to make things right," he whispered. He adjusted his hat and coat, gave Sandra one more smile, and began to walk down the asphalt driveway where a tall man stood by a long limousine with the back door open. Sandra watched him get into his car and looked on as the driver got in and drove out of sight.

Feeling light snowflakes hit her nose, Sandra turned to her children's resting place. "Mommy has to go now, but I promise that when this is all over, I will be back to tell you how brave and strong I was in finding the bad people who did this to us. Always know Mommy loves you both terribly. You two were the only people who really loved me and I will not let you down. Mommy will see and talk to you real soon. I promise." Sandra sat the teddy bears up straight on the tombstones and started to walk down the driveway.

She was halfway to the entrance when her phone rang. She pulled the phone from her purse and answered on the fourth ring. "Hello?...You motherfucker! I know what happened, you no good son of a bitch! Fuck you, you bastard! I don't want to hear shit from your ass! You just know this, you no good motherfucker, I know you killed my babies! You and those fucking dirty cops. You will all go to jail and rot like fucking animals, you son of a bitch!" Sandra's face was tomato red and spit shot from her mouth. Some people who were paying respect to their loved ones couldn't help but to stop and look at her go berserk.

Doug was in his truck in a parking lot listening to a woman that he had never heard use profanity before. He realized this was not the same woman he had abused, but he still tried to intimidate. "Fuck you and your dead kids, bitch! Who the fuck do you think you're talking to, bitch? I'm going to say this shit once, so listen closely! I want my discs back right fucking now, and if I don't get them back, Sandra, I promise you I will hunt your fucking ass down, open up your fucking throat myself, and watch your ass bleed to death, bitch!"

Sandra stood at the gated entrance with no tears coming down her face as she interrupted Doug. "Come get them, motherfucker! You're not anything but a fucking coward and a lowlife piece of shit! I'm not afraid of your ass, Doug, and you know what, your stupid ass had better watch your back, because unlike your dumb fucking ass, I have nothing to lose anymore. So you better hope you find me before these discs and I find someone else, you steroid-taking motherfucker!" Hanging up her phone, Sandra waved a cab down and got in.

In complete shock, Doug's hands began to tremble. When he regained some composure, he dialed a number on his cell phone and put it to his ear. "Bucky, listen to me, man. You've got to turn up the heat on finding Sandra. Use what resources you have, man, but you have to find her." He hung up his phone, started his car, and began to drive out of the parking lot. Suddenly he slammed on the brakes and just missed hitting a woman pushing her baby in a stroller. For the first time in Doug's life, a cold chill flooded his body. He tried shaking that feeling, but it was impossible.

Chapter Twenty-six

Tony Marino, Meet Sandra Lyte

While coming home from the cemetery, Sandra had the sudden urge for banana crunch ice cream, so instead of having the cab driver let her off at her basement apartment, she stopped at the supermarket. With the snow beginning to fall more rapidly along with a gusty wind, Sandra felt fortunate to find a cashier who was able to check her out quickly so she could get home. With her venomous conversation with Doug still on her mind, Sandra tried to focus on what her new friend Albert had said to her about her children. It was hard though, because she was thinking about Doug. She knew he was a persistent son of a bitch who had many associates in the city, and she began to wonder if it was safe for her to spend unnecessary time on the street. She looked at the items she had just purchased and decided to do her best to stay out of sight until she was ready to make her move with the discs. Covering her face from the wind and snow, Sandra hurried home.

* * *

Brushing herself off and stomping her feet, Sandra walked down the well-lit hallway that led to the door of her apartment, passing the slop sink closet and the electric meters. She was taking out her keys to unlock her door when she looked up and dropped her bag. She had a terrified look on her face, but she didn't scream or say a word; instead, she just looked at the six large Italian men who were all wearing expensive cashmere coats with suits to match. One of the men smiled at Sandra, walked over to her, and bent down to pick up her bag.

"Sandra, I didn't mean to frighten you," he said. "Please let me introduce myself. My name is Tony Marino and I was wondering if I could take up a few minutes of your time. I truly believe we have a lot in common, and if we put our heads together, we could help one another."

Sandra couldn't take her eyes off Tony's men, who were very large and intimidating. "I don't know you. And how did you find me?" Sandra asked.

"Sandra, I promise I will explain and answer all of your questions if you could give me just a minute of your time," Tony said, still maintaining the smile that revealed his perfectly white teeth. "I give you my word—you have nothing to fear. And besides, we would not want your ice cream to melt, now would we?"

Sandra knew she had no real choice in the matter and Tony was just trying to make her feel as if she did. She took a long, deep breath then exhaled. "Okay, Mr. Marino. But just for a few moments. And only you."

Tony nodded his head in agreement. "I fully understand, Sandra. Just me, and please call me Tony. Men, please give Sandra and me a little privacy."

With that command, the five men, who were obviously bodyguards, did as they were told and walked outside to their cars. As he held Sandra's bag, Tony watched her nervously open her door.She turned on the light and quickly put her groceries away as Tony stood and admired how Sandra had decorated such a small place so nicely. "Tony, I just have water and orange juice. May I offer you some?"

"No, thank you, I'm fine," Tony said, removing his gloves and looking around. "I really admire your creativity with your place. My wife would have a ball with your ideas."

Sensing that Tony was no associate of Doug's, Sandra felt a little more at ease and a brief smile flashed across her face.

"Please have a seat at the table and you can take your coat off," she offered.

Tony did as Sandra suggested, and she took a seat directly across from him. "Sandra, I am not one to mince words, so I will get right to the point. My heart goes out to you in your time of loss. I mean no disrespect to you and I don't mean to open up any wounds, but I am fully aware of what was done to your children and yourself. Tonight I am here to let you know that I not only feel your pain, but I also understand it."

He reached into his Armani suit jacket pocket and removed a 5"x7" photo of a closed white casket. "Sandra, this is the casket of my son, Anthony Michael Marino, Jr.—my only son—who was murdered a few days before your children faced their sad and untimely demise. I am here, Sandra, because I have discovered through hard work that the man responsible for my pain is also the man responsible for yours. Sandra, that man is Doug Gunner."

Sandra held the photo in her hand and stared at it in silence. "Sandra, I am not a stupid father, just a loving one. I know my son Michael was no angel of God, but he was still my son, and I cannot forgive or forget the way he died at Doug's hands. I am so sorry to bring my personal agendas to you during your trying times, but I really feel that we could help each other greatly."

Taking her eyes off the photo to look at Tony, Sandra couldn't help but to feel some compassion for the man. "Tony, I have not seen or heard from Doug since the day they admitted me into the hospital. No phone calls, visits, or letters. My girlfriend helped me home from the hospital, not Doug. I'm sorry about the loss of your son, and you have my deepest condolences. But I have no information to give you. I just hope for you and your family's sake that if Doug is responsible for our children's deaths, you'll make him suffer ten times as much as we have."

Tony reached into his pocket, removed a business card, and handed it to Sandra. "Listen, sweetheart, I have many associates and friends who, through the kindness of their hearts, have elected to offer me their help in locating Doug. I have searched and located many men for lesser deeds than his, so I know it's just a matter of time before I find him. But as I said to you before, any information that you gather and can pass on to me would be greatly appreciated."

Sandra read the card and then looked at the large but polite man. "I promise you that if I give you a call, it won't be a social one but an informative one."

Tony reached out and gently shook Sandra's hand before putting on his scarf and coat. "Take care, Sandra. You are a brave woman. May God continue to give you strength."

Nodding her head in acknowledgment, Sandra closed and locked the door. She went back over to the dinette table and picked up the business card. What could have possessed Doug to shoot and kill a mafioso's only son? Did he actually think this would just go away? Well, that was for Doug to figure out because what was on Sandra's mind was how she could use Tony as an asset, keeping Doug away from her while she figured out the safest way to get those discs to Maria Copper.

Sandra decided to simply sit down in front of her television in the dark and eat her bowl of banana crunch ice cream. It had been a long time since she had been able to enjoy any indulgence; and since this time could be her last, she wanted to savor it.

* * *

It had been about an hour since Sandra sat down with her ice cream to watch reruns of *The Jeffersons*, but the voice that said it would torment her resurfaced in her head and would not let her enjoy a small moment of relaxation, not even for a second. That voice wanted Sandra to know that she had work to do. "Now is not the time for enjoyment, Sandra," the voice said. "You have things to do and the planning must start immediately. Right now you control the board, and you must make your move. You have the bait. Now just put it on the hook. Doug is desperate and thinks you don't realize it because he has always regarded you as being stupid. Now is the time, Sandra. Show him how much he has underestimated you. Get on the phone and call him back."

Sandra listened until the voice slowly went back where it came from. The empty bowl in font of her still had the smell of banana crunch ice cream. She put the bowl in the sink and then got her cell phone. "Shit, I have to call the post office and get my mail sent to this address instead of Doug's," she said to herself. Wondering why she just said that, Sandra shook her head. Then just like that, the answer came to her. She was becoming more of a calculated thinker. She walked over to the sink, splashed her face with cold water, and wiped it dry with a paper towel. Then she sat at the dinette table, looking at her phone for a moment before dialing Doug's number and pressing send.

Doug was sitting in his living room with Jasmine's naked body on his lap, getting his groove on, when he heard his phone ring. His eyes were half closed and he was admiring the way Jasmine moved her hips from side to side. Slowly he reached for his phone and answered on the third ring. "Yeah, what's up?"

He quickly sat up and tossed Jasmine to the side, causing her to tumble and almost fall off the couch. "Damn, Doug!" Jasmine yelled. He raised the back side of his hand in a threatening motion and the woman quickly shut up.

Right away, Sandra recognized the voice of the woman that blew her only chance of escaping a while ago, posing to be a friend at the pantry. She could feel her anger begin to boil but knew she had to be cool for just about five minutes.

"Doug, please pay attention to me very carefully. I want to set up a meeting so I can give you back your discs. I realize what I did was wrong and I am way over my head. Doug, I don't want anything from you. All I ask is that you give me my freedom and allow me to move on with my life."

Doug listened very carefully to Sandra's voice. He didn't pick up any bad vibes or reason to believe she was lying, but he still had some doubts. After all, he never expected her to have the heart and the guts to steal the discs in the first place. "How the fuck do I know you're not trying to set me up, bitch? I mean you sounded very pissed off today with all of your fucking threats and all." Sandra clenched her teeth and did her best to hold it together. "You know what. Doug? You're going to have to trust me. All I want is my life back…nothing more and nothing less. I want to meet somewhere that is well exposed and well lit, where I can feel safe knowing that you will not hurt me. You know where the Valentine Avenue Park is across the street from public school nine? The same park I used to take your children to? I want to meet there next Sunday at noon on the corner. I will drop the discs inside a trash bin and walk away. Doug, I'm telling you that if anything happens to me, you'll regret it."Doug wanted to snap Sandra's neck for giving him directives, but he decided to remain cool and go along with her demand. Besides, he thought to himself, Sandra was nobody and knew nobody, so she was no threat. He would get what he wanted and regain his advantage over that slimy detective Tommy Davis. He got no bad vibe from this deal, so he decided to bite. "Okay, Sandra, you've got yourself a deal. And I promise I will let you walk away, scout's honor."

Sandra stood up at her dinette table. "Doug, you can play all you want and think I'm not serious, but I'm telling you—if anything happens to me, you are in a lot of trouble." She felt her heart pound faster and faster. "Okay, Doug. You'll see me on the corner dropping the discs off at noon. I will not call you anymore and please don't call me." She hung up her phone, located Tony Marino's card, and dialed his number.

* * *

Doug looked over at Jasmine, who was now sitting on the love seat smoking a joint. "I don't even need any backup for this shit. This will be like eating cake. All I want are my discs," he said quietly to himself. As he got up to go over to Jasmine, he heard the distinctive ring of the phone that his new organization had given him.

"Hello, Doug. Just calling to let you know that you will be picking up those three packages next Sunday starting at eight in the morning. I want the suitcase brought to me at The Plaza at three in the afternoon. Do you understand?"It felt like a million bullets of sweat were forming on Doug's forehead. He barely held it together when answering, "Yes, I fully understand. I will deliver the keys for the currency. You can count on me…yes, sir. I will see you at three." Hanging up the phone, Doug slowly exhaled and took a sip of cognac that sat on the coffee table. "Listen," he told Jasmine. "I'm busy all of a sudden. Get your shit on and get out." Without uttering a word, the woman did just that.

Chapter Twenty-seven

The Drop-off

It was a week later, Sunday morning, 7:30 a.m. to be exact, and Sandra, who probably hadn't slept three sound hours the night before, sat anxiously at her dinette table with her keys, cell phone, and the DVD case in front of her. She didn't have a sense of fear in her body or her mind, only transformation. She started to wonder to herself if she were stooping to Doug's diabolical level by going through with this plan. After all, there was a good chance that this would be the last day of Doug's life and she would be somewhat responsible. All throughout her life, she had been a good person who had never hurt anyone and had helped everybody who asked. By going through with this plan, was she becoming as evil as Doug was? As she sat at the dinette table and thought about the question, her inner friend showed up again.

"Sandra, I will make this short and sweet, okay? You are a good person who has suffered and endured much in the past seven years at the hands of a person who epitomizes evil. No one will miss him, and in some societies you would be a hero. Snap out of it and stop letting yourself feel sorry for this motherfucker. Remember, Sandra, revenge is a dish best served cold, and I'll be damned if I don't make sure you feed it to Doug straight out of the motherfucking freezer. I know and understand what you are feeling right now, but trust me—after you hear of his demise, you and your kids will rest easier."

As the voice exited her mind, Sandra looked at the photo of her children that sat atop the television and said, "Mommy will not turn back now."

* * *

As Doug drove to his first stop in the Bronx at the Executive Towers, he glanced over at the large silver-colored metal suitcase on the passenger seat. It would soon be loaded with a little over two million dollars that he was entrusted to deliver to his employer by three o'clock this afternoon. For the first time in a while, Doug felt needed; and he enjoyed the feeling. Never mind the fact that he didn't even know the three individuals he was delivering the special keys to—he just felt good knowing he was part of a special organization that trusted him with significant amounts of money. To top it off, he was getting his discs back and regaining his leverage.

Doug had never liked Sundays because of what they represented, but on this particular Sunday, it all just felt right.

* * *

At Tito Hernandez's apartment, two large bodyguards patted Doug down. He had two nickel-plated cannons located in the waist of his paints and he began to remove them until Tito waved him off.

"Let him keep his weapons. I can tell they make him feel safe," Tito said. Doug looked around the living room. Tito had a huge collection of gay porn neatly organized in a DVD case right next to his twenty-thousand-dollar home theater system.

"I have your key. Can we make this transaction now?" asked Doug.

"Sure, Dougie, but what's the rush? Sit with me and have a cup of java."

Trying to remember that this day would turn out great in a few hours, Doug held his temper. "My name is Doug and no thanks. Let's just get this over with, please."

Tito, who was wearing a skin-tight leather leopard suit, sucked his teeth and rolled his eyes at Doug while motioning to one of his large guards. The guard left the room and Tito continued to stare and smile at Doug, which made him extremely uncomfortable. The guard soon reentered the living room, rolling in a food server with stacks upon stacks of crisp one-hundred-dollar bills.

"Give me my key, you son of a bitch," Tito ordered Doug. "I thought you wanted to be my friend."

With his eyes now shooting .357 Magnum bullets at Tito, Doug was about one stupid comment away from pulling his steel and blasting gay Tito and his guards through the living room wall. He set his suitcase on the serving tray, opened it, and watched the guard put the money inside.

Reaching into his pocket, Doug handed over the red car key to Tito, making sure he never touched the man's hand.

"Now get the fuck out of here, Doug, because you make me very sick," demanded Tito. In the past Doug would have smoked Tito's ass in a second, but somehow he completed the transaction without violence and exited the apartment. As he walked to the elevator, Doug removed one of his guns and cocked it, just in case Tito got stupid.Back in his Navigator, Doug put the suitcase on the floor and looked at his watch. Seeing that it was 8:30 a.m., he felt good again knowing that the first pick-up was over. In another couple of hours, he would have completed what Mr. X had called a very important assignment *and* he would have his discs back. He started up his car and made his way to Brooklyn for his second stop.

* * *

At ten o'clock in the morning, Tony Marino was sitting in his private social club alongside four of his soldiers—Frankie, Sal, Johnny, and Vito—all loyal and respected workers. The men sipped on cappuccino and ate bagels as they inspected their weapons and listened closely to their capo.

"Sal, when she makes the drop, you start the car and get her out of there, understand?" Tony instructed.

"Yes, boss, I understand. Get her out and home as soon as she makes the drop. I have the red Town Car ready. It looks just like the cabs they drive up there."

Tony nodded his head with satisfaction, then addressed his other three men. "Remember my words, okay? He is no good to me dead or shot. When he returns to his car, you move in on him quickly and get it done without drawing too much attention. If he tries to put up a fight, stun him and carry him to the car. Under no circumstances do I want him dead, okay, Johnny?"

Johnny loaded the last bullet into his clip. "I know you want him alive, boss. I will do my best not to hurt him, yes." Feeling satisfied with his men, Tony held his glass of cappuccino in the air and toasted, "For Michael." His men looked at him with some sadness on their faces, held their glasses up, and responded as one, "For Michael."

* * *

At eleven o'clock in the morning, Sandra was taking small sips of water from a red glass, hoping that the water would quench her dry mouth; she was disappointed when it didn't. She remembered Tony telling her that the red Town Car's flashing rear lights were the signal for her to get in. Tony didn't want Sandra to look back at Doug because he might see something in her eyes. She looked at her watch and began to gather her coat and house keys. Glancing at the black DVD case, Sandra unzipped it for the fifth time and examined its contents. Feeling satisfied, she zipped it back up, looked at the clock on her wall, and waited until it read 11:30. The door in her head opened up and Sandra could hear it coming: "Be cool, Sandra. You can do this. In another ninety minutes, you will be back home starting a new chapter in your life. All you have to do is make it through the next ninety minutes. I know you are in a zone, so I will not stay long. I just wanted to let you know how proud I am of you." Her inner companion returned to the back of her mind and Sandra called a cab.

* * *

It was 11:30 a.m. and Doug was inspecting the large steel-like suitcase that sat on the passenger-side seat of his SUV. As he looked around Astoria Boulevard, he noticed the many people going to church. Focusing back on the money, he wondered to himself how two million dollars could fit so perfectly inside the case. It just reconfirmed how organized and precise his new employers were. He looked up at the sun and felt how warm it was becoming for a Sunday in the middle of winter.

He couldn't help but to let a good feeling inside him expose itself. The last two deliveries went beautifully, and he was right on schedule to get his discs back.

Doug had never felt guilt for anything he had done in his life, not even setting up his family. As far as he was concerned, all parties knew what they were getting into when they came together. No, it wasn't guilt he was feeling towards Sandra but strangely, compassion. That's why after picking up the last of the money, Doug decided that he would let Sandra walk. The way he saw it, what could she do to him? She was afraid and confused, probably planning to go back to Virginia. She was always weak and scared. Besides, Sandra knew that at any time, Doug could reach out from the streets and touch her. He knew she didn't want to live like that. He was sure that after their meeting in about twenty-five minutes, he would never see the woman he thought he loved again, so he decided it was okay to let her live.

* * *

It was 11:57 a.m. and Sandra was sitting in a cab on the corner of 183rd Street and Valentine Avenue, diagonally across from the park. Her heart started to race as she spotted Doug's red Navigator approaching. The man responsible for the deaths of the two people that loved her unconditionally had arrived. His truck slowly came to a stop on the corner of Valentine Avenue, right in front of public school nine.

In the opposite direction, the red Town Car that Tony had promised would be there to take her home sat waiting. Sandra squeezed her trembling hands together tightly in an effort to get them under control. *Be cool*, she thought as she firmly grabbed the leather case and paid the cab driver. Taking one more deep breath, Sandra slowly exited the cab.Doug watched the woman who had gone through eight hours of labor and prepared his meals every day for seven years, and tried his best to push away the memories of the first night he noticed her on the dance floor. He couldn't, because he now realized that no matter how cold-hearted a man could be, you never just erase seven years of memories from your life. "Snap out of it," Doug said softly to himself. He looked at Sandra's face and saw that she was no longer the smiling and bubbly Virginian woman that knocked his socks off; no, this woman was emotionless and battered. She had now transformed into a wounded and scarred victim that he was fully responsible for creating. Her green scarf lowered as she walked, and the white bandages meant to heal her neck were clear for Doug to see. This strengthened his decision even more—he would just let her go.

Sandra crossed the street, adjusting her scarf to conceal her bandages. As she got closer to the garbage can, she saw the flashing red lights of the car that would take her home in a few moments. "Be cool, Sandra," she said softly. She was now a few yards away from the garbage bin, and she quickly surveyed the area. No matter how calm this Sunday afternoon seemed, Sandra knew better than to underestimate Doug, who she could feel watching every step she made. Staying alert, she pulled the black case from under her arm and gently set it on top of the metal caged bin, which was piled high with beer bottles, fast food wrappers, and dirty snow. With her eyes circling the area at one hundred miles an hour, Sandra then made a sharp right turn and walked towards the red Town Car that was waiting for her with the engine running. Now ten feet away from the car, Sandra never took her eyes off Doug's vehicle, which was diagonally across from her direction. She grabbed the handle of the car's back door, firmly pulled it open, and quickly got inside."Excuse me, sir, can we go now, please?" she asked the neatly dressed gray-haired driver with a little quiver in her voice. Without looking back or saying a word to Sandra, Sal put the car in drive and pulled off. As they left, Sandra looked back through the smoked rearview window and stared at the red Navigator until she couldn't see it anymore. "Halfway there," she quietly said to herself. She sank into the plush leather seating of the Town Car and inhaled a deep breath of Sal's High Karate aftershave.

Although he could tell how easy this would be, Doug still made sure his guns were ready for use if needed. He put on his shades, unlocked his door, and stepped out into the bright sunshine that warmed his bald head. Looking around him as he slowly walked in the direction of the trash bin, Doug eyed every person that he passed with a little suspicion, trying not to get too comfortable. He jumped over a pile of water and slush, landing on the sidewalk. He was getting closer to his prized possession that would give him back the leverage he craved.

Now a few feet away from the trash bin, he could see the leather case sitting on top of garbage and snow. Letting a smile come to his face, Doug grabbed the package and admired it for a few moments before turning around to walk back to his vehicle. Stepping with some bravado, Doug hit his remote switch and unlocked the door of his SUV. He hopped inside and took a seat. With little regard to where the case had been sitting, Doug gave it a long kiss as if it were a woman's lips.

Sitting directly behind him in a black sedan, Frankie, Vito, and Johnny quickly checked for their weapons. Johnny removed a lead pipe from his shirt and slowly opened his door while Vito took out his stun gun and got out on his side of the car. Frankie, who was the driver, calmly started up the car and waited inside. Without saying a word, they quickly walked to Doug's SUV.

Doug reached for the keys that he had laid on the passenger seat while he was admiring his case, then he stuck the appropriate one into the ignition and started up his car. From the driver's side, his window suddenly exploded, causing what seemed like millions of glass particles to hit Doug in the face and land in his lap. "Oh shit!" he shouted as he covered his face and then tried to regain focus. From the corner of his right eye, he saw a baseball bat coming towards his passenger-side window. He covered his face again and there was another loud smash that shattered that window. As he reached for his gun, Doug's left hand was struck with a pipe.

"Oh shit, motherfucker!" Doug yelled out in pain. He felt as if his hand was broken. He looked to his right and saw a man pulling a funny-shaped gun from his coat. As the man reached inside the broken car window to open the door, Doug raised his right leg and kicked the intruder's hand with such force that he smashed it on broken glass, cutting it open. Letting out a loud yell, Vito pulled his hand back.

"Johnny, hit this fucking eggplant. Come on!" yelled Vito as he tried to point and aim the stun gun with his one good hand. Johnny, who was carrying more than his fair share of weight, gasped for air as he tried to get another clean strike but was thwarted by Doug, who grabbed the pipe. Johnny wrestled the pipe away from Doug, whose hand had swollen to the size of a grapefruit. Johnny hit Doug across the chest with the pipe, but not as hard as he'd hit him on the hand. Despite the pain of the blow, Doug grabbed Johnny by his hair and smashed his face into the steering wheel, causing the man's nose to split almost in half. Blood shot all over Doug's dashboard.

"Oh, fuck me!" Johnny yelled as he grabbed his now crimson-colored face and fell to the street in pain. With his good hand, Doug turned the ignition, started the SUV, and moved to put the gear in drive when Vito jumped through the passenger-side window, landing his upper body on top of the suitcase on the seat. Doug moved his right hand from the steering wheel to pound Vito as hard as he could on his neck and back.

"Get the fuck out, motherfucker!" Doug yelled. In his side-view mirror, he spotted another man getting out of the black sedan with a pistol. Using all of his strength, Doug lifted Vito up by his coat and pushed him back out the window. Then he quickly put his Navigator into drive and slammed down violently on the gas pedal, causing a loud screeching noise as his rear tires gave off smoke. Almost jumping the curb, Doug made a quick left on Valentine Avenue, running through a red light as he headed towards Fordham Road. Breathing hard and wiping glass particles away from his face, Doug checked his rearview mirror. It was clear; but thinking that the men might give chase, Doug pushed down harder on the gas, asking the SUV to release some of those three hundred horses. He looked again in his mirror but still didn't see them behind him. He quickly looked for his discs, which were lying on the floor. Feeling the throbbing in his left hand returning, he looked at it in total disgust; it was no longer dark brown but red and blue. Sweating and wide-eyed, Doug glanced at the passenger seat and instantly slammed on his brakes, stopping at the corner of Fordham Road.

"Oh shit! What the fuck!" He looked all throughout the SUV and smashed his good hand on the bloody steering wheel four times as he discovered that the steel suitcase with the two million dollars was gone. He let out a horrific scream that grabbed the attention of passersby who stopped and stared into the vehicle. Doug slowly shook his head as he quickly turned on Fordham Road and drove in the direction of his apartment.

* * *

With less than two hours before Mr. X expected delivery of the two million dollars, a dejected and exhausted Doug sat on his couch with a bag of ice covering his hand, which was throbbing with pain and had swollen hideously. Doug looked around his large and quiet living room, trying to put all of today's events together. He visualized the men who assaulted him this afternoon and couldn't figure out who they were or who they represented. One thing Doug was sure about though was that they didn't want him dead or they would have used their guns instead of pipes. Another thing that pounded at his head was why those cats showed up at his truck minutes after Sandra dropped off the discs. What could be the connection? Wiping sweat off his face, Doug couldn't find one simply because Sandra was a weak and stupid woman who had no guts or heart to attempt to plan something against anyone, especially not him.

"You just have to tell them the truth about getting robbed. Just tell them what happened," Doug said softly after glancing at his diamond-studded Movado watch. In his heart, however, he knew that this could be suicide. He would have to explain why he was sitting in his truck with a little over two million dollars in his possession instead of waiting at home with the money hidden in a secure place until the delivery. He couldn't explain it, so Doug decided he would go to this meeting prepared not only to die but also to take some people with him.Forgetting about his pain for a moment, Doug reached over, picked up the leather bag, and slowly unzipped it. Despite all the day's madness, he smiled knowing that he had his precious discs.

Without realizing it, Doug began to hyperventilate and his eyes got as large as saucers. As he slowly flipped through the book, Doug's eyes became very moist and his head felt like someone was hitting him repeatedly with an aluminum baseball bat. Now flipping through the book faster, Doug unconsciously smashed his swollen hand on the wooden coffee table. In front of him was the greatest collection of black films from the '70s: *Foxy Brown*, *Across 110th Street*, *Abby*, *Uptown Saturday Night*, *Three the Hard Way*, *Claudine*, *Cotton Comes to Harlem*, *Hell Up in Harlem*, and *Blacula*. All for Doug to enjoy while he tried to figure out how some weak and dumb chick made him look like the biggest jackass in the world.

He reached into his jacket, removed his nickel-plated semi-automatic Magnum, and held the barrel of the gun to his face, rubbing it slowly across his nose and near his mouth. Beginning to weep, the man with the body of granite slowly moved the gun back and forth, letting it hit his teeth and make a tapping noise. He looked back at the assortment of movies and then slowly slid the shaft of the gun until he could see the one bullet in the chamber. He sat all the way back on the couch, closed his eyes, and gently put the barrel of the gun in his mouth and cocked it.

There is no good reason, he thought as he let the taste of steel overtake his taste buds. As he leaned his head back, Doug envisioned himself sitting in a chair looking straight at a black chalkboard. With his index finger, he began to squeeze the trigger that would splatter his brains and skull all over the wall, when his father, Fred Gunner, entered the vision wearing his old bathrobe and the gray slippers that his wife bought him for Father's Day many moons ago. He was holding a piece of chalk in his hand. Doug tried to push his father out of the room, but, as usual, he couldn't. He had never been able to push his father out of the way.

With his finger still on the trigger, Doug listened to the deep baritone voice of his dad.

"Boy, what kind of man did I raise? I knew your ass was weak like your momma. Look at your stupid ass getting ready to let some bitch make you kill yourself like a goddamn coward. You pay all that damn money on that shrink because of all the shit I did to you and this is your answer for dealing with some country bitch?" Fred let out a loud, hard laugh from the bottom of his gut, causing Doug to weep louder.

"Oh, shut the fuck up, boy, and take that goddamn gun out of your mouth!" Fred demanded.

"Why can't you love me and look out for me? I love *you*!" Doug sobbed.

Fred shook his head and sucked his teeth. "'Cause I ain't shit, that's why! You ain't shit, yo' momma wasn't shit, and I never got love from nobody. So how the fuck could I give it to your dumb ass? Now I ain't got time for this shit, so if you want some revenge, you better pay attention and read, stupid."

Fred walked up to the chalkboard and began to write, and Doug slowly removed the gun from his mouth. After a few seconds, Fred moved to the side so Doug could see what he had written. On the board in white chalk was the underlined word "Friends," and under that were three names, "Carla," "Rose," and "Pamela." Doug studied what was on the board and then looked at his father, whose eyes were now flaming red, just like someone living in hell.

"Take your ass to that meeting and do whatever you have to do to buy you some time. And when you get that time, use it to flush Sandra out of her little hole before she leaves the city with your discs. Everybody has a weakness, stupid, and hers is love for her friends. Use them to get her out; and when she comes out, you had better reopen that gash on her throat. Now get your ass up and be the fucking man that I raised."

Doug watched his father leave the room and then studied the chalkboard, etching those names inside his head. Sitting up slowly from the couch, Doug looked at the DVD movies one more time before picking them up and violently tossing them across the living room. He looked at his watch and saw that he had about seventy-five minutes before his meeting. He got up and walked over to his closet, where he took out some fresh clothes along with a bulletproof vest. He looked at himself in a mirror that hung inside his closet door and said, "Thanks, Dad."

Chapter Twenty-eight

Meetings and Decisions

In Bensonhurst, Brooklyn, Tony sat in his social club office looking at Johnny and Vito, who were pretty beaten up physically and somewhat bruised emotionally. Trying not to catch Tony's eye, Frankie stood off on the far side of the room next to a jukebox.

"Somebody please explain to me how one man could get away when both of you were practically inside his car?" Tony fumed.

Everyone sat in silence with their heads pointed to the ground, until Johnny finally stood up. "Boss, on my son's eyes, we did everything the way you asked. I just feel he was expecting us."

Tony looked at his soldier. "Johnny, you are stupid. Please sit down. Who could have tipped him off? The only people who knew of our plan are the ones in this room." He walked over from his desk and stood in the middle of the room. Tony picked up a baseball bat and began to imitate a baseball player swinging in the "on deck" circle.

"You all understand he could be miles away now, don't you? The job was so simple and now I have to explain to my dead son's mother that her boy's killer is still on the loose. Do you understand how embarrassing that will be?"

Standing up from his chair, Vito looked somberly at his boss. "Tony, you have to know that Michael was like a son to all of us, and we would never do anything to screw up your plans on bringing that bastard to justice," he explained. "We honestly tried everything in our power to bring him in as you asked us, unharmed and not dead. I understand your disappointment, but put us back out there and let us bring him in."

Calmly walking over to a table that sat near his desk, Tony violently smashed the large silver suitcase that was taken from Doug's truck. The three men looked on nervously in silence, not daring to say a word to their furious leader. After about nine consecutive whacks, a sweating and heavy-breathing Tony stopped to look at the severely dented suitcase. "What the fuck is in this suitcase?" he asked.

"We have no idea, boss," Frankie answered from the back of the room. "During the fight, we were able to get our hands on it, so we grabbed it."

Tony walked over to his desk, opened the middle drawer, and removed a hammer. As he walked back over to the suitcase, Tony looked at his men, who stared back at him. Kneeling down and taking careful aim, Tony smacked the locks with the hammer until the latches popped open. With his men feeling a little more comfortable, they formed a small circle around the suitcase and waited for their boss to open it. Noticing the anticipation on their faces, Tony slowly pulled up the top portion of the suitcase and revealed neatly stacked and wrapped one-hundred-dollar bills totaling more than two million dollars. Tony let a small smirk come across his face. "We still got a chance," he told his men. "Doug ain't leaving town yet."

* * *

With some minor scratches on his face and his left hand heavily wrapped, Doug rode the elevator to the presidential suite of the Plaza Hotel in Manhattan. He felt for his gun in the back of his waistline and touched the bulletproof vest that covered his chest. He took a deep dose of oxygen while looking up at the red floor-indicator inside the elevator. With the sound of the bell, Doug took three steps forward. The doors opened and he walked towards suite 3211 where he would do his best in explaining the situation at hand. He walked down the beautifully painted hallway, which was decorated with pastel paintings on both sides of the walls and three-inch plush blue carpeting. He turned the corner and was about thirty feet away from the suite door, which was being guarded by two men Doug had never seen before. Stopping at the door, Doug looked at the guards, who were both wearing telephone headsets and long leather trench coats that, more than likely, concealed heavy artillery.

"Good afternoon. I am here for my three o'clock meeting with Mr. X."

Showing no expression, one of the guards looked at Doug and pressed a button on his headset.

"Sir, Mr. Gunner is here. May I send him in?"

Nodding to his partner, he opened the door for Doug using a magnetic card. As he walked past them and through the door, Doug was not surprised that they didn't frisk him since he had yet to give them any reason not to trust him. With the door closing behind him, a beautiful light-skinned female, looking to be in her early thirties, greeted him.

"Hello, Mr. Gunner. Would you like a drink?"

Blinded by the woman's beauty, Doug could only shake his head no.

"Well, okay, but if you change your mind, please don't hesitate to ask me. Now, if you would please follow me, I will take you to Mr. X," she said.

Doug followed the woman through the suite until he was facing two large mahogany doors with brass handles.

"Please, Mr. Gunner, go in. He's expecting you."

As the woman retreated to another section of the suite, Doug put on a face of coolness and entered the room.Sitting at a large desk and wearing a black pinstriped suit, Mr. X had a smile on his face and a lit cigar in his hand. At his side were two more guards that Doug had never seen before. *I have seventeen shots in my clip. So far I have seen four guards who are all probably armed and one female that I can't underestimate just because of her beauty. If this whole thing falls apart, I have to be prepared to fire first and ask questions later*, he thought. Looking at his smiling boss, Doug managed to exhale discretely.

"Doug, how are you? Glad to see you are on time, but I do have one question for you. I see that your hands are empty, which means my two million dollars is somewhere else. Can you explain to me why it is not here on my desk?"

Doug knew the situation was intense. The only thing left to do was to explain what happened, wait for Mr. X's reaction, and do his best to respond. Mr. X took a few slow puffs of his cigar without offering Doug a seat; he just motioned to him to answer his question.

* * *

It took Doug twenty minutes to explain to his boss what happened to him this afternoon in full detail, not hiding or leaving out anything, except Sandra. He figured that no matter what would go down, he had at least been honest to his boss about the money. Standing straight up and facing Mr. X, Doug waited for his response. Mr. X took another puff of the Cuban stogie and then turned away from Doug so that he was facing the window that overlooked the Manhattan skyline.

"Doug, I am in the business of transactions," he stated calmly, with his back still to Doug, "and today you gave three men three different keys that will open trunks to three different cars. In each of those trunks sits fifty-six kilos of pure Colombian cocaine, and each one of those men you dealt with today gave you $670,000 to pay for that cocaine. That's roughly two million dollars that you were supposed to deliver to me in what we call a transaction. According to you, though, there was a bump in the road that will not allow that transaction to take place today."

Standing and looking at the back of his boss's head, Doug had the urge to act first, blowing away the two guards standing at the sides of the desk and then pumping Mr. X full of lead, but he held his composure instead. He didn't feel nervous or anxious anymore, just upset. First, he was upset because his boss was speaking to him as if he were a child. Secondly, who was this person to turn his back on him? The way Doug saw it, no matter what the situation, you always looked another man in his eyes when dealing with him. It didn't matter if you were going to kill him or hug him—you did it with respect by looking in his eyes. With his hands at his side, Doug kept alert and waited.

"Doug, I'm going to be clear to you about this situation. Obviously, you did not take my advice when I told you to handle your business and personal affairs from your previous life before you became a part of this organization. So now a penalty must be paid," said Mr. X. Taking a quick glance at the guards, Doug figured he could get two shots off before they reached inside their jackets and just maybe he could get out of this suite alive. Finally turning around to face Doug, Mr. X continued, "Doug, from this moment on, you will not be allowed to earn money from this organization until your debt is paid or our money is found and returned. How long this situation lasts depends on you. You will have an unspecified amount of time to pay back your debt by working or simply finding our money. You must understand though that your time is limited. As usual, we will notify you when to make your drop-off, but your fifteen percent commission now belongs to us. So without wasting any more of our precious time, this meeting is adjourned."

Reaching into his desk drawer, Doug's boss pulled out a package and tossed it to him, which infuriated Doug even more. But believing that he might leave the suite with his life, he swallowed his pride and took the insult. "Doug, we will stay in touch. Now please show yourself out."

Trying not to show that he was suspicious of them, Doug walked past the guards posted outside the door and headed for the elevators, still not feeling totally secure.

A few minutes later he was sitting in his Navigator that still lacked side front windows. Doug looked at his work package and thought that he had no other option but to skim a little off the top and use that to survive until he could figure out how to get the money back. But first things first—he needed to spread some of his pain and frustration on to others.

* * *

It was 5:00 p.m. and Sandra was watching the news, or at least trying to watch it. With all that had happened today, she found it very hard to focus. She had not received a phone call from Tony Marino informing her of what had become of Doug, and she didn't feel like she had the right to call and ask him how everything went down. Even though it scared the hell out of her, she had no choice but to assume that Doug was still alive, which meant she had to be alert and act fast in turning over the discs. She had the urge to call her friend Pamela, who she had not spoken to or seen in about a week, but she put it off a little while longer because she knew other things had to be dealt with first. As she watched Maria Copper report on a special investigation involving credit card frauds on the elderly, she picked up her cell phone and dialed information for the telephone number for Channel 4 News. After getting the number, Sandra turned off the television and looked at the discs, which she had placed in a plastic bag.

"Okay, Sandra, this is it—the moment you have worked and planned for. All you have to do is make the phone call and get the instructions on how to go about getting the discs to Ms. Copper," she said to herself. Sandra understood that if Doug were alive, he would know she had something to do with him being set up. On top of that, he would be twice as furious after seeing what was inside that DVD case. Sandra knew she had to walk as quietly as possible on the streets because Doug would have everyone he knew out there on the lookout for her, and maybe a few of them would be out there to kill her on Doug's command. Whatever the case, she knew the stakes were high.

Sandra dialed the number the operator had just given her. "Hello, I am a concerned citizen with a question. How would I go about getting information to special investigator Maria Copper involving murder and corruption?"

Chapter Twenty-nine

Doug Strikes Back

Only getting three hours of sleep a night for the past two weeks, Doug had spent the other twenty-one hours putting together a plan to make things right and hustling to make twice the usual amount of money so he could repay his debt. Thinking of Sandra for the majority of his waking hours, Doug never reminisced about the days when they first met and how they shared many nights having fun and enjoying each other's time. No, Doug spent the majority of his time picturing Sandra sitting wherever she was, laughing at him and gloating to herself about how she made him look like a complete fool that Sunday afternoon. He hated her for rubbing it in his face that she was not as dumb as he thought she was. Doug also thought long and hard about how convenient it was for Sandra to leave the scene right before the ambush. Yes, Doug was beginning to put some things together while he labored his body and mind throughout most of the day.

He had clearly underestimated the feeble and dense woman from the south, but he promised himself that from this point on he would make sure that he utilized every second to make things right. It was time to make Sandra suffer for taking his discs, and Doug believed he knew just what to do. He planned to have some of his old friends causally hang around that food pantry in case Sandra was stupid enough to show her face. Doug also had a couple of his friends follow Pamela to the train station every morning so that he could learn her patterns and routes. One night, Doug explained his plan to his old pal Bucky and asked him to be ready on notice. He told Bucky it had to be fast and precise because time was of the essence. Always a loyal friend, Bucky assured Doug he would lend his assistance when needed.

As far as his debt went, Doug was spending a lot of his nightlife in the Wall Street area getting to know stock traders and executive wannabees who worked eighteen hours a day, always needing a jolt of energy to meet their deadlines. He discovered that with all their college degrees, they knew nothing about the economics of the drug game. They only had one objective, which was to get high at almost any price. Because he had the best-quality cocaine, Doug was able to charge them double what he was getting on the streets in Harlem. As his mentor Dollar Bill had told him, "The money is out there. You just have to sniff it out," and that's exactly what Doug did. He wanted to kick himself in the ass for not finding these pinstripe boys years ago. It was so easy. All he had to do was hang by the nearby coffee shop, making sure to give the owner a little piece, and like flies to shit, the zombies would come to him for nose candy. His new setup allowed Doug to pay back the organization twice as much as expected while keeping a little off the top for himself. Mr. X respected him for never complaining about his punishment of having to pay back the two million dollars. Doug's goal was to get back into the good graces of the organization. He also hooked up with a blue-eyed blonde-haired woman, who admired his hustle and his penis, and helped him invest five thousand a week into stocks and commodities. Yes, three hours of sleep a night was just fine for Doug because he was accomplishing a lot with his time.

* * *

It was Friday morning, and Doug sat in the back of the coffee shop looking over the *Wall Street Journal* and drinking a cinnamon latte. He checked on his new portfolio and saw that it was growing rapidly. Satisfied, he looked at his watch and then dialed a number on his cell phone. "Bucky, it's time to unleash hell. Spare no one who gets in the way and make sure you call me when you deliver them to the spot." He hung up the phone and watched the young server bring him an apple danish.

* * *

The pantry was three-quarters full this morning, more than likely because of the seasonable weather outside. Ms. Carla was helping a new girl named April serve breakfast, which consisted of oatmeal, milk, juice, and fruit. The people were quiet, knowing that Ms. Carla did not take kindly to loud chatter. Also helping, Rose poured fresh water into the glasses on the tables. Looking around at the men and women who ate at her pantry every morning, Carla stopped to admire the good work she had been allowed to do over the years. "Thank you, Lord, for giving me the strength to help those in need," she said quietly. As she helped April evenly divide the fruit into the plastic cups, a thunderous noise caused Carla to turn and grab her chest while April let out a scream. Everyone looked up as the main entry doors were being violently kicked open, and eight tall and muscular men walked into the pantry, led by Bucky. As three men covered the entrance door, five others made their way throughout the pantry, making sure no one escaped or got up from their seats. A cold and quiet fear had spread across the orange-painted pantry, where bright sunshine was spilling through the large windows. All of Bucky's men stood silently, holding automatic weapons at their sides. A few women, who had brought their children to the pantry to eat, began to shed tears as they sheltered and comforted their children, who were all terrified. Standing in the center of the room, Bucky smiled at the many faces that feared for their safety.

"Good morning, ladies and gentlemen. Please *do* be alarmed by the men that stand before you holding guns. I promise you that if anyone gets out of their seat and attempts to run, they will see their last bowl of oatmeal today. I give you my word, we will not be here for long and once we leave, you can carry on with your glamorous lives. So please just stay calm and this will be over in a moment."

Standing about six feet four inches tall, Bucky was wearing a black leather vest with nothing underneath. His huge arms were covered with tattoos of tigers and guns. He walked towards the large service table with the fresh oatmeal and cereal. Trying her best to hide her fear while leading her second family through this ordeal, Carla looked into Bucky's eyes not with defiance but with compassion. When he was just a few inches from the gray-haired woman he asked, "Are you Carla?"

She set the large oatmeal-stained wooden spoon on the table. "Yes, I am, young man," she answered, still giving comfort to a much-shaken April.

With a smile on his face, Bucky gently put one of his large arms around Carla's shoulder. "Carla, this will not take long. I just need to ask you a few questions in private. Is there a place where we can chat?"

Carla felt very nervous about the coldness in Bucky's touch, but she still continued to do her best in hiding her fear. "There is a coatroom right over there," she said, pointed to a green-colored room.

As Bucky led Carla to the room, April whimpered, "No, she didn't do anything. Why does she have to go back there?" Carla smiled at April and held her hand up in a gesture to show that everything would be fine.

Meanwhile, at the back of the pantry, Rose looked on in silence as one of the men stood directly to her left, holding a TEC-9 machine gun.Bucky slowly closed the door behind Carla and himself, and grabbed a metal chair so he could sit down while Carla remained standing.

"Carla, the first thing I want you to understand is that I am not one of those old-school cats who believes in respecting someone based on age and gender. So just because you are an old gray-haired woman, don't think for a fucking second I give a fuck about you. I am not here to learn how to bake cookies. I'm here for one reason and that is to find out where your good friend Sandra Lyte is hiding. Now, you have to understand that I am not leaving here without some information, so whatever useful info you give me will go a long way in ensuring not only your friends' safety but yours also."

Sitting with the chair turned backwards, Bucky removed a stick of gum from his vest and stuck it in his mouth, never removing it from the wrapper. "Sir, Sandra has not been here for a few months now and she never told me where she was going or staying so…"

Without letting her finish, Bucky quickly leapt out of his chair and pushed Carla violently into the coat rack, causing her to fall to the ground. He stood over her and spit the gum into Carla's face. Holding her chest, Carla struggled to catch her breath.

"I hope your heart is still in good condition because right now, lady, I am in a good mood, but you are not making this easy." Bucky reached down and grabbed Carla by one of her arms, forcing her to her feet and sitting her in the chair. Still breathing hard and fast, Carla, for the first time, had the look of fear in her eyes and Bucky could see it. "Where is Sandra, old woman?" Bucky asked again.

"Sir, please have mercy on me. I am not lying when I tell you she just volunteered her time. We never discussed personal matters."

Kneeling down to Carla, Bucky slowly rubbed his sausage-like fingers through her hair. "Is that your final answer?" he asked with a grin.

No longer able to hold back her tears, Carla began to sob. Twisting his head from side to side, Bucky, with the quickness of a rattlesnake, snapped his right fist on Carla's nose, breaking it and causing blood to spill from it. With tears filling her eyes, Carla's head snapped back and she almost fell from the chair, but Bucky prevented her from doing so. Her once-white apron was stained with blood.

"So, you really don't know anything, mama?" he asked.

Feeling as if her heart could give out at any moment, Carla looked up at the huge, smiling man and tried to regain her focus. "You are a piece of garbage. I promise you, God will make your soul burn in hell for what you have done." Letting her head slump back down, Carla remained silent.

Bucky was no longer smiling. He grabbed Carla by her hair and yanked her head up so she could look in his eyes. "Fuck you, old woman. My life is already hell and God can do no worse to me than I've already done to myself." Knocking Carla out of the chair and onto the floor, Bucky proceeded to kick her in the ribs with his steel-toe boots.

* * *

After a few moments, Bucky reappeared to the worried and frightened people, who still sat in silence. Upon seeing that he was alone and not with Carla, a few people started to cry. A man named Stanley, who was a retired veteran, slowly stood to his feet. "Where is Carla? What have you done to her?"

From behind, one of the gunmen smacked Stanley over the head, knocking him out cold. Little children started to cry and panic filled the pantry. Bucky took out a small photograph and started to scan the faces of the people like a hawk. Slowly moving his head from side to side, he brought it to a complete stop as he looked directly into the eyes of Rose.

"Come on over here, boo-boo," he said, smiling again. Rose looked around for help but got none from the frightened spectators. She got up slowly and began to cry as Bucky gently grabbed her by the hand and caressed her face with the gun he was holding.

"Don't cry, baby. Uncle Buck is going to take real good care of you. Just don't upset me, okay?" Looking at his watch, Bucky pointed to his men, who in turn harnessed their weapons.

"Okay, everyone, like I said earlier, if you all behaved, nobody would get hurt. As far as I can tell, only two people did not behave, that brother lying on the floor and your fearless fucking leader in the back. Therefore, without further ado, it's time for us to go. You better not leave your seats. I will have a person right outside looking in and he will shoot anyone who does not follow those rules. So good-bye, peasants, and enjoy your lumpy oatmeal." Squeezing Rose tightly by her slender shoulder, Bucky took the young woman out the pantry doors and his men followed.People still sat at their tables with concerned expressions on their faces, wondering what to do next. April looked towards the coatroom, then at the entrance doors, and then back at the others, who all remained still.

"I have to go and check on Ms. Carla, so stay in your seats," she told them.

A woman holding her two-year-old son whispered, "Ms. April, please, we don't know if that man was telling the truth about us being watched."

April shook her head at the woman. "You just stay in your seats. I'll be okay." Watching the door as she moved, April slowly made her way to the other side of the serving tables. She kept her eyes on the entrance doors and walked at a brisk pace until she reached the coatroom. Everyone continued to sit at their tables, and the man who was struck on the head began to regain consciousness. They all heard a faint scream from the coatroom as April discovered Carla's bloodied and lifeless body on the floor.

* * *

Some time had passed and the police were questioning some of the people who were inside the pantry. The paramedics rushed Carla into an ambulance on a stretcher, with April joining her. With the sound of the blaring sirens, the ambulance sped off as many people stood by the pantry crying loudly and wondering if their guardian angel would ever be the same again.

* * *

Pamela left the neighborhood 99-cent store and walked to her building, which was about a block and a half away. Being careful as she walked on the snow-covered ice, Pamela stayed close to the curb, never noticing the gray sedan that had been slowly moving alongside her. "Hi, Santiago," Pamela yelled at the man who owned the corner bodega. When she got closer to her building, she removed her keys with her sobriety-colored key holders from her pocket. The gray sedan pulled quickly in front of her building, coming to a screeching halt. Pamela stopped a few feet short of her courtyard and looked at the car. The doors quickly opened up and three large men wearing sunglasses jumped out, waving guns in their hands. The one named Sugar Bear led the charge towards Pamela, who dropped her bags and tried to run in the opposite direction.

"Somebody help me!" screamed Pamela. Sugar Bear ran up from behind her, grabbed her by her coat collar, and stuck a nickel-plated gun in her face.

"Bitch, if you scream again, I will blow your fucking brains out," he warned.

The two other men grabbed her and threw her into the waiting car. Sugar Bear looked around to see if they had been noticed. Not seeing any witnesses, he hurried into the driver's seat and took off down the street, heading to the club where Bucky awaited him.

* * *

In the basement of Doug's club, a small, poorly lit room reeked from the aroma of urine. The concrete floor was very cold and extremely damp. The room was no bigger than a cheap motel bathroom and a person standing six feet tall would have to bend down to walk inside. The lightbulb, which couldn't be any stronger than thirty-five watts, flickered, ready to burn out at any moment. Just below the paint-chipped ceiling, a water pipe dripped scalding hot water, one drop at a time, every five seconds. Inside this room, Rose Garden sat in a puddle of urine mixed with dirty water. Her mouth was battered and her left eye was swollen shut from the butt of Bucky's gun.

Rose's hands were tied in front of her with duct tape. Though her legs were free, she could barely walk on account of her right ankle, which was badly bruised from Bucky stomping on it a few hours earlier. Rose was shaking like a leaf and her stomach had been making rumbling noises since the moment they locked her inside the room. With her head slumped over into her chest, the young woman, just in her early twenties, made whimpering noises. Sobbing, "Please, just kill me, God; just kill me now," Rose waited for her prayers to be answered and grimaced with pain as the drops of scalding water continued to hit her back, creating a blister the size of a half-dollar.

Trying to ignore the pain of her ankle, Rose used every ounce of strength in her body to move a foot over to her right where the water no longer hit her back, but in the process, she badly scraped her knee on a small piece of glass. With a stinging sensation now coming from her knee, Rose gladly accepted the trade-off from the scalding water.

"Please God, just bring me to you. I cannot take anymore," pleaded Rose, who now sat up against the wall instead of on her knees. Closing her eyes, she began to rock her body back and forth. The flickering light was no more as it decided to quit and let darkness take over. Rose held her head up but saw nothing, so she continued to rock and cry, still hoping for the end to come. Shivering and shaking, she let out a quick scream as she felt a cold sensation on her neck. It was the breath of someone who smelled of rotting and burning flesh, which gave Rose hives all over her body.

"Hi, baby. How is Daddy's little girl?" the man who smelled like death asked. Slowly opening her eyes, Rose tried to scream but nothing came out. Her father, Butch, was kneeling about three inches away from her face.

He reached out and rubbed his daughter's face with his burnt and sticky, skinless hands. "Daddy misses his baby," he said with a smile. "Do you miss Daddy? I miss all of my children, especially you, baby." Slowly standing to his feet, Butch began to remove his clothes, revealing his charcoaled body. As his clothes came off, his remaining skin did as well, exposing his ribs and his pumping black heart. Now naked and standing over his daughter, who was unable to move, Butch smiled as he grabbed on to his smoldering penis, which fell from his body and into his hand.

"Daddy forgives you, baby. Just let daddy touch you one last time." Kneeling down to her, Butch opened his mouth and stuck out his black tongue, aiming it at Rose's mouth. As he got closer and closer, Rose let out a loud scream and smacked her father in the face, knocking his laughing head off his shoulders as his hands still reached out to her. Waving her bound hands wildly, Rose awakened to the flickering light in the empty room that still smelled like urine. Her entire body covered in sweat, the young woman could only continue to cry.

* * *

What felt like hours had only been thirty minutes. Rose was losing sensation in one of her legs as it lost circulation. Her mouth was completely dry and her stomach was aching tremendously from hunger. Her eyes widened as she saw a shadow from underneath the door and heard the shuffling of feet getting closer to the room. Though frightened, a sick joy overtook Rose's mind as she realized that this could be the end and she would be with her mother again. She was sweating and shaking, but she never took her eyes off the door as she heard the sound of keys. She heard the deadbolt lock turning and the door handle being pulled down. As the door opened, light from the hallway entered and Rose closed her one good eye, trying to adjust to the brightness. As she looked through the opening of her squinting eyelid, Rose made out a tall figure, which was obviously a man, and another figure that moved like a person just learning how to walk. A thunderous voice broke the silence of the tiny room, almost bursting Rose's eardrums.

"Hey, bitch. I brought you some company!" Still not able to make out any faces, Rose let out a yell as someone fell forward, landing on her sleeping leg. Straining her only good eye to gain focus, Rose could now see who was lying on her sore leg.

"Pamela? Pamela!" Rose yelled. Pamela was not bound in any way, but she was badly beaten throughout her body, probably for the same reason that had caused the assault on Rose—refusing to give any information about Sandra.

Reaching down with her bound hands, Rose gently felt for Pamela's swollen face and tried to rub it. She was aching and feeling weak but did her best to pull Pamela up into her arms, inch by inch, until she was able to cuddle her head and rock her gently. She heard Pamela trying to say something, so she held her ear as close as possible to Pamela's mouth and listened carefully.

"Don't be afraid, boo-boo. We ain't dead yet. Let's stay strong, okay?"

Looking at the battered and weak woman, Rose answered, "Okay, I will be strong. I promise."

* * *

Doug pulled up outside the club in his newly repaired truck. Bucky was waiting for him out front.

"We got both of them, baby, just like you asked," Bucky said as the two men greeted each other.

"Very good, partner. Now it's time to use the bait to catch the big fish. Once I catch that fish I'm going to fillet her ass for fucking with me." The two men laughed and entered the club.

Chapter Thirty

Do You Play Chess, Sandra?

On Monday morning, Sandra put on her coat and hid the discs in the waistline of her pants. It took almost ten days, but Sandra had finally gotten through to Maria Copper's assistant, Gail, and convinced her that she had something that would interest them very much. She didn't totally disclose what she had, but after about an hour on the phone, she had intrigued the assistant. Sandra would meet Gail at the loading dock of Channel 4 News. Then Gail would lead her to an unspecified location so she could explain what she possessed. If what Sandra possessed had anything that warranted news coverage, then and only then would she receive a one-time opportunity to met Maria Copper. Sandra and Gail exchanged cell phone numbers and agreed to speak again only when Sandra was five minutes away from the agreed meeting place. Sandra grabbed her keys and was headed for the door when her cell phone began to ring.

* * *

Inside Doug's office, a sweaty and trembling Pamela sat in a chair with a sawed-off shotgun held at her temple. Directly across from her, Rose's feet and hands were tied and her head was tilted to the side by a man holding a brand-new thirty-six-inch machete to her throat. Standing on the other side of Pamela, Doug held a cell phone to her mouth and instructed her on exactly what she was to say.

After the third ring, Pamela sobbed into the phone, "Hello, Sandra, this is Pamela. Can you please hear me out?" With his ear now to the phone, Doug could hear an upset Sandra on the other end asking Pamela what was going on. With her head nudged by the shotgun, Pamela sobbed heavily and continued, "Sandra, they have Rose and me tied up with guns and knives to our heads, threatening to kill us if you do not return the discs. Please, Sandra, help us; they say if you return the discs, they will let us go unharmed, but if you do not return them in forty-eight hours, we are dead. Sandra, we are so scared. Please help…"

Doug grabbed the phone from Pamela. To his delight, Sandra was crying hysterically on the other end. Looking at his two hostages, Doug said into the phone, "Okay, bitch, you know who this is and you know what I want, right? You almost got me a few weeks back on that Sunday morning…and those movies are classics. I had them sent to my father at his retirement home up in Westchester where he enjoys them with the rest of his elderly companions. However, I am not here to shoot the shit with you, Sandra. I want my fucking discs back, so let me explain the current scene to you. Your good friend and former neighbor who couldn't mind her fucking business is sitting in a puddle of piss with a shotgun pointed at her head by a friend of mine who shakes when he doesn't have his morning coffee. To my left, your little friend Rose—the one I had gang-banged on film—has a machete to her throat that, on my signal, my partner will use to take her head off like a hot knife slicing through butter. Finally, boo-boo, there's your friend Carla. You know her, right? Well, I had her fucked up and now she is in the hospital, so let me ask you, baby…Do you still think I am bullshitting about what I want?"

* * *

Sandra sat silently on her bed holding the discs in her hands as she listened to Doug. Already ten minutes off her schedule to meet Gail, she pictured her friends being brutally murdered if she didn't do as told.

"Okay, Doug, you win, all right? You just tell me when and where. But please, promise me you…""No baby, you get no promises or guarantees from me, you understand? The only thing you had better hope for is that you have my discs Wednesday morning, and I will call you with the location. Sandra, let me tell you something, okay. If you do not put my discs in my hand on Wednesday, guess what, boo-boo? You can have them, because I will send your two friends' heads to that fucking soup kitchen so that those animals who eat there can try something new and exotic. Therefore, Sandra, if you have any plans on contacting the police or going in another direction from what I tell you, then your friends will know just how much you cared about them the second before I kill them. I suggest your phone stay on and remain fully charged, Ms. Thickness, because I will be calling your ass very soon. Later."

* * *

Dropping her phone to the floor, Sandra held her head, which now throbbed with pain. Feeling anger, despair, and confusion, she could almost feel the end coming. Doug had her pinned in a corner and she didn't know how to escape. Feeling like a mouse in a maze that has no exit at the end, Sandra decided not to fool herself any longer; on Wednesday the end would be here. In her mind, she had put up a good battle and she hoped her children could someday forgive her, but this monster was just too evil to overcome. Sandra also realized that the chances were slim that Doug would ever let Pamela and Rose go once he had his discs. It ate at her mind that once again, because of her weakness, people she loved would die. "Just forget about it, Sandra," she thought to herself.

As she sat on the floor and looked at the dark cloudy day outside her window, Sandra could hear the door open as the footsteps walked from the back of her mind until they reached the front. She pounded her head in an attempt to send "the voice" back home, but to Sandra's disappointment, it didn't work.

"Don't you dare crumble, Sandra. Doug is stupid and egotistical. Just take some time to use your mind to recall everything he said to you a few moments ago. You have two days before you must return the discs for the slim possibility of saving your friends; however, you have one day to think about his words, which could possibly turn the tide back in your favor. But you must focus. I am leaving you at this time to think alone, but remember, I am always watching. Focus, Sandra. You can gain control of the board; you just have to focus."

The sweat on her forehead transferred to her hands as Sandra held her head and listened as the footsteps in her mind faded away. Using her bed as support, she lifted herself up and walked over to her window where she recalled every word spoken to her by Doug. Knowing that meeting with Gail was no longer an option, Sandra focused on regaining the upper hand, no matter how impossible that seemed. She walked over to her nightstand, pulled out the drawer, and removed a pencil and a piece of paper to transcribe every word from the phone conversation.

* * *

It had been two hours now and it was close to noon. Sandra continued to study her notes. As much as it hurt, she had pushed the terrifying images of Pamela and Rose out of her mind as she worked to decipher

Doug's speech. Feeling defeated and very frustrated, Sandra sighed, letting the paper fall to the floor as she gave up all hope. She had yet to find anything in Doug's words with great significance. She looked at the paper again and quickly sat up in her bed. The clue she had been looking for was staring her right in the face.

"Yes, can you locate the nearest car rental company in my area, please?" While on the phone with the operator, Sandra exchanged her address for the information that she needed. To Sandra's disappointment, the rental company informed her that she would need a driver's license and a credit card. With her credit card maxed out, no rental agency would help her. Through persistence, Sandra finally got in touch with a car service that charged by the hour to drive to distant locations. Feeling more energized than she had in a very long time, Sandra stopped in the middle of her kitchenette and recalled what she had said to herself a few months ago: *Do not become like Doug.*

The statement echoed inside her head repeatedly. Doug was a monster who was beyond repair, and Sandra had to consider if she wanted to cross over to that side, because it would change her life forever. Then something popped up in her head; it was from a detective show she had watched a while ago. A detective in search of a murderer said something that was a little strange but now made a lot of sense: "If you want to catch a monster, sometimes you have to become a monster." Knowing that she wanted desperately to put away Doug and the men responsible for her tragic loss, Sandra decided that only for this moment would she become that monster.

* * *

On Tuesday evening at 7:00 p.m., Sandra got inside a shiny black Cadillac CTS sedan that would cost her eighty-five dollars an hour. Reaching over to the driver, she handed him a one-hundred-dollar bill and said, "Besides what I am paying your company for their services tonight, if you can turn your head to a few things that may happen, there will be another one of those for you when this is over." The driver, a white man in his late forties, turned around and tried his best not to look at the horrible-looking scar on Sandra's neck. "Ma'am, I can't make any promises, but I have seen some crazy shit go on in that backseat. As long as you don't cross those lines, I don't see a problem in turning my head tonight." Giving the driver a smile, Sandra sat back in her seat and enjoyed the ride. After forty-five minutes, the car came to a stop in a parking lot. "Sir, I should not be long, so if you like, you can keep the car running," Sandra said as she gathered her belongings. The gray-haired driver looked back at Sandra and just nodded his head in acknowledgement as she exited the car.

* * *

As she looking around the large waiting area adorned with beautiful paintings and sculptures, Sandra's anger intensified. She couldn't figure out why Doug showed so much love and care for a man that he claimed never loved him. At this point, though, it didn't matter anymore because the day of reckoning was about to begin. Letting a smile come across her face, Sandra walked up to the reception desk where a black woman in her fifties was sitting.

"Good evening. My name is Sandra Lyte and I know it's late, but I have been cleared for a visit with Fred Gunner. He's not expecting me and I would really like to surprise him. If you like, you can confirm with Ms. Celeste Davis. I believe she's the head supervisor."

Sandra sat in the cafeteria, watching an orange-haired elderly woman sitting alone eating jello. The cafeteria was immaculately clean and was pleasingly decorated with the residents' craftwork.

As she moved on to admiring the luster of the furniture and the floors, she was startled by a deep, hoarse voice. "Who is here to see me?" asked Fred Gunner, who was sporting a gray sweat suit.

Regaining her composure, Sandra calmly turned to Fred with a smile on her face. "Good evening, Mr. Gunner, that would be me. My name is Sandra Lyte."

Still standing at the entrance of the cafeteria, Fred looked at Sandra with curiosity on his face, trying to figure out who she was. "Why are you here and what do you want?" he asked in a nasty tone.

Knowing how crucial this opportunity was, Sandra remained cool and tried to ease the tension between them. "Mr. Gunner, I mean you no harm. I'm your son's girlfriend and the mother of his children, Kareem and Chaka. I believe they visited you a short time before Christmas."

Fred seemed to be interested in what she had to say. He entered the cafeteria and took a seat next to her. "You are the one that my son had those damn kids with?" Fred asked.

Starting from her toes, rage filled Sandra's body as she continued to smile at Fred. "That's right, Mr. Gunner. Those are my kids, but I am not here to discuss them. I'm here to take you to see your son because he was injured and is home in bed. He sent me here because he wants to see you tonight, but we must make a stop before we go see him."

Fred pulled a pack of cigarettes from his pocket, lit one, and inhaled, blowing the smoke in Sandra's face. Still smiling at the old man, Sandra maintained her cool. "Mr. Gunner, there is no need to be rude to me. I am just here to get you to your son. If you have no desire to see him, that's fine; I will just gather myself together and leave." Sandra got up from the table and began to walk away.

"Hold on one damn minute, okay?" Fred demanded. Sandra turned around and looked at the man she perceived as Dr. Frankenstein. "I got a lot of pull in this motherfucker," he said. "I can leave here whenever I want. So, you know what, I'll take your little trip to see my son. That son of a bitch is late with my allowance. So, Sheila, or whatever the fuck your name is, let's go."

Nodding her head in agreement, Sandra responded calmly. "I will give you some time to gather a few things and clear things up with the supervisor, then we can leave. I have a car outside waiting for us as we speak." Within the next thirty minutes, Fred was ready to leave with Sandra. As he said, he seemed to have a lot of pull because no one asked questions as he and Sandra walked out of the front doors into the waiting car. Sandra opened the door for Fred, got in after him, and told the driver where they were going.

* * *

It was now 10:30 p.m. and Sandra's cell phone was down to the last bar on the battery indicator, but she still hadn't received a phone call from Doug. She retrieved her charger and plugged her phone into a wall outlet, making sure her signal was strong and that the phone was charging while Fred looked around her apartment as if he were standing in a garbage wasteland.

"Damn, you stay here in this hell hole? Where are your kids? Moreover, when are we going to see my son? I need my damn money."

Sandra walked over to the stove, turned on the kettle, and prepared to make two cups of tea. "My kids are with my mother until I can get a bigger place for us. Your son and I decided we needed to go our own ways but stay friends for the kids' sake. Mr. Gunner, I always have a cup of tea at about this time. Will you please join me for a cup? Then I promise we will go see Doug."

Fred put his foot on Sandra's dinette table and grabbed a magazine that was on the table. "Yeah, I don't give a shit. Make me a cup, and make sure you put honey in mine, you hear?"

With her back turned to Fred, Sandra clutched the spoon she was using with all of her strength. "No problem, Mr. Gunner…tea with honey coming right up in one minute." She reached up into the cabinet and grabbed two tea bags, honey, and a plastic bag that contained a yellow powder. She quickly looked behind her to make sure Fred wasn't looking at her as she opened the plastic bag and poured its contents into the cup that she would serve Fred.

"Damn, woman, how long does it take for you to give somebody a damn cup of tea? I see why Doug kicked your ass to the curb." Sandra walked over to the dinette table and put the cup of tea in front of Fred with a smile on her face. "You got any cookies or crackers?" he asked. Sandra walked back to the cabinet, grabbed a box of saltine crackers, and gave them to Fred, who was sipping on his cup of tea. As Sandra watched him enjoy his beverage, she took a seat directly in front of him and began to drink her tea. She smiled as Fred ate his crackers while rubbing his head.

"Damn, my head is killing me all of a sudden. Shit…" Fred complained.

Sandra put on a face of concern. "Oh my goodness, Fred. Would you like to lie across my bed? Come on, I'll help you." Sandra grabbed Fred by the waist and helped him to his feet. She gently laid him on the bed, taking off his shoes and positioning him facedown with his head on the pillow.

* * *

It was now 11:47 p.m. and Sandra sat on her bed, totally exhausted from the twenty-five minute workout with Fred Gunner. While the old man slept like a log on her bed, she had used some old sheets to make him a bed inside her tub. He weighed close to one hundred and eighty pounds, so it took Sandra every ounce of strength she could muster to drag Fred from the bed to the bathroom and put him inside the tub. She had propped him up against the back of the tub and did her best to stabilize his head. Once that was done, she gently handcuffed Fred's wrists and ankles; then she blindfolded him so he couldn't figure out were he was. Finally, for good measure, she duct-taped his mouth, making sure to cut a thin slit along the tape so that he could breathe but not scream.

She also duct-taped his thighs together to prevent him from walking. Before leaving the bathroom, Sandra checked her medicine cabinet and confirmed that she had more sleeping-beauty powder and a needle; she knew that the next time would have to be by injection. As she sat on her bed doing her best not to fall asleep, Sandra's arms ached like hell. She wanted to keep the phone near her in case it rang. She was dead tired and hanging on by a thread. Then she said to herself, "Get up and help your friends! They have guns and knives held on them. Get up and wait for that call." Her feet hit the floor and she stood and stretched her thick, firm body. She almost jumped right out of her skin at the sound of her phone ringing, its blue light illuminating after the second ring. She walked over to her nightstand and answered on the third ring.

* * *

It was midnight and Doug was sitting in his office inside his club, tossing cold French fries at his exhausted-looking hostages. Pamela and Rose were gagged and bound, sitting in chairs. "Okay, bitch, get a pencil and pad because I'm only saying this once. On Tremont and Webster Avenue, right across the street from Texas Fried Chicken, there's the old club where I took you a couple of times called Paradise. At exactly six in the morning you will walk through those doors, and I mean not a minute later. You will go to the back where the bar is and meet me there with my discs. When you give me my discs, I will give you your two friends and allow you to leave in a cab.

"Sandra, if you play any games with me or if I get the scent of cops or anyone else that should not be at this meeting, I'm walking out of the club and you can watch your friends' brains being blown from their heads. Do you understand me? Good. Fuck you very much, and I hope you screw this up tomorrow because it has always been a pleasure killing people you love."

Doug slammed the phone down on the receiver and looked at Pamela and Rose, who were sobbing. "I want both of you to think of a happy moment you spent with Sandra, because it will be your last. A few minutes after six this morning, she'll be dead, and by seven I will make you two watch each other get wasted. How's that?" asked Doug.

Rose continued to sob but Pamela now stared at Doug with a cold look of hatred that Doug could feel. Not liking her attitude, he calmly got up and walked over to Pamela, quickly hitting her with the back of his hand and busting her lip open.

"Who the fuck you staring at?" he asked. Pamela was obviously unable to answer. "I thought so," Doug mocked her as he exited his office to get a drink.

* * *

As she reviewed the instructions Doug had given her, Sandra tried to block the realization that she could possibly die tomorrow. After a few days, the landlord would come for his rent money and find Fred Gunner crying in the tub like a baby; and after that, a very tainted picture of her would emerge. She would possibly die a horrific death and still fail her children and her friends.

"No, push that bullshit out of your head. You will think like a monster and more importantly, you will think like Doug," Sandra said to herself as she got up from the chair. She went to the bathroom to check on Fred and to retrieve a bottle of rubbing alcohol.

* * *

It was 2:25 a.m. and Sandra had used almost the whole bottle of rubbing alcohol on her entire body. Because of it, she felt much better physically then she had earlier. Having checked on Fred, she was satisfied that he was doing well based on his breathing and the way he slowly moved his head when she stuck a feather in his ear. Sandra hoped Fred would sleep long enough, because the last thing she needed was to hear him whooping and hollering.

Out her window, Sandra could see how bright the sky was because of the full moon. For some reason, she felt compelled to do something that she had not done since her first week in New York almost eight years ago, and that was to pray. She didn't have the faith she had possessed many years ago, but she figured this was an opportune time. So on her knees, Sandra prayed quietly to her God and asked not for revenge or justice but simply for strength.

Chapter Thirty-one

Meet Me at the Club

Out across the sky, the sun was just beginning to send its rays of light across the borough of the Bronx. No businesses were serving the public and only a few cars drove by in either direction. With the cold wind hitting her face, Sandra checked her watch and saw that she was on time, just as Doug always liked. As she looked up at the old club, Sandra couldn't help but remember the many times Doug had taken her there for nights of dancing and drinking. The cold wind once again hit her face, causing it to freeze briefly and snapping Sandra back into reality, because beyond those doors her destiny awaited. The discs were inside her bag—Kareem and Chaka had used their own money to buy it for her a year ago for Mother's Day—and she held on to it tightly. With her free hand she grabbed on to a thick piece of cold chain that usually kept the doors of the club locked but had now been unhitched for her convenience or demise. Sandra pulled the doors open and entered.

The door slammed hard behind her and Sandra looked around the club, which was dusty and full of spider webs. Many of the windows were missing panes, which explained why it was so cold inside. In front of Sandra were burnt tables and chairs that surrounded a bar that served no more. Clutching her bag tightly, she had the urge to turn around and walk back out the door to save her own life, but that was not on the agenda today. The plan today was to take accountability for herself and to help those who needed her. So putting her best foot forward, Sandra walked towards the back of the club, trying to see clearly through all of the dust that filled the room.

She reached the back of the club where the women's and men's bathrooms were, but Sandra didn't see or hear anything but her heart pounding inside her chest. Taking a deep breath, she broke the silence. "Doug, I am here. Where are you?" she asked, and her echo questioned two more times. Not getting an answer, Sandra spoke a little louder. "Is anybody here?" Still not getting an answer, she clutched her bag even tighter and began slowly walking back towards the entrance doors, making sure she didn't bump into anything.

Sandra stopped suddenly and grabbed her chest so her heart would not jump out of it. A tall figure had emerged from behind one of the large columns and was walking towards the doors. Watching in fear and silence, Sandra listened as the figure grabbed and fondled the chains that weaved through the doors. She heard a loud clicking sound and it was clear to her that whoever was at the door was locking her inside. "Who is that?" Sandra asked with a quiver in her voice.

As she backed up a little, an old beer bottle by her foot caused her to roll backwards, lose her balance, and fall on her backside. Never taking her eyes off the dark figure that was now facing her, Sandra used her sore arms to help her quickly get back on her feet. She brushed off her pants and her hands. "Listen, Doug, is that you?" she demanded. "I am here like you asked, so why are you locking the doors?" Deep down inside, she knew the answer to that question, but she figured she would ask anyway, hoping to invoke an answer in order to make out who was speaking. Still looking straight at her company, Sandra's chest expanded larger and faster as the figure began to take his first steps towards her.

She wanted to run and dive through one of the windows, but Sandra could neither run nor jump because she was scared stiff as the figure's footsteps got closer and louder. The sun was now sending more rays through the windows and Sandra had to shield her eyes with her free hand, as the light limited her vision. She lowered her hand and was now clear about one thing: Doug did not show. Standing in front of her was Doug's henchman Bucky.

With her mouth halfway open and her body dwarfed by the man's size, Sandra managed to squeak, "Where is Doug? He told me he would be here." Not saying a word, Bucky slowly unbuttoned his long leather trench coat, one button at a time, never taking his eyes off Sandra. He removed his coat from his body and was wearing nothing but a leather vest. Sandra examined the large man from head to toe and saw that on the left side of his waist, he was wearing a holster that contained an eight-inch billy club. He reached inside his vest pocket and removed a stick of gum that he put inside his mouth. Looking at her while feeling his club, Bucky asked, "Sandra, do you have that package for Doug?"

"Who are you and where is Doug? This was not part of the agreement and neither was locking me in here."

Bucky blew and popped a bubble before responding, "Bitch, I'm only going to ask you one more time politely, and if you don't answer my question, I will come over there and smash your fucking skull in, have sex with your dead corpse, and just check for myself. Do you have Doug's package?"

For the second time in her life, Sandra smelled the stench of death in the air and it was consuming her mentally. She was finally grasping the reality of the situation: When she turned the discs over to this sick bastard, not only would he kill her, but he would also do what only a few perverted minds in this world would. Before Sandra would just give up and let that happen, she knew a stand would have to be made.

She reached down inside her bag, removed the Ziploc bag of discs, and held them above her head so Bucky could see them. "Yes, I have them right here," she answered.

Looking through the rays of sun, Bucky saw the shiny discs above Sandra's head. "Very good, now give them to me so we can get this over with," he said.

Sandra looked past the large man and at the chained door. "Listen, this is not right. Doug promised that my friends would be…"

Before Sandra could finish, Bucky picked up an old barstool and tossed it at Sandra angrily, striking her left leg. She screamed in pain and almost fell to the ground.

"Bitch, enough with the pleading and questions. Just give me the damn discs! I promise I will make this as quick and as painless as possible."

Holding her leg while her eyes filled with fear, Sandra put the plastic bag back inside her canvas bag, hopped to a broken window, and yelled for help. Because of the height of the window and the noise of the cars coming and going on Webster Avenue, her screams went unheard. She quickly turned and faced Bucky, who was now approaching. Sandra limped over to a flight of stairs that led to the upper level of the club. Letting out a loud and hearty laugh, Bucky slowly walked toward the stairs in pursuit of his prey.

"Go ahead, baby, make it interesting…it's cool. Your fate still remains the same; you will die and get screwed all within the same minute." As he walked up the stairs, Bucky removed the billy club from its holster. Holding a piece of broken wood that she found on the floor, Sandra quietly hid behind what used to be the DJ booth. She heard Bucky's loud footsteps come up the final few steps, and she gripped the piece of wood tightly with both hands, hoping she would get a chance to strike Bucky when he was not expecting it. Now on the second level, Bucky surveyed the floor, taking notice of all of the possible hiding places.

"Come out, come out, wherever you are, Sandra!" Bucky yelled. He picked up worn-out chairs and tossed them behind the bar and towards the jukebox. Sweating profusely, Sandra remained in her crouched position, waiting for her opportunity to strike. With dust stirring throughout the floor, she did her best not to sneeze or make any sudden noises. She held her head upward and wondered why she no longer heard him, because Bucky was a heavy man wearing boots. Trying to figure out where he could be, Sandra slowly and quietly peeped around the bottom of the booth. She pulled her braids from in front of her face and bit her lip, forcing herself not to scream as she found herself face-to-face with the back of Bucky's black combat boots. Not paying any attention to her now bleeding lip, Sandra slowly lifted her arms to strike him in the back of the leg when her face turned to pure red. There was no one in the boots. Shaking uncontrollably, she crawled backwards until her backside bumped into Bucky, who had quietly entered the booth from the opposite side, bootless. Letting out what had to be the loudest scream Bucky had ever heard, Sandra tried to make it to her feet; but he grabbed her by her braids and violently yanked her up from the floor.

"Where you going, baby? Were you going to stab me with that?" Bucky asked. Shaking and sweating, Sandra couldn't get anything out of her mouth, so she just shook her head no while letting go of the piece of wood. Still holding her tightly by the braids, Bucky was now inches away from Sandra's face and he began to sniff around her neck. He looked at her, slowly released her hair, and smiled. Still shaking, Sandra somehow managed to take one step away from Bucky, but that was all she managed because Bucky backslapped her so hard that she flew over the DJ booth and crashed onto the floor.

"You okay, baby? I'll come help you," he tormented as he slowly walked around the booth. He reached down and lifted a moaning Sandra off the ground by one of her arms. Looking at her with amusement, he flung her across the room, causing her to crash into a bunch of stacked chairs. On the floor and barely moving, Sandra reached for her back, which was throbbing with immense pain. Using her heels, she tried to crawl away from her approaching assailant, who continued to toy with her.

"Come here, baby, and get some more pain before I screw your dead ass," he said as he watched her crawl. Then he removed the billy club and hit Sandra across her back, causing her to scream without any sound ever leaving her mouth. Now face down on the floor, Sandra remained motionless, trying to take in little bits of oxygen. Satisfied that she was not going anywhere, Bucky calmly walked back over to the booth, retrieved his boots, and put them back on his feet. He looked behind the booth, grabbed Sandra's bag, and located the Ziploc bag that contains the discs. He glanced at Sandra, who was moving slightly but not enough to warrant any concern, then grabbed his cell phone and called Doug.

"Yo, dog, it's me. Listen, I got the package and I'm watching her lie flat on her face as we speak. Yeah, okay. I'll do her as soon as we get off the phone and then I'll call you back to let you know that it's over. I'll just put her body in the bathroom and chain the entrance back up when I'm done…Don't worry about that. My cousin is the supervisor, so when this place is demolished, he'll make sure all is cool. Okay, listen…let me get this over with and I'll call you back in a few so you can take care of those two on your side. Okay, dog…later." He hung up the phone and put it back inside his vest pocket. Then he walked over to Sandra, who had painfully turned on her side. Bucky shook his head with a grin on his face as Sandra managed to sit up and stare him in the eye.

"You know what, Sandra? I will say this about you, you have a lot of heart, baby. Too bad it has to end, though." Reaching down, Bucky grabbed Sandra by the collar of her coat and proceeded to drag her to a wall. The knees of Sandra's pants tore as they scraped against old broken glass bottles. Once at the wall, Bucky slammed her against it, causing Sandra to bang her head. Still maintaining her consciousness, she looked over at the discs that Bucky left on the table. Grabbing her by the throat, Bucky lifted Sandra two feet off the ground so that her feet dangled in the air and her eyes met with his. With his large black hands wrapped around her throat, Bucky squeezed slowly, causing Sandra to grasp for air and kick her feet frantically.

"Don't fight it, baby. It will be over very soon," Bucky said. Feeling queasy, Sandra gagged and spit into Bucky's face. She could see Kareem and Chaka from a distance getting closer, and her eyes were becoming bloodshot. With her last ounce of strength, Sandra reached up with her right hand and sliced Bucky under his left arm, between his armpit and his biceps, with a very sharp piece of glass that she had managed to pick up.

"Shit, what the fuck!" cried Bucky as he quickly dropped Sandra to the floor. Coughing uncontrollably while trying to regain oxygen in her body, Sandra watched a now panic-stricken Bucky stagger on his feet.

"Bitch, how the fuck did you just cut me?" he demanded. As the blood increasingly poured from his body, Bucky walked towards Sandra with bad intentions but fell about three feet short and landed on his knees, still holding his arm. Kneeling in a pool of his own blood, Bucky was losing his wits as he keeled over, mumbling, "Kill you bit…" He fell flat on his face, taking three last gasps of air before dying on the floor.

Sandra leaned against a column, barely able to move. She willed herself to stand on her two feet while giving support to her aching back. She looked down on her victim, then turned away and walked over to the table, grabbed the discs, and put them back inside her duffel bag. As she passed a cracked and dusty mirror that hung on the wall, Sandra looked at herself for a moment. She was running her hands through her braids when the voice returned from the back of her mind.

"You fought and you survived. Now you must hurry and get the hell out of here. You can't go through the front, so check for a back entrance or, as much as it will hurt, look for a bathroom window. Also, take his wallet and his billy club; they will be your trophies to remember this battle. Most importantly, take his cell phone. You'll know why soon enough. Hurry Sandra, the rent is due and you don't want that nosey-ass landlord to go in the apartment and find Fred, who more than likely is kicking and screaming like the bitch that he is. Pull yourself together and get out now!" said the voice. Then the footsteps faded away into the back of her mind once again.

More determined than ever, Sandra pushed the pain out of her mind and walked over to Bucky. She checked his pockets, finding his keys, wallet, and cell phone. She stood over his body and stared at the large man for about three seconds before putting all his possessions and the billy club in her canvas bag. Sandra hurried to the back of the club and looked for an exit. She turned to her right and saw a stack of chairs in front of a wall. Above the chairs, she made out a barely legible, dirty sign that read "EXIT." She rested her bag on the floor and steadily removed the chairs, one by one. With her children and her two friends on her mind, Sandra started to toss the chairs behind her with a little more gusto. With about fifteen more chairs in front of her, she could see a metal bar that she hoped would open the door. Moving five more chairs, enough to give her a path, Sandra grabbed her bag and put it on her bruised shoulder. Taking one deep breath, Sandra whispered, "Please open," and with every ounce of strength she had left, she pushed the door open, allowing brisk air and sunshine to engulf her face. Now with tears beginning to fall down her face, all Sandra could do was look up to the blue sky and say, "Thank you and please forgive me." Letting the door close behind her, Sandra looked both ways and saw a gas station about thirty feet away. Her pants and coat were filthy and torn, but that didn't faze her. What was important was that she was alive. She quickly limped towards the gas station where a Spanish man was filling up his cab.

Sandra walking over to him and managed to put a smile on her face before tapping him on the shoulder. "Good morning, sir. You working this morning?"

"Not right now. I'm going to breakfast."

Sandra removed a fifty-dollar bill from her pocket and flashed it in front of his face. "How about if I buy you breakfast?"

The man looked at his watch, then back at Sandra. He returned the gasoline pump back to the holder and nodded his head towards the car.

"Thank you," Sandra said with a smile, and then painfully slid into the backseat of the vehicle. As the car rolled away from the station and headed north on Webster Avenue, Sandra looked at the club until it was out of her sight. She leaned her head back and thought to herself, *No more tears,* as she headed home.

* * *

Having paid her rent, Sandra walked down to her apartment. Her watch read 7:35 a.m., which seemed almost impossible when she thought about all she had been through this morning. As she reached for her keys, Sandra followed her instincts and took out her new billy club, just in case Fred had miraculously escaped. She turned the keys inside the locks and slowly opened the door to her apartment. She stuck her head inside and saw that everything was the same as she had left it, so she entered. Once inside, she slowly opened the bathroom door and saw that the shower curtains were still drawn around the tub the way she had left them. She walked over with the billy club in her hand and slowly pulled back the shower curtains. There lay Fred Gunner, sweating, frightened, and smelling like urine. The elder Gunner turned his head towards Sandra and began thrashing about and mumbling under the duct tape that covered his mouth.

"Calm down, Fred. This will be over soon. I promise," Sandra said before walking out of the bathroom. She returned with a glass of water and a steak knife. Closing the door behind her, she removed the blindfold, cut the duct tape away from Fred's mouth, and gave him some water.

He took three large gulps and spat the water in her face. "You fucking bitch," he yelled, "you better let me go or I'll…"

"Or you'll what?" Sandra dared him, putting the steak knife to his throat. "You better shut your damn mouth because you don't have any idea what type of man you spawned, so you better not upset me." As she wiped the water from her face, Sandra heard a phone ringing. She left the bathroom and headed to the kitchen where she'd left her bag. She reached inside, grabbed Bucky's phone, and answered it on the fourth ring.

"Hello? No, Doug, you motherfucker, this is not Bucky. He won't be making it back to see you."

Doug stood in his office with his mouth wide open while Pamela and Rose discretely paid close attention to his every word. Trying to figure out what to say, Doug stumbled over his words. "Fuck you, Sandra," he spewed. "I have these two bitches right here and as soon as I hang up this phone, their asses are dead. You hear me!"

Without losing her cool, Sandra calmly listened to Doug as she walked back to the bathroom. She sat on the toilet seat and put the steak knife to Fred's throat. "Before you do that, Doug, I want you to say hello to somebody first, okay?"

Putting the phone to Fred's mouth, Sandra motioned for Fred to speak.

"Doug, come get me, son. She's crazy! She's gonna kill me!"

Sandra pulled the phone away from Fred with a fierce look on her face. "How much do you really love your punk-ass daddy?""Daddy? Please don't hurt my father!" Doug pleaded. Shaking, he quickly looked over at Pamela and Rose, who were staring at him with a little less fear on their faces. "Sandra, please do not hurt my father!"

Listening to the mighty Doug plead and whine like a little baby only gave Sandra more hope. "Oh, fuck you and your daddy. You just shut the fuck up and listen—and I mean listen closely—because I am only saying this once… and his life depends on it."

Chapter Thirty-two

The End of a Relationship

It was noon and Sandra had done the best she could in replenishing her body and mind. Having washed her body over the kitchen sink, bandaged her knees, and taken three extra-strength Tylenol caplets, she prepared to see Doug for the first time since Christmas Day and to fight for her friends' freedom. The meeting place Sandra had chosen was a newly renovated housing complex on the south side of the Bronx. Over the years she had become quite friendly with two of the security guards—they used to be homeless and had frequented the pantry back then; and now they would be the ones to let them into the complex. As far as the guards knew, Sandra and her guests would just be meeting to get a first-hand look at the new apartments.

The rules were simple: When the three women entered a cab, Doug would get his father and the discs. Sandra had explained to him that if he showed up with anyone, she would destroy his discs and slash his father's throat, just as he had attempted to have done to her.

Sandra had purchased a used wheelchair to transport Fred, and she had given him another injection fifteen minutes ago. She removed his handcuffs, sat him in the wheelchair, and rolled him to the door. She planned to put the handcuffs back on once they arrived at the complex. She had told Doug to meet her there at three o'clock, but she intended to be there two hours earlier.

While putting on her coat and grabbing her bag, Sandra's mind was not on the dangerous meeting that could blow up in her face or the realization that today could be the last day of her life. No, those things didn't enter her mind because Sandra wouldn't let them. She felt in her mind and soul that nothing was going to stop her from saving Pamela and Rose, not even Doug.

What was on her mind at this moment was how painful it was going to be wheeling Fred up the alleyway of her building. Knowing how steep the walkway was and how bad her arms ached, she would have to ask the cab driver to assist her to get him inside the cab. She unlocked the door and wheeled a drugged, unconscious Fred into the hallway. As she pushed the wheelchair to daylight, she could hear the sound of a car horn blowing.

* * *

It was now 1:00 p.m. and Sandra was pushing Fred across the large courtyard and eyeing the kids on the playground. None of them would ever have the chance to play with two of the happiest and most lovable children in the world: Kareem and Chaka. Determined not to let her emotions overcome her, Sandra quickly pushed the thought out of her mind. She was now about forty yards from building D, where she would have a bird's-eye view of Doug entering the complex, hopefully with her friends in tow. Looking up at the tall, newly constructed apartment buildings, Sandra figured the first floor would suit her just fine. Having reached the front of the building, she painfully used her arms to spin Fred around in the wheelchair and they entered through the glass doors.

* * *

It was 1:30 p.m. and Sandra had not taken her eyes off the main entrance of the complex. For a brief moment, she turned her attention to Fred, who seemed to be awakening as he slowly moved his hands and feet. As she looked at this man, Sandra couldn't help but wonder if he was the main reason Doug had become the person he turned out to be or if he was simply a father who had done all he could for a son that was born to be evil. She couldn't answer the question, but she knew who could.

Before moving from her perch, she looked hard to make sure Doug had not arrived. Satisfied that she would not miss him, she quickly walked over to the slop sink in an open closet nearby and filled up her empty soda bottle with cold water. She went back to the window and checked again, but she still saw nothing. So she turned back to Fred, who was beginning to moan, and slowly poured the wake-your-ass-up water all over his gray Afro, causing the man to shake and rattle inside the chair. Fred shook his head back and forth and opened one of his eyes. He spit water from his mouth and tried to gain some focus. He looked around with fear on his face, trying to figure out where he was.

"Let me go! You let me go! Where am I?" he yelled when his eyes met Sandra's. He moved his feet and arms and realized he was handcuffed. "Get these motherfucking cuffs off me and I will kick your ass! You have no right doing this to me. What have I done to you, bitch, huh?"

Sandra calmly walked over and stood in front of him. She removed a photo from her bag—a photo of Kareem and Chaka on their seventh birthday. She held the picture in front of Fred's wet face and just stared at him.

"So, what the fuck is that supposed to mean to me? Why are you showing me a picture of these two fucking kids?"

Looking down on Fred with a face of fury, Sandra reached back with all of her strength and smacked him across his face, snapping his head to one side. "The little boy's name is Kareem. He was a straight-A student who loved to play chess and dreamed of becoming an architect. He never let me carry a bag of groceries home and he promised me that when he became an architect, the first house he was going to build would be for me. This girl's name is Chaka. She planned to become a lawyer so that if her brother ever got in trouble, she could take care of him. She too was an 'A' student and she loved to help the struggling kids in her class with their homework. She loved to watch her mommy cook and always asked me, when we were alone, why her daddy didn't love us."

Fred stared at the photo and then looked away and stared at a nearby wall. Still burning with rage, Sandra yanked the man by his hair and turned his head so that once again they were eye to eye.

"You see this scar? It took one hundred and forty-two stitches to close it up. My friend gave me two pints of her own blood and I was close to dying for two days. All thanks to your fucking son who loved money and power over his own family and was planning all along to have us killed. My children were tossed out the fourth-floor window. Yes, these children—your grandchildren—were murdered by your son."

"So you think you're totally innocent in all of this shit?" he challenged. "What made you stay? You should have just left. You *did* know he was no shoe-sales clerk, right? He was a fucking hustler and you loved the life. So don't try to paint this picture of yourself as some innocent woman who didn't know what she was getting into. When did he ever tell you that he loved you? Nobody deserves what happened to those kids and you, but just read a newspaper every now and then—read how so many of you young girls are blinded by the fast money and the life. You have kids by these cats, thinking you can change them and make them settle down. They don't love you. You bitches are just trophies and when trophies start to tarnish, they get new ones."

Sandra wanted to twist his head until it ripped off his shoulders, but Fred had said something that was troublesome and weighed on her mind. Why didn't she try to walk away sooner? Sandra turned back to Fred, who was now staring out of the large glass window. "I stayed because I loved him and thought over time I could change him," she said, answering herself as well as Fred. "Simple as that, I just loved him. Judge me or call me stupid, but that is the only answer I have right now. My love for your son cost me what I loved most in this life—my children—and today his monkey ass is going to pay." Reaching inside her bag, Sandra removed a red handkerchief and tied it around Fred's mouth, deciding she had heard enough from Dr. Frankenstein. As they both stared out at the courtyard and waited for the monster to arrive, Fred didn't move in his chair and Sandra never uttered another word.

* * *

With a knife in her hand and her watch reading 3:00 p.m., Sandra now positioned herself behind Fred, who, in a strange way, sat up straight inside his wheelchair, almost with a sense of pride. It was almost as if he realized the end had now arrived. Sandra's eyes got a little misty but she made them stop. She could see Doug escorting Pamela and Rose, both weak-looking, across the courtyard towards the building. Wearing a brown leather coat and black pants, Doug held both women by their shirt collars as they walked without coats or sweaters. Sandra could see their hands tied together as they limped across the dirt.

Spotting Fred through the glass doors, Doug now stopped in the middle of the courtyard, looked up at the glass, and waved to his father, mouthing the words, "It's okay." Not believing what she was seeing, Sandra was infuriated. She held the twelve-inch butcher knife to Fred's throat and silently mouthed back, "No it's not." Fear spread across Doug's face as he pushed the women to hurry inside the building. Hearing the sounds of the door closing and footsteps getting closer, Sandra quickly rolled Fred to an apartment door marked 1A. With her back to the door, she reached with one of her hands, turned the doorknob, and slightly pushed it open. As the footsteps got closer from around the corner, Sandra's eyes widened and her hands tightened around the handle of the knife.

When the trio turned the hallway corner, Doug was holding Pamela and Rose, who were both badly bruised. Instantly, Doug's eyes met and locked with Sandra's, but neither one of them said a word. After a while, Sandra finally let herself exhale. "Release them right now," she demanded.

Doug violently pushed the two women to the side, where they tripped over each other and fell to the cold building's floor. Sandra watched her friends moan in pain, still shackled together. Doug was still mistreating those close to her, and Sandra decided to give him a taste of the feeling. She pressed the knife harder against Fred's throat, causing him to tremble as a trickle of blood dripped from his neck.

"No, Sandra, please!" Doug begged. "Listen, all I want is my father and the discs. Like I said, Sandra, I promise to let you and your friends go. I mean it this time." Looking at Doug without a trace of trust in her eyes, Sandra slowly opened the apartment door and rolled Fred into the large, empty apartment, never taking the knife away from his throat or her eyes off Doug.

"Sandra, come on, please. We don't have to do this. I promise to let..."

Doug watched the door close in his face and then looked back at Pamela and Rose, who still lay on the floor. "Doug, come get your father and the discs," he heard Sandra yell from the other side of the door. Now confused and sweating, Doug hesitantly reached for the apartment door while, at the same time, looking back at Pamela and Rose as if they might give him some type of advice. He grabbed on to the doorknob and slowly turned it while gently pushing the door open. He cautiously stuck his head inside.

"Sandra, where are you?" he called out. Not getting an answer, Doug removed his gun from the waistband of his pants. He stood inside the foyer area of the apartment and felt the cell phone he got from the organization vibrate. Immediately, Doug knew what that meant; Mr. X expected his payment today. Doug always answered the phone from the organization promptly, but right now he was in a precarious situation and wasn't sure what to do. He felt the vibration of his phone again and looked in the direction he thought his father could be, not knowing whether he was dead or alive. Doug ignored the vibration on his hip and walked towards the back of the apartment to find his father.

"Sandra, I'm here and your friends are safe. Now show me my fucking father," Doug demanded. He stood inside a large sunken living room with an entrance leading to a terrace and listened carefully for an answer.

"We're in here, Doug, inside the bedroom," Sandra responded from behind a door. Walking cautiously in the direction of Sandra's voice, Doug located the door and stood in front of it with his mouth almost touching the wooden barrier.

"Okay, Sandra, I'm coming in and my hands will be empty," he said, putting his gun in the back of his pants. He turned the doorknob and slowly opened the door. Sitting in the middle of the room inside the wheelchair, Fred was still handcuffed and gagged. Doug ran quickly to his father's aid. He was attempting to remove the handkerchief from around Fred's mouth when, from behind him, he heard the bedroom door slam, causing him to quickly turn around to face Tony Marino and eight of his henchmen. He reached for his gun, but one of Tony's men reacted to Doug, smacking him in the face with a black object that busted his nose.

Tony looked at Doug sprawled out over the floor and motioned for two of his men to get Doug on his feet. He pinned Doug to a wall and then walked over to Fred and removed the gag. "Sir, I believe this is your son?" Tony asked.

Petrified, Fred nodded his head up and down and looked over at his son, who was just regaining his sense of where he was. Sandra walked into the room holding her canvas bag. For the first time since she had known Doug, fear was all over his face.

Wearing a gray pinstriped suit, Tony calmly and coolly walked up to Doug and spat on him, leaving a glob of thick yellow saliva rolling down the middle of his face.

"Doug, my name is Tony Marino and I'm not big on speeches, so I will sum this up pretty quickly. A few nights before Christmas, you took away my wife's only son. He was no angel, but that doesn't matter because nobody is. You shot him three times, showing little or no mercy towards him and causing us to have a closed-casket funeral. Then you did the unthinkable to your own family and had your own children slaughtered for insurance money. You've gone beyond being a monster, Doug, and you are beyond reasoning to, so I am here to let you know that on behalf of my son, Sandra, her innocent children, and myself, you will die a horrible death today in front of your father. I will pass on to him what I now have to carry."

Holding his face, Doug just stared at his father, fully aware that his life would soon end.

Tony looked over at Sandra, who was observing Doug intensely. "Sandra, I need to get you out of here, but is there anything you would like to say to this man before he dies?"

Not saying a word, Sandra walked over to a pile of iron radiator pipes and picked up one that was about two feet long. She walked back over quickly towards a startled Doug, and Tony and his men made a path for her to pass.

"Sandra, I am so sorry. Please…"

Looking at him with fire in her eyes, Sandra reached back and swung the pipe forward, hitting Doug across his face and breaking his eye socket and nose, all with one shot. Doug grabbed his face and backpedaled until he hit a wall and fell to the floor. As she stood over the only man she had loved, Sandra got a flashback of her children reaching out to her for help on Christmas Day. In a fit of rage, she began beating Doug unmercifully while his father looked on in disbelief; and for the first time ever, Fred Gunner shed tears for his son. Doug held his arm up to protect his bloodied face, and with two more blows, Sandra broke his wrist and forearm.

"Oh God, Sandra. Please have mercy on me!" he begged.

Now beating on Doug's legs, Sandra screamed, "Fuck you mother-fucker, you son of a bitch!" She cracked Doug across his ribs and was going berserk when Tony and one of his men grabbed hold of her.

"Okay, sweetheart. I understand, but that is enough. That is not the person you are, Sandra. Let us do our job," Tony said to her. Then he turned to his men. "Make sure Doug and his father are allowed to speak to each other if they like. I will be back in a few minutes," he said before leading a furious Sandra out of the apartment.

Fred looked at his bloodied and injured son sprawled out on the floor. "Son, what did you get yourself into? You really had those kids murdered? Oh shit, Doug. May God have mercy on our souls." Inside the building hallway, Sandra ran over to Pamela and Rose, and hugged and kissed them all over their faces and heads. "Can you please help me get them loose?" she asked Tony, who nodded to one of his guards. The man pulled out a knife and cut Pamela and Rose free, then helped them to their feet.

"Go get the package from the car," Tony instructed, and the man hurried out of the building. Tony walked over to Sandra and put his hand around her shoulder.

"You are a very brave woman, Sandra. My wife and I would like to thank you for helping us bring closure to this situation. Your children would be very proud of you and I know these two women are."

Tony's guard ran back inside the building holding a black suitcase. He gave the suitcase to Tony and went back inside the apartment, leaving his boss with the three women.

"Sandra, in no type of way am I trying to tell you that this will bring your children back or make you forget them, but I am hoping that maybe it can provide a new beginning for you and your friends."

He opened the suitcase and revealed two million dollars to Sandra. She looked up at Tony, trying to find the right words, but he placed his finger across her lips. "Sweetheart, don't say a word, okay? You just get your friends and yourself out of here and go somewhere safe, like out of this city, and start your new life. I will never forget you and you will always have a friend in me."

As Tony and Sandra hugged each other, Pamela put her arms around Rose, who was still a little shaken up. Sandra let go of Tony, carried her bag and the suitcase over to her friends, and hugged them. Tony watching the three women as they exited the building, then he returned inside the apartment where Doug awaited his fate.

* * *

Some time had passed, and Tony Marino stood at the entrance of the living room holding the wheelchair of a still-handcuffed Fred, who was trying to turn his head away while one of Tony's men dismembered his son with a chainsaw. While Tony held Fred's head, the old man witnessed his son's body parts being tossed to the side as if they were chicken parts. The bedroom was crimson red with Doug's blood and guts splattered all over the walls. Walking out of the bedroom with Doug's head in his hand, Tony's henchman calmly placed the head in the old man's lap. Fred looked down and saw that his son never had the chance to close his eyes.

As Tony's men all began to exit the apartment, Tony bent down and whispered into Fred's ear, "Feel my pain." As Tony left the apartment, he could hear Fred's screams above the sound of a jumbo jet that was flying overhead.

* * *

To Doug's credit, he had prepared a document before his ill-fated meeting with Sandra, and he had instructed his Spanish mommy Jasmine to mail it express mail if she didn't hear from him at a specific time. Crying as she exited the post office, Jasmine did her last favor for Doug.

* * *

The old wall clock read 8:37 p.m. and Detective Tommy Davis was sitting alone in his office looking over open cases. He took one last puff of his cigarette and found an express delivery package on his desk. Looking puzzled, the detective opened the envelope and removed a one-page letter.

Tommy, If you have received this letter, it means that more than likely I am dead...and if you don't hurry, you and your precinct are fucked. From the time I met you, we have been involved in some shady shit. To your credit, you have always been on the up and up with me for these many years, but as you know, a brother can never be too sure. So, I am writing to let you know that during these wild times of ours, while you and your crew partied at my secret hideaway in the Bronx, I recorded all of the dirty shit on to DVD discs; just in case you ever tried to squeeze me, I had leverage. Well, possibly in death, I have to give you the bad news: Those discs are in the hands of Sandra Lyte, the bitch that I paid you to take care of along with her kids.

Well, brother, Sandra is not as dumb and weak as we thought because she is still alive and well, and she has the discs. The chances are good that she watched those discs and at any moment, possibly even while you are reading this letter, she could be on her way to expose everyone involved. Tommy, I fucked up, partner, by underestimating her. Therefore, I just want to say good-bye, hoping you find her before she can find someone important to watch those discs. Good-bye...Doug.

Falling backwards into his chair, Tommy began to tremble as his face turned beet red. He picked up his cell phone and began to call all of those involved to meet up with him. They needed to find and kill Sandra at all costs.

Chapter Thirty-three

APB on Sandra Lyte

On Thursday evening, Sandra, Pamela, and Rose were sitting on a carpeted floor between two queen-sized beds, listening to the sounds of the passing cars on I-95. The room smelled of cinnamon and strawberries from the foaming bath product the women had used when they each took a long, hot bath—each doing her best to wash away the sins of Doug and very possibly her own.

"I am so sorry for what you all had to go through for me. I hope over time your wounds will heal," Sandra said, breaking the silence.

Pamela reached across Rose and touched Sandra's badly bruised thigh. "Please don't say sorry, Sandra. It's because of you that we all sit here right now. I just think at some point in time, we all need to thank God for keeping us alive and helping us cope with the horrors we've all endured."

Sandra's eyes fixated on the window where a neon sign was flashing. "Sometimes I feel so disconnected from God. It's almost as if I don't have the right to speak to Him about anything. My life at this moment compared to where it was ten years ago makes me feel so dirty and unworthy."

In a soft, clear voice, almost like a jazz vocalist from the fifties, Rose interjected, "Our righteousness is just filthy rags before the Lord and no matter how hard we try, we will always fall short of His glory. We must accept the gift that He has given us and not take it for granted. Let's not focus on the suffering we all have gone through but believe God never left us and that He is the one who kept us alive. We all have lost so much, but we need to focus on the fact that even through all of the pain and sorrow, we sit inside this room together for a reason. We are not sure for what reason, but it is according to His plan that we are together and safe."

Sandra and Pamela looked at Rose in silence as tears ran down their faces. Having spoken volumes and now quieted down, Rose climbed into one of the beds, which felt much better than the hallway steps she usually slept on. Comforted by the softness of the mattress and the cozy feel of the new pajamas Sandra had purchased for her, she soon fell fast asleep. Sandra and Pamela helped each other up from the floor, sat on the other bed, and watched Rose sleep for about an hour, never saying another word for the rest of the night.

* * *

The next morning, Pamela and Rose were eating pancakes with beef sausages along with orange juice to wash it down. Pamela touched Rose's long silk-like hair, trying to figure out what style of cornrows she would braid in her hair. Sitting on the bed with the discs by her side, Sandra was about to use her cell phone when she asked, "How does Phoenix sound to you two?"

"Arizona? I heard it's hot as hell all year round out there," Pamela responded, delaying the forkful of pancakes she was about to put in her mouth.

"No big deal. We'll just get us a big pool in the backyard of our house. Moreover, I'll make sure we have an air conditioner in every room. So, I'll ask again—how does Phoenix sound to you two?"

"It sounds good to me," Pamela said with a smile while an ecstatic-looking Rose quickly answered, "Please, can we go now?" Sandra and Pamela laughed loudly.

"Sure, baby, we can leave here as soon as possible. But there is still one thing that must be put to rest before we leave," Sandra said, fingering the discs. She picked up her cell phone and dialed the number for Gail, the assistant to Maria Copper at Channel 4 News. On the fourth ring, Sandra got an answer.

"Hello, Ms. Smothers, you may not remember me, but my name is Sandra Lyte and not too long ago, I contacted you about some information pertaining to police corruption and murder..."

* * *

The newsroom was alive and kicking as people ran around like chickens without heads as they shared information about a manhunt going on in the city. Looking to find a place that was less noisy, Gail entered a supply room and closed the door behind her.

"This is Sandra Lyte? Yes, I remember our conversation and that you didn't show up that morning. Sandra, I understand that you want to speak to Maria Copper, but do you realize what's going on this morning? Sandra, are you near a television set? Sweetheart, you need to turn it on right now," Gail advised.

* * *

Pamela and Rose stopped talking when they saw how confused and upset Sandra was. They all sat in silence as Sandra turned to channel four where a story about her was running. Looking at the screen, Pamela and Rose quickly jumped out of their chairs and huddled next to their shocked friend. On the television screen was a picture of Sandra's face with the words "Wanted for Murder" under her picture. Turning the sound up on the television, the women heard that Sandra was armed and dangerous with no regard for the law. With her phone still held to her mouth, a frightened Sandra could only whisper, "That's not true. I didn't kill Doug. He was responsible for my babies being murdered, but I didn't kill him. That's not true."

* * *

Listening to every word that Sandra was saying, Gail was also quickly running to Maria Copper's office where the special investigative reporter had just arrived sporting a gray sharkskin two-piece suit. The olive-skinned Cuban woman had distinctive brown eyes and long brown curly hair that reached all the way to the bottom of her back. She glanced up from the messages she was reviewing when she saw her wild-eyed assistant waving to her through her glass office door.

Looking somewhat amused by the excitement in Gail's eyes, Maria waved her in. Gail held her hand over the receiver of the phone and said, "You are not going to believe this, but I have Sandra Lyte on the other end right now. She claims she has information concerning major corruption that she wants to bring in to only you."

Maria's eyes grew wide and she gestured for the phone.

"Hello, this is Maria Copper. To whom am I speaking?"

* * *

Sandra stood by the hotel window looking at the traffic and, more importantly, looking for police cars. "Ms. Copper, my name is Sandra Lyte," she started, "and I don't know if you've seen what's on the news right now, but I didn't kill anyone, and I can prove it if you give me the chance. Ms. Copper, I am not turning myself in to police custody because honestly, I will not make it through the night. I have evidence that will shatter the foundation of the New York City Police Department. Certain officers who have much to lose would definitely kill me to keep things quiet. That's why they say I am armed and dangerous—so that some trigger-happy cop can have an excuse to blow my damn head off as soon as I make a sudden move.

"Now, Ms. Copper, I have great respect for all the good you have done for the small people in this city. I know you have no reason whatsoever to believe me, but I am telling you I have major proof on video that will clear my name and bring to justice those responsible for murdering my children. You remember that story on Christmas Day, don't you, Ms. Copper?"

Maria twirled a fountain pen between her fingers. "Yes, Sandra. I know who you are and what happened to your children," she answered, still looking at her assistant. "I am so sorry, but you do understand that I cannot officially interfere in police matters. Sandra, this is a serious police matter that will come to a head one way or another. Therefore, I will say this with no intention of hurting you or leaving you out there in the cold.

"At five o'clock this evening, for my Friday report, I am supposed to go on the air to report on fraudulent jewelry shop owners. If you can somehow make it to my assistant at a specified location, I promise I will look at what you have. And if what you have is as explosive as you claim, then I will lead in tonight's broadcast with your story.

"As I said, though, I will not help you elude the police. That will be strictly up to you. Get a pen and paper because I'm going to give you my personal cell phone number so you can contact me directly, but you are only to use the number when you are near Rockefeller Center in Manhattan."

Sandra grabbed a piece of paper and a pen and wrote down all the information Maria gave her. "Yes, Ms. Copper. I understand everything you said and I appreciate you giving me this chance to tell my story. I hope to see you later on today. Good-bye, Ms. Copper."

When she hung up the phone, Sandra turned to Pamela and Rose, who had been sitting on the bed taking in the whole conversation.

* * *

Maria hung up and looked silently at Gail for a moment. "I want you to drop all you are doing right now, okay? I need you to run a background check on this woman and tell me what comes up. Because if she is on the up and up on what she claims, this could blow us right past our other two rivals on the block and very possibly push me up this station's chauvinistic ladder. So, Gail, as always, help me out," she said as she tossed Gail's phone back to her.

"Yes, Ms. Copper, right away," Gail responded with excitement in her voice. As Gail exited the office, Maria planted her seven-hundred-dollar crocodile shoes on the desk and said quietly, "Okay, Sandra, make me shine."

* * *

Sitting on the bed with her friends, Sandra grabbed each of them by the hand. "Okay, we all know the truth and we all know what that means to the police: nothing. I'm a wanted woman, which means you two cannot be seen with me at any time."

Rose jumped up from the bed, visibly upset. "No, we have to stick together and not let them scare us, Ms. Sandra."

Pamela gently grabbed Rose by the arm and pulled her back down on the bed. "Sandra, I understand what must be done," she assured her friend. "You need to understand though, that these cops are nothing like the cops in Virginia. I have seen too many of us 'mistakenly' gunned down because a shiny object was supposedly seen in our hands. Baby, the only way you're going to make it is by staying low and buried in the cracks of the streets."

Sandra took a deep breath and nodded her head in agreement. "I have to get rid of these clothes and maybe do something different with my hair. Even though we used cash for this room, I still don't trust staying here much longer because the clerk at the desk might remember our faces."

"Let me run out and get a few things to make you look a little different, and then we can quickly decide what our plan is."

"No, Pamela, *my* plan, not ours, okay? Once we leave this room, yes, we can agree to meet someplace and hopefully leave this city. But, sweetheart, if for any reason I don't make it back..."

Now crying, Rose jumped up from the bed. "Don't say that, Ms. Sandra. You have to make it back! Remember what you promised—the house, the pool, and us living with each other forever?"

Sandra reached out and pulled Rose close to her. "Yes, baby, I remember. And I promise to do all that I can to make that happen for all of us," she said. Then she turned to Pamela. "When we leave, we'll decide where you and Rose will stay. If I don't return by midnight tonight, take that suitcase; it holds two million dollars that I want you to take to start a new life with Rose. Make sure she goes to college...and buy a house with a pool. You understand, sister?"

Fighting back the tears, Pamela nodded. "Yes, sister, I understand." She sniffled and then regained her composure. "Listen, time is not on our side right now. I better run out and get your things." As Pamela smiled and headed out the motel door, Sandra grabbed her by the arm and pulled her close so that they could share an embrace.

Chapter Thirty-four

The Gauntlet

Inside a poorly lit room in the basement of police headquarters, Detective Tommy Davis stood in front of his fellow comrades, Sam Daniels, Joseph McCarthy, and Tony Harris. All four men were putting on bulletproof vests and loading unregistered guns. Wearing dark shades and leather jackets, they were all very intimidating looking with emotionless expressions on their faces. Tommy walked in front of each man and handed him a photo of Sandra and an i730 phone so they could communicate with one another.

"It's very simple, men. The situation as we know it has taken a turn for the worst. We all know what's at stake here. She must be disposed of immediately. Sam and Joe, you two buddy up while Tony and I work together. We will stay in constant contact, paying close attention to radios and scanners. Also remember, we have blues at our disposal and they are under strict orders to stay in contact with us if we need them. Finally, men, once she's caught, we shoot and plant immediately. Okay, everyone stay alert and be careful. Let's go." Tommy opened up the large black door leading to the stairs and watched his fellow officers leave with death in their eyes.

* * *

At 10:30 a.m., Sandra, Pamela, and Rose were almost ready to leave the motel. Standing in front of a full-length mirror, Pamela admired the camouflage job she had performed on Sandra, whose long black braids were now cut down to the top of her shoulders and dyed blonde. Wearing baggy carpenter jeans and a thick blue hooded sweatshirt, Sandra decided to go without a coat because the weight might hamper her and the temperature was expected to rise to the mid fifties. On her head was a blue fitted baseball cap and on her face was a pair of black sunglasses. Sandra's cell phone was clipped securely to her belt and the discs were taped to her back under her sweater. Pamela looked at her watch and said, "It's time for us to go."

The three friends gathered together, hugged, and grabbed their possessions. "Remember what we agreed on, okay? A minute past midnight, you two go to the airport. No waiting. Agreed?" Pamela and Rose looked at each other and nodded their heads slowly in agreement. The women exited with Pamela holding the suitcase and Sandra holding Rose's hand.

The sun was shining brightly on the street as Sandra quickly entered a blue cab while Pamela and Rose got into a green one that was right behind Sandra's. As the two cars pulled off, Sandra went towards the Henry Hudson while the other cab took Pamela and Rose to a Holiday Inn one hundred feet from JFK Airport.

* * *

At 254th Street and Broadway, Sandra's driver merged with traffic to get on the southbound side of exit twenty-two. Sandra looked at her watch and allowed a small smile to come on her face. In about an hour, she would be at the news station pursuing justice. Then, for the first time since she met Doug, she could attempt to put her life back in order. As she gazed at the scenery overlooking the Hudson River, she imagined being with her new friends and hoped that one day she would laugh again. More importantly though, Sandra imagined someday finding some peace.

Feeling her back, Sandra slid her hand across the plastic bag that would put the corrupt cops away for a very long time. If they had families, they too would feel a little of what Sandra was feeling: pain and suffering. As the driver continued to drive smoothly along, Sandra removed her shades and looked ahead at the traffic leading to the tollbooths. She glanced at her watch again. "Excuse me, sir," she said to the driver, "it's just a little past eleven. Is the traffic always backed up like this at this time?"

The driver had also been eyeing the scene ahead of him. "Absolutely not. I come across this highway three or four times a week, and I have never seen it this backed up at this time."

Sandra's heart was pumping rapidly. She took a deep breath and was able to calm herself down, minimizing the traffic delay's effect on her fragile optimism. With the cars in all three lanes inching ahead, the driver could see the tunnel, which was now about three hundred feet in front of him. "I can't be sure because my vision is not that great, but it looks like the police have created some type of check point," he said.

Sandra rubbed her hands slowly but tightly together, took a deep breath, and stretched her head forward, trying to get a glimpse as they continued to inch forward. Her eyesight was better than the driver's was and her heart was now racing much faster with no way of slowing it down. Their car was about 150 feet from the tunnel, and Sandra could see flashing lights ahead. Six police officers with flashlights were walking around near the tunnel. Sandra wondered how long have they had been out here and why they were on this particular highway.

"Excuse me, sir, I'm sorry for disturbing you again, but is there a way that we can get off this highway and maybe take the scenic route?"

The driver pointed to his right in the opposite direction. "That was the last exit before the toll and there is no way I would ever try to back up. Besides, there's gotta be at least three hundred cars behind us."

The cab inched closer to the tunnel leading to the tollbooths and Sandra now saw police officers looking inside cars, and two of them had dogs. With her anxiety building, Sandra took forty dollars out of her pocket. "Sir, I know this is an inconvenience, but I need to get out of your cab, so can you please stop?"

The driver turned around slowly and looked at Sandra as if she had lost her mind. "Lady, are you crazy? We're on the damn highway and if I let you out, I could lose my license. Besides, we're almost there and we haven't done anything wrong. They will just look in the car then let us continue. Please just relax, okay?"

While the driver was giving Sandra his rationale, she had gathered one hundred dollars and she now reached over to the front seat and dropped it in his lap. "Sir, that is one hundred dollars for a ten-minute ride. Now let me out of this damn car, or when the cops get to us, I will tell them you're kidnapping me. I mean it. Now open this fucking door," she demanded.

The driver brought the car to a complete stop with only forty feet separating them from the tunnel. "You're sick. Get the hell out of here. I hope you get run over."

Sandra felt her back and made sure her discs were still there. Then she gently stepped one foot out on the highway. She adjusted her shades and hat and began to walk quickly back to the previous exit, half-crouched over. She ducked and weaved between slow-moving cars that honked at her as she passed. She finally made it over to the left lane; the exit leading up to Riverdale Avenue was now a hundred feet away. Sweat was pouring down her face and Sandra started to remove her sunglasses until she thought better of it.

She was huffing and trying to gather fresh air into her body to fight the exhaust fumes when she heard a loud, long whistle. Knowing for a fact that it was in regard to some fool running against traffic on a major highway, she didn't bother to turn around when she heard, "Police, halt!"

The exit was now about twenty feet away and it was packed with cars. Cramps were starting to overtake her body, but Sandra fought the tears and the pain. Already exhausted, she was no longer running but limping along while holding her ribs, which felt as if someone had crushed them with a baseball bat. Sandra gritted her teeth together and began to lug her body up the incline. She checked behind her and saw three officers; one officer was in pursuit and gaining on her, along with his police dog.

Now on a walkway, Sandra was halfway up the ramp but was beginning to slow down because every step brought the urge to vomit. Taking a peep behind her, she saw one of the officers saying something on his radio. She hurried on, letting out grunts as she moved. She stumbled and almost fell on her face but held herself up by bracing on the trunk of a green Town Car. When she moved her hand, she noticed the car's bumper sticker: Flamingo Cab #44 - Call 718-555-8989. She banged on the driver's window, which scared him half to death. The Dominican man rolled down his window and yelled, "No working! Going home, mommy!"

Still unable to speak, Sandra looked back and saw the officers weaving through the cars and running towards her with their guns drawn. Quickly fumbling through her pocket, Sandra removed a knot of hundred-dollar bills and shoved them in the driver's face. He looked at the money and then at Sandra and said, "Come now! Hurry now!"

The door locks popped open and Sandra quickly jumped inside the cab and slammed the door behind her. Her body was running on empty for lack of oxygen. "Trying…to kill…me…please go!" she moaned.

Without hesitation, the cabby made a sharp right, which caused the right front and rear tires to jump on the walkway. With half of the car on a tilt, the driver began passing cars in front of him while blowing his horn. Still breathing very hard and feeling queasy, Sandra lifted her body up and looked through the rear window where she saw the police standing and talking on their radios as they had stopped giving chase.

"Mommy, where you going?"

"Rockefeller Center at Forty-eighth Street in Manhattan, please. Here, take this one hundred-dollar bill, just hurry," Sandra sputtered between coughs.

Now clutching the money inside his stubby hands, the driver made a left, headed towards 230th Street and Broadway. He weaved through traffic and made a quick right towards the Grand Concourse and 205th Street. "Are you sure you know where you're going, mister?" Sandra asked.

Taking a quick look back at her, he answered confidently, "I know the city, lady. You no worry. What happen back there? Who going to kill you?"

Sandra wiped her face with her sweater. "Some very bad people," she answered as she laid her head back on the headrest.

* * *

Detectives Tommy Davis and Tony Harris were riding south on Broadway and 238th Street, paying close attention to their police scanner, which could pick up cab dispatcher frequencies. They heard over their radio that there was a perp on the Henry Hudson Parkway. Tommy went with his gut and assumed that it was Sandra. They got the details of the cab that the perp had jumped into—the color of the car, the company, and a partial plate number—then Tony radioed Sam and Joseph, telling them to play close attention. Turning up his scanner, Tommy listened carefully when he heard the Flamingo dispatcher calling for car number forty-four. He pulled his car to the side and brought it to a halt, hoping to pick up something useful.

* * *

The driver picked up the handle of his car radio and answered his dispatcher. "Yes, I am on one nine five Grand Concourse going south to Rockefeller Center. Come back, Manny, you break up." He tapped the radio receiver on the dashboard but still couldn't make out what his dispatcher was saying, so he tossed the receiver on the passenger seat of the cab. He looked back at Sandra, who was focusing on the numbered street signs that descended with each passing block. "Don't worry, mommy. We make on time, okay?"

Looking at him with a slight bit of confidence in her eyes, Sandra gave him a small smile while nodding her head. She looked up at the street sign as they came to a red light. They were now on 188th Street and the Grand Concourse, right next to the now-closed Loews Paradise Theater.

* * *

Breathing fast and hard, Tommy grabbed his i730. "Sam, listen up. What's your twenty?"

Two quick beeps came in on his phone and then Tommy heard, "Right now we're riding south on Webster Avenue and 202nd Street, getting close to Fordham Road."

Tommy pressed the button on his phone. "Listen, when you get to Fordham, make a left and blast your siren. They're on the Grand Concourse driving a green Town Car from the Flamingo Cab Company, car number forty-four. I know this bitch is heading to Manhattan to turn those discs over to someone in the media. We're heading that way also. Go, Sam, go!" Tommy threw his phone on the dashboard, hit his siren, and took off, heading south on Broadway.

* * *

"Mommy, I take a shortcut at one forty-nine street and go across the one forty-five street bridge that put us back near Broadway, okay?" the driver suggested when he noticed the traffic picking up at 161st Street.

"Whatever, mister. Just please hurry up," Sandra said as she looked at her watch. Nodding his head up and down, the cabby drove towards 149th Street.

* * *

Inside a room at the Holiday Inn, Pamela sat on the bed, watching the television intently as the news at noon was about to begin. Rose stood silently looking out the window, frightened but somewhat amazed at how close the airplanes were flying near their window. She turned her attention to Pamela, who had not spoken for the past fifteen minutes. "Do you think she will make it back to us?" Rose asked as she walked over and sat on the bed next to Pamela, "because I don't think it would be right if we went without her. We all promised that we would be a family."

Pamela turned away from the television, looked deeply into Rose's eyes, and stroked her gently across the head. "Yes, sweetheart, I do believe she will make it back. No matter what, Rose baby, Sandra will always love us and hold us dear to her heart until the bitter end. Do you understand?"

Rose nodded and then laid her head on Pamela's shoulder. They both then focused on the twelve o'clock news.

* * *

The traffic light turned green and Sandra's cab gradually picked up speed. They were now at the corner of 149th Street, where they made a right turn. As they rode down the bumpy street, Sandra exhaled when she saw the 145th Street Bridge getting closer. With the static noise coming from his radio again, the driver picked up his receiver. "Manny, I no hear nothing good, okay? I'm going on one forty-five and Lenox. I call when I coming back." The driver put on his sunglasses and drove to the end of the bridge, where he made a left. As they continued down Lenox Avenue, Sandra had flashbacks of when she had rented a room not too far from the area. As they approached Harlem Hospital, the car was slowing down for a yellow traffic light when Sandra's body was suddenly thrown against the driver's seat because a car smashed them from behind. The driver, who had almost banged his head on the steering wheel, looked behind him and yelled, "Oh shit, what the hell!"

Holding and rubbing her neck, Sandra looked out the back window and saw a black sedan with two white male occupants sitting inside. She looked closer and saw one of them loading a gun. She was breathing hard and her heart was racing as the man on the passenger side stuck half his body out the window and pointed his gun.

"Mister, go! Oh shit! Please, mister, they have guns…drive!" Sandra yelled. Still rubbing his chest, the driver looked in his rearview mirror just as shots rang out and smashed the rear window.

"Oh my God," he yelled as he stepped down hard on his gas pedal, causing a loud screeching noise from his tires.

Sandra dived to the floor of the car, but she could hear the screams of people who were witnessing what was going on. Holding her head between her elbows, Sandra yelled to the driver, "Mister, please don't stop…They're going to kill me! Please just keep driving!" The car swerved from side to side and Sandra squeezed her hands together, trying not to cry. "Mister, please do not let them catch us!" Four more shots rang out and Sandra heard the driver crying and saying a prayer in his native tongue. Two more shots were fired, totally shattering the rear window and showering Sandra with broken glass. Still not picking her head up, Sandra screamed when she felt the car hit a bump. The car was swerving wildly now and she could hear the blasting of several different horns.

"Mister, are you okay? Mister?" Sandra yelled. Not getting an answer, she slowly tilted her head upward and let out a frantic yell. The driver's bloody headrest had brain and skull fragments all over it. In a state of panic, Sandra eased herself up from the floor and looked frantically around the car. Not only was the driver dead but his foot was still on the accelerator. They were speeding down Lenox Avenue in the wrong direction, just missing oncoming cars.

"Oh shit!" Sandra yelled as she dived over the top of the passenger seat, grabbing on to the steering wheel in an attempt to keep it straight. As cars swerved out of her way, Sandra used one hand to try to move the driver's foot off the pedal. Not being able to, she focused back on the street just as a food vending truck came towards her. She couldn't turn quickly enough, and the truck clipped the right side of the cab, causing it to veer to the right, jump the curb, and head right towards a large pile of garbage.

"Oh God, help me!" Sandra yelled as she released the steering wheel and buried her head in the passenger seat. She heard screaming people who she hoped were running out of the way. Then the car hit the garbage and a fire hydrant, finally coming to a stop and deploying its air bags. Recovering quickly, Sandra looked around for her sunglasses and her hat; she could hear people milling around near the car. Someone opened the passenger-side door and she covered her eyes with her wounded left hand.

"Miss, are you okay? Oh shit, this guy's head is blown open… somebody call the cops!" a black man yelled. Reaching inside the car, the tall, well-built man grabbed Sandra by her waist and gently pulled her out.

"Stay calm, lady, I got you," he said.

A crowd of people began to gather around the car and a Spanish man stepped up to help get Sandra to the steps of a nearby building. Her back ached badly as she reached behind to feel for her discs. They were still there and were seemingly undamaged. She grabbed on to the rail, wincing in pain as she slowly lifted herself up. An old woman who was standing near Sandra said, "No, sweetheart. You stay still now; an ambulance is on its way. Harlem Hospital is only a few blocks away and the police are coming. Did you know there was a dead man in the car?"

"Where is the train station, miss?" Sandra asked, ignoring the woman's advice and wrapping a handkerchief someone had given her around her injured hand. A little Spanish boy pointed up the block towards the

135th Street station. Sandra stumbled down the steps and, to everyone's amazement, began to slowly trot in that direction.

"Hey, lady, where the hell are you going!" yelled the man who had helped her out of the car. Determined to get to the train, Sandra ignored the yells of the bystanders, who started to turn in the opposite direction when they heard the ambulance's siren getting closer to the scene. After making a hard U-turn and coming to a screeching stop, Detectives Tommy Davis and Tony Harris quickly exited their car with their badges around their necks and their guns drawn. Tommy ran over to the crashed car and looked inside the vehicle where he discovered the dead driver. He also found Sandra's sunglasses. He looked angrily at the crowd of people. "Where is the woman that was inside this car?" he demanded. The crowd gave the officers the silent treatment, so Tommy turned to his partner. "Where's the nearest train station?" Tony looked around his surroundings and focused on the direction of the hospital. "The number-two train is on 135th Street, three blocks that way." Tommy grabbed his phone and paged Sam. "Daniels, listen to me, okay? You and McCarthy get over to the 125th Street Metro-North terminal and stay there just in case she shows her face. We're heading underground at one three five, you got me?"

The phone beeped and Tommy listened for Sam's response. "That's a copy. We'll be at the Metro-North terminal until further notice, over." Tommy and Tony took one more look at the driver before running back over to their car. Tommy grabbed his official radio and sent out a call to the transit police to look out for Sandra at the Harlem Hospital train station. Quickly getting inside their car, the two detectives drove off in that direction.

In the meantime, a police car and an EMS truck were now pulling up to the scene. The brother that pulled Sandra out of the car quietly said to himself, "Run, sister, run."

* * *

Sandra was now standing at the front of the downtown platform with her head lowered in an attempt to conceal her face. She looked at her hand and saw that the bleeding had stopped, so she tossed the bloody handkerchief onto the tracks and got nervous when she saw no sign of a train approaching. She glanced at her watch, which read 12:47 p.m., and almost jumped out of her skin when she heard from the uptown side of the platform, "Hey, lady, why did you just litter on the tracks?"

Slowly, Sandra lifted her head and peered in the direction of the voice. Standing there on the uptown side of the platform were two uniformed police officers. Deciding not to say a word, Sandra turned her attention back to the platform floor when she heard a transmission coming from one of their radios. She looked up again, and she and the officer on the radio caught each other's eyes. He whispered something to his partner, who was now leaving the uptown side of the tracks to join Sandra on the downtown side. The officer that was on his radio unsnapped his gun holster as he slowly walked down the platform so that he would be directly in front of her.

Taking a quick glance down the tracks again, Sandra only saw people who were frustrated with the delay of the downtown number-two train. She looked back at the officer on the uptown platform as he slowly raised his hands, saying, "Don't you fucking move, lady. I mean it; don't you fucking move." She looked down the platform and spotted the other officer, who was walking towards her; and standing by the turnstiles right behind him were Detectives Davis and Harris, who already had their weapons drawn.

Some of the bystanders waiting for the train had just noticed what was taking place, causing a few to hurry back outside while others remained in place, watching the scene unfold. Breathing hard, Sandra took a few steps backwards, never taking her eyes off the two detectives, especially Tony, who was slowly raising his weapon in her direction.

"Lady, just fall to your knees with your hands up and all of this will be over," said the uniformed officer who was now thirty feet away from Sandra.

Sandra focused on Tony, who had death in his eyes. "I didn't do anything. If I do as you say, do you promise not to hurt me?"

The uniformed officer had now stopped walking towards Sandra. He raised his hands to signify that everything would be all right and said, "I promise you, nobody will hurt you."

The officer looked over at his partner on the uptown platform and motioned to him to relax, failing to notice the two detectives behind him because of their plain clothes. Sandra was getting on her knees with her hands in the air when she saw the dragon take aim. "No!" she screamed as she took three steps towards the edge of the platform and jumped onto the wet and dirty train tracks. The sound of two bullets cracked the air as they left Detective Harris's gun, both just missing Sandra's head.

"What the fuck are you doing, Tony! Not here, you fucking idiot!" yelled Detective Davis, who quickly flashed his badge at the uniformed officers who had turned towards them and were a split second away from returning fire.

"Officer, hold your fire! We are NYPD. Hold your fire!" he yelled, holding his shield in the air as he weaved through the panic-stricken people who were screaming and running.

The officer on the uptown platform now had his gun drawn. "She's in the tunnel! Pete, she's in the tunnel," he yelled. "Radio in to command station to kill the third rail! I'm going in after her!" Officer Pete, who was looking at Tommy with a very pissed-off stare, grabbed his radio and did what his partner had requested.

* * *

Scared and nervous, Sandra held her hands out in front of her as she ran in the middle of the downtown track with no idea of where she was going. Feeling her sneakers getting soaked with what smelled like a combination of urine and sewage water, Sandra covered her mouth with one of her hands and tried to push that morning's breakfast back down her throat. Breathing heavily, she picked up her speed and after a few more steps, she tripped over a loose bolt, which caused her to fall on her hands and knees. She was lying in brown sewage water and moaning in pain. As she tried to lift herself up she heard, "Lady, stop running. You're going to get yourself killed!"

Sandra turned her head in the direction of the voice and made out a small beam of light that had to be a flashlight. When she turned her head back around in front of her, she let out a blood-curdling scream. Standing on its hind legs, two feet from her face, there was a fourteen-inch rat that had to weigh at least four pounds.

"Oh shit!" she yelled while using every muscle in her body to lift herself up. As she made it to her feet, the monster rat scurried away from her and hid under the third rail. Now on her feet and knowing more than ever that she wanted out of this dark sea of puss called a tunnel, Sandra ignored every ache and pain throughout her body and quickened her pace, hoping to see a ray of light.

* * *

Looking at his partner with disgust and anger, Tommy smacked Tony hard on the shoulder. "You stupid ass. I told you we do this my way. I'm telling you, asshole, if she gets away, we might as well put bullets in our fucking heads ourselves. Now come on, let's go." Hurrying through the turnstiles, the detectives ran upstairs to their car, leaving the lone uniformed officer on the platform.

As they entered their car, Tommy picked up his i730 and paged Sam, who was at the 125th Street Metro-North station.

"Sam, listen partner, all hell just broke loose down here. Sandra Lyte has just taken off into the one three five tunnel heading south. You two need to get to one two five and Lenox; I know she is going to come out from that side. You guys move your asses, fast!"

The phone beeped and Tommy heard Sam respond, "That's a copy. We're moving over to said location right now, over." Tommy threw the phone back on the dash, started up his car, and headed to 125th Street.

* * *

The pain of her cramps was flaring and Sandra held the left side of her rib cage as she continued to move. She now only heard the officer's voice faintly, making Sandra conclude that he had given up on chasing her. Regardless, she pressed on. She looked ahead and saw a blue lightbulb in a fixture to her right, about twenty feet away. As she got closer, she ignored the stench of the tunnel and let a glimmer of hope enter her mind because above the blue light was a sign that read "EXIT." Stopping and looking at the large red letters, Sandra listened in silence to hear if anyone or anything was near.

With reassurance that she was still alone, she gazed up at an opening that looked like it contained stairs. Realizing now that she was about five feet down on the tracks, Sandra used her hands to brace herself on the cold and dirty ledge as she tried to lift herself up, but she was unsuccessful in her first attempt. Breathing hard but feeling determined, she took a couple of steps back and tiptoed quickly to the ledge. She jumped with all the springs that her thick but tired legs would give her. She got the upper half of her body on the ledge while her legs swung and dangled in the darkness.

"Please, please, please," Sandra squealed through her clenched teeth. As she fought to get the rest of her body on the ledge, she felt a large hand touch her hip and push her up onto the walkway.

"Oh God, please don't hurt me!" she yelled as she quickly turned around. She grabbed her chest and tried to control the fear that was running through her body as she looked into the eyes of a tall white man who had a long dirty beard and smelled like garbage.

"Please, don't be afraid. I won't hurt you. My name is Winthrop and I am cousins with the Duke of Earl. Are you looking for a place to sleep? I have many rooms in my mansion."

Sandra looked straight into Winthrop's eyes. "No, Winthrop," she answered softly. "I don't need a place to sleep. I'm just looking for a way to get back to the streets."

"Why do you want to get back to the streets? They will only hurt you out there. Why do you think…hey, I know you! You're the woman I saw on TV before they kicked me out of the restaurant this morning. They say you killed some people, but I don't believe them because all they do is lie."

Standing up and bracing herself on the ledge and wall, Sandra was now looking down on Winthrop when she said, "That's right, Winthrop, they *are* telling lies, but the only way that I can help myself is to get out of here. Do you think you can help me, please?"

Winthrop looked up and down the dark tunnel and then gazed at Sandra with pitiful eyes. "The younger ones try to set me on fire when I sleep and nobody cares anymore that all I have to eat is fur."

Sandra felt antsy and frustrated, and she wanted to get away from Winthrop in the worst way, but something was keeping her in that one spot. "What do you mean eating fur and people trying to set you on fire?"

Reaching into a dirty, half-ripped pocket of his jacket, the man pulled out a half-eaten rat, causing Sandra to turn her face in disgust. With her head still turned, Sandra said, "Winthrop, I promise that if you help me, I will help you so that you can eat and sleep somewhere nice, okay?"

Winthrop looked at Sandra with skepticism. "The chief of the city always says that he will help us but he never does. I just want to feel hot water again. I have the right to taste chicken soup again, right?"

Sandra could identify with Winthrop's waning self-respect. "Help me, Winthrop, and then I can help you; but we have to hurry. Please, I beg you."

Winthrop grabbed the ledge and pulled himself up onto the concrete walkway. Sandra was about one foot shorter then he was.

"You really need my help?"

"Yes, I do," Sandra answered. She was speaking the truth but she also knew that this man needed to feel wanted.

"Come this way. I know a way to the streets where the soldiers of this tunnel won't see you. Just follow me." The tall man walked into a doorway and Sandra cautiously followed behind him.Winthrop pointed out a set of metal steps and Sandra looked up in the direction to which they led. A cautious smile came to her face when she saw a very small ray of light.

"You follow me up, miss, and I will open it for you so that you can tell them the truth." As the man began to climb the steps, Sandra reached out and grabbed his dirty and bruised hand.

"I want you to have this, Winthrop, and I want to thank you for helping me. I want you to feel good, okay?" Sandra gave the man ten crisp twenty-dollar bills and Winthrop closed his hand around the money. "By the way, my name is Sandra."

As Winthrop led her up the steel steps, Sandra felt her back to make sure the discs were still in place. Now at the top of the steps, Winthrop positioned himself so that he would be able to use his back as leverage when pushing up on the grating.

"You get ready, Sandra, because I don't know how long I can hold this up." Sandra nodded her head in agreement as she held on to the guardrail and watched Winthrop. He grunted and strained as he pushed with all of his strength. Sandra wondered if he would be successful because the grating seemed so heavy.

More light from outside began to shine inside, allowing Sandra to see Winthrop's weather-beaten face. Letting out a louder and heavier grunt, Winthrop opened the grating enough so that Sandra could make it through. "Go, Sandra. I cannot hold it much longer," he warned, with redness overtaking the dirt on his face.

Sandra quickly squeezed her thick body past Winthrop and through the grating. Now standing on 129th Street and Lenox Avenue, Sandra took in as much fresh air as possible. She looked down at the grating where Winthrop stood underneath, looking back up at her.

"Go tell the truth, Sandra, and be free," he said.

"I will, and thank you," Sandra whispered. She looked around 129th Street, then at her filthy clothes, then back down towards the grating to say something to Winthrop, but just like that, he was gone. She brushed dirt from her hair then looked at her watch. It was now 1:26 p.m.

She looked around again, hoping to find a store, and noticed a few people staring at her. Her eyes scanned past her audience and spotted a bodega on the corner of 129th Street, which caused her to let out a sigh of relief—she was dying for a bottle of water. As she walked slowly towards the bodega, Sandra heard a loud *WHOOP, WHOOP*. Continuing to walk towards the store, she acted as if she never heard the sound. Then a voice came from a speaker: "You—lady with the blonde hair—come over here to this car right now." Sandra took a quick look at the car then turned and began to walk in the opposite direction of the police.

"I said stop right there and do not move, lady," the officer repeated into the speaker as the police car pulled to a stop. The officers started to get out and Sandra made a fast dash for it, running north on Lenox Avenue. The two officers were not far behind her when she looked across the street and spotted a social club. She quickly dashed across the street, swung the door open, and walked to the back of the club, totally ignoring the forty men in motorcycle gear sitting at the bar and at a few tables. The men, who had been watching a DVD of a motorcycle exhibition, were now staring at Sandra, who sat in a corner at the back of the club, dirty and exhausted. The bartender walked from behind the bar to the back where Sandra sat.

A few of the men were pointing at Sandra and quietly talking amongst themselves. One of these men, whose name was Hawk, said to a fellow Black Nightfalcon member, "Yo, I seen her around here a while back. My baby sister said her kids got thrown out of the window this past Christmas."

The other member named Eddie shook his head from side to side. "Damn, Hawk, you serious? She's probably fucked up in the head roaming the streets now and just wandered in here."

Sandra looked at her cell phone and saw that she was down to two bars. She saw the time on her phone and pounded her fist on her thigh.

"Running out of time…I have to keep going," she mumbled to herself, not noticing the shadow that was cast over her. She wiped her face with some napkins that were lying on the table.

"Excuse me, miss, but are you okay?" asked Biscuit, the bartender.

Finally noticing her surroundings, Sandra looked up and scooted away from the giant of a man. "I'm sorry, sir. Please don't hurt me; I'm leaving right now, okay?"

"Whoa, my sister, calm down," Biscuit said, holding his hands up in retreat. "Nobody here is going to hurt you." Feeling a tap on his shoulder, Biscuit turned around and was face-to-face with Hawk, who whispered in Biscuit's ear as Sandra looked on. "Miss, is someone after you? Is that the reason you ran in here and hid in the corner?" Biscuit asked with compassion.

"Some policemen are trying to kill me and right now I don't have time to explain my story to you. If you could be so kind, just let me wash my face in your restroom and then let me leave through the back exit, and I promise you will never see me again."

Biscuit took out his keys and walked over to a closet. He opened the door and turned on a light. When he came back out, he had a washcloth and an extra-large sweatshirt with the Black Nightfalcon's emblem on the front. "It's a little big for you, but you can have it," he said as he handed both items to Sandra. "There's a sink with some soap inside. Go clean yourself up and then you are free to leave."

"Thank you very much," Sandra said, closing the door behind her.

Hawk watched the exchange and then began to walk back to his seat when Detectives Davis, Harris, Daniels, and McCarthy entered the club with their badges exposed around their necks. The club was completely silent except for the sound of bikes coming from the television.

"Good afternoon, gentlemen. I'm Detective Davis and I will make this short and sweet so that even you will understand. Over my radio a few moments ago, I heard a call about a female perp who goes by the name Sandra Lyte. She's a brown-skinned woman about five foot four inches and weighing one hundred and forty pounds. She was last seen running down this block wearing a blue hooded sweatshirt and her hair is blonde. Can anyone help me?"

As the detectives looked around the bar, all the club members remained silent until Biscuit spoke up. "No, detective. I've been here all day. No one fitting that description has entered my establishment. If you would like to leave your card, I will be sure to contact you if anyone happens to see her."

Detective Davis looked over to Hawk who was opening the door where Sandra was. "Excuse me, my man, but where are you going?" asked Davis.

Hawk looked at Davis as if he were no one important. "Detective, I'm going to the men's room. There's no crime in that, is there?"

Davis gave Hawk a long dirty look. "Not at this moment, but watch your fucking mouth, my friend."

Turning away from Davis, Hawk entered the bathroom. With his finger pressed against his lips, Hawk motioned to a petrified Sandra to calm down. He gently grabbed her by the arm and pulled her close to him, whispering, "We have three minutes to get you out of here before they wonder what is taking me so long, okay?"

Still shaking from the sound of Davis's voice, Sandra whispered, "They killed my babies, mister. Please help me." Hawk totally believed Sandra. With compassion in his eyes, he led her to a window and proceeded to open it. He stepped on the toilet bowl and quickly pushed his thin but very muscular body through the window, and jumped to the ground three feet below.

He watched as Sandra pushed half her body out of the window, then he reached up and grabbed her two hands. As he pulled her gently through the window, Sandra screamed, "He's got my legs! Help me, he's pulling my legs!"

Hawk looked up quickly and saw somebody violently yanking at Sandra's leg. "Oh shit!" he yelled as he used all of his muscles to pull Sandra as hard as he could through the window while the officer inside yelled, "Tommy, help me! I got her, help me!"

Sandra screamed in pain as her stomach rubbed across the metal windowsill. Fighting through the pain, she used her left leg to thrust back and kick the dragon in his face, knocking him backwards onto Detective Davis and causing them both to fall to the bathroom floor.

"Pull me, please!" Sandra yelled to Hawk, who did so and got her out the window and onto the ground.

"Come on, Sandra, get up!" Hawk yelled as he pulled her towards his gray Suzuki Hayabusa 1300 motorcycle. He grabbed his helmet and quickly put it on Sandra's head, then he jumped on his bike and started it up. He grabbed Sandra by the arm, got her on the bike, and asked, "Where are we going?"

Holding on tight to his waist, Sandra yelled through the helmet, "Rockefeller Center."

As Hawk got ready to speed off, he came face-to-face with the four detectives, who were yelling at him to halt as they started to remove their weapons. Quickly spinning the bike around on its front wheel, Hawk took off in the opposite direction. Detective Davis grabbed his radio and called all cars in the area for back up, describing the bike and the direction in which it was heading. Then the detectives ran from the back of the club to their cars, yelling at each other for letting Sandra get away.

"Listen, they are heading towards Broadway. You two get on Seventh because there is less traffic and we'll continue down Broadway. They can't get that far ahead with all of this fucking traffic," Tommy yelled at Sam before entering his car.

As the detectives started their engines and got ready to drive off, Sam looked at Joseph and said, "That dumb ass Tony can't do anything right. If he would have cut her throat the right way, we wouldn't be in this shit."

Joseph nodded his head in agreement. "He's a brain-dead son of a bitch."

* * *

Sandra held on to Hawk's waist tightly as they swerved in and out of traffic heading south on 121st Street and Seventh Avenue. Looking at the congestion ahead, Hawk started to make a right on 120th Street but quickly put on his brakes when he saw a patrol car right in his pathway. Maneuvering the bike, he ran a red light and continued down Seventh Avenue with the patrol car on his tail with sirens blasting. He looked back at Sandra and yelled, "If they start shooting, you just hold on because things will get a little hairy on the back of this bike!"

Sandra just nodded the helmet up and down in agreement. Hawk realized that he wouldn't be able to utilize the bike's speed in this traffic, so he rode the lines of the street, dodging cars while briefly looking back to see how close the patrol car was.

* * *

Maria was sitting in her office listening to the transmission of the police chase. She turned on her computer and logged on to her GPS system to track the area where Sandra was. She looked up at her door because Gail had just entered. "Come on in and sit down," Maria requested. "I have something to ask you."

Gail sat across from Maria's desk and paid close attention to her boss.

"Gail, a few things bother me about this whole manhunt for this woman. First, they say she is the main suspect of a murder—then why is Sandra running to me and not trying to flee the city? I mean, let's get serious, anybody with half a brain who knows that they're going to prison is not sticking around, right? They're going to make a run for it. Something else puzzles me, Gail. I contacted the detective that's covering Sandra's case. His name is Tommy Davis and every time I spoke to him about the case, I always got the same answer with a different level of hostility each time: 'We're working on it.' Finally—and this has nothing to do with journalistic hunches, just common sense—Sandra Lyte is one woman. Tell me two things: Why is the entire NYPD out chasing this one woman and why is it so difficult to catch her? Well as corny and stupid as this may sound, I will tell you why. Sandra has something very important that she wants to show me and it's destiny keeping her free. Gail, what I'm about to do will jeopardize my life and my job. Can I continue to trust you as I have for the past nine years?"

Gail looked at her boss, who had never been so serious in all the time they had known each other. "Yes, Ms. Copper, you know you can trust me. But what are you about to do?"

"Level the playing field," Maria answered as she picked up her cell phone and started dialing.

"Hello, this is Maria Copper. May I speak with my brother, Agent Ricky Copper? Yes, I can hold."

* * *

It was now 2:23 p.m. and Hawk and Sandra were riding on 86th Street and Broadway with the same patrol car on their tail. The car was totally out of its jurisdiction and, for some reason, its sirens were not sounding off like they had been in Harlem. Though the car was keeping up at a steady pace, it had not attempted to run them off the street. As the car's lights continued to flash inside the car, patrol officers Randy Thompson, a black man from Queens, and Stanley Combs, a white man from Staten Island, listened for instructions from Detective Davis. They were both sweating profusely.

"Randy, I just got on the force, man. I have a family and a new house. I'm on those discs having sex with fucking prostitutes. If this shit leaks out, man, I am done. I never should have listened to you."

Randy glanced angrily at his partner as he continued driving. "Oh, fuck you. Nobody twisted your arm to go with me to that damn party. You could not stop talking about it. Now act like you have a pair of balls and just get ready to smoke these two when Davis gives us the word."

* * *

At Seventy-fourth Street, the traffic had cleared up enough for Hawk to pick up a little speed, but when he got to the corner of Seventy-second Street, Detectives Davis and Harris pulled up right next to him. Both men had menacing looks on their faces as they began to steer closer to the bike. Hawk looked in his side mirrors and saw that the patrol car was now speeding up on his left in an attempt to box him in. As people looked on at the chase, which was now becoming more intense by the moment, Hawk fought to keep the bike steady as Detective Davis bumped him on his rear tire. Davis looked ahead and saw that all the lights were now turning green and figured that Hawk would likely make a speed move. "Tony, quick—take his tires out! Hurry up!" he ordered.

Jumping into the backseat of the car, Tony quickly rolled down the left rear window, stuck half his body out, and aimed his gun. Sandra looked through the visor of the helmet and let out a scream when she saw the tattoo on Tony's arm as he pointed the gun in her direction. Hawk looked to his right and saw the gun also. He put the bike in a faster gear, leaving the patrol car and the detectives behind just as Tony let off two rounds, causing people watching the scene to run in panic. The first shot missed, but the second hit Hawk on the left side of his upper back.

"Shit, I'm hit!" he yelled as he lost control of the bike, causing them to swerve to the right, near the sidewalk on Sixty-sixth Street and Broadway. Stopping the bike completely, Hawk got Sandra and himself off safely. Grimacing with pain, he fell to one knee as crowds of people gathered around and somebody screamed for someone to call an ambulance. Still on one knee and barely able to breathe, Hawk could see that the two cars were only about a block and a half away. He reached out to Sandra, grabbed the helmet off her, and looked her in the eyes. "Run, sister! Hurry up and get out of here. Go expose the truth!"

Sandra looked back and saw the cars getting closer. "Come on, get up. We can make it together! Get up! I can't leave you!"

"Run, Sandra. Damn it, run now!" he yelled as he pushed Sandra away and then collapsed to the ground. Sandra started running down Broadway but looked back one more time. The patrol car had stopped and the two officers got out and ran towards Hawk with their guns drawn. Because of the crowd that had gathered, Detectives Davis and Harris were blocked and had to get out of their car to pursue Sandra on foot.

Now on Sixty-fourth Street and Broadway, Sandra dodged through the many people who were on the street. She reached for her cell phone, flipped the receiver up, and saw that she was down to her last battery bar. She knew that Maria had told her that she should not call until she was at their agreed location, but Sandra felt she had no choice simply because she couldn't run anymore. Holding her right side because of the extreme pain, she pressed the redial button and held the phone to her ear while hopping across Sixty-second Street with Davis and Harris not far away on Sixty-third Street.

* * *

Maria was standing by her desk with Gail and quickly answered her cell phone. "Okay, Sandra. Calm down and tell me where you are. I know where that is. How far are the men that are chasing you? My God, Sandra, just keep going and do your best to blend in with the crowd, okay? Tell me what you're wearing...Okay, get off the phone. I'm going to do everything I can, but you just keep going."

Hanging up from Sandra, Maria dialed her brother directly. "Ricky, where are you? Okay, your people are going to have to hurry! She called me from Sixty-second and Broadway so she should be somewhere in that area..."

* * *

Detectives Harris and Davis were gaining on Sandra as they were now just a half a block away from her on Sixtieth Street. "Sam, where the fuck are you guys?" Davis said into his two-way. "She's now running on Fifty-ninth Street. I'm still a half a block away from her. Where are you? Forget it, I see you. She's the blonde woman running straight towards you. Grab her ass quickly and get her to your car!"

Halfway down the block, Sandra slowed down, visibly anguished. She was twenty-five feet away from Detectives Daniels and McCarthy, who were holding out their badges and holding up the palms of their hands, motioning Sandra to halt. Daniels was smiling as he silently mouthed, "It's over, bitch," as he walked slowly towards her. She looked behind her and saw Detectives Davis and Harris slowly approaching, trying not to cause a scene that would alarm the shoppers around them. Detective Harris, looking hard into Sandra's eyes, took his finger and slowly slid it across his throat. As the four men walked towards Sandra, she backed up towards the street, confused and unsure of where to go. With a look of desperation on her face, Sandra yelled, "Somebody help me! They're going to kill me!"

With people stopping to assess the situation, the four detectives realized they had to move in quickly. As they got ready to pounce on Sandra, an unmarked black van pulled up directly in front of her. The door slid open and two agents dressed in black quickly grabbed her and pulled her inside. As the detectives looked on in shock, Tony Harris ran towards the van yelling, "Stop! No! Halt!" but to no avail; the speeding van headed down Broadway. Sandra looked around the dark but neat van, but she couldn't say a word because of the fear running through her body. A tall, well-built man handed her a bottle of water and said, "Just stay calm, Ms. Lyte. Everything will be okay; you're safe now. I'm federal agent Ricky Copper and I'm taking you to my sister Maria."

Slowly and cautiously taking the water, Sandra looked at the four agents that sat with her and said, “Thank you, you just saved my life.” She took a long deserving drink of water.

Chapter Thirty-five

Opening a Can of Worms

As Sandra, Maria, Ricky, and Lou Peterson, the newsroom chief, watched the DVDs, Gail entered the room, bringing Sandra a turkey sandwich and a bottle of iced tea. Maria rubbed Sandra on the shoulder as she looked at her from the corner of her eye and shook her head slowly with admiration. "Sandra, are you sure you're okay watching this again? I can only imagine the pain you're feeling."

Taking a sip from the cold glass of iced tea that tasted so good going down, Sandra answered, "I'm fine, thank you. Besides, I need to watch."

"Lou, we're leading with this in twenty minutes, right?"

Lou stared at Maria as if she had lost her senses. "Are you serious, Maria? You are damn right we're leading with this."

"Excuse me, Agent Copper, I realize that I am going to have to answer some questions that could lead well into the night. Do you think it would be okay if I call my two friends? I really need to let them know that I'm okay."

"Absolutely, Sandra," Agent Copper answered as he got up from his chair. "Let's go to Maria's office where it's quiet."

* * *

Inside their hotel room, Pamela and Rose were sitting at the dining table working on a crossword puzzle. The cell phone rang and startled both of them. Pamela quickly flipped the receiver and answered, "Hello? Oh Sandra! Please tell me you are okay!"

Pamela fell back into her chair weeping. "Baby, Sandra made it," she told Rose. "She is doing fine! She says to tell you that she misses you and very soon we will all be together."

Rose bit her lower lip and couldn't keep her emotions in check as she too began to cry.

"No, Sandra, it's okay. We understand that you have much to do. You just please stay brave and stay in contact. Please call me so I can tell you where we are. Okay, Sandra, we love you too. Bye."

When Pamela put down the receiver on the phone, she and Rose embraced.

* * *

The hairdresser fussed with Maria's hair as the reporter looked over her notes. The producer let her know with his fingers that they were going live in ten seconds. Maria shuffled her papers one more time, the lights went on, and the theme music played. Backstage, Sandra watched intently as Maria led the five o'clock evening news.

"Good evening, welcome to Channel 4 News. I am Maria Copper and what we are about to show you tonight involves extortion, sodomy, illegal drug use, attempted murder, and the horrific murders of two innocent children. My fellow New Yorkers, these crimes you must understand, were not committed by typical criminals but by individuals who, when exposed, will rock the core of the New York City Police Department. That's right; the alleged crimes all involve high-ranking officers, from detectives all the way down to uniformed officers. Viewers, this is not hearsay or speculation. Many of the crimes I speak of are caught on digital recorded discs, and I must warn you that much of the footage you are about to see is graphic and strong. So, if you have children or are easily offended, I advise you to please turn away, because what we are about to show will shock and anger you."

* * *

The whole hour had been dedicated to Sandra's discs and Maria had chronicled everything that had been shown on camera. Sandra was relieved to see that the technicians were able to block out Rose's face as she performed sex acts in front of the cops. They were also able to enhance the sound and picture quality perfectly so that the whole city was able to watch all of the officers doing the evil things that could send them away for a very long time. The laughing and smiling images of Doug made Sandra wonder what had become of him and his father, but the thought only lasted for a split second.

* * *

Inside Gracie Mansion, the mayor of New York City was beet red in the face as he and his aides watched the story of his police force spread like wildfire. He picked up a telephone as his staff looked on in silence and shame. "Chief Brown, I want you, Captain Clarke, and Lieutenant Jackson in my office in thirty minutes. Do I make myself clear?"

Getting his answer, the mayor calmly hung up the phone and looked to his press aide, Yvette Jackson. "Okay, Yvette, how do we handle this with the press?"

* * *

It was 7:35 p.m. on Friday and Sandra was sitting inside a room along with a court-appointed attorney, four detectives, and a criminal reporter. Detective Frank Zeigler was recording the session.

"Sandra, I want you to take your time and ask for anything you may need—a beverage, some food, or just rest time—and we will be glad to give it to you. We just want you to relax and answer our questions to the best of your ability, because I am here to let you know that you are not on trial here. No ma'am, in my opinion, you are a hero."

Taking a deep breath, Sandra began her five-hour-long session.

* * *

The mayor had ordered a special task force of the best-decorated police officers to make major sweeps of all the cops that were seen on the discs. The unit consisted of fifty highly trained men working under the command of the mayor and the chief of police. At exactly 8:00 p.m., they were going to swoop down like avenging angels and bring in all nine officers by night's end.

* * *

At 8:20 p.m. in Bensonhurst, Brooklyn, Detective Joseph McCarthy was being led out of his single-family brick home in handcuffs as his neighbors looked on. His wife Judy was holding their six-month-old daughter and screaming at the officers while being restrained by her father. As he was led to the police car, McCarthy silently mouthed, "I am sorry," before being taken away.

* * *

At 8:45 p.m. in the Bronx, Detective Sam Daniels was being handcuffed in the living room of his two-bedroom apartment. Kim, his wife of twenty-four years, looked on in tears as she hugged their crying daughter, Wendy, who one hour ago had surprised her parents by coming home from college for the weekend. While Daniels was being led out the door, Wendy fell to her knees, grabbing her father's leg to keep him home. Three officers gently took the distraught nineteen-year-old to another room.

* * *

At 8:50 p.m. in Elmhurst, Queens, five police officers wearing riot gear were being led by their sergeant to the door of Detective Tony Harris. They knocked on the door, announcing themselves as police officers, and Tony responded from the other side of his door, "Come on in." Following the instructions of their sergeant, the officers entered cautiously with their weapons exposed. Once inside the roach-infested apartment, the officers lowered their weapons as they observed Tony Harris sitting on his couch with nothing on but a pair of boxers. He held a half-empty quart of Jack Daniel's in his hand.

"Before you take me in, brothers, let me first say this: I'm a fucking warrior that has been dealing with the scum of this city for twelve years now. You, my brothers in arms, are taking me away because some fucking whore claims that we are bad people. No, my friends, I am not bad! I was trying to do all of us a favor by getting rid of that bitch before she could hurt us and stop us from doing the job! So, take me in. I don't give a damn, because I'm not ashamed of who I am or what I've done, because I was doing it for us, my brothers."

Staring at the drunken and disorientated Tony, the sergeant said, "Detective, please put some clothes on so we can take you in."

Tony tossed his bottle of whisky to the side and held out his hands. "Fuck that. Take me in just like this, in all my glory," he slurred. The officers handcuffed the detective and led him out of the apartment.

* * *

At 9:05 p.m., Detective Tommy Davis was sitting in a small rental fishing boat in the waters of City Island, about one hundred feet from shore. Smiling, Tommy stopped paddling the nine-foot rowboat and let the currents take over. He reached inside a small black shaving bag and removed three detectives' badges, setting them neatly on the floor of the boat. The badges belonged to his father, Jack Davis, his grandfather Benny Davis, and him. He also removed from the bag a blue rosary that he laid across all three badges.

Tommy looked up at the half moon. "On this night, I want to apologize for the dishonor and disgrace I have brought to you two. You taught me the rules and I swore that I would always honor them. I have disgraced the force that I represent, while ruining fifty years of our name on that force. For that, I accept punishment. I love you both, and I am sorry. Please forgive me." After completing the sign of the cross, Tommy removed a revolver from his bag and gently put the barrel in his mouth. Taking one more look at the badges, he closed his eyes and pulled the trigger, breaking the silence of the night for a split second. As the current continued to control the boat, Tommy lay motionless with his eyes staring straight up at the heavens.

* * *

On Saturday at 1:35 a.m., Pamela and Rose were waiting anxiously by the main entrance of the Holiday Inn in Queens. Holding Rose by her shoulder, Pamela's eyes widened as she spotted a police car coming towards them. The car came to a stop and an officer got out to open the back door for an exhausted but jubilant Sandra. She walked very slowly towards Pamela and Rose because her body was in pain. The police officer watched for a moment, then he returned to his car and drove off. Sandra, Pamela, and Rose engaged in a loving embrace. For the first time in a while, they all felt safe.

Chapter Thirty-six

The Jury of Your Peers

On April 24th, four weeks into the explosive trial that rocked the city, Sandra was sitting inside a packed Bronx courtroom, listening as the defense made its last stance for the dirty cops, Detectives Sam Daniels, Joseph McCarthy, and Tony Harris. Throughout the trial, Sandra and the officers had not taken their eyes off each other. Sandra looked for closure and justice while the detectives looked for their attorney, Alvin Peachtree, to pull off a miracle while proving that Sandra was no angel. Sandra's attorney, Dorothy White, a black woman in her late forties who dressed out of *Vogue* magazine, listened closely to Peachtree, a tall, lanky man in his mid fifties, who specialized in defending drug dealers and organized crime members.

"Ladies and gentlemen of the jury, before I close out the questioning in defense of my clients, I would like to make one last crucial point, if I may. These men, who have worked so hard to protect and serve the public for so many years, *may* have committed a horrible crime, but only you can decide if that is true in this court of law. But ladies and gentlemen, another crime is being overlooked here today, and that crime was committed by Sandra Lyte."

With hisses and mumbles coming from the packed courtroom, the judge banged his gavel. "Order! I said order in this courtroom!"

"Objection!" Attorney White quickly stood up from her chair. "Your Honor, my client is not on trial here and furthermore, she has not been accused of any wrongdoing. I request that Mr. Peachtree please close his argument so that we may send the jury to deliberate their decision."

"Mr. Peachtree, I am getting quite tired of your antics. What's your point here?" the judge asked after taking a long breath.

"Yes, Your Honor, I do have a point...and it may prove that it should not just be my clients being charged for murder but also Ms. Lyte, for kidnapping and accessory to the murder of Doug Gunner. Your Honor, I would like to call Fred Gunner to the stand."

The courthouse doors swung open and Fred Gunner entered the courtroom walking with a cane and wearing a black two-piece polyester suit. He walked up to the stand, put his hand on the Bible, and took his oath. Shivering inside her body, Sandra did her very best to hide the fear she was feeling at this moment. Setting his cane by his side, Fred looked at the desk where Sandra was sitting and strangely gave her a quick grin. Sandra felt her head spinning by the second and could also see the walls crashing down around her.

Attorney Peachtree smiled at Fred. "Mr. Gunner, I understand the anguish you must be going through right now and I promise that this will not take long."

People in the courtroom began sucking their teeth and letting out sighs. Pamela, who was looking on quietly, mumbled, "Fuck him and Doug," as she looked at Rose, who stared angrily at Fred.

"Mr. Gunner, please tell the court the same exact account you gave me of what happened to you on the evening of February twenty-first at approximately seven o'clock that evening. And sir, it's okay; we understand if you speak a little slowly."

Fred looked at the judge and then out into the crowd. He leaned into the microphone and cleared his throat to answer. "Just like I explained to you, sir, when I was watching television that night…I saw a big bright light come through my window, and it hit my body, not allowing me to move or call for help."

Attorney Peachtree stared at Fred with a perplexed look on his face then looked over at the judge, who was staring at Fred as if he had lost his mind. Sandra was looking at her attorney while Ms. White was doing her best not to burst out in laughter. The jury was looking at each other while laughter came from the crowd in attendance.

"Order! I said order right now!" Mr. Peachtree walked over to the bench where Fred sat. "Mr. Gunner, that is not what you told me, and must I remind you, sir, that you are under oath!" he said angrily.

Fred looked out at the crowd again and caught the glance of an Italian woman sitting to his right in the middle of the crowd. The woman wearing all white gave Fred a gentle wink of her eye. Fred couldn't take his eyes off the woman who had paid him a little visit a week ago while he sat in a coffee shop. Connie Marino, the wife of Tony, had a little sit-down with Fred, explaining to him why it would be in his best interest if he forgot about the encounter between Sandra and himself because she now considered Sandra a friend of the family.

"Mr. Gunner, please complete your statement," the judge requested, knocking Fred back into reality.

"Like I told him, Judge, I woke up in a room where the aliens held me and made me watch while they chopped up my son in little pieces. Then they put me back on my own private ship, sending me away…"

Banging his gavel once again to quiet the crowd, the judge looked at Attorney Peachtree with little respect. "Mr. Peachtree, do you have any more case-blowing witnesses for us today?"

Looking at Fred and never taking his eyes off him, he answered, "No, Your Honor, I have no further questions."

Looking over at Fred, the judge said, "You may step down, Mr. Gunner."

With the assistance of his cane, Fred stepped down from the witness stand and walked out of the courtroom, never again looking at Sandra.

"Ladies and gentlemen of the jury, you have heard testimonies from both sides and now the fate of these defendants is in your hands. I ask that you carefully review all of the evidence before you and return with a decision that is fair and just. We will proceed on Monday at nine o'clock in the morning," the judge said.

* * *

It was now 2:22 p.m. on April 27th. Outside the courtroom, news trucks and news reporters waited anxiously because the rumor spreading like wildfire was that the jury had reached a verdict. About twenty police cars lined the street as seventy uniformed police officers stood along the courtroom steps in solidarity.

Inside, Sandra was sitting with her attorney. She shivered as the jury foreman led the jury into the room, which was full to capacity. Pamela and Rose reached across the railing and held on to Sandra's shoulders.

"Ladies and gentlemen of the jury, have you reached a verdict?" The male foreman stood. "Yes, Your Honor, we have."

"What is your verdict?"

The juror read from the paper in his hand, "We, the jury, find defendants Anthony J. Harris, Samuel D. Daniels, and Joseph P. McCarthy on the charges of murder in the first degree…guilty."

The courtroom exploded with screams of joy and the judge banged aggressively on his gavel. "One more outburst and I will hold this entire courtroom in contempt," he warned. "Juror, you may continue."

"In the charge of attempted murder, we find the defendants…guilty."

When the decisions for the other charges were announced, Sandra, her attorney, and her two friends were ecstatic. As the officers who were involved in lesser but still career-ending acts awaited their fate, the guilty detectives were led out of the courtroom. They stared at Sandra, who stared right back at them. Opening up her collar, Sandra revealed the lifelong scar inflicted on her and pulled from underneath her shirt a necklace that contained a wallet-sized picture of Kareem and Chaka. She stuck it forward so that Tony Harris, especially, could see it. Sandra watched until the convicted felons disappeared behind the courtroom doors.

"Can we go away and start over now?" Rose asked with tears in her eyes.

Sandra put her arms around Rose's shoulder and smiled. "As soon as we get out of here, sweetheart."

As Sandra's attorney led them out of the courtroom, hordes of reporters and supporters began screaming questions at the victorious party.

Final Chapter

A New Beginning

It was July 15th and Tempe, Arizona, was like an egg in a hot skillet. Sandra, Pamela, and Rose parked their blue Lexus GS430 in front of the Arizona State University bookstore. As the women exited the car, Rose nervously looked over a list.

"I am so afraid. It has been so long since I've been in a classroom," she confessed.

"Rose, we have complete faith in you and we know you will do well," Sandra said. "With all that we had just been through, you bounced right back and got your GED in no time. I know this will be a piece of cake for you. Now, get inside and buy those books. We'll be right here when you come out."

Smiling and shaking her head confidently, Rose happily jogged inside the crowded bookstore with her list in her hand.

"Sandra, I am really happy that you've decided to attend those counseling sessions," Pamela said as he leaned next to Sandra in the Lexus. "I know it has only been two weeks, but I really see a difference in the way you're carrying yourself, and I am happy for you. In addition, I think what you did concerning Kareem and Chaka was nothing short of incredible. I know they are happy you did."

Sandra looked at Pamela with pure happiness, something she had not felt in a while. "Well, I would have never been able to find my mental and spiritual well-being if it were not for God, Rose, and you, so I want to thank you for everything. As far as my babies go, it was the least I could possibly give back to them as their mother."

"Sandra, I also meant to ask you yesterday—for the past couple of days, you've been spending a lot of time at the Big Top supermarket—what's up with that?"

"Just wanted to take care of someone who took care of me and taught me so much when I was lost, that's all. Hey, when she comes out, how about we drive over to the mall for some shopping and banana crunch ice cream, and then we can head on home to take a swim in our really big pool?"

"Sounds like a plan to me," Pamela said laughing.

* * *

It was 3:30 p.m. in the Bronx and Ms. Carla was instructing her three new volunteers, Angela, Christine, and Esther, on where to set the food and beverages for the patrons. A tall and large man entered the pantry. He was sweating and holding an invoice.

"Excuse me…I'm looking for a Carla Smith."

Ms. Carla glanced up from the very large can of fruit cocktail she was opening. "Good afternoon, sir, I'm Carla. Can I do something for you?"

"Ma'am, I'm with the Big Top Food Corporation and I really think you need to come outside, because someone has sent you something that you need to see."

"Ladies, you keep preparing the food, okay? I will be right back." Carla grabbed her cane and followed the man outside. When she stepped into the hot, humid street, men, women, and children were already gathering for dinner.

"Ma'am, this is for you and it comes with a note." The driver led Carla to two eighteen-wheelers. The driver waved at another man who walked to the back of his truck. Simultaneously, both men opened the back of the trailers.

Both trucks were filled to their maximum capacities with nothing but food. Carla was shocked and confused. There was so much food that she wouldn't have to worry about how she would feed her friends for a very long time. The driver couldn't help but smile. "Someone must really like you," he said as he handed her a letter.

Carla slowly unfolded it and read silently to herself.

By the time you have this letter in your hands, I hope God has blessed you by restoring your good health and keeping your loving heart. There is no way I can ever put into words how much I love you and what you will always mean to me. When I did not have a mother or a place to hide, you became that mother for me, and that I will never forget. I just want you to know that I am doing much better and have learned to take life one day at a time. In addition, Rose is doing great and she speaks about you all the time. She has just started college and she said that as soon as she gets her classes together, she'll mail you a picture.

You have brought so much love and joy to so many people. I hope this food helps at the pantry. Maybe one day real soon we can talk, but right now I am just getting myself settled and I need a little time before I can pick up a phone again. But you can be assured that when I do get the courage to call someone, that someone will be you, Ms. Carla.

With love and blessings for you always, I love you and will never forget you…
Your daughter, Sandra.

Carla couldn't stop the tears from falling from her eyes. Through her tears she saw four of her regular patrons who came to eat every day. "Excuse me, fellas, do you think you could give me a hand unloading this into the pantry?"

In an instant, not only did the four men run over and begin to empty the trailers but so did the women and children. Within minutes, more than forty people were unloading the trailers and taking the boxes of food inside the pantry. Standing back and watching the people help her while laughing and smiling with one another, Carla looked up to the sky and quietly said, "I love you too, Sandra, and no matter what, we will see each other again, either in this life or in the next. God bless you, baby."

* * *

It was now three o'clock in the morning and the Arizona temperature was around fifty degrees. Sandra was standing sixty feet from the back of her home. In front of her were two handcrafted marble tombstones, one pink and the other blue. Before Sandra left New York, she had her children's bodies dug up and removed from the one-hundred-dollar pine boxes Doug had originally used to bury them. She paid top dollar to have their bodies restored as best they could be, and Sandra made sure Kareem and Chaka had the proper burial they deserved. Getting on her knees, Sandra looked closely at the tombstones. They each had an eight-inch square with the corresponding child's picture encased within six-inch thick glass. In the middle of each tombstone, a constant blue flame burned in each child's memory. "Hey boo-boos, Mommy couldn't sleep so I figured I would come out here and pay my babies a visit. As always, I miss you and love you. I hope that you two are doing well and that you're getting ready for the day when Mommy will be able to see you again. You will never leave my heart or my soul because we are one, and no one will ever separate us." She bent down to kiss the top of each tombstone. As she walked back towards the house, Sandra could see Rose, who had watched the whole scene. Sliding the patio doors open, Sandra hugged her around the neck and gave her a kiss on the forehead as Rose revealed a deck of cards so that she and Sandra could play the memory game.

To all the readers who purchased my book, I want to thank you for your support.

Before you put this book down, let's have some fun!

If The Mouse that Roared was ever made into a motion picture here are my picks:

Sandra Lyte	Taraji P. Henson from *Hustle and Flow*
Doug Gunner	Michael Jai White from *Spawn*
Pamela Brown	Tichina Arnold from the sitcom *Martin*
Fred Gunner	Danny Glover from *The Color Purple*
Rose Garden	Camille Winbush from the sitcom *The Bernie Mac Show*
Tommy Davis	Kevin Bacon from *Stir of Echoes*
Tony Harris	Christopher Meloni from series *Oz* and *Homicide*
Ms. Carla	Della Reese from *Touched by an Angel*
Bucky	Stu "Large" Riley from *Shaft*
Tony Marino	Chazz Palminteri from *A Bronx Tale*

For more information and upcoming publications, or to tell me what your picks are for the "motion picture", you can contact me at

Dwayne Murray, Sr.
Madbo Enterprises
1444 East Gunhill Road, Suite 32
Bronx, New York 10469

Or visit my website at:

WWW.MADBOENTERPRISES.COM
WWW.Myspace.com/madbo726

Click on either my guestbook or email address, I would love to read your opinions about the book.